MIDNIGHT UNDER THE BIG TOP

•••• ⋗≽⫙≼⋖ ••••

MIDNIGHT UNDER THE BIG TOP

TALES OF MURDER, MADNESS, AND MAGIC

EDITED BY
BRIAN JAMES FREEMAN

Cemetery Dance Publications
❖ Baltimore ❖
2023

LIST OF ATTRACTIONS

ACT ONE:

INTERMISSION: POETRY

ACT TWO:

ACTONE

THE NIGHT OF THE TIGER

by Stephen King

I first saw Mr. Legere when the circus swung through Steubenville, but I'd only been with the show for two weeks; he might have been making his irregular visits indefinitely. No one much wanted to talk about Mr. Legere, not even that last night when it seemed that the world was coming to an end—the night that Mr. Indrasil disappeared.

But if I'm going to tell it to you from the beginning, I should start by saying that I'm Eddie Johnston, and I was born and raised in Sauk City. Went to school there, had my first girl there, and worked in Mr. Lillie's five-and-dime there for a while after I graduated from high school. That was a few years back…more than I like to count, sometimes. Not that Sauk City's such a bad place; hot, lazy summer nights sitting on the front porch is all right for some folks, but it just seemed to itch me, like sitting in the same chair too long. So I quit the five-and-dime and joined Farnum & Williams' All-American 3-Ring Circus and Side Show. I did it in a moment of giddiness when the calliope music kind of fogged my judgment, I guess.

So I became a roustabout, helping put up tents and take them down, spreading sawdust, cleaning cages, and sometimes selling cotton candy when the regular salesman had to go away and bark for Chips Baily, who had malaria and sometimes had to go someplace far away, and holler. Mostly things that kids do for free passes—things I used to do when I was a kid. But times change. They don't seem to come around like they used to.

We swung through Illinois and Indiana that hot summer, and the crowds were good and everyone was happy. Everyone except Mr. Indrasil. Mr. Indrasil was never happy. He was the lion tamer, and he looked like old pictures I've seen of Rudolph Valentino. He was tall, with handsome, arrogant features and a shock of wild black hair. And strange, mad eyes—the maddest eyes I've ever seen. He was silent most of the time; two syllables from Mr. Indrasil was a sermon. All the circus people kept a mental as well as a physical distance, because his rages were legend. There was a whispered story about coffee spilled on his hands after a particularly difficult performance and a murder that was almost done to a young roustabout before Mr. Indrasil could be hauled off him. I don't know about that. I do know that I grew to fear him worse than I had cold-eyed Mr. Edmont, my high school principal, Mr. Lillie, or even my father, who was capable of cold dressing-downs that would leave the recipient quivering with shame and dismay.

When I cleaned the big cats' cages, they were always spotless. The memory of the few times I had the vituperative wrath of Mr. Indrasil called down on me still have the power to turn my knees watery in retrospect.

Mostly it was his eyes—large and dark and totally blank. The eyes, and the feeling that a man capable of controlling seven watchful cats in a small cage must be part savage himself.

And the only two things he was afraid of were Mr. Legere and the circus's one tiger, a huge beast called Green Terror.

As I said, I first saw Mr. Legere in Steubenville, and he was staring into Green Terror's cage as if the tiger knew all the secrets of life and death.

He was lean, dark, quiet. His deep, recessed eyes held an expression of pain and brooding violence in their green-flecked depths, and his hands were always crossed behind his back as he stared moodily in at the tiger.

Green Terror was a beast to be stared at. He was a huge, beautiful specimen with a flawless striped coat, emerald eyes, and heavy fangs like ivory spikes. His roars usually filled the circus grounds—fierce, angry, and utterly savage. He seemed to scream defiance and frustration at the whole world.

Chips Baily, who had been with Farnum & Williams since Lord knew when, told me that Mr. Indrasil used to use Green Terror in his act, until one night when the tiger leaped suddenly from its perch and almost ripped his head from his shoulders before he could get out of the cage. I noticed that Mr. Indrasil always wore his hair long down the back of his neck.

I can still remember the tableau that day in Steubenville. It was hot, sweatingly hot, and we had a shirtsleeve crowd. That was why Mr. Legere and Mr. Indrasil stood out. Mr. Legere, standing silently by the tiger cage, was fully dressed in a suit and vest, his face unmarked by perspiration. And Mr. Indrasil, clad in one of his beautiful silk shirts and white whipcord breeches, was staring at them both, his face dead-white, his eyes bulging in lunatic anger, hate, and fear. He was carrying a currycomb and brush, and his hands were trembling as they clenched on them spasmodically.

Suddenly he saw me, and his anger found vent. "You!" He shouted. "Johnston!"

"Yes, sir?" I felt a crawling in the pit of my stomach. I knew I was about to have the wrath of Indrasil vented on me, and the thought turned me weak with fear. I like to think I'm as brave as the next, and if it had been anyone else, I think I would have been fully determined to stand up for myself. But it wasn't anyone else. It was Mr. Indrasil, and his eyes were mad.

"These cages, Johnston. Are they supposed to be clean?" He pointed a finger, and I followed it. I saw four errant wisps of straw and an incriminating puddle of hose water in the far corner of one.

"Y-yes, sir," I said, and what was intended to be firmness became palsied bravado.

Silence, like the electric pause before a downpour. People were beginning to look, and I was dimly aware that Mr. Legere was staring at us with his bottomless eyes.

"Yes, sir?" Mr. Indrasil thundered suddenly. "Yes, sir? Yes, sir? Don't insult my intelligence, boy! Don't you think I can see? Smell? Did you use the disinfectant?"

"I used disinfectant, yes—"

"Don't answer me back!" He screeched, and then the sudden drop in his voice made my skin crawl. "Don't you dare answer me back." Everyone was staring now. I wanted to retch, to die. "Now you get the hell into that tool shed, and you get that disinfectant and swab out those cages," he whispered, measuring every word. One hand suddenly shot out, grasping my shoulder. "And don't you ever, ever, speak back to me again."

I don't know where the words came from, but they were suddenly there, spilling off my lips. "I didn't speak back to you, Mr. Indrasil, and I don't like you saying I did. I—resent it. Now let me go."

His face went suddenly red, then white, then almost saffron with rage. His eyes were blazing doorways to hell.

Right then I thought I was going to die.

He made an inarticulate gagging sound, and the grip on my shoulder became excruciating. His right hand went up…up…up, and then descended with unbelievable speed.

If that hand had connected with my face, it would have knocked me senseless at best. At worst, it would have broken my neck.

It did not connect.

Another hand materialized magically out of space, right in front of me. The two straining limbs came together with a flat smacking sound. It was Mr. Legere.

"Leave the boy alone," he said emotionlessly.

Mr. Indrasil stared at him for a long second, and I think there was nothing so unpleasant in the whole business as watching the fear of Mr. Legere and the mad lust to hurt (or to kill!) mix in those terrible eyes.

Then he turned and stalked away.

I turned to look at Mr. Legere. "Thank you," I said.

"Don't thank me." And it wasn't a "don't thank *me*," but a "*don't* thank me." Not a gesture of modesty but a literal command. In a sudden flash of intuition—empathy if you will—I understood exactly what he meant by that comment. I was a pawn in what must have been a long combat between the two of them. I had been captured by Mr. Legere rather than Mr. Indrasil. He had stopped the lion tamer not because he felt for me, but because it gained him an advantage, however slight, in their private war.

"What's your name?" I asked, not at all offended by what I had inferred. He had, after all, been honest with me.

"Legere," he said briefly. He turned to go.

"Are you with a circus?" I asked, not wanting to let him go so easily. "You seemed to know—him."

A faint smile touched his thin lips, and warmth kindled in his eyes for a moment; "No. You might call me a—policeman." And before I could reply, he had disappeared into the surging throng passing by.

The next day we picked up stakes and moved on.

I saw Mr. Legere again in Danville and, two weeks later, in Chicago. In the time between I tried to avoid Mr. Indrasil as much as possible and kept the cat cages spotlessly clean. On the day before we pulled out for St. Louis,

I asked Chips Baily and Sally O'Hara, the red-headed wire walker, if Mr. Legere and Mr. Indrasil knew each other. I was pretty sure they did, because Mr. Legere was hardly following the circus to eat our fabulous lime ice.

Sally and Chips looked at each other over their coffee cups. "No one knows much about what's between those two," she said. "But it's been going on for a long time, maybe twenty years. Ever since Mr. Indrasil came over from Ringling Brothers, and maybe before that."

Chips nodded. "This Legere guy picks up the circus almost every year when we swing through the Midwest and stays with us until we catch the train for Florida in Little Rock. Makes old Leopard Man touchy as one of his cats."

"He told me he was a policeman," I said. "What do you suppose he looks for around here? You don't suppose Mr. Indrasil—?"

Chips and Sally looked at each other strangely, and both just about broke their backs getting up. "Got to see those weights and counter weights get stored right," Sally said, and Chips muttered something not too convincing about checking on the rear axle of his U-Haul.

And that's about the way any conversation concerning Mr. Indrasil or Mr. Legere usually broke up—hurriedly, with many hard-forced excuses.

We said farewell to Illinois and comfort at the same time. A killing hot spell came on, seemingly at the very instant we crossed the border, and it stayed with us for the next month and a half, as we moved slowly across Missouri and into Kansas. Everyone grew short of temper, including the animals. And that, of course, included the cats, which were Mr. Indrasil's responsibility. He rode the roustabouts unmercifully, and myself in particular. I grinned and tried to bear it, even though I had my own case of prickly heat. You just don't argue with a crazy man, and I'd pretty well decided that was what Mr. Indrasil was.

No one was getting any sleep, and that is the curse of all circus performers. Loss of sleep slows up reflexes, and slow reflexes make for danger. In Independence Sally O'Hara fell seventy-five feet into the nylon netting and fractured her shoulder. Andrea Solienni, our bareback rider, fell off one of her horses during rehearsal and was knocked unconscious by a flying hoof. Chips Baily suffered silently with the fever that was always with him, his face a waxen mask, with cold perspiration clustered at each temple.

And in many ways, Mr. Indrasil had the roughest row to hoe of all. The cats were nervous and short-tempered, and every time he stepped into the Demon Cat Cage, as it was billed, he took his life in his hands. He was feeding the lions inordinate amounts of raw meat right before he went on, something that lion tamers rarely do, contrary to popular belief. His face grew drawn and haggard, and his eyes were wild.

Mr. Legere was almost always there, by Green Terror's cage, watching him. And that, of course, added to Mr. Indrasil's load. The circus began eyeing the silk-shirted figure nervously as he passed, and I knew they were all thinking the same thing I was: *He's going to crack wide open, and when he does—*

When he did, God alone knew what would happen.

The hot spell went on, and temperatures were climbing well into the nineties every day. It seemed as if the rain gods were mocking us. Every town we left would receive the showers of blessing. Every town we entered was hot, parched, sizzling.

And one night, on the road between Kansas City and Green Bluff, I saw something that upset me more than anything else.

It was hot—abominably hot. It was no good even trying to sleep. I rolled about on my cot like a man in a fever-delirium, chasing the sandman but never quite catching him. Finally I got up, pulled on my pants, and went outside.

We had pulled off into a small field and drawn into a circle. Myself and two other roustabouts had unloaded the cats so they could catch whatever breeze there might be. The cages were there now, painted dull silver by the swollen Kansas moon, and a tall figure in white whipcord breeches was standing by the biggest of them. Mr. Indrasil.

He was baiting Green Terror with a long, pointed pike. The big cat was padding silently around the cage, trying to avoid the sharp tip. And the frightening thing was, when the staff did punch into the tiger's flesh, it did not roar in pain and anger as it should have. It maintained an ominous silence, more terrifying to the person who knows cats than the loudest of roars.

It had gotten to Mr. Indrasil, too. "Quiet bastard, aren't you?" He grunted. Powerful arms flexed, and the iron shaft slid forward. Green Terror flinched, and his eyes rolled horribly. But he did not make a sound. "Yowl!" Mr. Indrasil hissed. "Go ahead and yowl, you monster. Yowl!" And he drove his spear deep into the tiger's flank.

Then I saw something odd. It seemed that a shadow moved in the darkness under one of the far wagons, and the moonlight seemed to glint on staring eyes—green eyes.

A cool wind passed silently through the clearing, lifting dust and rumpling my hair.

Mr. Indrasil looked up, and there was a queer listening expression on his face. Suddenly he dropped the bar, turned, and strode back to his trailer.

I stared again at the far wagon, but the shadow was gone. Green Terror stood motionlessly at the bars of his cage, staring at Mr. Indrasil's trailer. And the thought came to me that it hated Mr. Indrasil not because he was cruel or vicious, for the tiger respects these qualities in its own animalistic way, but rather because he was a deviate from even the tiger's savage norm. He was a rogue. That's the only way I can put it. Mr. Indrasil was not only a human tiger, but a rogue tiger as well.

The thought jelled inside me, disquieting and a little scary. I went back inside, but still I could not sleep.

The heat went on.

Every day we fried, every night we tossed and turned, sweating and sleepless. Everyone was painted red with sunburn, and there were fistfights over trifling affairs. Everyone was reaching the point of explosion.

Mr. Legere remained with us, a silent watcher, emotionless on the surface, but, I sensed, with deep-running currents of—what? Hate? Fear? Vengeance? I could not place it. But he was potentially dangerous, I was sure of that. Perhaps more so than Mr. Indrasil was, if anyone ever lit his particular fuse.

He was at the circus at every performance, always dressed in his nattily creased brown suit, despite the killing temperatures. He stood silently by Green Terror's cage, seeming to commune deeply with the tiger, who was always quiet when he was around.

From Kansas to Oklahoma, with no letup in the temperature. A day without a heat prostration case was a rare day indeed. Crowds were beginning to drop off; who wanted to sit under a stifling canvas tent when there was an air-conditioned movie just around the block?

We were all as jumpy as cats, to coin a particularly applicable phrase. And as we set down stakes in Wildwood Green, Oklahoma, I think we all knew a climax of some sort was close at hand. And most of us knew it would involve Mr. Indrasil. A bizarre occurrence had taken place just prior to our first Wildwood performance. Mr. Indrasil had been in the Demon Cat Cage, putting the ill-tempered lions through their paces. One of them missed its balance on its pedestal, tottered and almost regained it. Then, at that precise moment, Green Terror let out a terrible, ear-splitting roar.

The lion fell, landed heavily, and suddenly launched itself with rifle-bullet accuracy at Mr. Indrasil. With a frightened curse, he heaved his chair at the cat's feet, tangling up the driving legs. He darted out just as the lion smashed against the bars.

As he shakily collected himself preparatory to re-entering the cage, Green Terror let out another roar—but this one monstrously like a huge, disdainful chuckle.

Mr. Indrasil stared at the beast, white-faced, then turned and walked away. He did not come out of his trailer all afternoon.

That afternoon wore on interminably. But as the temperature climbed, we all began looking hopefully toward the west, where huge banks of thunderclouds were forming.

"Rain, maybe," I told Chips, stopping by his barking platform in front of the sideshow.

But he didn't respond to my hopeful grin. "Don't like it," he said. "No wind. Too hot. Hail or tornadoes." His face grew grim. "It ain't no picnic, ridin' out a tornado with a pack of crazy-wild animals all over the place, Eddie. I've thanked God mor'n once when we've gone through the tornado belt that we don't have no elephants.

"Yeah," he added gloomily, "you better hope them clouds stay right on the horizon."

But they didn't. They moved slowly toward us, cyclopean pillars in the sky, purple at the bases and awesome blue-black through the cumulonimbus. All air movement ceased, and the heat lay on us like a woolen winding-shroud. Every now and again, thunder would clear its throat further west.

About four, Mr. Farnum himself, ringmaster and half-owner of the circus, appeared and told us there would be no evening performance; just batten down and find a convenient hole to crawl into in case of trouble. There had been corkscrew funnels spotted in several places between Wildwood and Oklahoma City, some within forty miles of us.

There was only a small crowd when the announcement came, apathetically wandering through the sideshow exhibits or ogling the animals. But Mr. Legere had not been present all day; the only person at Green Terror's cage was a sweaty high-school boy with clutch of books. When Mr. Farnum announced the U.S. Weather Bureau tornado warning that had been issued, he hurried quickly away.

I and the other two roustabouts spent the rest of the afternoon working our tails off, securing tents, loading animals back into their wagons, and making generally sure that everything was nailed down.

Finally only the cat cages were left, and there was a special arrangement for those. Each cage had a special mesh "breezeway" accordioned up against it, which, when extended completely, connected with the Demon Cat Cage. When the smaller cages had to be moved, the felines could be herded into the big cage while they were loaded up. The big cage itself rolled on gigantic casters and could be muscled around to a position where each cat could be let back into its original cage. It sounds complicated, and it was, but it was just the only way.

We did the lions first, then Ebony Velvet, the docile black panther that had set the circus back almost one season's receipts. It was a tricky business coaxing them up and then back through the breezeways, but all of us preferred it to calling Mr. Indrasil to help.

By the time we were ready for Green Terror, twilight had come—a queer, yellow twilight that hung humidly around us. The sky above had taken on a flat, shiny aspect that I had never seen and which I didn't like in the least.

"Better hurry," Mr. Farnum said, as we laboriously trundled the Demon Cat Cage back to where we could hook it to the back of Green Terror's show cage. "Barometer's falling off fast." He shook his head worriedly. "Looks bad, boys. Bad." He hurried on, still shaking his head.

We got Green Terror's breezeway hooked up and opened the back of his cage. "In you go," I said encouragingly.

Green Terror looked at me menacingly and didn't move.

Thunder rumbled again, louder, closer, sharper. The sky had gone jaundice, the ugliest color I have ever seen. Wind-devils began to pick jerkily at our clothes and whirl away the flattened candy wrappers and cotton-candy cones that littered the area.

"Come on, come on," I urged and poked him easily with the blunt-tipped rods we were given to herd them with.

Green Terror roared ear-splittingly, and one paw lashed out with blinding speed. The hardwood pole was jerked from my hands and splintered as if it had been a greenwood twig. The tiger was on his feet now, and there was murder in his eyes.

"Look," I said shakily. "One of you will have to go get Mr. Indrasil, that's all. We can't wait around."

As if to punctuate my words, thunder cracked louder, the clapping of mammoth hands.

Kelly Nixon and Mike McGregor flipped for it; I was excluded because of my previous run-in with Mr. Indrasil. Kelly drew the task, threw us a wordless glance that said he would prefer facing the storm and then started off.

He was gone almost ten minutes. The wind was picking up velocity now, and twilight was darkening into a weird six o'clock night. I was scared, and am not afraid to admit it. That rushing, featureless sky, the deserted circus grounds, the sharp, tugging wind-vortices, all that makes a memory that will stay with me always, undimmed.

And Green Terror would not budge into his breezeway.

Kelly Nixon came rushing back, his eyes wide. "I pounded on his door for 'most five minutes!" He gasped. "Couldn't raise him!"

We looked at each other, at a loss. Green Terror was a big investment for the circus. He couldn't just be left in the open. I turned bewilderedly, looking for Chips, Mr. Farnum, or anybody who could tell me what to do. But everyone was gone. The tiger was our responsibility. I considered trying to load the cage bodily into the trailer, but I wasn't going to get my fingers in that cage.

"Well, we've just got to go and get him," I said. "The three of us. Come on." And we ran toward Mr. Indrasil's trailer through the gloom of coming night.

We pounded on his door until he must have thought all the demons of hell were after him. Thankfully, it finally jerked open. Mr. Indrasil swayed and stared down at us, his mad eyes rimmed and oversheened with drink. He smelled like a distillery.

"Damn you, leave me alone," he snarled.

CHADBOURNE

"Mr. Indrasil—" I had to shout over the rising whine of the wind. It was like no storm I had ever heard of or read about, out there. It was like the end of the world.

"You," he gritted softly. He reached down and gathered my shirt up in a knot. "I'm going to teach you a lesson you'll never forget." He glared at Kelly and Mike, cowering back in the moving storm shadows. "Get out!"

They ran. I didn't blame them; I've told you—Mr. Indrasil was crazy. And not just ordinary crazy—he was like a crazy animal, like one of his own cats gone bad.

"All right," he muttered, staring down at me, his eyes like hurricane lamps. "No juju to protect you now. No grisgris." His lips twitched in a wild, horrible smile. "He isn't here now, is he? We're two of a kind, him and me. Maybe the only two left. My nemesis—and I'm his." He was rambling, and I didn't try to stop him. At least his mind was off me.

"Turned that cat against me, back in '58. Always had the power more'n me. Fool could make a million—the two of us could make a million if he wasn't so damned high and mighty…what's that?"

It was Green Terror, and he had begun to roar ear-splittingly.

"Haven't you got that damned tiger in?" He screamed, almost falsetto. He shook me like a rag doll.

"He won't go!" I found myself yelling back. "You've got to—"

But he flung me away. I stumbled over the fold-up steps in front of his trailer and crashed into a bone-shaking heap at the bottom. With something between a sob and a curse, Mr. Indrasil strode past me, face mottled with anger and fear.

I got up, drawn after him as if hypnotized. Some intuitive part of me realized I was about to see the last act played out.

Once clear of the shelter of Mr. Indrasil's trailer, the power of the wind was appalling. It screamed like a runaway freight train. I was an ant, a speck, an unprotected molecule before that thundering, cosmic force.

And Mr. Legere was standing by Green Terror's cage.

It was like a tableau from Dante. The near-empty cage-clearing inside the circle of trailers; the two men, facing each other silently, their clothes and hair rippled by the shrieking gale; the boiling sky above; the twisting wheat fields in the background, like damned souls bending to the whip of Lucifer.

"It's time, Jason," Mr. Legere said, his words flayed across the clearing by the wind.

Mr. Indrasil's wildly whipping hair lifted around the livid scar across the back of his neck. His fists clenched, but he said nothing. I could almost feel him gathering his will, his life force, his id. It gathered around him like an unholy nimbus.

And, then, I saw with sudden horror that Mr. Legere was unhooking Green Terror's breezeway—and the back of the cage was open!

I cried out, but the wind ripped my words away.

The great tiger leaped out and almost flowed past Mr. Legere. Mr. Indrasil swayed, but did not run. He bent his head and stared down at the tiger.

And Green Terror stopped.

He swung his huge head back to Mr. Legere, almost turned, and then slowly turned back to Mr. Indrasil again. There was a terrifyingly palpable sensation of directed force in the air, a mesh of conflicting wills centered around the tiger. And the wills were evenly matched.

I think, in the end, it was Green Terror's own will—his hate of Mr. Indrasil—that tipped the scales.

The cat began to advance, his eyes hellish, flaring beacons. And something strange began to happen to Mr. Indrasil. He seemed to be folding in on himself, shriveling, accordioning. The silk shirt lost shape, the dark, whipping hair became a hideous toadstool around his collar.

Mr. Legere called something across to him, and, simultaneously, Green Terror leaped.

I never saw the outcome. The next moment I was slammed flat on my back, and the breath seemed to be sucked from my body. I caught one crazily tilted glimpse of a huge, towering cyclone funnel, and then the darkness descended.

When I awoke, I was in my cot just aft of the grainery bins in the all-purpose storage trailer we carried. My body felt as if it had been beaten with padded Indian clubs.

Chips Baily appeared, his face lined and pale. He saw my eyes were open and grinned relievedly. "Didn't know as you were ever gonna wake up. How you feel?"

"Dislocated," I said. "What happened? How'd I get here?"

"We found you piled up against Mr. Indrasil's trailer. The tornado almost carried you away for a souvenir, m'boy."

At the mention of Mr. Indrasil, all the ghastly memories came flooding back. "Where is Mr. Indrasil? And Mr. Legere?"

His eyes went murky, and he started to make some kind of an evasive answer.

"Straight talk," I said, struggling up on one elbow. "I have to know, Chips. I have to."

Something in my face must have decided him. "Okay. But this isn't exactly what we told the cops—in fact we hardly told the cops any of it. No sense havin' people think we're crazy. Anyhow, Indrasil's gone. I didn't even know that Legere guy was around."

"And Green Terror?"

Chips' eyes were unreadable again. "He and the other tiger fought to death."

"Other tiger? There's no other—"

"Yeah, but they found two of 'em, lying in each other's blood. Hell of a mess. Ripped each other's throats out."

"What—where—"

"Who knows? We just told the cops we had two tigers. Simpler that way." And before I could say another word, he was gone.

And that's the end of my story—except for two little items. The words Mr. Legere shouted just before the tornado hit: *"When a man and an animal live in the same shell, Indrasil, the instincts determine the mold!"*

The other thing is what keeps me awake nights. Chips told me later, offering it only for what it might be worth. What he told me was that the strange tiger had a long scar on the back of its neck.

TWITTERING FROM THE CIRCUS OF THE DEAD

by Joe Hill

WHAT IS *TWITTER*?

"*Twitter* is a service for friends, family, and co-workers to communicate and stay connected through the exchange of quick, frequent answers to one simple question: ***What are you doing?*** …Answers must be under 140 characters in length and can be sent via mobile texting, instant message, or the web."

—from *twitter.com*

 ## TYME2WASTE

TYME2WASTE I'm only trying this because I'm so bored I wish I was dead. Hi Twitter. Want to know what I'm doing? Screaming inside.
8:17 PM February 28th from Tweetie

TYME2WASTE My didn't that sound melodramatic.
8:19 PM February 28th from Tweetie

TYME2WASTE Lets try this again. Hello Twitterverse. I am Blake and Blake is me. What am I doing? Counting seconds.
8:23 PM February 28th from Tweetie

(more)

TYME2WASTE Only about 50,000 more until we pack up and finish what is hopefully the last family trip of my life.
8:25 PM February 28th from Tweetie

TYME2WASTE It's been all downhill since we got to Colorado. And I don't mean on my snowboard.
8:27 PM February 28th from Tweetie

TYME2WASTE We were supposed to spend the break boarding and skiing but it's too cold and won't stop snowing so we had to go to plan B.
8:29 PM February 28th from Tweetie

TYME2WASTE Plan B is Mom and I face off in a contest to see who can make the other cry hot tears of rage and hate first.
8:33 PM February 28th from Tweetie

TYME2WASTE I'm winning. All I have to do to make Mom leave the room at this point is walk into it. Wait, I'm walking into room where she is now...
8:35 PM February 28th from Tweetie

TYME2WASTE She's such a mean bitch.
10:11 PM February 28th from Tweetie

TYME2WASTE @caseinSD, @bevsez, @harmlesspervo yay my real friends! I miss San Diego. Home soon.
10:41 PM February 28th from Tweetie

TYME2WASTE @caseinSD Hell no I'm not afraid Mom is going to read any of this. She's never going to know about it.
10:46 PM February 28th from Tweetie

TYME2WASTE After she made me take down my blog, it's not like I'm ever going to tell her.
10:48 PM February 28th from Tweetie

more

TYME2WASTE You know what bitchy thing she said to me a couple hours ago? She said the reason I don't like Colorado is because I can't blog about it.
10:53 PM February 28th from Tweetie

TYME2WASTE She's always saying the net is more real for me and my friends than the world. For us, nothing really happens till someone blogs about it.
10:55 PM February 28th from Tweetie

TYME2WASTE Or writes about it on their Facebook page. Or at least sends an instant message about it. She says the internet is "life-validation."
10:55 PM February 28th from Tweetie

TYME2WASTE Oh and we don't go online because it's fun. She has this attitude that people socially network 'cause they're scared to die. It's deep.
10:58 PM February 28th from Tweetie

TYME2WASTE She sez no one ever blogs their own death. No one instant messages about it. No one's Facebook status ever says "dead."
10:59 PM February 28th from Tweetie

TYME2WASTE So for online people, death doesn't happen. People go online to hide from death and wind up hiding from life. Words right from her lips.
11:01 PM February 28th from Tweetie

TYME2WASTE Shit like that, she ought to write fortune cookies for a living. You see why I want to strangle her. With an Ethernet cable.
11:02 PM February 28th from Tweetie

more

TYME2WASTE Eric asked if I could blog about him having sex with a certain goth girl from school to make it real but no one laughed.
11:06 PM February 28th from Tweetie

TYME2WASTE I told Mom, no, the reason I hate Colorado is 'cause I'm stuck with her and it's all waaaaay too real.
11:09 PM February 28th from Tweetie

TYME2WASTE And she said that was progress and got this smug bitch look on her face and then Dad threw down his book & left the room.
11:11 PM February 28th from Tweetie

TYME2WASTE I feel worst for him. A few more months and I'm gone forever but he's stuck with her for life and all her anger and the rest of it.
11:13 PM February 28th from Tweetie

TYME2WASTE I'm sure he wishes he just got us plane tickets now. Suddenly our van is looking like the setting for a cage match duel to the death.
11:15 PM February 28th from Tweetie

TYME2WASTE All of us jammed in together for 3 days. Who will emerge alive? Place your bets ladies and germs. Personally I predict no survivors.
11:19 PM February 28th from Tweetie

TYME2WASTE Arrr. Fuck. Shit. It was dark when I went to bed and it is dark now and Dad says it's time to leave. This is so terribly wrong.
6:21 AM March 1st from Tweetie

more

TYME2WASTE We're going. Mom gave the condo a careful search to make sure nothing got left behind, which is how she found me.
7:01 AM March 1st from Tweetie

TYME2WASTE Damn knew I needed a better hiding place.
7:02 AM March 1st from Tweetie

TYME2WASTE Dad just said the whole trip ought to take between thirty-five and forty hours. I offer this as conclusive proof there is no God.
7:11 AM March 1st from Tweetie

TYME2WASTE Writing something on Twitter just to piss Mom off. She knows if I'm typing something on my phone I'm obviously engaged in a sinful act.
7:23 AM March 1st from Tweetie

TYME2WASTE I'm expressing myself and staying in touch with my friends and she hates it. Whereas if I was knitting and unpopular...
7:25 AM March 1st from Tweetie

TYME2WASTE ...then I'd be just like her when she was 17. And I'd also marry the first guy who came along and get knocked up by 19.
7:25 AM March 1st from Tweetie

TYME2WASTE Coming down the mountain in the snow. Coming down the mountain in the snow. 1 more hairpin turn and my stomach's gonna blow...
7:30 AM March 1st from Tweetie

TYME2WASTE My contribution to this glorious family moment is going to come when I barf on my little brother's head.
7:49 AM March 1st from Tweetie

---

more

TYME2WASTE **If we wind up in a snowbank and have a Donner Party, I know whose ass they'll be chewing on first. Mine.**
7:52 AM March 1st from Tweetie

TYME2WASTE **Of course my survival skilz would amount to Twittering madly for someone to rescue us.**
7:54 AM March 1st from Tweetie

TYME2WASTE **Mom would make a slingshot out of rubber from the tires, kill squirrels with it, stitch a fur bikini out of 'em and be sad when we got saved**
7:56 AM March 1st from Tweetie

TYME2WASTE **Dad would go out of his mind because we'd have to burn his books to stay warm.**
8:00 AM March 1st from Tweetie

TYME2WASTE **Eric would put on a pair of my pantyhose. Not to stay warm. Just 'cause he wants to wear my pantyhose.**
8:00 AM March 1st from Tweetie

TYME2WASTE **I wrote that last bit 'cause Eric was looking over my shoulder.**
8:02 AM March 1st from Tweetie

TYME2WASTE **But the sick bastard said wearing my pantyhose is the closest he'll probably come to getting laid in high school.**
8:06 AM March 1st from Tweetie

TYME2WASTE **He's completely gross but I love him.**
8:06 AM March 1st from Tweetie

TYME2WASTE **Mom taught him to knit while we were snowed in here in happy CO and he knitted himself a cocksock and then she was sorry.**
8:11 AM March 1st from Tweetie

---

more

TYME2WASTE I miss my blog which she had no right to make me take down.
8:13 AM March 1st from Tweetie

TYME2WASTE But Twittering is better than blogging because my blog always made me feel like I should have interesting ideas to blog about.
8:14 AM March 1st from Tweetie

TYME2WASTE But on Twitter every post can only be 140 letters long. Which is enough room to cover every interesting thing to ever happen to me.
8:15 AM March 1st from Tweetie

TYME2WASTE True. Check it out.
8:15 AM March 1st from Tweetie

TYME2WASTE Born. School. Mall. Cell phone. Driver's permit. Broke my nose playing trapeze at 8—there goes the modeling career. Need to lose 10 lbs.
8:19 AM March 1st from Tweetie

TYME2WASTE Think that covers it.
8:20 AM March 1st from Tweetie

TYME2WASTE It's snowing in the mountains but it's not down here snow falling in the sunlight in a storm of gold. Goodbye beautiful mountains.
9:17 AM March 1st from Tweetie

TYME2WASTE Hello not so beautiful Utah desert. Utah is brown and puckered like Judy Kennedy's weird nipples.
9:51 AM March 1st from Tweetie

TYME2WASTE @caseinSD Yes she does have weird nipples. And it doesn't make me a lesbo for noticing. Everyone notices.
10:02 AM March 1st from Tweetie

----

more

TYME2WASTE Sagebrush!!!!!! W00t!
11:09 AM March 1st from Tweetie

TYME2WASTE Now Eric is trying on my pantyhose. He's bored. Mom thinks its funny but Dad is stressed.
12:20 PM March 1st from Tweetie

TYME2WASTE I dared Eric to wear a skirt in the diner to get our takeout. Dad says no. Mom is still laughing.
12:36 PM March 1st from Tweetie

TYME2WASTE I promised him if he does it I'll invite a certain hot goth to the pool party in April so he can see her in her tacky bikini.
12:39 PM March 1st from Tweetie

TYME2WASTE Theres no way he'll do it.
12:42 PM March 1st from Tweetie

TYME2WASTE ohmigod hes doing it. Dad is going into the diner with him to make sure he isn't killed by offended Mormons.
12:44 PM March 1st from Tweetie

TYME2WASTE Eric came back alive. Eric saves the day. I'm actually glad to be in the van right now.
12:59 PM March 1st from Tweetie

TYME2WASTE Dad says Eric sat at the bar and talked football with this big trucker guy. Trucker guy was fine with the skirt and pantyhose.
1:03 PM March 1st from Tweetie

TYME2WASTE He's still wearing it. The skirt. He's probably a total closet tranny. Sicko. Course that would be fun. We could shop together.
1:45 PM March 1st from Tweetie

------

more

TYME2WASTE @caseinSD Yes we do have to invite a certain goth to the pool party now. She probably won't even come. I think sunlight burns her.

2:09 PM March 1st from Tweetie

TYME2WASTE Every time I start to fall asleep the van hits a bump and my head falls off the seat.

11:01 PM March 1st from Tweetie

TYME2WASTE Trying to sleep.

11:31 PM March 1st from Tweetie

TYME2WASTE I give up trying to sleep.

1:01 AM March 2nd from Tweetie

TYME2WASTE Oh fuck Eric. He's asleep and he looks like he's having a wet dream about a certain goth chick.

1:07 AM March 2nd from Tweetie

TYME2WASTE Meanwhile I'd have a better chance of sleeping if there were only steel pins inserted under my eyelids.

1:09 AM March 2nd from Tweetie

TYME2WASTE I'm so happy right now. I just want to hold this moment for as long as I can.

6:11 AM March 2nd from Tweetie

TYME2WASTE I just want to be home. I hate Mom. I hate everyone in the van. Including myself.

8:13 AM March 2nd from Tweetie

TYME2WASTE Okay. This is why I was happy earlier. It was 4 in the morning and Mom pulled into a rest area and then she came and got me.

10:21 AM March 2nd from Tweetie

---

more

TYME2WASTE She said it was my turn to drive. I said my permit is only for driving in Cali and she just said get behind the wheel.
10:22 AM March 2nd from Tweetie

TYME2WASTE She told me if I got pulled over to wake her up and we'd switch and everything would be all right.
10:23 AM March 2nd from Tweetie

TYME2WASTE So she went to sleep in the passenger seat and I drove. We were down in the desert and the sun came up behind us.
10:25 AM March 2nd from Tweetie

TYME2WASTE And then there were coyotes in the road. In the red sunlight. They were all over the interstate and I had to stop.
10:26 AM March 2nd from Tweetie

TYME2WASTE Their eyes were gold and the sun was in their fur and there were so many, this huge pack. Just standing there like they were waiting for me.
10:28 AM March 2nd from Tweetie

TYME2WASTE I wanted to take a picture with my cell phone, but I couldn't figure out where I left it. While I was looking for it they disappeared.
10:31 AM March 2nd from Tweetie

TYME2WASTE When Mom woke up I told her all about them. And then I thought she'd be mad I didn't shake her awake to see them so I said I was sorry.
10:34 AM March 2nd from Tweetie

more

TYME2WASTE And she said she was glad I didn't wake her up, because that moment was just for me. And for like three seconds I liked her again.
10:35 AM March 2nd from Tweetie

TYME2WASTE But then in the place we ate breakfast I was looking at my e-mail for a sec. & I heard Mom saying to the waitress, we apologize for her.
10:37 AM March 2nd from Tweetie

TYME2WASTE I guess the waitress was standing there waiting for my order and I didn't notice.
10:40 AM March 2nd from Tweetie

TYME2WASTE But I didn't sleep all night and I was tired and zoned out and that's why I didn't notice, not 'cause I was looking at the phone.
10:42 AM March 2nd from Tweetie

TYME2WASTE And Mom had to trot out her stories about being a waitress herself and that it was demeaning not to be acknowledged.
10:45 AM March 2nd from Tweetie

TYME2WASTE Just to rub it in. And she can be completely right and I can still hate the way she makes me feel like shit at every opportunity.
10:46 AM March 2nd from Tweetie

TYME2WASTE I napped but I don't feel better.
4:55 PM March 2nd from Tweetie

TYME2WASTE Dad of course has to go the slowest possible route by way of every backroad. Mom says he missed a turn and added 100 miles to the trip.
6:30 PM March 2nd from Tweetie

---

more

TYME2WASTE **Now Mom and Dad are fighting. OMG I want out of this van.**
6:37 PM March 2nd from Tweetie

TYME2WASTE **Eric I am psychically willing you to find some reason for us to get off the road. Put on the pantyhose again. Say you have to pee.**
6:49 PM March 2nd from Tweetie

TYME2WASTE **Anything. Please.**
6:49 PM March 2nd from Tweetie

TYME2WASTE **No no no no. When I was sending you psychic signals, I was not signaling to you to pull over for this.**
6:57 PM March 2nd from Tweetie

TYME2WASTE **Mom doesn't want to pull over either. Write it down, kids, first time in two years we've agreed on anything.**
7:00 PM March 2nd from Tweetie

TYME2WASTE **Oh Dad is being a prick now. He says there was no point in taking backroads if we weren't going to find some culture.**
7:02 PM March 2nd from Tweetie

TYME2WASTE **We are driving up to something called The Circus of the Dead. The ticket guy looks really REALLY sick. Not funny sick. SICK sick.**
7:06 PM March 2nd from Tweetie

TYME2WASTE **Sores around his mouth and few teeth and I can smell him. He's got a pet rat. His pet rat dived in his pocket and came out with the tickets.**
7:08 PM March 2nd from Tweetie

TYME2WASTE **No it wasn't cute. None of us want to touch the tickets.**
7:10 PM March 2nd from Tweetie

---

more

TYME2WASTE Boy, they're really packing them in. Show starts in 15 min. but the parking lot is 1/2 empty. The big top is a black tent with holes in it.
7:13 PM March 2nd from Tweetie

TYME2WASTE Mom says to be sure to keep doing whatever I'm doing on my phone. She wouldn't want me to look up and see something happening.
7:17 PM March 2nd from Tweetie

TYME2WASTE Oh that was shitty. She just said to Dad that I'll love the circus because it'll be just like the internet.
7:18 PM March 2nd from Tweetie

TYME2WASTE Youtube is full of clowns, message boards are full of fire-breathers and blogs are for people who can't live without a spotlight on them.
7:20 PM March 2nd from Tweetie

TYME2WASTE I'm going to tweet like 5 times a minute and make her insane.
7:21 PM March 2nd from Tweetie

TYME2WASTE The usher is a funny old Mickey Rooney type with a bowler and a cigar. He also has on a hazmat suit. He says so he can't get bitten.
7:25 PM March 2nd from Tweetie

TYME2WASTE I almost fell twice on the walk to our seats. Guess they're saving $ on lights. I'm using my iPhone as a flashlight. Hope there isn't a fire
7:28 PM March 2nd from Tweetie

TYME2WASTE God this is the stinkiest circus ever. I don't know what I'm smelling. Are those the animals? Call PETA.
7:30 PM March 2nd from Tweetie

more

TYME2WASTE **I can't believe how many people there are. Every seat is taken. Don't know where this crowd came from.**
7:31 PM March 2nd from Tweetie

TYME2WASTE **They must've had us park in a second-ary parking lot. Oh, wait, they just flipped on a spotlight. Showtime. Beating heart, restrain yourself.**
7:34 PM March 2nd from Tweetie

TYME2WASTE **Well that got Eric and Dad's attention. The ring mistress came out on stilts and she's practically naked. Fishnets and top hat.**
7:38 PM March 2nd from Tweetie

TYME2WASTE **She's weird. She talks like she's stoned. Did I mention there are zombies in clown outfits chasing her around?**
7:40 PM March 2nd from Tweetie

TYME2WASTE **The zombies are waaay gross. They have on big clown shoes, and polka dot outfits, and clown makeup.**
7:43 PM March 2nd from Tweetie

TYME2WASTE **But the makeup is flaking off, and beneath it they're all rotted and black. Yow! They almost grabbed her. She's quick.**
7:44 PM March 2nd from Tweetie

TYME2WASTE **She says she's been a prisoner of the circus for six weeks and that she survived because she learned the stilts fast.**
7:47 PM March 2nd from Tweetie

TYME2WASTE **She said her boyfriend couldn't walk on them and fell down and was eaten his first night. She said her best friend was eaten the 2nd night.**
7:49 PM March 2nd from Tweetie

----

more

TYME2WASTE She walked right up to the wall under us and begged someone to pull her over and rescue her, but the guy in the front row just laughed.
7:50 PM March 2nd from Tweetie

TYME2WASTE Then she had to run away in a hurry before Zippo the Zombie knocked her off her stilts. It's all very well choreographed.
7:50 PM March 2nd from Tweetie

TYME2WASTE You can totally believe they're trying to get her.
7:51 PM March 2nd from Tweetie

TYME2WASTE They rolled a cannon out. She said here at the Circus of the Dead we always begin things with a bang. She read it off a card.
7:54 PM March 2nd from Tweetie

TYME2WASTE She walked up to a tall door and banged on it and for a minute I didn't think they were going to let her out of the ring, but then they did.
7:55 PM March 2nd from Tweetie

TYME2WASTE Two men in hazmat suits just led a zombie out. He's got a metal collar around his neck with a black stick attached.
7:56 PM March 2nd from Tweetie

TYME2WASTE They're using the stick to hold him at a distance so he can't grab them.
7:57 PM March 2nd from Tweetie

TYME2WASTE Eric says he has fantasies about a certain goth girl putting him in a rig like that.
7:58 PM March 2nd from Tweetie

more

TYME2WASTE This show would be a great date for the two of them. It's got a hint of sex, a whiff of bondage, and it's really really morbid.

7:59 PM March 2nd from Tweetie

TYME2WASTE They put the zombie in the cannon.

8:00 PM March 2nd from Tweetie

TYME2WASTE Auuuughhh! They pointed the cannon at the crowd and fired it and fucking pieces of zombie went everywhere.

8:03 PM March 2nd from Tweetie

TYME2WASTE The guy in the row in front of us got smashed in the mouth with a flying shoe. He's bleeding and everything.

8:05 PM March 2nd from Tweetie

TYME2WASTE Fucking yuck! There's still a foot inside the shoe! It's totally realistic looking.

8:08 PM March 2nd from Tweetie

TYME2WASTE The guy sitting in front of us just walked off w/his wife to complain. Same dude who laffed at the ringmistress when she asked for help.

8:11 PM March 2nd from Tweetie

TYME2WASTE Dad had a zombie lip in his hair. I am so glad I didn't eat lunch. Looks like a gummy worm and it smells like ass.

8:13 PM March 2nd from Tweetie

TYME2WASTE Naturally Eric wants to keep it.

8:13 PM March 2nd from Tweetie

----

more

TYME2WASTE Here comes the ringmistress again. She says the next act is the cat's meo
8:14 PM March 2nd from Tweetie

TYME2WASTE OMG OMG that was not funny. She almost fell down and the way they were snarling
8:16 PM March 2nd from Tweetie

TYME2WASTE The men in hazmat suits just wheeled in a lion in a cage. Yay, a lion! I am still girl enough to like a big cat.
8:17 PM March 2nd from Tweetie

TYME2WASTE Oh that's a really sad sick looking lion. Not fun. They're opening the cage and sending in zombies and he's hissing like a housecat.
8:19 PM March 2nd from Tweetie

TYME2WASTE Roawwwwr! Lion power. He's swatting them down and shredding them apart. He's got an arm in his mouth. Everyone cheering.
8:21 PM March 2nd from Tweetie

TYME2WASTE Eeeuuuw. Not so much cheering now. He's got one and he's tugging out its guts like he's pulling on one end of a tug rope.
8:22 PM March 2nd from Tweetie

TYME2WASTE They're sending in more zombies. No one laughing or cheering now. It's really crowded in there.
8:24 PM March 2nd from Tweetie

TYME2WASTE I can't even see the lion anymore. Lots of angry snarling and flying fur and walking corpses getting knocked around.
8:24 PM March 2nd from Tweetie

more

TYME2WASTE **OH GROSS. The lion made a sound, like this scared whine, and now the zombies are passing around organ meat and hunks of fur.**
8:25 PM March 2nd from Tweetie

TYME2WASTE **They're eating. That's awful. I feel sick.**
8:26 PM March 2nd from Tweetie

TYME2WASTE **Dad saw I was getting upset and told me how they did it. The cage has a false bottom. They pulled the lion out through the floor.**
8:30 PM March 2nd from Tweetie

TYME2WASTE **You really get swept up in this thing.**
8:30 PM March 2nd from Tweetie

TYME2WASTE **The Mickey Rooney guy who led us back to the seats just showed up with a flashlight. He says we left the headlights on in the van.**
8:31 PM March 2nd from Tweetie

TYME2WASTE **Eric went to turn them off. He has to pee anyway.**
8:32 PM March 2nd from Tweetie

TYME2WASTE **The fireswallower just came out. He has no eyes and there's some kind of steel contraption forcing his head back and his mouth open.**
8:34 PM March 2nd from Tweetie

TYME2WASTE **One of the men in the hazmat suits is FUCK ME.**
8:35 PM March 2nd from Tweetie

TYME2WASTE **They shoved a torch down his throat and now he's burning! He's running around with smoke coming out of his mouth and**
8:36 PM March 2nd from Tweetie more

TYME2WASTE fire in his head coming out his eyes like a jack o lante
8:36 PM March 2nd from Tweetie

TYME2WASTE They just let him burn to death from the inside out. Realest thing I've ever seen.
8:39 PM March 2nd from Tweetie

TYME2WASTE What's even realer is the corpse after the hazmat guys sprayed it down with the fire extinguishers. It looks so sad and shriveled and black.
8:39 PM March 2nd from Tweetie

TYME2WASTE The ringmistress is back. She's really weaving around. I think something is wrong with her ankle.
8:40 PM March 2nd from Tweetie

TYME2WASTE She says someone from the audience has agreed to be tonight's sacrifice. She says he will be the lucky one.
8:41 PM March 2nd from Tweetie

TYME2WASTE He? I thought the sacrifice was usually a girl in this sort of situation.
8:41 PM March 2nd from Tweetie

TYME2WASTE Oh no he did not. They just wheeled Eric out, cuffed to a big wooden wheel. He winked on the way past. Psycho. Go Eric!
8:42 PM March 2nd from Tweetie

TYME2WASTE They hauled out a zombie and chained him to a stake in the dirt. There's a box of hatchets in front of him. Don't like where this is going.
8:43 PM March 2nd from Tweetie

------

more

TYME2WASTE Everyone's laughing now. The lion scene was a little grim, but we're back to funny again. The zombie threw the first hatchet into the crowd.

8:45 PM March 2nd from Tweetie

TYME2WASTE There was a thunk, and someone screamed like they got it in the head. Obvious plant.

8:45 PM March 2nd from Tweetie

TYME2WASTE Eric is spinning around and around on the wheel. He's telling the zombie to kill him before he throws up.

8:46 PM March 2nd from Tweetie

TYME2WASTE Eeeks! I'm not as brave as Eric. A knife just banged into the wheel next to his head. Like: INCHES. Eric screamed too. Bet he wishes now

8:47 PM March 2nd from Tweetie

TYME2WASTE OMGOMEO

8:47 PM March 2nd from Tweetie

TYME2WASTE Okay. He must be okay. He was still smiling when they wheeled him out of the ring. The hatchet went right in the side of his neck.

8:50 PM March 2nd from Tweetie

TYME2WASTE Dad says it's a trick. Dad says he's fine. He says later Eric will come out as a zombie. That it's part of the show.

8:51 PM March 2nd from Tweetie

TYME2WASTE Yep, looks like Dad's right. They've promised Eric will reemerge shortly.

8:53 PM March 2nd from Tweetie

TYME2WASTE Mom is wigging. She wants Dad to check on Eric.

8:54 PM March 2nd from Tweetie

---

more

TYME2WASTE She's being kind of crazy. She's talking about how the guy who sat in front of us never came back after he got hit by the shoe.
8:55 PM March 2nd from Tweetie

TYME2WASTE I don't really see what that has to do with Eric. And besides, if I got hit by a flying shoe...
8:55 PM March 2nd from Tweetie

TYME2WASTE Okay, Dad is going to check on Eric. Sanity restored.
8:56 PM March 2nd from Tweetie

TYME2WASTE Here comes the ringmistress again. This is why Eric agreed to go backstage. With the fishnets and black panties she's very goth-hot.
8:56 PM March 2nd from Tweetie

TYME2WASTE She's being weird. She isn't saying anything about the next act. She says if she goes off script they don't let her out of the ring.
8:57 PM March 2nd from Tweetie

TYME2WASTE But she doesn't care. She says she twisted her ankle and she knows tonight is her last night.
8:58 PM March 2nd from Tweetie

TYME2WASTE She says her name is Gail Ross and she went to high school in Plano.
8:59 PM March 2nd from Tweetie

TYME2WASTE She says she was going to marry her boyfriend after college. She says his name was Craig and he wanted to teach.
9:00 PM March 2nd from Tweetie

more

TYME2WASTE She says she's sorry for all of us. She says they take our cars and dispose of them while we're in the tent.
9:01 PM March 2nd from Tweetie

TYME2WASTE She says 12,000 people vanish every year on the roads with no explanation, their cars turn up empty or not at all and no one will miss us.
9:02 PM March 2nd from Tweetie

TYME2WASTE Creepy stuff. Here's Eric. His zombie make-up is really good. Most of the zombies are black and rotted but he looks like fresh kill.
9:03 PM March 2nd from Tweetie

TYME2WASTE Still got the hatchet in the neck. That looks totally fake.
9:03 PM March 2nd from Tweetie

TYME2WASTE He's not very good at being a zombie. He isn't even trying to walk slow. He's really going after her.
9:04 PM March 2nd from Tweetie

TYME2WASTE oh shit I hope that's part of the show. He just knocked her down. Oh Eric Eric Eric. She hit the dirt really, really hard.
9:05 PM March 2nd from Tweetie

TYME2WASTE They're eating her like they ate the lion. Eric is playing with guts. He's so gross. He's going totally method.
9:07 PM March 2nd from Tweetie

TYME2WASTE Gymnastics now. They're making a human pyramid. Or maybe I should say an INhuman pyramid. They're surprisingly good at it. For zombies.
9:10 PM March 2nd from Tweetie

more

TYME2WASTE Eric is climbing the pyramid like he knows what he's doing. I wonder if they gave him backstage training or
9:11 PM March 2nd from Tweetie

TYME2WASTE He's up high enough to grab the wall around the ring. He's snarling at someone in the front row, just a couple feet from here. Wait
9:13 PM March 2nd from Tweetie

TYME2WASTE no lights fuck thta was stupid whyd they put out the
9:14 PM March 2nd from Tweetie

TYME2WASTE someones screaming
9:15 PM March 2nd from Tweetie

TYME2WASTE this is really dangerous its so dark and lots of people are screaming and getting up. im mad now you don't do this to people you don't
9:18 PM March 2nd from Tweetie

TYME2WASTE we need help we areacv
9:32 PM March 2nd from Tweetie

TYME2WASTE gtttttgggtttggtttttttttgggbbbnnnfrfffgt
9:32 PM March 2nd from Tweetie

TYME2WASTE I cant say anything theyll hear. were beinb ver y qiuet wevegot a plas
10:17 PM March 2nd from Tweetie

TYME2WASTE were off i70 mom says it was exit 331 but we drove a long way the last town we saw was called ucmba
10:19 PM March 2nd from Tweetie

---

more

TYME2WASTE cumba
10:19 PM March 2nd from Tweetie

TYME2WASTE the people in the stands were all dead except for us and a few others and they were roped together tethered
10:20 PM March 2nd from Tweetie

TYME2WASTE please someone send help call UT state police not making this up
10:22 PM March 2nd from Tweetie

TYME2WASTE @caseinSD lease help you know me you know I wouldnt isnta joke
10:23 PM March 2nd from Tweetie

TYME2WASTE have to be quiet so I can't call got the ringer is turned off
10:24 PM March 2nd from Tweetie

TYME2WASTE AZ state police mom says its arizona not UT our van is a white econlein
10:27 PM March 2nd from Tweetie

TYME2WASTE its quiet less screaming now less growling
10:50 PM March 2nd from Tweetie

TYME2WASTE theyre dragging people into piles
10:56 PM March 2nd from Tweetie

TYME2WASTE eating theyre eating them
11:09 PM March 2nd from Tweetie

TYME2WASTE the man who got hit by the shoe earlier walked by but he isn't like he was he hes dead now
11:11 PM March 2nd from Tweetie

more

TYME2WASTE just mom and me i love my mom shes so brave i love her so much so much i never ment it none of the bad things not one i am with her i am
11:37 PM March 2nd from Tweetie

TYME2WASTE imso csared
11:39 PM March 2nd from Tweetie

TYME2WASTE theyresearching to see if anyone is left with flashlights the men in hazmat soups i say go out mom says no
11:41 PM March 2nd from Tweetie

TYME2WASTE were here were waiting for help please forward this to everyone on twitter this is true not an internet prank believe believe believe pleves
12:03 AM March 3rd from Tweetie

TYME2WASTE ohgod it was dad went by mom sat up and said his name and mom and dad and mom and dad
12:09 AM March 3rd from Tweetie

TYME2WASTE notdad oh my oh bnb nnnb ;;/'/.,/;'././/
12:13 AM March 3rd from Tweetie

TYME2WASTE /'/.
12:13 AM March 3rd from Tweetie

TYME2WASTE Were you SCARED by this TWITTER FEED???!?!?
9:17 AM March 3rd from Tweetie

TYME2WASTE The FEAR—and THE FUN—is only just BEGINNING!
9:20 AM March 3rd from Tweetie

more

TYME2WASTE "THE CIRCUS OF THE DEAD" featuring our newest RINGMISTRESS the SEXY & DARING BLAKE THE BLACK-HEARTED.
9:22AM March 3rd from Tweetie

TYME2WASTE Watch as our newest QUEEN OF THE TRAPEEZE introduces our PERVERSE & PERNICIOUS performers...
9:23 AM March 3rd from Tweetie

TYME2WASTE ...while DANGLING FROM A ROPE ABOVE THE RAVENOUS DEAD!
9:23 AM March 3rd from Tweetie

TYME2WASTE A CIRCUS so SHOCKING it makes the JIM ROSE CIRCUS look like THE MUPPET SHOW!
9:25 AM March 3rd from Tweetie

TYME2WASTE Now touring with stops in ALL CORNERS OF THE COUNTRY!
9:26 AM March 3rd from Tweetie

TYME2WASTE Visit our Facebook page and join our E-MAIL LIST to find out when we'll be in YOUR AREA.
9:28 AM March 3rd from Tweetie

TYME2WASTE STAY CONNECTED OR YOU DON'T KNOW WHAT YOU'LL MISS!
9:30 AM March 3rd from Tweetie

TYME2WASTE "THE CIRCUS OF THE DEAD"...Where YOU are the concessions! Other circuses promise DEATH-DEFYING THRILLS!
9:31 AM March 3rd from Tweetie

TYME2WASTE BUT ONLY WE DELIVER! (Tix to be purchased at box office day of show. No refunds. Cash only. Minors must be accompanied by adult.)
9:31 AM March 3rd from Tweetie

more

CHADBOURNE

THE FACTS IN THE CASE OF THE DEPARTURE OF MISS FINCH

by Neil Gaiman

T o begin at the end: I arranged the thin slice of pickled ginger, pink and translucent, on top of the pale yellowtail flesh, and dipped the whole arrangement—ginger, fish, and vinegared rice—into the soy sauce, flesh-side down; then I devoured it in a couple of bites.

"I think we ought to go to the police," I said.

"And tell them what, exactly?" asked Jane.

"Well, we could file a missing persons report, or something. I don't know."

"And where did you last see the young lady?" asked Jonathan, in his most policemanlike tones. "Ah, I see. Did you know that wasting police time is normally considered an offense, sir?"

"But the whole circus…"

"These are transient persons, sir, of legal age. They come and go. If you have their names, I suppose I can take a report…"

I gloomily ate a salmon skin roll. "Well, then," I said, "why don't we go to the papers?"

"Brilliant idea," said Jonathan, in the sort of tone of voice which indicates that the person talking doesn't think it's a brilliant idea at all.

"Jonathan's right," said Jane. "They won't listen to us."

"Why wouldn't they believe us? We're reliable. Honest citizens. All that."

"You're a fantasy writer," she said. "You make up stuff like this for a living. No one's going to believe you."

"But you two saw it all as well. You'd back me up."

"Jonathan's got a new series on cult horror movies coming out in the autumn. They'll say he's just trying to get cheap publicity for the show. And I've got another book coming out. Same thing."

"So you're saying that we can't tell anyone?" I sipped my green tea.

"No," Jane said, reasonably, "we can tell anyone we want. It's making them believe us that's problematic. Or, if you ask me, impossible."

The pickled ginger was sharp on my tongue. "You may be right," I said. "And Miss Finch is probably much happier wherever she is right now than she would be here."

"But her name isn't Miss Finch," said Jane, "it's — —" and she said our former companion's real name.

"I know. But it's what I thought when I first saw her," I explained. "Like in one of those movies. You know. When they take off their glasses and put down their hair. 'Why, Miss Finch. You're beautiful.'"

"She certainly was that," said Jonathan, "in the end, anyway." And he shivered at the memory.

There. So now you know: that's how it all ended, and how the three of us left it, several years ago. All that remains is the beginning, and the details.

For the record, I don't expect you to believe any of this. Not really. I'm a liar by trade, after all; albeit, I like to think, an honest liar. If I belonged to a gentlemen's club I'd recount it over a glass or two of port late in the evening as the fire burned low, but I am a member of no such club, and I'll write it better than ever I'd tell it. So here you will learn of Miss Finch (whose name, as you already know, was not Finch, nor anything like it, since I'm changing names here to disguise the guilty) and how it came about that she was unable to join us for sushi. Believe it or not, just as you wish. I am not even certain that I believe it anymore. It all seems such a long way away.

I could find a dozen beginnings. Perhaps it might be best to begin in a hotel room, in London, a few years ago. It was 11:00 AM. The phone began to ring, which surprised me. I hurried over to answer it.

"Hello?" It was too early in the morning for anyone in America to be phoning me, and there was no one in England who was meant to know that I was even in the country.

"Hi," said a familiar voice, adopting an American accent of monumentally unconvincing proportions. "This is Hiram P. Muzzle dexter of Colossal

Pictures. We're working on a film that's a remake of *Raiders of the Lost Ark* but instead of Nazis it has women with enormous knockers in it. We've heard that you were astonishingly well supplied in the trouser department and might be willing to take on the part of our male lead, Minnesota Jones…"

"Jonathan?" I said. "How on earth did you find me here?"

"You knew it was me," he said, aggrieved, his voice losing all trace of the improbable accent and returning to his native London.

"Well, it sounded like you," I pointed out. "Anyway, you didn't answer my question. No one's meant to know that I was here."

"I have my ways," he said, not very mysteriously. "Listen, if Jane and I were to offer to feed you sushi—something I recall you eating in quantities that put me in mind of feeding time at London Zoo's Walrus House—and if we offered to take you to the theater before we fed you, what would you say?"

"Not sure. I'd say 'Yes' I suppose. Or 'What's the catch?' I might say that."

"Not exactly a catch," said Jonathan. "I wouldn't exactly call it a *catch*. Not a real catch. Not really."

"You're lying, aren't you?"

Somebody said something near the phone, and then Jonathan said, "Hang on, Jane wants a word." Jane is Jonathan's wife.

"How are you?" she said.

"Fine, thanks."

"Look," she said, "you'd be doing us a tremendous favor—not that we wouldn't love to see you, because we would, but you see, there's someone…"

"She's your friend," said Jonathan, in the background.

"She's *not* my friend. I hardly know her," she said, away from the phone, and then, to me, "Um, look, there's someone we're sort of lumbered with. She's not in the country for very long, and I wound up agreeing to entertain her and look after her tomorrow night. She's pretty frightful, actually. And Jonathan heard that you were in town from someone at your film company, and we thought you might be perfect to make it all less awful, so please say yes."

So I said yes.

In retrospect, I think the whole thing might have been the fault of the late Ian Fleming, creator of James Bond. I had read an article the previous month, in which Ian Fleming had advised any would-be writer who had a book to get done that wasn't getting written to go to a hotel to write it. I had, not a novel, but a film script that wasn't getting written; so I bought a plane ticket to London, promised the film company that they'd have a finished script in three weeks' time, and took a room in an eccentric hotel in Little Venice.

I told no one in England that I was there. Had people known, my days and nights would have been spent seeing them, not staring at a computer screen and, sometimes, writing.

Truth to tell, I was bored half out of my mind and ready to welcome any interruption.

Early the next evening I arrived at Jonathan and Jane's house, which was more or less in Hampstead. There was a small green sports car parked outside. Up the stairs, and I knocked at the door. Jonathan answered it; he wore an impressive suit. His light brown hair was longer than I remembered it from the last time I had seen him, in life or on television.

"Hello," said Jonathan. "The show we were going to take you to has been canceled. But we can go to something else, if that's okay with you."

I was about to point out that I didn't know what we were originally going to see, so a change of plans would make no difference to me, but Jonathan was already leading me into the living room, establishing that I wanted fizzy water to drink, assuring me that we'd still be eating sushi and that Jane would be coming downstairs as soon as she had put the children to bed.

They had just redecorated the living room, in a style Jonathan described as Moorish brothel. "It didn't set out to be a Moorish brothel," he explained. "Or any kind of a brothel really. It was just where we ended up. The brothel look."

"Has he told you all about Miss Finch?" asked Jane. Her hair had been red the last time I had seen her. Now it was dark brown; and she curved like a Raymond Chandler simile.

"Who?"

"We were talking about Ditko's inking style," apologized Jonathan. "And the Neal Adams issues of *Jerry Lewis.*"

"But she'll be here any moment. And he has to know about her before she gets here."

Jane is, by profession, a journalist, but had become a best-selling author almost by accident. She had written a companion volume to accompany a television series about two paranormal investigators, which had risen to the top of the best-seller lists and stayed there.

Jonathan had originally become famous hosting an evening talk show, and had since parlayed his gonzo charm into a variety of fields. He's the same person whether the camera is on or off, which is not always true of television folk.

"It's a kind of family obligation," Jane explained. "Well, not exactly *family*."

"She's Jane's friend," said her husband, cheerfully.

"She is *not* my friend. But I couldn't exactly say no to them, could I? And she's only in the country for a couple of days."

And who Jane could not say no to, and what the obligation was, I never was to learn, for at the moment the doorbell rang, and I found myself being introduced to Miss Finch. Which, as I have mentioned, was not her name.

She wore a black leather cap, and a black leather coat, and had black, black hair, pulled tightly back into a small bun, done up with a pottery tie. She wore makeup, expertly applied to give an impression of severity that a professional dominatrix might have envied. Her lips were tight together, and she glared at the world through a pair of definite black-rimmed spectacles—they punctuated her face much too definitely to ever be mere glasses.

"So," she said, as if she were pronouncing a death sentence, "we're going to the theater, then."

"Well, yes and no," said Jonathan. "I mean, yes, we are still going out, but we're not going to be able to see *The Romans in Britain*."

"Good," said Miss Finch. "In poor taste anyway. Why anyone would have thought that nonsense would make a musical I do not know."

"So we're going to a circus," said Jane, reassuringly. "And then we're going to eat sushi."

Miss Finch's lips tightened. "I do not approve of circuses," she said.

"There aren't any animals in this circus," said Jane.

"Good," said Miss Finch, and she sniffed. I was beginning to understand why Jane and Jonathan had wanted me along.

The rain was pattering down as we left the house, and the street was dark. We squeezed ourselves into the sports car and headed out into London. Miss Finch and I were in the backseat of the car, pressed uncomfortably close together.

Jane told Miss Finch that I was a writer, and told me that Miss Finch was a biologist.

"Biogeologist actually," Miss Finch corrected her. "Were you serious about eating sushi, Jonathan?"

"Er, yes. Why? Don't you like sushi?"

"Oh, I'll eat *my* food cooked," she said, and began to list for us all the various flukes, worms, and parasites that lurk in the flesh of fish and which are only killed by cooking. She told us of their life cycles while the rain pelted down, slicking night-time London into garish neon colors. Jane shot me a sympathetic glance from the passenger seat, then she and Jonathan went back to scrutinizing a handwritten set of directions to wherever we were going. We crossed the Thames at London Bridge while Miss Finch lectured us about blindness, madness, and liver failure; and she was just elaborating on the symptoms of elephantiasis as proudly as if she had invented them herself when we pulled up in a small back street in the neighborhood of Southwark Cathedral.

"So where's the circus?" I asked.

"Somewhere around here," said Jonathan. "They contacted us about being on the Christmas special. I tried to pay for tonight's show, but they insisted on comping us in."

"I'm sure it will be fun," said Jane, hopefully.

Miss Finch sniffed.

A fat, bald man, dressed as a monk, ran down the pavement toward us. "There you are!" he said. "I've been keeping an eye out for you. You're late. It'll be starting in a moment." He turned around and scampered back the way he had come, and we followed him. The rain splashed on his bald head and ran down his face, turning his Fester Addams makeup into streaks of white and brown. He pushed open a door in the side of a wall.

"In here."

We went in. There were about fifty people in there already, dripping and steaming, while a tall woman in bad vampire makeup holding a flashlight walked around checking tickets, tearing off stubs, selling tickets to anyone who didn't have one. A small, stocky woman immediately in front of us shook the rain from her umbrella and glowered about her fiercely. "This'd better be gud," she told the young man with her—her son, I suppose. She paid for tickets for both of them.

The vampire woman reached us, recognized Jonathan and said, "Is this your party? Four people? Yes? You're on the guest list," which provoked another suspicious stare from the stocky woman.

A recording of a clock ticking began to play. A clock struck twelve (it was barely eight by my watch), and the wooden double doors at the far end of the room creaked open. "Enter...of your own free will!" boomed a voice, and it laughed maniacally. We walked through the door into darkness.

It smelled of wet bricks and of decay. I knew then where we were: there are networks of old cellars that run beneath some of the overground train tracks— vast, empty, linked rooms of various sizes and shapes. Some of them are used for storage by wine merchants and used-car sellers; some are squatted in, until the lack of light and facilities drives the squatters back into the daylight; most of them stand empty, waiting for the inevitable arrival of the wrecking ball and the open air and the time when all their secrets and mysteries will be no more.

A train rattled by above us.

We shuffled forward, led by Uncle Fester and the vampire woman, into a sort of holding pen where we stood and waited.

"I hope we're going to be able to sit down after this," said Miss Finch.

When we were all settled the flashlights went out, and the spotlights went on.

The people came out. Some of them rode motorbikes and dune buggies. They ran and they laughed and they swung and they cackled. Whoever had dressed them had been reading too many comics, I thought, or watched *Mad Max* too many times. There were punks and nuns and vampires and monsters and strippers and the living dead.

They danced and capered around us while the ringmaster—identifiable by his top hat—sang Alice Cooper's song "Welcome to My Nightmare," and sang it very badly.

"I know Alice Cooper," I muttered to myself, misquoting something half-remembered, "and you, sir, are no Alice Cooper."

"It's pretty naff," agreed Jonathan.

Jane shushed us. As the last notes faded away the ringmaster was left alone in the spotlight. He walked around our enclosure while he talked.

"Welcome, welcome, one and all, to the Theater of Night's Dreaming," he said.

"Fan of yours," whispered Jonathan.

"I think it's a *Rocky Horror Show* line," I whispered back.

"Tonight you will all be witnesses to monsters undreamed-of, freaks and creatures of the night, to displays of ability to make you shriek with fear—and laugh with joy. We shall travel," he told us, "from room to room—and in each of these subterranean caverns another nightmare, another delight, another display of wonder awaits you! Please—for your own safety—I must reiterate this!—Do not leave the spectating area marked out for you in each room—on pain of doom, bodily injury, and the loss of your immortal soul! Also, I must stress that the use of flash photography or of any recording devices is utterly forbidden."

And with that, several young women holding pencil flashlights led us into the next room.

"No seats then," said Miss Finch, unimpressed.

The First Room

In the first room a smiling blonde woman wearing a spangled bikini, with needle tracks down her arms, was chained by a hunchback and Uncle Fester to a large wheel.

The wheel spun slowly around, and a fat man in a red cardinal's costume threw knives at the woman, outlining her body. Then the hunchback blindfolded the cardinal, who threw the last three knives straight and true to outline the woman's head. He removed his blindfold. The woman was untied and lifted down from the wheel. They took a bow. We clapped.

Then the cardinal took a trick knife from his belt and pretended to cut the woman's throat with it. Blood spilled down from the knife blade. A few members of the audience gasped, and one excitable girl gave a small scream, while her friends giggled.

The cardinal and the spangled woman took their final bow. The lights went down. We followed the flashlights down a brick-lined corridor.

The Second Room

The smell of damp was worse in here; it smelled like a cellar, musty and forgotten. I could hear somewhere the drip of rain. The ringmaster introduced the Creature—"Stitched together in the laboratories of the night, the

Creature is capable of astonishing feats of strength." The Frankenstein's monster makeup was less than convincing, but the Creature lifted a stone block with fat Uncle Fester sitting on it, and he held back the dune buggy (driven by the vampire woman) at full throttle. For his pièce de résistance he blew up a hot-water bottle, then popped it.

"Roll on the sushi," I muttered to Jonathan.

Miss Finch pointed out, quietly, that in addition to the danger of parasites, it was also the case that bluefin tuna, swordfish, and Chilean sea bass were all being overfished and could soon be rendered extinct, since they were not reproducing fast enough to catch up.

The Third Room

went up for a long way into the darkness. The original ceiling had been removed at some time in the past, and the new ceiling was the roof of the empty warehouse far above us. The room buzzed at the corners of vision with the blue-purple of ultraviolet light. Teeth and shirts and flecks of lint began to glow in the darkness. A low, throbbing music began. We looked up to see, high above us, a skeleton, an alien, a werewolf, and an angel. Their costumes fluoresced in the UV, and they glowed like old dreams high above us, on trapezes. They swung back and forth, in time with the music, and then, as one, they let go and tumbled down toward us.

We gasped, but before they reached us they bounced on the air, and rose up again, like yo-yos, and clambered back on their trapezes. We realized that they were attached to the roof by rubber cords, invisible in the darkness, and they bounced and dove and swam through the air above us while we clapped and gasped and watched them in happy silence.

The Fourth Room

was little more than a corridor: the ceiling was low, and the ringmaster strutted into the audience and picked two people out of the crowd—the stocky woman and a tall black man wearing a sheepskin coat and tan gloves—pulling them up in front of us. He announced that he would be demonstrating his hypnotic powers. He made a couple of passes in the air and rejected the stocky woman. Then he asked the man to step up onto a box.

"It's a setup," muttered Jane. "He's a plant."

A guillotine was wheeled in. The ringmaster cut a watermelon in half, to demonstrate how sharp the blade was. Then he made the man put his hand under the guillotine, and dropped the blade. The gloved hand dropped into the basket, and blood spurted from the open cuff.

Miss Finch squeaked.

Then the man picked his hand out of the basket and chased the ringmaster around us, while the *Benny Hill Show* music played.

"Artificial hand," said Jonathan.

"I saw it coming," said Jane.

Miss Finch blew her nose into a tissue. "I think it's all in very questionable taste," she said. Then they led us to

The Fifth Room

and all the lights went on. There was a makeshift wooden table along one wall, with a young bald man selling beer and orange juice and bottles of water, and signs showed the way to the toilets in the room next door. Jane went to get the drinks, and Jonathan went to use the toilets, which left me to make awkward conversation with Miss Finch.

"So," I said, "I understand you've not been back in England long."

"I've been in Komodo," she told me. "Studying the dragons. Do you know why they grew so big?"

"Er..."

"They adapted to prey upon the pygmy elephants."

"There were pygmy elephants?" I was interested. This was much more fun than being lectured on sushi flukes.

"Oh yes. It's basic island biogeology—animals will naturally tend toward either gigantism or pygmyism. There are equations, you see..." As Miss Finch talked her face became more animated, and I found myself warming to her as she explained why and how some animals grew while others shrank.

Jane brought us our drinks; Jonathan came back from the toilet, cheered and bemused by having been asked to sign an autograph while he was pissing.

"Tell me," said Jane, "I've been reading a lot of cryptozoological journals for the next of the *Guides to the Unexplained* I'm doing. As a biologist—"

"Biogeologist," interjected Miss Finch.

"Yes. What do you think the chances are of prehistoric animals being alive today, in secret, unknown to science?"

"It's very unlikely," said Miss Finch, as if she were telling us off. "There is, at any rate, no 'Lost World' off on some island, filled with mammoths and Smilodons and aepyornis...."

"Sounds a bit rude," said Jonathan. "A what?"

"Aepyornis. A giant flightless prehistoric bird," said Jane.

"I knew that really," he told her.

"Although of course, they're *not* prehistoric," said Miss Finch. "The last aepyornises were killed off by Portuguese sailors on Madagascar about three hundred years ago. And there are fairly reliable accounts of a pygmy mammoth being presented at the Russian court in the sixteenth century, and a band of something which from the descriptions we have were almost definitely some kind of saber-tooth—the Smilodon—brought in from North Africa by Vespasian to die in the circus. So these things aren't all prehistoric. Often, they're historic."

"I wonder what the point of the saber teeth would be," I said. "You'd think they'd get in the way."

"Nonsense," said Miss Finch. "Smilodon was a most efficient hunter. Must have been—the saber teeth are repeated a number of times in the fossil record. I wish with all my heart that there were some left today. But there aren't. We know the world too well."

"It's a big place," said Jane, doubtfully, and then the lights were flickered on and off, and a ghastly, disembodied voice told us to walk into the next room, that the latter half of the show was not for the faint of heart, and that later tonight, for one night only, the Theater of Night's Dreaming would be proud to present the Cabinet of Wishes Fulfill'd.

We threw away our plastic glasses, and we shuffled into

The Sixth Room

"Presenting," announced the ringmaster, "The Painmaker!"

The spotlight swung up to reveal an abnormally thin young man in bathing trunks, hanging from hooks through his nipples. Two of the punk girls helped him down to the ground, and handed him his props. He hammered a six-inch nail into his nose, lifted weights with a piercing through his tongue, put several ferrets into his bathing trunks, and, for his final trick, allowed the taller of the punk girls to use his stomach as a dartboard for accurately flung hypodermic needles.

"Wasn't he on the show, years ago?" asked Jane.

"Yeah," said Jonathan. "Really nice guy. He lit a firework held in his teeth."

"I thought you said there were no animals," said Miss Finch. "How do you think those poor ferrets feel about being stuffed into that young man's nether regions?"

"I suppose it depends mostly on whether they're boy ferrets or girl ferrets," said Jonathan, cheerfully.

The Seventh Room

contained a rock-and-roll comedy act, with some clumsy slapstick. A nun's breasts were revealed, and the hunchback lost his trousers.

The Eighth Room

was dark. We waited in the darkness for something to happen. I wanted to sit down. My legs ached, I was tired and cold, and I'd had enough.

Then someone started to shine a light at us. We blinked and squinted and covered our eyes.

"Tonight," an odd voice said, cracked and dusty. Not the ringmaster, I was sure of that. "Tonight, one of you shall get a wish. One of you will gain all that you desire, in the Cabinet of Wishes Fulfill'd. Who shall it be?"

"Ooh. At a guess, another plant in the audience," I whispered, remembering the one-handed man in the fourth room.

"Shush," said Jane.

"Who will it be? You sir? You madam?" A figure came out of the darkness and shambled toward us. It was hard to see him properly, for he held a portable spotlight. I wondered if he were wearing some kind of ape costume, for his outline seemed inhuman, and he moved as gorillas move. Perhaps it was the man who played the Creature. "Who shall it be, eh?" We squinted at him, edged out of his way.

And then he pounced. "Aha! I think we have our volunteer," he said, leaping over the rope barrier that separated the audience from the show area around us. Then he grabbed Miss Finch by the hand.

"I really don't think so," said Miss Finch, but she was being dragged away from us, too nervous, too polite, fundamentally too English to make a scene. She was pulled into the darkness, and she was gone to us.

Jonathan swore. "I don't think she's going to let us forget this in a hurry," he said.

The lights went on. A man dressed as a giant fish then proceeded to ride a motorbike around the room several times. Then he stood up on the seat as it went around. Then he sat down and drove the bike up and down the walls of the room, and then he hit a brick and skidded and fell over, and the bike landed on top of him.

The hunchback and the topless nun ran on and pulled the bike off the man in the fish-suit and hauled him away.

"I just broke my sodding leg," he was saying, in a dull, numb voice. "It's sodding broken. My sodding leg," as they carried him out.

"Do you think that was meant to happen?" asked a girl in the crowd near to us.

"No," said the man beside her.

Slightly shaken, Uncle Fester and the vampire woman ushered us forward, into

The Ninth Room

where Miss Finch awaited us.

It was a huge room. I knew that, even in the thick darkness. Perhaps the dark intensifies the other senses; perhaps it's simply that we are always processing more information than we imagine. Echoes of our shuffling and coughing came back to us from walls hundreds of feet away.

And then I became convinced, with a certainty bordering upon madness, that there were great beasts in the darkness, and that they were watching us with hunger.

Slowly the lights came on, and we saw Miss Finch. I wonder to this day where they got the costume.

Her black hair was down. The spectacles were gone. The costume, what little there was of it, fitted her perfectly. She held a spear, and she stared at us without emotion. Then the great cats padded into the light next to her. One of them threw its head back and roared.

Someone began to wail. I could smell the sharp animal stench of urine.

The animals were the size of tigers, but unstriped; they were the color of a sandy beach at evening. Their eyes were topaz, and their breath smelled of fresh meat and of blood.

I stared at their jaws: the saber teeth were indeed teeth, not tusks: huge, overgrown fangs, made for rending, for tearing, for ripping meat from the bone.

The great cats began to pad around us, circling slowly. We huddled together, closing ranks, each of us remembering in our guts what it was like in the old times, when we hid in our caves when the night came and the beasts went on the prowl; remembering when we were prey.

The Smilodons, if that was what they were, seemed uneasy, wary. Their tails switched whiplike from side to side impatiently. Miss Finch said nothing. She just stared at her animals.

Then the stocky woman raised her umbrella and waved it at one of the great cats. "Keep back, you ugly brute," she told it.

It growled at her and tensed back, like a cat about to spring.

The stocky woman went pale, but she kept her umbrella pointed out like a sword. She made no move to run in the torchlit darkness beneath the city.

And then it sprang, batting her to the ground with one huge velvet paw. It stood over her, triumphantly, and roared so deeply that I could feel it in the pit of my stomach. The stocky woman seemed to have passed out, which was, I felt, a mercy: with luck, she would not know when the bladelike fangs tore at her old flesh like twin daggers.

I looked around for some way out, but the other tiger was prowling around us, keeping us herded within the rope enclosure, like frightened sheep.

I could hear Jonathan muttering the same three dirty words, over and over and over.

"We're going to die, aren't we?" I heard myself say.

"I think so," said Jane.

Then Miss Finch pushed her way through the rope barrier, and she took the great cat by the scruff of its neck and pulled it back. It resisted, and she thwacked it on the nose with the end of her spear. Its tail went down between its legs, and it backed away from the fallen woman, cowed and obedient.

There was no blood, that I could see, and I hoped that she was only unconscious.

CHADBOURNE

In the back of the cellar room light was slowly coming up. It seemed as if dawn were breaking. I could see a jungle mist wreathing about huge ferns and hostas; and I could hear, as if from a great way off, the chirp of crickets and the call of strange birds awaking to greet the new day.

And part of me—the writer part of me, the bit that has noted the particular way the light hit the broken glass in the puddle of blood even as I staggered out from a car crash, and has observed in exquisite detail the way that my heart was broken, or did not break, in moments of real, profound, personal tragedy—it was that part of me that thought, *You could get that effect with a smoke machine, some plants, and a tape track. You'd need a really good lighting guy, of course.*

Miss Finch scratched her left breast, unselfconsciously, then she turned her back on us and walked toward the dawn and the jungle underneath the world, flanked by two padding saber-toothed tigers.

A bird screeched and chattered.

Then the dawn light faded back into darkness, and the mists shifted, and the woman and the animals were gone.

The stocky woman's son helped her to her feet. She opened her eyes. She looked shocked but unhurt. And when we knew that she was not hurt, for she picked up her umbrella, and leaned on it, and glared at us all, why then we began to applaud.

No one came to get us. I could not see Uncle Fester or the vampire woman anywhere. So unescorted we all walked on into

The Tenth Room

It was all set up for what would obviously have been the grand finale. There were even plastic seats arranged, for us to watch the show. We sat down on the seats and we waited, but nobody from the circus came on, and, it became apparent to us all after some time, no one was going to come.

People began to shuffle into the next room. I heard a door open, and the noise of traffic and the rain.

I looked at Jane and Jonathan, and we got up and walked out. In the last room was an unmanned table upon which were laid out souvenirs of the circus: posters and CDs and badges, and an open cash box. Sodium yellow light spilled in from the street outside, through an open door, and the wind gusted at the unsold posters, flapping the corners up and down impatiently.

"Should we wait for her?" one of us said, and I wish I could say that it was me. But the others shook their heads, and we walked out into the rain, which had by now subsided to a low and gusty drizzle.

After a short walk down narrow roads, in the rain and the wind, we found our way to the car. I stood on the pavement, waiting for the back door to be unlocked to let me in, and over the rain and the noise of the city I thought I heard a tiger, for, somewhere close by, there was a low roar that made the whole world shake. But perhaps it was only the passage of a train.

THE GIRL IN THE CARNIVAL GOWN

by Kelley Armstrong

W e're riding our bikes to school when the carnival passes, and with a shared look, the three of us decide we don't really need to go to school today. Trailers clunk and shuffle along the dusty road. Dismantled amusement park rides lie jumbled in unrecognizable pieces. Ragged tarps cover other trailers, leaving us vying to peek through the holes. Across each vehicle, a banner proclaims Blackrose Carnival! Opening Tonight! No specific information is given, the banners recycled for every stop, all of them tattered, one nearly ripped through. In our flyspeck town, we know only carnivals like this, tiny operations that arrive unannounced for Friday night and depart Sunday morning, on to another town, indistinguishable from ours.

We pedal madly after the procession, as if we could somehow lose them along the half-mile downtown stretch. As expected, they pull into the supermarket. The owner will go inside and negotiate with Mr. Cole, hoping to convince the old man that he should pay *them* for the sheer glamor of having a carnival in his parking lot. He'll listen, and then he'll demand a hundred dollars for the inconvenience. They'll haggle, but in the end, Mr. Cole will be counting his five twenties and ordering his staff to set up food stands out front to take advantage of the hungry crowds.

We drop our bikes beside the supermarket and lope toward the collection of trailers. Reggie strides off on reconnaissance. His twin brother, Ray, follows me, Def Leppard blasting from his Walkman headphones.

I'm cutting behind a trailer when I spot a dog. It's a huge beast, a mastiff crossbreed bound by a rusty chain that barely allows it room to turn around.

71 | ● ● ● ●

When the dog spots me, it whines and lies down, head on its paws. There's no sign of a water bowl despite a blistering June sun baking the asphalt. Bare skin flanks the dog's studded collar where its fur has rubbed away. Scars crisscross its back.

I hunker down and croon under my breath, and the dog whines again.

Reggie strides around the corner, saying something, but the slap of a door cuts him off.

"Hey!" a man shouts. "You trying to get your face bit off, boy?"

I rise, and he realizes I'm not a boy. His gaze slides over me in a way that raises my hackles. Reggie sees it, too, and he surges forward. A look from me stops him. I pull the bill of my ball cap down, as if that'll hide me.

The carnie is in his early twenties. A scraggly mustache and beard tries and fails to hide a serious lack of dental hygiene, and his hands and hair compete to see which can hold the most grease.

"We were wondering—" I begin.

"Step away from that dog, girl," the man says. "She's a killer."

I look at the dog, head still on her big paws, brown eyes turned up to me.

Reggie snorts. "Yeah, she'd kill for a good meal. When's the last time you fed her?"

The man steps toward him. "Maybe you wanna grow up a little, boy, before you talk like that."

Reggie's twelve, but he's already nearly as tall as the man, lean and lanky, and he fixes the carnie with a stare that has the guy hesitating midstep and then planting his foot hard, as if to avoid withdrawing.

"You boys get on out of here," he says. "If your cute little friend wants a look around, I'll give her the tour."

I'm ready to cut off Reggie's inevitable retort when a man walks around the trailer. He's in his forties, wearing an old-fashioned waistcoat pulled tight over his belly. He beams with the smile of a used-car salesman running behind on his monthly quota.

"Well, well, our first customers," he says. "You're a little early, kids, but I hope Charlie here was properly regaling you with the delights to come."

"We were just talking about your dog," I say. "She hadn't gotten her water yet, and I was offering to fill her bowl, knowing how busy you are setting up."

The man tilts his head, his eyes glinting with something deeper than his salesman's smirk. He studies me a moment. Then he says, "Charlie will obtain the necessary water and kibble. And I'll find you a few game tickets in thanks for noticing poor Dixie's plight. I'm Theodore Blackrose, owner of this fair festival. Barker, ringmaster, magician, and…" He winks with a look at the departing Charlie. "Carnie wrangler."

"I'm Esmerelda," I say. "But everyone calls me Ezzi."

"Ezzi?" His brows shoot up in mock horror. "What a tragic debasement of such a magnificent moniker. I shall call you Esmerelda. And your companions?"

"Reggie," I say because he really hates being called Reginald. "And his brother, Raymond." Ray nods without taking off his headphones. "Game tickets would be great, sir, but we were actually wondering if you might have some work for us."

"How can I refuse such a polite request? The extra help would be immensely appreciated. Come this way, please, and I'll take you to our foreman."

THE FOREMAN is more than happy to take advantage of three kids dumb enough to offer their services. We haul fifty-pound bags of popcorn kernels to the snack kiosks. We unpack prize boxes so tightly packed that the tiny stuffed toys spring out like confetti. We scrub dust from those tattered banners and rehang them below the supermarket sign. We even assemble a couple of midway rides…and make mental note of which ones, so we don't ride them.

It's backbreaking work, but I love the chance to dig below the surface and see how a carnival works. Reggie does, too, and he's right in there, the two of us asking questions until the carnies feign laryngitis. Ray never takes off his headphones, and it might look as if he's bored, but we're twelve—if we're bored, we say so…or, in Ray's case, he would just wander off midtask to sit on a picnic bench. He's enjoying himself, though, and works in silence alongside us.

When we're finished, we collapse on the narrow strip of mowed grass that passes for landscaping. Mr. Cole gave us iced lemonade and watermelon—in return for slipping him the carnival food prices so he can undercut them—and we're enjoying those while waiting for the foreman to bring our pay. He finally comes over and hands us each a ticket.

"Free admittance to the carnival tonight," he says.

Reggie stares down at the stub. "A five-dollar ticket? For eight hours of work?"

The foreman reaches into his pocket and peels off three dollar bills. He passes them out with a snide, "Don't spend it all in one place."

I catch sight of Mr. Blackrose and glance over, my expression enough to bring him striding our way.

"What seems to be the problem?" he asks.

"Nothing," I say. "We were just thanking your foreman for our payment. Admission tonight and a dollar bill."

There's no sarcasm in my voice, yet the ringmaster's eyes glint again with that knowing look, appreciation for my technique.

"Well, now, I'm glad you're such good sports," he says, "but that's just our foreman's idea of humor. I have your proper payment." He reaches into his pockets and takes out a handful of two-day tickets. Then he pauses. "You three don't still need parental accompaniment, do you?"

We all shake our heads.

"Excellent. Then let me magically transform these"—he flicks his wrist, and the handful of blue paper turns into three gold pieces of cardboard—"into all-access weekend passes, complete with front-row seats to my Saturday night magic show." He winks at me. "I think I've already found a lovely local assistant to join my fair Annabelle."

We take the passes with thanks.

I CHECK on the dog—Dixie—before we leave. Her chain is empty. There are bowls with water and food, but both are so grimy that I'd like to serve Charlie *his* dinner in them. There's a hose nearby, so I surreptitiously empty, clean and refill the bowls.

As I head to where Reggie and Ray wait, whispers snake out from the magician's tent, drawing me to it. The black canvas is painted like a midnight sky with oddly shaped constellations. When I peer at the constellations, I realize they're roses. Black roses, like the carnival's name.

The whispers continue, low and urgent, and something in the tone sets my hackles rising, like when Charlie gave me that gross once-over. It's not his voice, though. It's a girl's.

I step closer still, hoping to make out the words, but all I can catch is that murmur with gaps of silence, as if she's speaking to someone who's talking lower still. I reach to touch the midnight-black canvas. It's cold and clammy, and I shiver. The girl's voice comes again, and tendrils of fear waft out, wrapping around me, rooting me in place as I strain to listen.

The voice fades before I catch a single word. I stand there a moment, staring at those odd constellations. Then Reggie whistles, a double high-pitched signal that they're ready to go. I reluctantly step back from the tent. Then I turn and run.

AS SOON as I get home, I tell my mom that I skipped school. She's fine with that. It was the last day, mostly games and stuff that we're too old for anyway. My parents are strict, but as long as I follow the rules, there's wiggle room to make my own decisions, and I'm encouraged to do that.

Ray and Reggie's mom will say the same thing. They live right next door, and our parents have been friends since they were kids. We're a tight-knit group here just beyond the edge of town, a rural cul-de-sac of families joined by either kinship or friendship, often both.

At dinner, my parents want to hear all about my day. My sixteen-year-old brother doesn't say anything—he's too busy wolfing down his food, as always. That's Zeke, short for Ezekiel. Yep, our parents like old names. At least they don't make us use them.

When I finish talking about the carnival, I tell my parents about the passes, and they exchange a look.

"Does this mean you want to go alone?" Dad asks.

I nod, my mouth full of mashed potato.

Another shared look, and then Mom says, "*Fully* alone? Or drop-you-off-and-stay-out-of-your-way alone?"

I swallow my mouthful. "We can handle it."

"I'll take them," Zeke says. "Me and the guys—"

"Alone," I say. "That means no parents *or* big brothers."

Silence. Defense prepared, my guts strum, as if I'm about to step on stage for a public-speaking assignment. I play it cool, though, fork-cutting my meatloaf into bite-size pieces and then lifting one to my mouth, hesitating at the last second to be sure I won't need to launch my defense midchew.

"You said it's at the supermarket?" Mom asks.

I nod.

"There's a pay phone," she says. "If I dig up a few dimes, will you promise to save them for calls?"

My look reminds her I'm not five, so careless I'd spend my emergency money on candy floss.

"You know, this might be a fine idea," Dad says. "Zeke got his chance with that traveling circus when he was only a year older than Ezzi. She can handle this, and tell us all about it when she gets home."

Mom adds, "Is it all right if Zeke and his friends go tonight? They won't bother you. Then you'll have Saturday evening all to yourselves."

I glance at Zeke. As my older brother, he's supposed to be a pain in the ass, so I'll refuse, and then he'll be a jerk about it and show up anyway and harass us all night. That's how it always goes in the movies. In reality, Zeke and I get along just fine. He can be overprotective, but that's just his nature.

When Mom makes her suggestion, I glance at Zeke. He grunts, as if to say he's not thrilled about the idea of me being alone at the carnival Saturday night, but when our parents speak, we obey. His nod promises he'll give me my space. I thank him with a smile and tell Mom that sounds fine by me.

WE END up going to the carnival with Zeke and his friends, one of whom is Ray and Reggie's older brother. We ride in the back of Zeke's pickup, and then we hang out together, our little pack roaming the carnival, playing games and going on rides in two separate groups but within sight of one another. That satisfies Zeke's protective streak, and it's not like anyone would give him crap for hanging out with his little sister. No one gives Zeke crap about anything.

More than once that night, I'm drawn to the midnight-rose magic tent, hoping to hear the girl again, hoping to settle my fluttering anxiety. It's closed up tight, though.

The carnies we met earlier today treat us like strangers, and I'm glad for that. Tonight I want to *be* a stranger and explore the public side of the carnival. I've peered behind the curtain. Now, I'd like to see the other side and piece the two together in my mind. It's a fascinating experience. I note how the flashing strobe lights hide the peeling paint and rotting wood on the game booths. How the aroma of fresh popcorn masks the stink of mildew on the old tents. How the booming music covers the unsettling creaks and groans of the ancient Tilt-A-Whirl.

What I notice most, though, are the carnies. They've cleaned up, of course. I have, too, wearing a sundress, with my hair plaited and my lips regularly refreshed with roll-on lipgloss that tastes of raspberry. But with the carnies, it's more than clean clothes and scrubbed hands. Charlie flatters each woman with a disarming grin and saves his leers until they've passed. The foreman who gave us those fifty-pound sacks of kernels and "forgot" to mention the wheelbarrow rushes to offer free bags and carrying trays to anyone struggling with their purchases. The two women who'd mocked us lugging the bags now coo and trill at Zeke and his friends as they try their hands at the games of skill. Every carnie wears a mask for the crowds, their true faces showing only when they slip a hand into an untended pocket. They also show those faces when Zeke and his friends win one too many prizes, the carnies strongly "suggesting" they go try the games of chance instead.

A few times, I slip off to visit Dixie. I've brought her scraps of meatloaf wrapped in aluminum foil and a bone Mom had put aside for broth but let me take.

The last time I go to check the dog, her chain lies coiled and empty. I'm wondering where she'd be when a trailer door opens, and I see the girl. It's impossible *not* to see her. She wears a dress striped in green, yellow, red and blue like a circus big top, the skirt billowing with what must be crinolines, a word I've only encountered in books. A strip of black fabric circles the base of the skirt, and on it ride white silhouettes of carousel beasts, everything from horses to lions to griffons.

If I saw the dress in a store window, I'd think it was meant for a small child, a fantastical piece of clothing too ridiculous for anyone over the age of five. But the girl is my age, and on her, it is magical. A costume fit for a masquerade. She's coming out of a trailer, and her face is turned away. Long blond hair streams down her back in a perfect waterfall that would last five seconds on me.

When she turns, I see she actually is dressed masquerade-style, the upper half of her face hidden behind a black mask embossed with roses. Our eyes meet, and the hairs on my neck rise. It's like looking into Dixie's brown eyes, a haunted emptiness, as if whatever is inside has retreated to some safe and dark corner.

"Esmerelda," a voice says, and Mr. Blackrose exits the trailer behind the girl. He lays a hand on her shoulder. "Annabelle, meet a young lady with a name even more exquisite than your own."

The girl blinks, and I think she's insulted, but what passes behind those dark eyes shimmers with inexplicable fear.

"Annabelle," Mr. Blackrose says, his voice sharp with warning.

The girl starts, as if slapped, and gives an old-fashioned curtsy and a "Pleased to make your acquaintance, Esmerelda."

"Ezzi, please," I say.

Her lips quirk in a smile that seems as much a surprise to her as it is to me.

Mr. Blackrose says, "Annabelle is my assistant and my daughter."

I don't mean to register my surprise at the latter—they look nothing alike—but he laughs and says, "Thankfully, Annabelle takes after her dearly departed mother. We're just about to retire for the evening, but I do hope you'll be joining us onstage tomorrow night for my magic show."

"I will."

He whisks a single black rose from behind his back. "Then I will see you at nine thirty. The show begins at ten sharp after the rides and the games close."

I take the rose and assure him I'll be there, and he swoops the girl off into the night.

AFTER DINNER the next evening, Reggie, Ray and I return to the carnival. Zeke grumbles about staying behind, but Mom and Dad haven't changed their minds. I'm old enough to try this on my own. If anything goes wrong, I'll probably be in college before I'm given this kind of responsibility again. No pressure.

CHADBOURNE

We stash our bikes behind the supermarket. Then we enjoy our free passes, which give us access to all the shows and rides. I've brought more meat for Dixie, and I keep an eye out for the girl in the carnival gown. I don't see her, and I'm too busy reveling in an evening of total freedom to look very hard. She'll be at the show later.

Mr. Blackrose told me to come to the tent at nine thirty to get ready. I arrive at 9:25 to be punctual…and maybe because I can't wait to get a look inside. It's been closed all weekend, with a sign on the door announcing the magic show and noting that it's an additional fee with limited seating. There's been a big Sold Out! banner over it since yesterday.

I ignore the sign marked Authorized Personnel Only. I am authorized. Kind of. Opening the flap, I slip into a cool, dark space that smells of wood shavings and sweat. It's pitch dark at first. Then the midway lights filter through the rose constellations, the tent becoming a night sky that allows just enough illumination for my eyes to adjust.

The tent is no big top. It might seat a hundred people, and even then, they'll be packed in tight enough to violate the local fire code. Benches form a semicircle in front of the stage. I cross to it, wood shavings crunching underfoot. Then I hop up onto the stage and peel back the curtain to see a trailer door.

Ah-ha. That explains why I couldn't hear more than muted voices Friday. Annabelle must have been inside the trailer, which is backed up to the tent.

Voices sound again, and this time, the words come clear. It's nothing interesting, just Mr. Blackrose talking to Charlie about the takedown, which they'll start after closing tonight.

I rap on the door. Mr. Blackrose opens it, his face gathering for an angry bark at whoever dared venture past that sign. Then he sees me and expels that bark in a too-loud, too-jovial, "Good evening, Miss Esmerelda."

He pivots with a wave, ushering me into a small room where Charlie lounges. The carnie flashes me a jackal-smile, yellow teeth glinting as his gaze rakes over me. He's seen me often enough to know exactly what I look like, and the look was never about actual interest anyway. It's as predatory as his smile, a way to make me feel small. I meet it with a steady look that, after a moment, has him snorting and turning aside, as if he's lost interest in the game.

Mr. Blackrose explains the show and my role in it. Then he walks toward the two closed doors at the back, opens the left one and flicks on a light to reveal a dressing room.

"You'll find your gown in here," he says.

"Gown?"

He smiles. "To match fair Annabelle, of course."

I nod and step inside. The door clicks shut behind me. I affix the lock and look around. A floor-to-ceiling mirror covers the interior wall. Beside it hangs a dress that is the reverse image of Annabelle's. Instead of bright-colored stripes and white carousel beasts, this dress has black and gray and white stripes with a jeweled carousel along the bottom.

I finger the fabric. It looks nicer than it feels, starchy and cheap. I take the dress down and hold it in front of me. As I do, I catch a faint hiss. At first, I think it's the rasp of my fingers on the rough material, but when I stop moving, the hissing continues. I cock my head and listen. There's a click. Then another one. Clicks like the mandibles of some giant beetle, underscored by that steady, unnatural hiss.

I touch the fabric again and shiver. Then I hang the dress up and open the door.

Mr. Blackrose is adjusting his comb-over in a mirror. He puts on his top hat. Looks in the mirror. Takes off the hat and readjusts his hair, as if his work isn't completely hidden by the hat, anyway.

When I clear my throat, he glances over. He's prepared to gush, his features arranging for the appropriate expression, words ready to rush out as soon as he opens his mouth. He stops himself, and his lips purse in pique.

"I'm allergic to polyester fabrics," I say. "I'm so sorry, sir. I really should have mentioned it, but I never imagined you'd let me wear one of your beautiful gowns, and now I feel awful. I completely understand if you don't want me on stage like…"

I glance down at myself, as if I'm dressed in a canvas sack rather than a pretty new summer dress, one that I'm sure has polyester in it somewhere.

"That's fine, my dear," he says, finding his smile. "Your dress is lovely."

"I'm sorry again. It was such a pretty gown, too."

A pause. Then he snaps his fingers. "Why don't you and Annabelle have a little dress-up party after the show? She has so many outfits that I'm certain you'll find something. You can tell your parents we'll have you home before midnight." He pauses. "Speaking of your parents, will they be here tonight?"

I shake my head. "They let me come by myself."

"Your friends, then? I can make sure they get front-row seats for your performance."

I shake my head. "They have a ten p.m. curfew. But the dress-up party sounds like fun. May I run to the pay phone and call my mom to let her know I'll be late?"

He beams. "Absolutely."

THE MAGIC show is... Well, it's a magic show. When Reggie, Ray and I were little, we went to every magic show we could until we discovered it was all fake. Then we kept going until we figured out all the tricks. After that, curiosity sated, our interest had waned.

I hope Mr. Blackrose will have a trick or two I haven't seen, one I can figure out, especially given my new vantage point on stage. Alas, he performs the same tired illusions I cracked years ago, and I must console myself with the fresh experience of being an assistant.

After the show, Mr. Blackrose and Annabelle sign autographs. The kids want mine, too, even though they see me practically every day. Tonight, I am special. Tonight, I am a star.

As we finish, the carnies usher the stragglers out and even help them carry their souvenirs to their cars, making sure no one lingers.

Once they're gone, Mr. Blackrose says, "Now, Annabelle, take Esmerelda inside, and show her your dresses. She'd like to try them on. We'll use the Polaroid and take photographs for our dear guest to remember her special night."

Annabelle's head snaps up. "Wh-what?"

Mr. Blackrose repeats it, annoyance edging into his words.

"N-no," she says. "We can't. There isn't time. We have to break camp, and Ginny needs help packing and—"

"—and if I say there's time, then there's time. Take Esmerelda—"

"No." Annabelle whirls on me. "Go. Just...go."

She's about to say more when Mr. Blackrose's hand grips her shoulder hard enough for her to flinch.

"Please excuse my daughter, Miss Esmerelda. She's overtired and being unspeakably rude. She can rest a moment to recover herself while you try on a dress. I think I know exactly the right one for you."

He takes us inside where Charlie waits, and he passes Annabelle to the carnie. The girl has slumped, not fighting or even looking my way. Charlie propels her through the door on the right, the one beside the dressing room. Mr. Blackrose follows them. Low murmurs sound, the two men speaking, Annabelle starting to say something only to be cut short.

Mr. Blackrose appears with a princess dress, high-waisted and elegant. "This doesn't seem to contain any polyester. Why don't you try it on, and we'll go back out to the stage for a photograph. Perhaps by then my daughter will feel more herself."

I carry the gown into the dressing room. I'm examining the dress when someone raps hard on the trailer door. A carnie tells Mr. Blackrose that a guest is demanding to see the man in charge.

"Esmerelda?" Mr. Blackrose calls. "I'll be back in a few minutes."

"Don't rush," I call back. "It'll take me a while to do up all these buttons."

The carnie says, "The lady claims Charlie picked her pocket. She wants to see him, too."

Mr. Blackrose's sigh ripples through the trailer, but he gets Charlie. Once they're gone, the trailer goes silent. Or so it seems until I pick up that hum again.

I ease open my door and creep to the one they took Annabelle through. It's locked. I fix that and step into an office with a desk, a chair and a fax machine. There's no sign of the girl.

I look around, keeping one ear tuned for the sound of the door. A window covers the interior wall, which is weird. Then I look closer. Through the "window" I see the dressing room. The dressing room mirror is one-way glass.

The whirring noise comes from in here, and I track it to a mounted video camera pointed at the one-way glass. Beside it, a regular camera is hooked up to some kind of timer. It clicks, that insect mandible sound I heard earlier, as it takes a picture of whoever is on the other side of the glass. Videos and photos of me when I was supposed to be changing into the dress. I eye the cameras, not quite sure what I've discovered.

I turn to the desk. Two of the drawers are locked. I break one open to find typed sheets with mailing addresses. The second drawer contains photographs and video cassette tapes. I pick up one of the photos, glance at the picture and drop it as if scorched.

I blink and give my head a sharp shake. Then I have to pick up the photo again. I don't want to, but I need to be sure of what I'm seeing.

I was not mistaken. It's a photo of Annabelle without her carnival gown. Without any gown at all. I take two sharp breaths and then force myself to sift through the photographs. Most are Annabelle. A few are other girls our age in their underwear as they pull on dresses.

I close the drawer and look around. Did Charlie take Annabelle with them? He must have.

I'm standing at the rear wall when I hear stifled crying. I move aside a wall hanging to reveal a narrow door. I snap the lock and open it.

A metallic clink comes from the darkness within. I squint until my eyes adjust to the windowless room. Then I see Annabelle. She's sitting upright on a metal cot, and when she moves, a chain whirs against the metal. That chain binds her like a dog, and she's gagged with a dirty cloth.

I hold up a finger and slip out. I'd seen a key in the drawer with the mailing list. Sure enough, it fits the lock securing Annabelle's chains.

As I free Annabelle, voices sound out outside the tent, and she gives a stifled yelp.

"Stay in here," I whisper. "Wait until I tell you it's safe to go." I take a wad of bills from my pocket and put them on the bed. "There's a bus stop in town."

I hurry out, closing doors as I go, and I barely get back into my dressing room before the door opens.

"You done yet, girl?" Charlie calls.

"I was unbuttoning the dress so I can get into it," I say.

"Well, hurry it up."

I give him time to take up his position on the other side of the mirror. He expects me to be undressing, so I pull my dress off. Then I drape it over the mirror and smile at his grunt of frustration as I back into the corner to change.

A few minutes later, he calls, "You *done?*"

I reach out as carefully as I can and yank the dress down while staying away from the mirror. Then I wait.

A minute passes.

"What the hell are you doing in there, girl?"

I thump against the wall and groan. Charlie's chair scrapes the floor. His footsteps cross the trailer. I watch as my door opens.

"Are you—?" he begins.

He stops. He stares. A volley of profanity follows, ending with, "Who the hell let a dog in—?"

I leap. He falls back, hands rising. I hit him square in the chest, and he drops with me on him. He opens his mouth to shout, but the sound comes in a garbled cry as I rip out his throat.

As Charlie dies, lifeblood soaking the floor, I throw back my head and howl. Annabelle's door creaks open. Her footsteps slide across the office. She looks out the next door and sees Charlie, still twitching in death. Then she spots me.

Annabelle starts backing into the office. Our eyes meet. She swallows, uncertain. I back up and wave my muzzle, grunting for her to go.

As she stumbles forward, the door flies open. Annabelle squeaks. Mr. Blackrose sees me. Sees Charlie. His mouth opens. I lunge and take him down. Behind him, a brown wolf tears into the tent. It's Zeke.

When I rip out Mr. Blackrose's throat, Zeke grunts, acknowledging I'm okay. He glances at Annabelle, frozen behind me. Then he steps back, muzzle-waving her out of the trailer. She hesitates and then totters forward, staggering around us before racing out.

When Annabelle's gone, I snarl, telling Zeke he can leave, but he searches the trailer to be sure it's empty. The overprotective big brother, as always. When he returns, I nod toward Charlie, telling Zeke he can feed on the carnie, but he snorts and takes off to find his own dinner. I wait until he's gone. Then I begin to eat.

WHEN I go outside, I'm in human form. The others are mostly still wolves and still feeding. A few have shifted back and are dismantling the carnival. They come over to congratulate me, hug me, pat me on the back for a job well done. I staked out the carnival and set everything in motion. I had help, of course, like Reggie and Ray's mom, who'd claimed Charlie picked her pocket to get them out of the trailer. But my parents let me handle the prep work, and my success raises my status to a full adult member of our pack.

After tonight, it'll be another year or two before we feed on humans again. The rest of the time, we make do with deer and rabbits. That only keeps our instincts at bay for so long, though, and eventually, we must do this, or we risk losing control and slaughtering innocents.

We *have* slaughtered some innocents tonight. My pack never sugarcoats that reality. But this is a choice we can live with. I can live with it even more than usual, thinking of the tapes and photographs stuffed in my bag for burning later.

Beyond the supermarket parking lot, the town is quiet and dark and still. Someone would have heard a scream or two. As efficient as we are, someone still screams. Yet tonight, the town keeps its curtains pulled and its ears plugged. Our pack founded this place, generations ago, and we have a silent bargain with the humans who've settled here. We keep them safe, and what happened here tonight means they are safe from *us*, too, from our instincts.

Speaking of safe, Annabelle is gone. My parents explained her situation to the pack, and they gave me money and assurances no wolf would touch her. I see no sign of her now as I walk behind the trailers.

Dixie is there, whining uneasily. I remove her too-tight collar. Rust sticks the clasp, but I snap that as easily as I did the locks inside. Then I bend to look her in the eye, and rub her neck, and tell her she's free if that's what she wants. She can also come with me, but the choice is hers.

When I stand, she falls in beside me, so close she brushes my thighs as I walk, as if she fears being left behind. I head to where I left my bike. Reggie and Ray are there waiting, Ray licking a last bit of blood from his cheek before he turns on his Walkman.

As we set out, we pass our dads, driving the trucks that pull the carnival trailers. They wave and tell us to go straight home, and we promise we will.

We ride so fast that Reggie nearly collides with a figure stepping from behind a tree. His bike stops with a squeak, which he echoes in a grunting growl.

"Annabelle," I say.

"It's Annie," she says, her voice quavering. "It was always Annie."

I nod. "You can go home now. You're safe. A bus comes through every morning."

We don't warn her not to tell what she saw. Who'd believe her if she did?

When she doesn't move, Reggie glances at me, eager to be going, and Dixie whines, wanting to get away from this place.

"What if I don't want to go?" Annabelle—Annie—asks, barely above a whisper. "What if I want to stay?"

"Your family—"

"I ran away. That's how he…" She trails off with a swallow. Then she meets my gaze. "Take me with you. I won't be any trouble. I can do chores, work the fields, whatever you need. Just take me and…" A harder swallow, and her voice comes firmer as she straightens. "Show me how to do what you did. How to be what you are. I want that."

Reggie looks at me. I nod, and he shifts forward on his banana seat, motioning for Annie to climb on. She does, and we continue home, taking our strays with us.

HERD IMMUNITY
by Tananarive Due

A man was far ahead of her on the road. Walking and breathing. So far, so good.

That he was a man, Nayima was certain. His silhouette against the horizon of the rising roadway showed his masculine height and the shadow of an unkempt beard. He pulled his belongings behind him in an overnight suitcase like a business traveler. Maybe she trusted him on sight because of the unmistakable shape of a guitar case slung across his back. She'd always had a thing for musicians.

"*Hey!*" she screamed, startling herself with her bald desperation.

He paused, his steady legs falling still. He might have turned around. She couldn't quite make out his movements in the quarter-mile or more that separated them. The two of them, alone, were surrounded on either side by the golden ocean of central California farmland, unharvested and unplowed, no trees or shade in sight as the road snaked up the hillside.

His attention gave her pause. She hadn't seen anyone walking in so long that she'd forgotten the plan that had kept her alive the past nine months: Hide. Observe. Assess.

But fuck it.

She waved and called again, so he would be certain she wasn't a mirage in the heat.

"Hey!" she screamed, more hoarsely. She tried to run toward him, but her legs only lurched a stagger on the sharp grade. She was dizzy from heat and modulated hunger. The sky dimmed above her, so she stopped her pathetic chase and braced her palms against her knees to calm the cannon bursts from her heart. The world grew bright again.

He walked on. She watched him shrink until the horizon swallowed him. She remembered a time when terrifying loneliness would have made her cry. Instead, she began following him at the pace her body had grown accustomed to. He didn't seem afraid of her; that was something. He hadn't quickened. He was tired and slow, like her. If she was patient, she would catch up to him.

Nayima hadn't planned to stay on State Road 46 toward Lost Hills. She had wanted to follow the last highway sign—one of the few conveniences still in perfect working order—toward a town just ten miles east. But she decided to follow the man instead. Just for a while, she'd told herself. Not so far that she'd run too low on water or go hungry.

Nayima followed him for three days.

She wasted no energy or hope checking the scattered vehicles parked at odd angles for fuel or food, although most still had their keys. She was far too late for *that* party. Cars were shelter. Handy when it rained. Or when it was dark and mountain lions got brave, their eyes glowing white in her flashlight beam. ("Bad, bad kitty," she always said.)

The cars on SR-46 weren't battered and broken like the ones in Bakersfield, witnesses to riots or robberies. For a time, carjacking had been the national hobby. She'd jacked a car herself trying to get out of that hell-hole—with a sprained ankle and a small mob chasing her, she'd needed the ride more than the acne-scarred drunk sleeping at the wheel. On the 46, the pristine cars had come to rest, their colors muted by a thin veil of burial dust.

Nayima missed her red Schwinn, but she'd hit a rock the day before she'd seen the man on the road—the demon stone appeared in her path and knocked her bicycle down an embankment. She'd been lucky only to bump her elbow hard enough to make her yell. But her bike, gone. Crumpled beyond salvage. Nayima didn't allow herself to miss much—but damn. And this man, her new day job, meant she didn't have time to peel off to look for tucked-away farmhouses and their goodies. Too risky. She might lose him. Instead, Nayima walked on, following her ghost.

She imagined how they would talk. Testify. Teach what little they knew. Start something. Maybe he could at least tell her why he was on the 46, what radio broadcast or quest had beckoned. She hadn't heard anything except hissing on radios in three months. She didn't mind walking a long distance if she might arrive somewhere eventually.

Each morning she woke from her resting place—the crook of a tree, an abandoned car that wasn't a tomb, in the cranny beneath the inexplicably locked cab of an empty eighteen-wheeler parked ten yards off the road like a beached whale—and wondered if the man had gone too far ahead. If he'd walked the whole night just to shake her. If he'd found a car that had sung him a love song when he caressed her and turned the key.

But each day, she saw signs that he was not lost. He was still walking ahead, somewhere just out of sight. Any evidence of him dampened her palms.

He left a trail of candy wrappers. Chocolate bars mostly, always the minis. Snickers, Twix, Almond Joy (her favorite; that wrapper made her stomach shout at the sight). Her own meals were similarly monotonous, but not nearly as colorful—handfuls of primate feed she'd found overlooked at a vet's office outside Bakersfield. Her backpack was stuffed with the round, brown nuggets. Monkey Balls, she called them. They didn't taste like much, but they opened up her time for walking and weren't nearly as heavy as cans.

On the third morning, when the horizon again stretched empty, and sinking dread bubbled in her stomach, the road greeted her with a package of Twizzlers, six unruined sticks still inside. The Twizzlers seemed fresh. She could feel his fingertips on the wrapper. The candy was warm to her tongue from the sun. So good it brought happy tears. She stood still as long as she dared while the sweetness flooded her dry mouth, coated her throat. Feeling anything was a novelty.

She cried easily over small pleasures: a liquid orange sunset, the wild horses she'd seen roaming a field, freed to their original destiny. She wondered if he had left her the Twizzlers in a survivors' courtship rite, until she found a half-eaten rope of the red candy discarded a few steps away. A Red Vines man, then. She could live with that. They would work it out.

By noon on Twizzlers Day, she saw him again, a long shadow stretching only half a mile ahead of her. Time was, she could have jogged to catch up to him easily, but the idea of hurry made her want to vomit. Her stomach wasn't as happy with the candy feast as the rest of her.

So she walked.

He passed a large wooden sign—not quite a billboard, but big—and when she followed behind him, she read the happy script:

COUNTY LINE ROAD FAIR!!!!
June 1-30 2 MI

Beneath that, cartoon renderings of pigs with blue ribbons, a hot dog grinning in his bun, and a Ferris wheel. A dull fucking name for a fair, she thought. Or a road, for that matter. She vowed that when the renaming of things began, she and the man on the road would do better. The Fair of Ultimate Rainbows, on Ultimate Rainbow Road. A name worthy of the sign's colors.

She was nearly close enough to touch the sign before she made out the papers tacked on the right side, three age-faded, identical handbills in a vertical line:

RESCUE CENTER

Stamped with a Red Cross insignia.

Red Crap. Red Death. Red Loss.

Nayima fought dueling urges to laugh and scream. Her legs nearly buckled in rebellion. The sun felt ten degrees hotter, sizzling her neck.

"You have got to be goddamn kidding," she said.

The man on the road could not hear her.

She cupped her hands to her mouth. *"Do you still believe there's a Wizard too?"*

Moron.

But she kept the last word silent. She shouldn't be rude. They needed to get along.

He didn't stop walking, but he gave her a grumpy old man wave over his shoulder. Finally—communication. Candor was the greatest courtesy in the land of the 72-Hour Flu, so she told him the truth. "They're just big petri dishes, you know! Best way to get sick is in evac camps! Was, I mean. Sorry to bear bad news, but there's no rescue center here!"

Nine months ago, she would have believed in that sign. She'd believed in her share. Back when the best minds preached hope for a vaccine that would help communities avoid getting sick with precautions, she'd heard the term on the CDC and WHO press conferences: *herd immunity.* As it turned out, the vaccine was a fable and herd immunity was an oxymoron.

Only NIs were left now: naturally immune. The only people she'd seen since June were other NIs floating through the rubble, shy about contact

CHADBOURNE

for fear of the attacks of rage and mass insanity. Nayima had escaped Bakersfield, where anyone walking with pep was a traitor to the human experience. Nayima had seen radiant satisfaction on the face of an axe-wielding old woman who, with her last gasps of breath, had split open the skull of the NI nurse offering her a sip of water. No good deed, as they say. This man was the first NI she'd met on the road in the three months since.

The formerly populated areas would be quieter now. That was the thing about the 72-Hour Flu: it settled disputes quickly. The buzzards were building new kingdoms in the cities, their day come at last.

"*The dead can't rescue the living!*" Nayima shouted up the godless road.

Her new friend kept walking. No matter. He would be stopping in two miles anyway.

She could smell the fair already.

SHE THOUGHT *maybe, just maybe*—not enough to speed her heart, but enough to make her eyes go sharp—when the rows of neatly parked cars appeared on the west side of the road. A makeshift parking lot, with rows designated in letter-number pairs on new cedar poles, A-1 through M-20. Because of the daylight's furious glare across the chrome and glass, the cars seemed to glitter like fairy-tale carriages. It was the most order Nayima had seen in months.

Then she saw the dust across their windows.

Everywhere she went, too late for the party. Even at the fair.

Buzzards and crows sat atop the COUNTY LINE ROAD FAIR—FREE PARKING banner, bright white and red, that hung across the gravel driveway from SR-46. The Ferris wheel stood frozen beyond, marking where the fair began, but it was so small it seemed sickly. The cartoon had been so much grander. Everything about the sign had been a lie.

The sound of mournful guitar came—picking, not strumming. She had never heard the melody before, but she knew the song well. "The 72-Hour Blues."

In the parking lot, she glanced through enough rear windows to start smiling. The Corolla had a backpack in plain sight. A few had keys in their ignitions. One was bound to have gas. This was a car lot Christmas sale. The cars on the road were from the people who'd given up on driving and left nothing behind. These cars were satisfied at their destination, although their drivers had left unfinished business inside. A few cars with windows cracked open stank of dead pets; she saw a large dog's white fur carpeting the back-seat floor of a Ford Explorer. A child's baseball cap near the fur made her think of a pudgy-cheeked boy giving his dog a last hug before his parents hurried him away.

The cars screamed stories.

She saw her own face in the window. Hooded. Brown face sun-darkened by two shades. Jaw thin, showing too much bone. *You gotta eat, girl*, Gram would say. Nayima blinked and looked away from the stranger in the glass.

Tears. Damn, damn, damn.

Nayima dug her fingernails into her palm, hard. She drew blood. The cars went silent.

The guitar player could claim he'd found the treasure first, but there was enough to share. She had a .38 if he needed convincing, but she hoped it wouldn't come to that. Even the idea of her .38 made her feel sullied. She didn't want to hurt him. She didn't want him to try to hurt her. She wanted the opposite; someone to keep watch while she slept, to help her find food, to keep her warm. She couldn't remember the last time she'd wanted anything so badly.

The music soothed the graveyard in the parking lot. The guitarist might be the best musician she would ever know; just enough sour, not too much sweet. He was playing a song her grandmother might have hummed but had forgotten to teach her.

Dear Old Testament God of Noah, please don't let him be another asshole.

He was out of sight again, so she followed the music through the remains of the fair.

The Ferris wheel wasn't the only no-frills part of the County Line Road Fair, which had been named right after all. She counted fewer than a dozen rides—the anemic Ferris wheel was the belle of the ball. The rest was two kiddie fake pony rides she might have found at a good-sized shopping mall, a merry-go-round with mermaids among the horses (that one actually wasn't too bad), a spinner ride in cars for four she'd always hated because she got crushed from centrifugal force, and a Haunted Castle with empty cars waiting to slip into the mouth of hellfire. A giant with a molten face guarded the castle's door, draped in black rags. Even now the Haunted Castle scared her. As she passed it, she spat into one of the waiting cars.

Crows scattered as she walked.

This fair was organized like all small fairs—a row of games on one side, food vendors on the other. Birds and scavengers had picked over the empty paper popcorn cups and foil hot dog wrappers, but only a few of the vendors had locked their booths tight with aluminum panels. A large deep fryer stood in plain sight at Joe's Beef Franks as she passed—nothing but an open door-way between them—so she was free to explore. Cabinets. Trash. Counters. So many possibilities. Now her heartbeat did speed up.

With a car and enough essential items, she could think about a future somewhere. The guitar seemed to agree, picking up tempo and passion. The music reminded her that she didn't have to be alone in her getaway car.

Words were nearly useless now, so she didn't speak right away when she found his camp alongside the elephant ear vendor's booth. He had laid out a sleeping bag in the shade of the awning promising "Taysteee Treets," his back supported against the booth. She stood across the fairway by the ring-toss and took him in.

First surprise: he was wearing a dust mask. A summer look for the fall. Ridiculous.

The mask was particularly disappointing because it was already hard to make out his face beneath his hair and the dirt. He had light brown skin, she guessed, a dark tangle of thinly textured hair, a half-fed build to match hers. He looked nearly a foot taller, so he would have an advantage if they had to fight. Nayima slipped her hand to the compartment in her backpack she kept in easy reach. She took hold of the gun slowly, but she didn't pull it out.

"Guitar's mine to keep, and nothin' else is worth taking," he said. His voice was gravel. "Grab your pick of whatever you find here and move on."

"You think I followed you three days to rob you?"

"I don't try to guess why."

Nayima shook off her light jacket's hood. She'd shaved her head in Bakersfield so she wouldn't be such an obvious rape target. Most of her hair was close to her scalp—but she had a woman's face. She imagined his eyes flickering, just a flash.

"I'm Nayima," she said.

He concentrated on his guitar strings. "Keep your distance."

"You're immune." Dummy. She didn't call him names, but it dripped in her voice.

He stopped playing. "Who says?"

"You do," she said. "Because you're still breathing."

He went back to playing, uninterested.

"Let me guess," she said. "Everyone in your family got sick and died—including people you saw every day—but you never got even a tummy-ache."

"I was careful."

"You think you're still alive because you're smarter than the rest?"

"I didn't say that." He sounded angry. "But I was very careful."

"No touching? No breathing?"

"Yes. Even learned how to play with these on." He held up his right hand. She hadn't seen his thin, dirty gloves at first glance.

"Your fingertips never brushed a countertop or a window pane or a slip of paper?"

"Doing my best."

"You never once got unlucky."

"Until now, I guess," he said.

"Bullshit," she said. Now she felt angry. More hurt, but angry too. She hadn't realized any stranger still held the power to hurt her feelings, or that any feelings were still so raw. "You're living scared. You're like one of those Japanese soldiers in World War II who didn't know the war was over."

"You think it's all over. In less than a year."

"Might as well be. Look how fast the UK went down."

His eyes dropped away. Plenty had happened since, but London had been the first proof that China's 72-Hour Virus was waging a world war instead of only a genocide. Cases hadn't appeared in the U.S. until a full two days after London burned—those last two days of worry over the problems that seemed far away, people that were none of their business. The televisions had still been working, so they had all heard the news unfolding. An entire tribe at the fire, just before the rains.

"What have you seen?" Finally, he wasn't trying to push her away.

"I can only report on Southern and Central California. Almost everybody's gone. The rest of us, we're spread out. You're the only breather I've seen in two months. That's why it's time for us to stop hiding and start finding each other."

"'Us?'" he repeated, hitched brow incredulous.

"NIs," she said. "Naturally Immunes. One in ten thousand, but that's a guess."

"Jesus." A worthy response, but Nayima didn't like the hard turn of his voice.

"Yes." She realized she didn't sound sad enough. He might not understand how sadness made her legs collapse, made it hard to breathe. She tried harder. "It's terrible."

"Not that—you." He sang the rest. "*Welcome, one and all, to the new super race...*"

Song as mockery, especially in his soulful, road-toughened tenor, hurt more than a physical blow. Nayima's anger roiled from the memory of rivulets of poisoned saliva running down her cheeks from hateful strangers making a last wish. "They spit in my face, whenever they could. They tried to take me with them—yet here I stand. You can stop being a slave to that filthy paper you're wearing, giving yourself rashes. We're immune. Congratulations."

"Swell," he said. "I don't suppose you can back any of that up with lab tests? Studies?"

"We will one day," she said. "But so far it's you, and me, and some cop I saw high-tailing out of Bakersfield who should not have still been breathing. Believe me when I tell you: This bad-boy virus takes everybody, eventually. Except NIs."

"What if I just left a bunker? A treehouse? A cave?"

"Wouldn't matter. You've been out now. Something you touched. It lives on glass for thirty days, maybe forty-five. That was what the lab people in China said, when they finally started talking. Immunity—that's not a theory. There were always people who didn't get it when they should've dropped. Doctors. Old People."

"People who were careful," he said.

"This isn't survival of the smartest," she said. "It's dumb luck. In our genes."

"So, basically, Madame Curie," he said, drawing out his words, "you don't know shit."

Arrogant. Rude. Condescending. He was a disappointment after three days' walk, no question about it. But that was to be expected, Nayima reminded herself. She went on patiently. "The next one we find, we'll ask what they know. That's how we'll learn. Get a handle on the numbers. Start with villages again. I like the Central Valley. Good farmland. We just have to be sure of a steady water supply." It was a relief to let her thoughts out for air.

He laughed. "Whoa, sister. Don't start picking out real estate. You and me ain't a village. I'll shoot you if you come within twenty yards."

So—he was armed. Of course. His gun didn't show, but she couldn't see his left hand, suddenly hidden beneath a fold in his sleeping bag. He had been waiting for her.

"Oh," she said. "This again."

"Yeah—this," he said. "This is called common sense. Go on about your business. You can spend the night here, but I want you gone by morning. This is mine."

"Rescue's coming?"

He coughed a shallow, thirsty cough—not the rattling cough of the plague. "I'm not here for rescue. Didn't know a thing about that."

"I have water," she said. "I bet there's more in the vendor booths." Let him remember what it felt like to be fussed over. Let him see caring in her eyes.

His chuckle turned into another cough. "Yeah, no thanks. Got my own."

"If you didn't come here to get rescued, then why? Jonesing for hot dog buns?"

He moved his left hand away from his gun and back to his guitar strings. He plinked.

"My family used to come," he said. "Compete in Four-H. Eat fried dough 'til we puked. Ride those cheap-ass rides. This area's real close-knit, so you'd see everybody like a backyard party. That's all I wanted—to be somewhere I knew. Somewhere I would remember."

The wind shifted. Could be worse, but the dead were in the breeze.

"Smells like their plan didn't work out," Nayima said.

"Unless it did." He shrugged. "You need to leave me alone now."

Coming as it did at the end of the living portrait he'd just painted, the theft of his company burned a hole in her. She needed him already. Father, son, brother, lover, she didn't care which. She didn't want to be without him. Couldn't be without him, maybe.

His silence turned the fairgrounds gloomy again. This smell was the reason she preferred the open road, for now.

"At least tell me your name," she said. Her voice quavered.

But he only played his fantasy of bright, spinning lights.

WITH ONLY two hours left before dark, Nayima remembered her situation. She was down to her last two bottles of water—so there was that. She noted every hose and spigot, mapping the grounds in her mind. Even with the water turned off, sometimes the reserves weren't dry.

Nayima went to search for a car first, since that would decide what else she needed. She didn't break into cars with locked doors during her first sweep. She decided she would only break a window if she saw a key. Glass was unpredictable, and her life was too fragile for everyday infections. The first vehicles she found with keys—the first engines she heard turn—had less than an eighth of a tank. Not enough.

Then she saw the PT Cruiser parked at B-7. Berry purple. The cream-colored one she'd driven in college at Spelman had been reincarnated in her favorite color, calling to her. Unlocked door. No stench inside. Half a bottle of water waiting in the beverage cup, nearly hot as steam from the sun. No keys in the ignition, but they were tucked in the passenger visor, ready to be found. The engine choked complaints about long neglect, but finally hummed to life. And the gas tank, except by a hair, was full. Nayima felt so dizzy with relief that she sank into the car's bucket seat and closed her eyes. She thanked the man on the road and his music in the sky.

She could pack a working car with enough supplies for a month or more. With so much gas, she would easily make it to the closest town. She would stake out the periphery, find an old farmhouse in the new quiet. Clean up its mess. Rest with a proper roof.

Nayima's breath caught in her throat like a stone. Her first miracle in the New World.

The rest of her searching took on a leisurely pace, one step ahead of the setting sun. Nayima avoided the guitar player while she scouted, honoring his perimeter. She drove from the parking lot to the fairway, her slow-moving wheels chewing the gravel. Her driver's seat was a starship captain's throne.

Weather and dust were no match for the colors at the County Line Road Fair. Painted clowns and polar bears and ringmasters in top hats shouted red, blue, and yellow from wildly named booths promising sweet, salty, and cold. In the colors and the guitar music, ghostly faces emerged, captured at play. The fairground teemed with children. Nayima heard their carefree abandon.

For an instant, she let in the children's voices—until her throat burned. The sky seemed ready to fall. She held her breath until her lungs forced her to suck in the air. To breathe in that smell she hated. The false memory was gone.

As she'd expected, airtight packages of hot dog buns looked fresh enough to last for millennia. She found boxes of protein bars in a vendor's cabinet and a sack of unshelled peanuts so large she had to carry it over her back like a child. She stuffed the PT Cruiser with a growing bounty of clean blankets, an unopened twenty-four pack of water bottles and her food stash—even a large purple stuffed elephant, just because she could. The PT Cruiser, her womb on wheels, cast a fresh light on the world.

But there was the question of the passenger seat, still empty. The *may, maybe, might* part was making her too anxious to enjoy her fair prizes.

Then Nayima saw the stenciled sign:

RESCUE CENTER ➔

The arrow pointed away from the vendors' booths, toward the Farm World side of the fair, with its phantom Petting Zoo and Pony Rides in dull earth tones; really more an alleyway than a world. On the other end, a long wood-plank horse stall like one she had seen at the Kentucky Derby stood behind an empty corral, doors firmly shut.

Nayima climbed out of her PT Cruiser, pocketing her precious keys. She followed the dried tracks of man and beast side by side, walking on crushed hay. On the Farm World side, she could barely make out the sounds of the guitar. She felt like she had as a kid swimming in the ocean, testing a greater distance from shore. He might stop playing and disappear. It seemed more and more likely that she had only dreamed him.

But she had to see the rescue center. Like the driver from the PT Cruiser who had left her water bottle half full, she followed the sign. In her imagination, Nayima melted into scuffling feet, complaining children, muffled sobs.

The signs were posted on neatly spaced posts. Each sign, helpful and profound.

FAMILIES SHOULD REMAIN TOGETHER
YOUR CALM HELPS OTHERS STAY CALM
SMILE—REMOVE YOUR MASK

The smell worsened with each step toward the looming structure. In front of the closed double doors stood two eight-foot folding tables—somewhat rusted now. Sun-faded pages flapped from a clipboard. Nayima glanced at a page of dull bureaucracy: handwritten names and addresses: Gerald Hillbrandt, Party of 4. As she'd guessed, a few hundred people had come.

SHOES →

Nayima's eyes followed the next sign to the southwest corner of the stall, where she found rows of shoes neatly paired against the wall. Mama Bear, Papa Bear, Baby Bear, all side by side. Cheerfully surrendered. Nayima, who wore through shoes quickly, felt a strange combination of exhilaration and sorrow at the sight of the shoes on merry display.

ENTRANCE →

The next sign pointed around the corner, away from the registration table and cache of shoes. The entrance to the intake center had been in the rear, not the front. The rear double barn doors were closed, but they also had tables on either side, each with a large opaque beverage dispenser half-filled with a dark liquid that could be iced tea.

A refreshments table, she thought—until she saw the signs.

MAKE SURE EVERYONE IN YOUR PARTY TAKES A FULL CUP
PARENTS, WATCH YOUR CHILDREN DRINK BEFORE DRINKING YOURSELF
MAKE SURE CUPS ARE EMPTIED BEFORE ENTERING
TRASH HERE, PLEASE

Beneath the last sign, a large garbage can halfway filled with crumpled plastic cups. Nayima stared. Some cups were marked with lipstick. Several, actually. Had they come to the Rescue Center wearing their Sunday best? Had they dressed up to meet their maker?

The smell, strongest here, was not fresh; it was the smell of older, dry death. The door waited—locked, perhaps—but Nayima did not want to go inside. Nayima laid her palm across the building's warm wooden wall, a communion with whoever had left her the PT Cruiser. And the shoes she would choose. What visionary had brought them here in this humane way? Had they known what was waiting? Her questions filled her with acid grief. She was startled by her longing to be with them, calm and resting.

Just in time, she heard the music.

"**LOOK WHAT** I found," she said, and held up the sign for him to see.

"Can't read that from here."

"I can come closer."

"Wouldn't do that."

So, nothing had changed. She sighed. "It says—'Smile, Remove Your Mask.'"

He laughed. She already loved the sound. And then, the second miracle—he tugged his mask down to his chin. "Hell, since it's on the sign." He pointed a finger of judgment at her. "You stay way over there, I'll keep it off."

His voice was clearer. It was almost too dark to see him now, but she guessed he couldn't be older than fifty, perhaps as young as forty. He was young. Young enough. She wasn't close enough to see his eyes, but she imagined they were kind.

"I'm Kyle," he said.

She grinned so widely that she might have blinded him.

"Easy there, sister," he said. "That's all you get—my name. And a little guitar, if you can be a quiet audience. Like I said, you're moving on."

"Some of the other cars have gas. But this one has a full tank."

"Good for you," he said, not unkindly.

"You'll die here if you're afraid to touch anything."

"My cross to bear."

"How will you ever know you're immune?" she said.

He only shrugged. "I expect it'll become clear."

"But I won't be here. I don't know where I'll be. We have to..." She almost said *We have to fight back and make babies and see if they can survive.*

"…stay together. Help protect each other. We're herd animals, not solitary. We always have been. We need each other."

Too much to comprehend lay in his silence.

"All you need is a full tank of gas," he said at last. "All I need is my guitar. Nothing personal—but ever hear of Typhoid Mary?"

Yes, of course she had heard of Typhoid Mary, had lived under the terror of her legacy. In high school, she'd learned that the poor woman died in isolation after thirty years, with no one allowed close to her. Nayima had decided long ago not to live in fear.

"We have immunity," she said. "I won't get you sick."

"That's a beautiful idea." His voice softened practically to a song. "You'll be the one who got away, Nayima."

She couldn't remember the last time anyone had called her by name. And he'd pronounced it as if he'd known her all her life. Not to mention how the word beautiful cascaded up and down her spine. While her hormones raged, she loved him more with each breath. Nayima was tempted to jump into her PT Cruiser and drive away then, the way she had learned to flee all hopeless scenarios.

Instead, she pulled her car within fifteen yards of him and reclined in the driver's seat with her door open, watching him play until he stopped. The car's clock said it was midnight when he finally slept. Hours had melted in his music. She couldn't sleep, feverish with the thought of losing him.

At first, she only climbed out of the car to stretch her limbs. She took a tentative step toward him. Then, another. Soon, she was standing over him while he slept.

She took in his bright guitar strap, woven from a pattern that looked Native American. The wiry hairs on his dark beard where they grew thick to protect his pink lips. The moonlight didn't show a single gray hair. He could be strong, with better feeding. Beneath his dusty camo jacket, he wore a Pink Floyd concert shirt. He could play her all of the old songs, and she could teach him music he didn't know. The moonlight cradled his curls across his forehead, gleamed on his exposed nose. He was altogether magnificent.

Nayima was sure he would wake when she knelt beside him, but he was a strong sleeper. His chest rose and fell, rose and fell, even as she leaned over him.

Was the stone rolling across her chest only her heartbeat? Her palms itched, hot. She was seventeen again, unexpectedly alone in a corner with Darryn Stephens at her best friend's house party, so aware of every prickling pore where they touched. And when he'd bent close, she'd thought he was going to whisper something in her ear over the noise of the world's last dance. His breath blew across her lips, sweet with beer. Then his lips grazed hers, lightning strikes down her spine, and the softness…the softness…

Kyle slept on as Nayima pressed her lips to his. Was he awake? Had his lips yielded to her? It seemed so much like Kyle was kissing her too, but his eyes were still closed, his breathing uninterrupted even as she pulled away.

She crept back to her PT Cruiser, giddy as a twelve-year-old. Oh, but he would be furious! The idea of his anger made her giggle. She dozed to sleep thinking of the gift of liberation she had given Kyle. Freedom from masks. Freedom from fear. Freedom to live his life with her, to build their village.

BY DAWN, Nayima woke to the sound of his retching.

She thought she'd dreamed the sound at first—tried to will herself to stay in her happy dream of singing "Kumbaya" with well-groomed strangers in the horse stalls, hand in hand—but she opened her eyes and saw the guitar player hunched away from her. He had pushed his guitar aside. She heard the splatter of his vomit.

Nausea came first. Nausea came fast.

Shit, she thought. Her mind was a vast white prairie, emptied, save that one word. She remembered his laughter, realized she would never hear him laugh again now.

"I'm sorry," she said. "I thought for sure you were like me. An NI."

She wished her voice had sounded sadder, but she didn't know how. She wanted to explain that he might have contracted the virus somewhere else in the past twenty-four hours, not necessarily from her. But despite the odds and statistics on her side, even she didn't believe that.

It's only a mistake if you don't learn from it, Gram would say. Nayima clamped her fingernails into both palms. Her wrist tendons popped out from the effort. Hot pain. The numbness that had thawed with his music and 4-H stories crept over her again, calcified.

The man didn't turn to look at her as she stood over him and picked through his things. His luggage carrier held six water bottles and a mountain of candy bars. The necessities. She left him his candy and water. His 9mm had no ammo, but she took it. She left his guitar—although she took the strap to remember him by. She might take up guitar herself one day.

The man gagged and vomited again. Most people choked to death by the third day.

"I'm leaving now," she said, and knelt behind him. She searched for something to say that might matter to him. "Kyle, I found that Rescue Center over in Farm Land—Farm *World*—and it looks nice. Somebody really thought the whole thing through. You were right to come here. Where I grew up, they just burned everything."

Even now, she craved his voice. Wanted so badly for him to hear her. To affirm her. To learn her grandmother's name and say, "Yes, she was." Yes, you were. Yes, you are.

The man did not answer or turn her way. Like the others before him, he was consumed with his illness. Just as well, Nayima thought as she climbed back into her car. *Just as well.* She glanced at her visor mirror and saw her face: dirt-streaked, unrepentant. She blinked and looked away.

Nayima never had been able to stomach the eyes of the dead.

PICKLED PUNKS AND THE SUMMER OF LOVE

by Lisa Morton

Pat had been working at the carnival for exactly one hour when he found the dead body.

It was 10 a.m. on a June Saturday in 1967, and the crowds were a sunset away. Kurt the Patch had assigned him to clean up trash left over from last night. He was bending to retrieve a crushed popcorn box when he saw the man sprawled on the steps leading up to the pickled punks trailer.

Pat, still only 15, had never seen a corpse before, but he knew instantly that this man was dead. The body was upside-down, head on the ground, back on a slant up the stairs, legs inside the trailer. There was thick, crusted blood under the dead man's nose and down one cheek. A dark stain surrounded the head. The eyes were wide in terror.

He located Kurt near the beat-up Winnebago that passed for the carnival's business office, paying off two more cops in passes. As soon as the cops walked away, Pat told Kurt what he'd found.

"Aw, fuck me," Kurt muttered. "Okay, show me."

Kurt examined the body quickly and then went to find the same cops he'd just bribed. Within an hour there were uniformed cops and homicide detectives and photographers and medical examiners. The M.E. looked the body over and told the anxious carnies that there was no obvious sign of malicious intent, that chances were the man had been drunk and fallen down the steps.

Pat heard one cop mutter, "Maybe, but…look at his eyes."

As the body was carried away on a stretcher, Kurt turned to Pat and asked if he was okay. Pat nodded, numb. Kurt slipped him a five-dollar bill as he pulled him aside for a chat. When he'd agreed to give Pat the job yesterday, he'd said he couldn't afford to keep an underaged kid more than a week. Now he confessed to Pat that this was the fourth man who'd been found dead near the pickled punks trailer in as many months; although the deaths all looked accidental, it wouldn't be long before the cops would start investigating more seriously.

"Hey, look, I understand all about how bad a place home can be," he told Pat, "but this carny can't be your home neither, kid. I'm sorry, but that's just how it's gotta be."

Pat nodded and shoved the fiver in a pocket and tried to not to think about the dead man's terror, forcing himself to focus instead on what he was going to do with his own life.

TWO NIGHTS ago Pat had decided he'd had enough.

His mother, drunk again, had thrown an empty whiskey bottle at Pat when he'd told her he was too young to buy her more booze. Fortunately the bottle hadn't broken, but it'd left Pat with a goose egg and fresh determination. He'd gone to his room and thrown a few pieces of clothing, his transistor radio and his beat-up copy of *The Lightbulb Kids Mystery #1* into his duffel bag. Then he'd walked out the front door, past the slurred questions and insults of his mother. He'd kept on walking until he realized his feet had brought him to the carnival.

The Lupo Brothers show had arrived earlier in the week. It was a medium-sized carnival, too small to have a daredevil motorcyclist act but big enough to have games, food stands, half-a-dozen rides, a girlie show and a freak tent (which Pat soon learned the carnies called the "ten-in-one"). When the carnival had set up, some of Pat's friends had been hired as extra local help, and had been paid in passes; they said the carnival looked "cool" and this guy called Kurt the Patch was in charge and was "far out."

So Pat showed up, asking for Kurt the Patch. The carnies didn't laugh at him; they just nodded or pointed wearily. The man he found was in his early thirties, dark-haired and -skinned, with an energy that threatened to detonate any instant.

"Trouble at home, huh, kid? I get one like you in almost every town. Nice goose egg, by the way." Kurt sighed and then offered Pat ten dollars for the week plus room and board, as long as Pat didn't mind bunking in a trailer and could be gone at the end of seven days. He introduced Pat to Vinnie, a smiling 20-year old who worked on the midway, before running off to take care of a small disaster brewing elsewhere.

Vinnie punched Pat's arm in a comradely fashion, then led him to a trailer lined with bunk beds. He gently prodded his companion for the story, not pushing, letting Pat reveal as much or as little as he wanted. Later, Pat would look back and realize this was a basic part of the carny way of life.

Pat stowed his bag in an unused bunk, and Vinnie introduced him to Cool Daddy, a fortyish black man who roused himself from his hangover long enough to look up and grunt before rolling over in his bunk, turning his back to them.

"He don't look like much now," Vinnie whispered, "but nobody's a better mechanic and all-around fixer."

After Vinnie had shown him around the lot, they stopped at the cook tent for early dinner. Pat had been to the carnival last year as a guest, but now he was officially a J.C.L. (after a cook had laughingly called him that, Vinnie had explained it was carny slang, short for "Johnny-Come-Lately"). Pat was astonished at how sundown transformed a sparsely populated, dusty collection of trailers and plywood stalls into a world of densely-packed glamour and mystery. He paused to watch the barker in front of the ten-in-one ("see the two strangest women on earth, Zelda and her parasitic twin!"). He felt the undeniable lure of the jam auctioneer, who offered incredible deals. He yearned to plunk down his two bits and try his luck at the rifle range.

Then he came to Rowdy's Revue.

Rowdy's Revue ("Featuring the Most Beautiful Girls in the World") was the token carnival kootch show. The talker in front of the tent promised "sights you will never see at home, fellahs!", and stepped aside as a line of three curvaceous young women shook their ample (and barely covered) breasts at the eager men. Within seconds money was furiously exchanging hands, as tickets were bought and men entered the tent, already sweating in anticipation.

Pat, however, was no longer watching the spieler or the girls or the marks; in fact, everything else had faded away the instant *she* stepped on the stage.

She was the most beautiful woman Pat had ever seen. Pat thought she was even more gorgeous than that woman on the British spy show he liked, the new one on ABC. She had shoulder-length dark hair, high cheekbones, a full mouth, and eyes that looked deeper and more alluring than a pirate treasure cave. It didn't matter to Pat that she wasn't as well built as some of the other dancers, that she didn't really smile and could barely dance; he only knew he would give everything he owned to see her up close, without the presence of the hooting mob around him. He thought she deserved more respect.

Pat was suddenly aware of someone beside him, and a voice whispered into his ear, "She's somethin', ain't she?"

He turned, nearly stumbling backwards over his own feet when he looked up and saw a leering white-and-red clown face above him. But the friendly hand that reached out reassured him.

"Hey, sorry, kid, it's me, Vinnie."

Pat peered closer, and saw that it was his friend under the strange makeup. "Wanna go watch me work?"

Pat turned back to the stage, reluctant to leave *her* behind, but she'd already vanished into the tent. Pat felt disappointed, but he nodded to Vinnie. The clown took his arm and began steering him through the crowd.

"Don't tell me you already got a crush on Ember, huh?"

"Ember?"

"Ember L'Amour. 'Course that's just her stage name, like mine's Bozo. She's the most gorgeous hunk'a flesh on the whole carny circuit. Not much of a dancer, but with that face who cares, right? Hey, you know what a Bozo does?"

Pat shook his head. He wanted to know more about Ember; he wanted to know her real name. He wanted to know if Vinnie was her friend.

He tried to watch Vinnie in action, as he sat in a wire-mesh cage and insulted marks until they handed over bills for a chance to hurl a softball at a target and dunk the offensive clown in a tub of water. But all he could think about was Ember.

Finally, at midnight, an exhausted Pat staggered off to his bunk. Cool Daddy was already back, snoring away, but what kept Pat awake wasn't the older man's rumbling.

It was the image of her face, and her name.

Ember.

THE NEXT evening, even though he was supposed to be looking for somewhere else to go—even though the murder should have scared him away Pat hung around the lot. He liked the feel of the carnival around him, a big protective cocoon keeping him insulated from the painful realities of life in suburbs haunted by drunken single parents. He liked the smells of food and sweat and machine oil, the noise of laughing, yelling voices, the sight of hundreds of light bulbs and balloons and toys.

He wanted to stay here. Contrary to what the Patch had told him, Pat thought he could make the carnival his home. It didn't matter to him that he wouldn't finish high school, or have a normal life. His mother—and the father who'd left when he was born—had made sure he'd never had that anyway.

He had nowhere else to go. No relatives who he really knew; there was an aunt in Denver who'd been kind to him the one time they'd met, but he couldn't imagine asking her to take him in.

He thought about the four mysterious deaths that Kurt had mentioned, and how unlikely it was that they were truly accidental. He'd asked Vinnie about it, and Vinnie had told him that all four victims had been men, townies who could have easily been pushed down the stairs, or even killed somewhere else and left there.

Before today, Pat had only known murder through fiction. In his books, the Lightbulb Kids—a brother and sister team named Chance and Wendy— always solved the crimes by the end of the story and became heroes.

What if he solved the mystery of the carnival deaths? Wouldn't he become a hero? Patch would have to let him stay.

And maybe Ember would talk to him.

So it was that Pat found himself returning to the trailer. There was still yellow police tape across the steps leading up, still dark reddish stains on the steps, but he could see the door was slightly open, and this area of the carnival was almost completely deserted, away from the revelry and crowds. Figuring that his first step would be to find out what was inside the "pickled punks" trailer, he sidled beneath the tape and moved cautiously up the stairs, trying to avoid stepping in the dried blood. He prodded the door with one finger, making it squeal as it swung inward on rusty hinges. He went up one step, then two, and tried to peek into the trailer, but the interior was dark, too dark to see anything. He felt the wall just inside the door and was rewarded with a light switch. With a last look around, he flipped the switch—and gasped at what he saw.

The main floor space of the trailer was empty, but the walls were lined with shelves, and on the shelves were glass jars. Some of the jars were almost as big as five-gallon water jugs, and there were things floating inside all of them.

Some of the things might have been human.

Pat walked up to the display nearest him. The only lights in the trailer were cheap overhead tubes, and all the glass had the sickly green tint of fluorescents. The first held a two-headed puppy. A plaque beneath it stated that the dog had been born alive, but lived only a few hours.

Next to the puppy was a snake with no tail, only a head on either end. It was coiled around its jar of formaldehyde several times. Its plaque said that it had led a normal life and died after many years on display in Browning's Museum of Unnatural History.

The rest of that wall held a panoply of deformed animals, most embryonic, a few skeletal.

But the other wall held humans.

There were only three displays. One showed a five-month-old embryo with four arms, the extra set sprouting from the sides of its tiny concave chest. One showed a pair of Siamese twins joined at the backs of their heads. Their plaque said they'd been born prematurely and lived for a day. The last showed a monster with a head so outsized that it dwarfed the entire body.

Its eyes were open.

Pat jerked back in alarm before looking again and realizing that he'd seen an optical illusion; the thing's skin was so translucent over the eyes that they looked open, large black pupils and glassy corneas seemingly staring out at Pat. There was no plaque beside this one; Pat wondered if it had been purchased on the sly, from a devious hospital worker who had simply provided the carcass, not a story to accompany it. Pat gazed at its tiny fingers and toes, feeling sorrow, feeling—

Sick. He was abruptly sweating, trembling, stomach churning, head light. His ears buzzed. He staggered back, struggling to think, to hang on—

CHADBOURNE

The door squealed and someone else entered the trailer.

He whirled, almost calling out, but his throat closed when he saw…her.

Ember was halfway into the trailer when she spotted him and froze. She was as beautiful here, ten feet away from him, as she'd been on the stage. She wore a bathrobe over her skimpy costume; she still had on her glittering stage makeup.

"Oh," she breathed out, her voice husky, "I thought this was closed…" Then, looking away from him, she said, "*No.*"

Pat lurched forward as his symptoms vanished and his tongue worked again. "No, it is closed. I'm…I'm new here—working for the carnival, I mean and I found the body this morning, and I just wondered—"

"You found the body today?"

Pat nodded.

Her eyes darted past him, around the trailer's walls. "Did you…find anything else?"

He shook his head. "No."

She seemed to relax, a tension disappearing from her shoulders. "Good. I mean, the fuzz would love a reason to close this trailer down. Did Kurt tell you this is one of the last pickled punks exhibits on the circuit?"

"What are pickled punks?" he asked.

She stepped the rest of the way into the trailer, and Pat tried not to stare at her with the intensity he felt. She glanced at the displays around them. "They are. It's carny slang, you know? Because they're preserved in jars of formaldehyde. Like they're pickled."

Pat got it, laughing slightly. He was pleased when she gave him a half smile. "So why is it one of the last?"

Ember shrugged. "Some folks think it's offensive. They want to ban 'em. Most of the other shows now just have pictures. I don't want to lose ours."

He nodded as if he understood, even though he didn't. Then he remembered that they hadn't formally met, so he stepped forward, extending a hand. "Sorry, I'm Pat."

She took his hand, and he felt a firm, dry grasp. "Kate."

Kate. He knew "Ember" didn't fit her. Kate did.

"Hello, Kate. Nice to meet you."

A few seconds later, Pat realized he was still holding her hand and he released it, feeling heat rising in his face, hoping it wasn't suddenly vivid red. "I better go," he mumbled, starting to edge past her.

As he walked away from the trailer, he heard her call to him: "Pat—"

He turned back, and saw her leaning out of the doorway. "If you ever want to talk…well, I'm up earlier than most of the other folks on the lot, and I'll bet you are, too. Just ask Kurt or Vinnie to point out my trailer. Do you like coffee?"

He'd had it once and hated it. He nodded vigorously.

"Me, too. See you."

Then she went back into the trailer.

Pat stepped down to the ground, where he hesitated, considering. Why had she come to the trailer tonight, and why was she still there now? What was the "anything else" she'd asked if he'd found? And what had happened to him in there?

He was debating whether to stay and spy on her when he saw movement in the dark: Someone was watching him, crouched in the shadows of a truck thirty feet away. Unsure whether to run or stay and protect Ember, Pat froze, his heart hammering, until his observer stepped into the light.

Pat saw a man covered with thick, scaly, gray skin, his face a mass of stony wrinkles that gave him a permanent scowl. It took him only a second to remember the name from a banner: Leo the Alligator-Skinned Man was one of the main attractions in the ten-in-one. As he slouched forward, Pat saw he was shirtless and holding a nearly-empty bottle of whiskey in one hand.

"What're you doin' out here, sonny?" His voice was a hoarse croak, rasped by both genetics and liquor.

Pat managed only, "I…"

"Shouldn't be here. Not near this trailer. People keep dyin' here, ya know that?"

"But Ember—I mean Kate—"

"She's fine here. You're not. Now get the hell out of here."

Pat turned and took two steps, then looked back, thinking he should try to talk to Leo…but one look at the alligator-skinned man's steel-edged glare sent a jolt of adrenaline through Pat and he kept moving. He walked away quickly, trying not to run, hoping he wouldn't feel Leo's cracking fingers on his arm, smell his hot whiskey breath behind—

He risked one glance back and saw Leo going into the trailer, the door closing softly behind him. Then he gave in to his impulse and ran all the way back to the sanctuary of his bunk.

THE NEXT day, Pat decided it was time to take Kate up on her offer.

He found her outside her trailer, almost as if she'd been expecting him. She smiled and invited him inside. They had coffee and a nice chat that made Pat feel as if he'd known her forever. They talked about the other carnies, who could be trusted and who couldn't; they talked about their favorite bands (Kate liked the Beatles, but Pat liked a new band from California called The Doors), they talked about the hippies and the War and the protests and riots. Kate found out about Pat's mother, and Pat heard about the stifling Midwest farm upbringing Kate had happily left behind. Pat confessed that he wanted to make the carny his home, and Kate hoped Patch would let him stay. But when he told her he wanted to solve the pickled punks murders, she turned away, uncomfortable, and Pat had enough sense to shut up.

Vinnie caught Pat leaving his new friend's trailer and he began softly singing "She Loves You." Pat blushed three shades of crimson, then rushed to assure Vinnie they were just friends. Vinnie laughed and slapped Pat on the back.

Later, Pat asked Vinnie what he couldn't get up the nerve to ask Kate himself: If she had a real boyfriend or husband. Vinnie frowned, and the answer surprised Pat: Some of the other dancers in Rowdy's Revue thought Ember/Kate was just stuck up. She never flirted with the marks beyond what the job required; she never picked up extra money by turning a quick trick in a carny donniker; she never went into town with the other carny dancers, looking for handsome townies. But others remembered that business that happened two years ago, when two men had fought over her and one had wound up dead. Something had happened to Kate that night, something that had changed her forever. She'd left the carny for a few months; when she came back, she'd become withdrawn, solitary. When every show was done she left promptly, presumably to return to her trailer alone.

But Pat thought he knew where she went.

To be sure, he secretly followed her again that night. He felt guilty spying on someone he could now consider a friend, but it never occurred to him that Kate was any kind of suspect. In fact, he rationalized tailing her by telling himself that he was watching over her, keeping her safe from whatever—or whoever—was causing people to die near the trailer.

She was in there maybe fifteen minutes, then left. Pat waited until she was gone; after looking around to make sure he was alone, he ventured into the trailer himself.

He switched on the fluorescents, blinking in the flickering glare. There was no evidence left to mark her presence there, nothing to indicate if it was one display in particular that drew her. He glanced at all of the jars carefully, not stopping until he came to the baby with the grotesquely huge head. Then he blinked, staring, furiously trying to remember…

…because he was sure the thing had been moved since the last time he'd been in the trailer.

He tried to recall; he thought the jar was in the same place on the shelf, but that the long-dead entity within had somehow been shifted, its foot-wide face now staring sightlessly in a different direction.

Pat felt his stomach clench in fear. Why would she move the dead thing? Unless…

…unless she hadn't moved it.

But that was ridiculous. Wasn't it?

Pat left the trailer quickly, rubbing the goosepimples away as he turned off the lights, jumped down the steps and ran for the safety of his bunk.

TWO NIGHTS later, another town.

It was summer in the south, hot and muggy; marks swatted mosquitoes away even as they reached for their wallets.

Kurt had reluctantly let Pat stay, but told him again it could only be for a week. Now Pat waited behind the kootch show tent, thinking about how his time was running out, how he'd decided to simply ask Kate about her connection to the pickled punks trailer, to see if she could help him find the solution that would grant him a future with the carnival.

But Kate wasn't alone as she left the kootch tent.

There was a man with her. He was young, huge, hulking; from the way he staggered Pat knew he was stinking drunk, maybe even high. It was also clear that Kate didn't want him around; she shook her head furiously, then finally turned on him, her expression vicious.

The man reacted by slapping her.

Pat's feet were carrying him forward before he even knew what was happening. His mouth was open, and words of warning were coming out—then he was flying backwards, blood in his mouth and pain in his cheek. It took him a few seconds to realize he'd been hit and was sitting in the carny dirt.

He struggled to his feet, but Kate was there, holding his arm, holding him back, before he could charge his assailant.

"Don't, Pat, I'll take care of this. Okay?! I can handle this. Trust me."

Pat stared at her, then at the muscle-bulging giant behind her. "He'll hurt you—"

"No, he won't, not again. He's just a mark, okay? Trust me, Pat. Now go over to Kurt and get something on that cheek. Just do me a favor and don't tell him what really happened. Can you do that for me?"

Pat was hurt; all he knew was that she didn't want his protection. He would have happily given every tooth in his head to keep her safe. Instead, she was sending him away.

He nodded and turned away. Behind him, the mark taunted, "Yeah, ya little shithead, git on home ta yer mama, and leave this one to a *real* man."

The last thing he heard was the man saying, "C'mon, baby, I got money." Then he ran to his bunk, buried his disgrace in his pillow and cried.

"Be careful with that one, boy," Cool Daddy muttered at him once.

When he saw the bully again the next day, he was dead inside the pickled punks trailer.

HE DIDN'T find the body this time; that privilege went to Leo. The alligator-skinned man had been heading for the ten-in-one when he'd passed the trailer and noticed the door hanging open. Pat had been part of a group who'd heard Leo's shouts. He and Kurt and Vinnie had run for the trailer and seen the man inside. And the blood.

It was thick this time, on the man, on his clothes, on the floor around him. His arms were in stiff, outstretched positions, the fingers bent as if clawing the trailer's steel floor. His eyes were open, staring at the right-hand wall.

At the huge-headed thing in the jar.

Kurt had told Pat to go call the police; he'd been happy to comply, because he didn't want his expression to give away what he knew, about who the dead man on the gruesome floor had last been with.

The scene was the same as before—fuzz, dicks, M.E.'s. Despite the blood, the examiner was once again unable to find an injury. The corpse was carted away, the blood cleaned up, Leo was questioned, providing surly answers as the cops openly stared at him—and the pickled punks trailer closed up again.

That night Pat waited behind the kootch show tent, ignoring the other girls who walked by him, offering their affectionate gibes and taunts; he waited until Kate appeared. She saw him, walked to him silently, and took him by the arm.

"I want to show you something," was all she said.

They crossed the lot, now past closing and nearly empty; Pat knew the path all too well.

"We can't go in there," he told her.

She ignored him. When they reached the pickled punks trailer a voice assailed them.

"Kate…"

Pat knew those grating tones without even looking, but then Leo reared up in the dark, next to him.

"It's all right, Leo," she told him.

There was a pause before Leo said, in little more than a whisper, "He's just a kid."

Pat was shocked at Kate's forceful response. "I said it's all right, Leo. Leave us alone."

The alligator-skinned man paused, then reluctantly shambled off.

Kate reached up, tore aside the police tape, turned on the lights, and went in. Pat followed her, and she closed the door behind them.

Although the trailer had been scrubbed, the metallic tang of blood lingered in the stale air. "Kate," he began, "I just want you to know—whatever happened to that guy, he deserved it—"

"Sit down, Pat." She sat cross-legged in the middle of the floor; he followed her example and waited while she decided what to say.

When she finally spoke, she didn't look at him. Her voice was very soft, and he found himself leaning forward to hear. "Two years ago there was a man, one night after the show. He wasn't like the others; he wasn't loud or drunk or sweaty. He was young, and handsome, with black hair and green eyes. His name was Ian. And he…" She trailed off before looking up at Pat with an expression he'd never seen on her before. "You won't believe me."

"I'll believe you," he said in a gentle tone that he hoped would convince her.

Apparently it worked; she smiled at him and went on. "He could talk to me without speaking. They call it telepathy. It's like what Janky the Mentalist says he can do, but this was for real. Okay?"

He just nodded, believing it only because it was her saying it.

"He spoke to me up here," she pointed to her head, "and he told me I was the most beautiful thing he'd ever seen, and that he wanted to take care of me. And I believed him."

She struggled for a few seconds, finally going on: "We slept together that night. He was the first man I'd been with since I was a teenager; and now he's the last man I was with."

Even though Pat's skin felt as if it were aflame, he shivered.

"He told me he would always take care of me, and I believed him. Except…" Her perfect features tightened in pain and the first tear escaped.

"There was a guy working here at the time named Hector. He was a roughie, and he…had a thing for me, I guess. Anyway, he saw us, me and Ian, in the morning, coming out of the trailer, and he just went crazy. He was a big guy, very strong—could drive a tent peg into the hardest ground with one hammer swing. The thing is…he went after me. Ian was as good as his word—he managed to fight Hector off, but he…"

One tear escaped and trickled down her cheek, and Pat felt his eyes welling. "Oh my god, Kate. I'm sorry."

Kate nodded, and reached out for Pat's hand. "Even while he was dying, there in the dirt next to my trailer, I heard him in my mind, telling me again that he'd always take care of me."

A sudden chill coursed through Pat, and he looked up, startled, because the temperature in the trailer *was* dropping.

She continued, unheeding. "They arrested Hector, of course. And a month later I found out I was pregnant. I was glad at first, because it was a part of him. I left the carny and went home, expecting to raise my child there. But then—it started going wrong."

The overhead lights throbbed, not their usual light flicker but a distinct, rhythmic pulsing. Pat's gut twisted in dread. He wanted very badly to leave the trailer, but forced himself to stay seated, to listen to her.

"The pregnancy was painful, more than they're supposed to be. I had morning sickness, and vomited up blood. I began to have strange dreams, dreams that I knew weren't my own, dreams of rushing blood and struggling for breath. I was four months along when I miscarried."

Pat heard a metallic click just then, a sound like a cannon shot in the quiet between her sentences. After a second, he realized what the sound had been: A bolt being driven into a lock. The door to the trailer had just been locked from outside. He was trapped here now.

Kate rose to her feet, stepped to Pat and extended a hand down to him. "Come on, Pat, there's someone I want you to meet."

Pat accepted her hand and allowed her to lead him across the trailer, until they stood in front of the huge-headed embryonic monster.

"This is my son."

The thing's massive head tilted until it was gazing at Pat through its translucent eyelids.

And then Pat felt it inside him. It was like emerging from darkness to gaze at a white-hot light, a sharp stab of pain that pierced the center of Pat's brain. He reeled back, pulling his hand from Kate's.

"Pat—!"

What was in his head wasn't words, it wasn't intellect or sound, it was pure emotion. And the emotion was killing rage.

Pat felt something like a sledgehammer blow, and he knew the sudden warmth he felt on his chin and neck was his own blood.

He suddenly understood what had killed the other men in the pickled punks trailer. With the same abrupt clarity he knew that he would die here, too. He'd die full of rage that wasn't his own, his life exploding out of him—

Then he was outside, on his back, Kate bending over him in concern. "Pat! Pat, can you hear me?!"

He thought he nodded. He must have, because she cried out in relief. "Can you stand up?"

He sat up and the world spun away from Pat, and he let it go.

LATER, HE found out that it had been Leo who'd carried him back to his bunk.

But when he woke up it was Vinnie he saw, looking down at him in concern. He told Pat that he'd been sick for three days, with high fever and delirium. Pat asked if he'd said anything while he was out; he was relieved when Vinnie told him it was nothing intelligible.

Then Vinnie broke the news: Kate/Ember had disappeared the same day Pat had gotten sick. Her trailer was still on the lot, but her clothes were gone and so was she.

When he could walk, Pat made his way to the pickled punks trailer.

Kurt found him there, staring at what was left. The jars were all gone, replaced with two-dimensional photos. Pat asked what had happened to the exhibits; Kurt told him that, with the recent deaths linked to the pickled punks, he couldn't pay off the cops any longer to look the other way, and so they had complied with state laws and removed the "offending material." The animals had been sold to a museum; two of the babies had received burial. The third had disappeared.

Pat didn't have to ask which one.

Later that day Pat told Kurt and Vinnie he was leaving the carnival. Kurt gave him enough money for a bus ticket home, plus some extra. Vinnie gave him a home address, where he lived during the carny's off-season, and told Pat to look him up. Pat said he would.

The last person he saw before he left was Leo.

"You knew, didn't you?" Pat asked.

Leo answered by lifting the ubiquitous whiskey bottle. "It's one'a the reasons for this, kid."

No other words were necessary between them. They exchanged a short nod, then Pat left the carnival. He got a lift into town, where he bought his bus ticket home.

During the ride, he thought about his mom; he thought she might be glad to see him. He thought he could make things different now; he was older and knew things his mother would never guess at.

But most of all he thought of Kate. He already missed her; he missed her face and trust in him and her coffee; he missed the fact that he'd never gotten to kiss her, or even stroke her face; but he didn't pity her or worry about her. He'd kept her safe by leaving; he wouldn't be around the carnival to blurt out what he knew, to endanger her by giving away her terrible secret. He would have given her more than that, if he could have.

And wherever she was, whatever strange changes the future brought, he felt some comfort from knowing that she and her son would always be safe.

COURTING THE QUEEN OF SHEBA

by Amanda C. Davis

We were still setting up for the matinee when Billy came tearing into the grassy back lot, face aglow. He strode right past me and stopped before Arthur Whitman, our clown. "You got to see this," he panted. "There's a new outside show, and it's got a dead girl."

Mr. Whitman and I passed back and forth a look of weary tolerance, as would a set of overtaxed parents. As a lady rider I had been with Prince's Hippodramatic Show for three years; Mr. Whitman, for two. We knew better than to fuss over the games and exhibitions that poached our customers and took advantage of our advertising for their own profit. But Billy was the newest rider in the show. He had yet to learn.

"A dead girl?" said Mr. Whitman, who had the voice of a droll Easterner when not greased up in whiteface. "Waxworks, more like."

Billy shook his head vehemently. "Not *new* dead—*old* dead. And it's real as Alice's—uh—" Luckily at that moment he noticed me nearby, and he stammered into silence. Mr. Whitman's eyebrows piqued (whether at Billy's claim or the evaded vulgarism) and he agreed to join Billy for a closer look. I, not yet in my costume and therefore properly attired for a public appearance, followed.

The "dead girl" was housed in a canvas tent not far across the inn yard from our own. The proprietor sat on a collapsible chair near the entrance, beside a wooden marquee: SEE THE QUEEN OF SHEBA, FIVE CENTS. A fair price if she was as advertised, but outside shows never are, so Mr. Whitman offered the proprietor a free ticket to our matinee in exchange for entry, and the man relented. Had he made it to the circus, it would have made him a splendid bargain: seats could be had for a quarter. With all parties thinking they had made a shrewd deal, we slipped inside the tent to pay homage to the Queen of Sheba.

The tent was small; the Queen fit it snugly. She lay in a box with a glass top, barely five feet from head to toe, and every inch of her had shriveled to paper. Most of her body was wrapped in brittle cloth the color of sand that looked as if it might break at a touch, although I could see part of her shrunken hand and much of her skull, to which still clung several wisps of light-colored hair.

"The Queen of Sheba," said Billy, in a satisfied tone. "She ain't the beauty she's made out to be."

Mr. Whitman bent over the case, deep in scrutiny. "Sheba or not, she has been very classically preserved. The weave of the linen is remarkably like those I have seen abroad—" Whether Mr. Whitman had ever been abroad was unconfirmed, but he listed several cities in Africa and Europe. I thought the linen remarkably like what we saw every day in cheap hotels. "Look at the narrowness of her torso below the rib cage. The internal organs have undoubtedly been removed. Billing her as the Queen of Sheba—a typical humbug. But she may well be a genuine Egyptian mummy."

When we had seen our fill, we filed into the bright summer sun.

"It's remarkable," I said, as we were leaving, "that the proprietor let us stay as long as he did. Most men would have called us out long ago."

"He knows we're showmen," said Billy confidently. "Did right by us, didn't you, feller?" He delivered the proprietor a friendly blow to the arm.

The proprietor tipped to one side, slid from the chair, and fell to the ground, stone dead.

Billy's face went white as bone. Mr. Whitman had more sense. In a flash, he took the proprietor under the shoulders and dragged him into the tent to lay beside the box with the Queen of Sheba. He nearly didn't fit. We picked up the sign (so as to discourage others from disturbing us) and stuffed ourselves into the tent: three living souls, and two dead ones.

Billy had his hand over his mouth. I suppose it was all he could do to stand. Mr. Whitman gave him a bracing shake of the shoulders.

"Keep hold of your senses," Mr. Whitman said to him. "No man dies of a bruised arm. Obviously, our friend perished quite naturally while we were within his exhibit. See, his face bears the signs of some heart trouble."

I avoided the face of the proprietor, instead gazing into the desiccated face of the Queen. "I wonder, was he alone?"

"Alone?" joked Mr. Whitman. "He traveled with the Queen!"

"Heart trouble," said Billy. He still looked quite pale. "I thought I was a murderer."

"Only a fool," said Mr. Whitman. "Come. We will leave this unlucky man with his display and alert Mr. Prince. He is our employer, after all, and to be frank, dealing with corpses is far beyond my level of pay."

At the word "pay" Billy roused slightly. "Hang on," he said. You could see the mossy water-wheel of his brain slowly churn up his thoughts. "This poor old feller was chargin' a half-dime a person just to come in an' look. Say we got a thousand people here and everyone wanted to see. That's—that's—"

"Quite a sum," said Mr. Whitman.

I saw what they were aiming at and felt obliged to intervene. "We cannot claim this man's property just because he died in our presence."

To our eventual detriment, Mr. Prince did not agree.

I MUST say this in our defense: we saved the proprietor from the potter's field. In between the matinee and the evening show we managed to bribe the local Methodists into laying him out in preparation for burial in their churchyard the following Sunday. It cost a small fortune, but Mr. Prince was happy to pay it—we were, after all, expecting to rake in thirty to forty dollars per day showing the Queen. I think the arrangements slaked his conscience. They did not slake mine.

A paper inside the proprietor's jacket told us his name had been Harold Collins. Billy went quite overboard in pretending to mourn "dear old Harry." I didn't speak to him all day. The situation turned my stomach. We had made Collins's death into profit, his funeral into a play. Then again, he was—as Billy had noted—a showman. Perhaps he would have wanted to participate in one last spectacle.

The circus put on an impressive show that night. We riders performed tricks and tableaux, saddled and bareback, that left the audience gasping. Mr. Whitman capered beautifully. Our acrobats were Mercury; our strongman, Atlas. Quite simply, we astounded them.

We retired to our hotel, boarded the horses, ate late, and claimed our rooms. As a rule I boarded with another rider called Kathleen. Our habits suited one another. We turned in early. I am sure I fell asleep first. It must have been hours, but it seemed to be mere minutes before I awoke to the sound of Kathleen turning restlessly beside me in bed, whispering to herself.

This disturbance being rare, I murmured into my pillow: "Hush, dear." When she did not cease, I raised my head a little, hoping to rouse her by my own movements. "Wake up, Kathleen." My voice must have been weak—I sleep soundly and wake with difficulty—for the tossing and the whispering did not stop.

I had resolved to bear it out when her whispers grew clearer. "Gone and gone and gone...days and days...will it never end? Oh will it never end?"

"Kathleen," I said, still not quite willing to open my eyes, "please..."

Fingers like dead grapevines brushed my shoulder. *"I'm so hungry."*

Without warning, the fingers dug hard and deep into the dent at the corner of my collarbone. I cried out. Now fully awakened, I rolled to confront Kathleen—

—only to see the corpse of the Queen of Sheba lying beside me in her place, staring at me through long-dried eye sockets and grinning with long yellow teeth!

Needless to say, I screamed—from the depths of my chest, with all my breath. Before I knew it, half a dozen performers crowded into my room, some with candles, most in bedclothes...and myself, in bed in my nightgown with the sheets to my chin, with no corpse beside me and no explanation for why I had awoken nearly the entire hotel.

To my equal shame and relief, Mr. Prince pushed through the gathering crowd, all bombast and authority; and when he asked what disturbed me, and I sheepishly admitted it was naught but a dream, he cleared out the room as efficiently as he might have cleared out sneak-ins from beneath the tiered seating. Soon we were alone.

"See here," he said, "you're sensible, Alice, and a good rider. I'll forgive a night terror or two. Only don't make a habit of it." As he closed the door he added, so that only the two of us could hear, "And when Kathleen comes

back, tell her for God's sake to be more discreet. Our reputation is poor enough as it is."

He had spoken of what I had noticed but dared not acknowledge; Kathleen was not here. I had never heard her voice, never felt her touch. Yet I was never alone.

I lit a candle and lay on my back for the rest of the night, cruelly and inescapably awake.

WELL BEFORE dawn we were roused for the journey to the next town. (Kathleen was back by then, indecently tousled and wholly immune to my cold shoulder.) We dressed mechanically and met in the dining room for breakfast, more sleep-dogged than usual. Before I sat Mr. Whitman approached me privately.

"I hear," he said, "that you had some trouble this past night."

"A very little," I said. The long night and terrible shock must have worn on my nerves, because I added, "I suppose you rushed to my aid only to find a silly girl having a bad dream."

He cleared his throat. "I did not, in fact," he said. "At the moment you—ah—alarmed the troupe, I was suffering some alarm of my own."

"Speak plainly," I snapped.

He licked his lips. "You saw her too?"

I did not answer. I did not need to.

Billy entered the dining room. His eyes were sunken in his face. The chandelier man called to him: "Hi! Billy! Are you hungry?"

Billy skittered like a foal. "What'd you say? G--d---, I never want to hear that word again!" He took his place at the table looking sullen.

"H'm," said Mr. Whitman.

"Hungry," I said, raising a hand to my mouth. "She said—"

"'I'm so hungry,'" he finished.

My own appetite vanished. I saw the same sentiment reflected in Arthur Whitman's face. "Oh, what have we done?"

He said nothing; and between his troubled silence and Billy's sullenness, breakfast was solemn indeed.

AS ALWAYS, the crewsmen had gone on hours before to set up the new site—leaving us to a long drive in the dim morning. We stopped at the town borders to clean the wagons and change into our costumes. Then the band played, the wagons aligned, and we made the grand entrée.

Nowadays you may find entertainment on any corner, but then we offered the brightest a country farmer might hope to see. Sleek showhorses; painted carts; gay music from the bandwagon; sequins shining on our costumes. Mr. Whitman, already "greased," gamboled along, a living marionette. There were many difficulties in circus life, many inconveniences. But so few people know the heaven of wholehearted applause.

We rode through town to the lot and directly to the tent. The audience followed. While Jones the treasurer sold tickets and we prepared for the performance, Mr. Prince had several of the workers set up the tent and coffin of the Queen of Sheba.

It was to be our first day to display her, and Mr. Prince fairly bounced with anticipation. After much agonizing, he assigned Jones the treasurer to sit outside her tent collecting dues in between shows. Shame upon us all! We even used poor Harry Collins's sign, and charged the same price he had set.

We all took turns sneaking to visit Jones outside his tent, and by the end of the day it was clear: the Queen of Sheba was a tremendous money-maker. The town may not have been a wealthy one, but curiosity is a powerful force against financial discretion. Hundreds paid their half-dime to see the Queen. "No wonder those penny-showmen are so keen to follow us!" Mr. Prince cackled, when Jones had counted the take. "If this keeps up, she'll earn us an elephant."

Despite my weariness, I dreaded the setting sun. As Kathleen and I settled into our hotel I begged her to stay the night. She agreed, in her own fashion ("Sure I'll be stayin' the night, what do you take me for?"). Small comfort, but I took it to heart.

Dark fell. Sleep hovered over me. The Queen of Sheba seemed further away, less clear in my memory. I let my eyes flicker shut, relaxed into steady breath...

...and woke—in a terrible turnabout—to the sound of a piercing shriek from not so far away.

Almost before Kathleen and I were dressed enough to investigate, Mr. Prince came knocking with the news. I had rarely seen him so serious. "Jones is dead," he said. "His poor wife woke to find him—" He broke off, whether for propriety or the sake of his nerves.

"Wasn't his heart that killed him?" asked Kathleen.

"Ah…" said Mr. Prince. "The cause of death is not…immediately obvious. That is to say…"

"POOR FELLER was dried up like a winter potato," said Billy.

He sat across from us in the wagon, bouncing with every rut in the road, and though the sun had yet to rise, for once none of us tried to sleep.

"How'd ye get in see him?" said Kathleen, eyes bright.

"Don't be prurient, dear," I said. It was no use, of course. I gave Billy a look from beneath my eyelashes to let him know I didn't truly want him to stop telling his tale.

"Got there first," Billy bragged to Kathleen. "So's no one could keep me out. There was Mrs. Jones in her night-cap and Jones laying there—and I about half didn't know him—because Jones never was *that* thin!"

"*Thin*," I said.

"Skin and bone," said Billy. The grin faded from his face. I suppose that was the moment the realization truly struck him. "Skin and bone."

Kathleen shivered and leaned on my shoulder. "Will we be havin' another funeral?"

"Not us," said Mr. Whitman, in his deep glum voice. He sat not too far from Billy, but I had not thought he was listening. "Jones and the new widow have been left behind pending their journey home. I believe Mr. Prince has arranged for a casket and transport. We, of course, will 'play out the play'."

"Can't even take a day off when your treasurer dies," said Billy in disgust.

But missing a day off did not trouble me as much as did Billy's description of Jones's corpse. I could not shake from my mind the memory of my nightmare—or else vision.

I had heard the pleas of the Queen of Sheba.

And Jones died looking very hungry.

THE TREASURER managed a thousand vital tasks, but none of them to do with the performance itself, so his absence did not prevent us from putting on our usual show. (It did, however, make us mutter to one another about when and whether we would have our pay.) Mr. Prince himself sold tickets. He ordered the chandelier man, who managed our lighting, to sell showings to the Queen of Sheba.

I would like to tell you that we outdid ourselves with every show, but in truth every day brought a fresh audience—so our acts rarely varied. The audience left; the take was counted; the tent was dismantled, the center pole discarded. One variation tonight: the next day being Sunday, the crew did not leave immediately for the next town but stayed the night. We did not perform on Sundays. Public opinion did not allow it.

We woke early intending to go to church (a matter of piety for some, a matter of appearance for others). At breakfast, however, I noticed that one of our number was staring at his plate rather than emptying it: the chandelier man, who had spent the previous day with the Queen of Sheba. Mr. Whitman caught my gaze. He had noticed too. As soon as possible he took the man aside. I carried on bright conversation with the others, ever watching from the corner of my eye. When Mr. Whitman came to beg my company, I excused myself immediately and followed him to a quiet corner.

It had cost Mr. Whitman much patience and some of his whiskey before the chandelier man gave up his story, but when he did, it went like this: He (the chandelier man) boarded with one of the drivers. The driver, we all knew, was a stout little man fond of drink and food, a chewer of tobacco, and he liked to carry some bread or an age-wrinkled apple with him, as he said, "to carry him to breakfast." This he kept beside the bed. Both men fell asleep quickly. (Circus folk always did; sleep we found more scarce than gold.) Sometime during the night, the chandelier man woke to the sound of weeping.

("I heard no weeping," I said. "I did," said Mr. Whitman.)

In the dim light the chandelier man saw a slim figure by the bed. He would not reveal who he thought it might be, but he was not alarmed until it laid a hand on his arm. The fingers, he said, were tough as wood, rough as bark. It leaned its face down and whispered—

"I'm so hungry," I said, at the same time Mr. Whitman did. He nodded gravely.

Only then did the chandelier man begin to see the face—or understand whose it was. He said his heart went mad in his ribs. He told Mr. Whitman of a gaping mouth, eyes sunk so deep they might not remain in their sockets, hollow cheeks, flaking skin. They stared at one another for some moments. Then the chandelier man—rigid with fear—cried: "Hungry, are you? Why— have a bite!"

And he lunged across the sleeping driver, snatched up the age-wrinkled apple, and hurled it at the Queen's gawping face.

The Queen's mouth closed with a hard snap. Like the last wisp of smoke from a dead candle slipping through a window, she vanished.

The chandelier man barely had time to recover before the driver, who had seen nothing and knew only that he had been lunged upon in the middle of the night, started a large quarrel over what was going on and why they were both unpleasantly awake. To compound matters, the driver's apple could not be found. As of breakfast it did not seem that the chandelier man had been forgiven.

Mr. Whitman and I regarded each other for a somber moment. Then he said—as a barbecue-goer remarking on the mild weather—"I'm beginning to believe we have a problem on our hands."

He startled a laugh from me; then, a scowl. "You're suggesting—"

"I am," he said quietly.

"It's preposterous."

"Perhaps," he said. "Miss Monroe, please listen. For all my songs and japes in the ring, I am a scholar at heart. To link these recent events to our new acquisition...I admit it is preposterous. But I fear that not to do so may be far worse."

I stared at him: Mr. Whitman, the droll Easterner; Mr. Whitman, the prancing jester. "I won't be made a fool, Mr. Whitman."

Again he grew quiet. "I would never presume."

I have known a man or two who thought they might slide the wool over a pretty girl's eyes; I have also been fortunate to know sincerity. Mr. Whitman radiated it. And something else: something far more convincing. In his sincerity I detected restrained but genuine fear.

"You sound as if you may have a plan," I said.

"I do," he said, his countenance clearing to hear me come to his side. He nodded his head toward the others in their Sunday best. "I'm afraid it will make heathens of us for a day."

I tossed my head. "I am a lady rider with a traveling circus," I said, in a haughty voice that, following my intent, made him laugh. "I can hardly be worse."

IN THE space of ten minutes we became both heathens and criminals: ignoring the church bell in order to hitch two horses to our smallest wagon and abandon our employer with the corpse of a Queen hidden beneath a quilt. I, who traveled almost without ceasing, felt the old thrill of the road rise anew. It must have been the illicit aspect that excited my sensibilities; that, or the freedom. I traveled daily. But I always traveled where someone else demanded I go.

Mr. Whitman explained himself as we drove. The Queen's nocturnal appearances, he said, had too much in common to come from our individual imaginations. He and I had only discussed the phrase "I'm so hungry" among ourselves; Billy, as far as he could ascertain, never admitted hearing it to anyone, though he reacted strongly enough to the word that morning. The chandelier man, then, had not heard it from us. Either we four had invented the phrase independently or it had a common source.

"As for poor Jones," he added, "who can say what he might have seen or heard?"

"Billy said he looked thin."

"Thin as a starveling," he said.

So Mr. Whitman determined the validity of his—our—visions. Jones' death, and the chandelier man's threatening visitation, convinced him of the danger. Those performers who spent time near the Queen became the objects of her wrath. To him the course seemed clear. The Queen of Sheba must be gotten rid of. And who would know how to do so but the original proprietor?

"But," I said, coloring, "the proprietor—Mr. Collins—is dead."

"So is the Queen," he said. "The fact has failed to quiet her. And Mr. Collins is not yet in his grave."

We had an appointment with a dead man. And we were bringing a dead woman to meet him.

THE JOURNEY took most of the morning. Not far from town we heard the pealing of church bells.

"I do feel heathen," remarked Mr. Whitman.

Something in the character of the anthem gave me pause. "No," I said slowly, recalling hundreds of church bells in hundreds of towns across America. "Those are funeral chimes."

"Collins," we said together, and he urged the horses toward the sound of the bells.

We reached the church just in time to see a procession from the church, with six men bearing the coffin toward its final resting place. I could not imagine that so many people had turned out for a funeral for a man none of them had properly met, but then I remembered—our business thrived upon the scarcity of spectacle. Surely the funeral of a stranger counted as a spectacle worth seeing.

Mr. Whitman pulled the horses to a halt. I leapt down nimbly enough to turn a few heads; he followed less prettily and hurried around the cart. "Stop!" I cried, running toward the funeral party.

The men bearing pall stopped, as one does when hearing the word "Stop" cried in a high woman's voice; at once I was the center of attention. I sought the preacher. His eyes lit up at the sight of me, and I knew he recognized me—from the show or from our prior delivery of Mr. Collins's body, I could not guess. "Do not bury this man yet," I pleaded, with the whole town looking on. "We—we must add something to the coffin." There were looks all around.

The preacher took me around the shoulders. "It would not do to open the coffin now," he said, under his breath. "Give his effects to the poor. We should carry on."

"No," said Mr. Whitman, coming up behind us. The pastor turned—and he let out a start: for Mr. Whitman had laid the glass coffin containing the Queen of Sheba at his feet.

No performance of ours could have commanded the utter attention as did this simple act. *Oh*, I thought; *if Mr. Prince knew the show we were giving for free!* But I did not speak. The preacher drew away from me, and he bent low over the coffin. "Is this—is this—a *girl?*"

"Please open the coffin," I said again.

He stood, with a face like he had been smacked by an iron. "Let the coffin down," he said, in a hoarse voice, to the pallbearers. "Gentlemen, please take your ladies home." No one moved. "Then—please—open the coffin."

The six bemused men obeyed. Someone procured a hammer, and the nails were pried free; the coffin lid came open with a stench and a grisly sight, though not so much as I had feared for a man three days dead. Mr. Whitman took up the Queen under his arm—that is how small she was—and brought her coffin alongside Collins's in the thick churchyard grass. He found the latch upon the glass and, gently as a mother peeling back a blanket from her child, laid open the casket so that the two dead souls lay side by side under the blue sky.

Then—with a hiss of a kettle left too long on the fire—the Queen of Sheba *rose*.

She lurched up in her coffin, shroud tearing at her mouth so that it gaped wide as a scream, turning her head from side to side blindly. The air filled with cries of horror. We could not have planned a better show! Her bone-thin wrists arched as she scrabbled to take hold of her coffin walls; then her groping fingers fell upon the coffin nearby, and further still she crawled, until the brittle hands took hold of Collins within his coffin.

She hissed, wordlessly. Her voice was like dry wind. By spasms she jerked her way to join him in the coffin.

The mouth-rent in her shroud opened wider. Like spiders the dry fingers clutched his jaws. Then she drew herself down, down, to his face, and her tiny teeth showed and then—the teeth tore into his dead flesh, over and over, and the hiss of her voice became a gurgle, a terrible glugging, and her breath bubbled with gore.

I screamed; we all screamed, I am sure. Heedless of us, the dead Queen feasted.

"Bury them!" I shrieked. "Bury them both!"

Mr. Whitman leapt forward to Collins' coffin. Laying his shoulder to it he shoved the box along the grass until it came to the hole that had been laid open for it. "Help me!" he roared. One brave soul came to his side. Together they hurled the coffin, and the pair joined within in awful union, six feet deep.

Mr. Whitman scrambled for the shovel and began throwing dirt over the Queen and her prey; I dashed to his side and did the same with my hands. Before I knew it, others had joined. We rained grave dirt upon them until we could see them no longer, then until the dirt stopped moving, then until the earthen mound beside the stone was unexpectedly gone.

I fell back and felt Mr. Whitman's arms catch me. "She is gone," he said. His hands shook, but they held mine firmly nonetheless. "I suspect she is hungry no more."

"Then let us leave her here," I whispered.

And while the crowd of good Christians made mob among themselves, trying to understand what we or they had done, we left behind the buried dead, the empty coffin, and the best audience of our lives.

That was our adventure. Of course we had trouble from Mr. Prince when at last we returned, late that evening, as all prepared to move along to our next engagement the following day. Mr. Whitman took him aside and made the argument that by disposing of the Queen we had in fact preserved the entire circus. He did not go so far as to call us heroes. But we did it privately to one another.

His argument worked; we kept our jobs. Mercifully, we had no more deaths or nightmares. Mr. Prince did take some revenge from our salaries, but this did us little harm in the long run: we extorted much of the difference from Billy, whose life we insisted that we had saved. And as Mr. Whitman and I learned soon enough, while we wintered between traveling seasons and I took his name as my own, the old adage is true: Two may live as cheaply as one.

And for that happy discovery, I can thank no one but the Queen of Sheba!

THE CIRCUS REBORN

by Nayad Monroe

itting alone on a bench in the city's largest park on a Tuesday, Addison tried to keep herself from crying…until the tears pushed out anyway, and then she tried to hide the fact that she was crying. She knew it wasn't working; the people passing by were seeking a pleasant time outdoors after work in the warm, extended late June evening light, and choosing to stay in their don't-see-you bubbles to avoid eye contact with problems. Addison could have wailed out loud, sitting there with all the belongings she had left, otherwise known as the contents of the purse she'd taken along on her job search that morning. She could have jangled the useless keys to the apartment where she'd never been on the lease, which held the possessions her shitty Craigslist roommates had stolen when they changed the lock to kick her out. All because she didn't pay her part of the rent yet. She'd told them she would pay them back. No one in this city ever listened to her. Even if Addison jumped up on the bench and screamed, the city people on the park path would stride on by, treating her like a ghost. She gave up and let audible sobs chase the tears and black mascara running down her face.

With her vision blurred, it took a moment to notice the change as a unicycle rider approached from the left, passed in front of her, but then reversed and returned, pedaling in place. Addison gradually took in the odd, frilly white one-piece suit with enormous red buttons, and then the rider's old-fashioned-style clown face: white as the suit, nose red and mouth exaggerated, with bright blue eyes beaming at her from within the blackened ovals of his eye sockets. Wide and frizzled hair of the classic clown orange supported a tall, white conical hat. Addison stared as the clown tilted his head slightly and raised his thickly-drawn eyebrows at her, unicycling back and forth. He reached into the gap between two of the buttons on his torso, and extracted a rectangle—an envelope—which he extended toward her.

Addison shook her head.

The clown shook his head in return. He waved the lavender envelope back and forth, wheeling himself closer, and reached forward to offer it again. This time, Addison looked at the envelope, thought about it. She had nothing. The envelope was something. It was pretty, with even a hint of shimmer in the paper. A mild scent wafted from it—summery, floral. She took it. The clown somehow, while keeping the unicycle upright, bowed at the waist. He straightened and gave her a flourishy wave, and then pedaled away down the path.

Addison lifted the weighty envelope toward her face and inhaled its perfume. The scent flowed into her nose and brought something magical along with it, up into her mind with a rush of fascination. Whatever was in the envelope, it had to be good and she had to see what it was.

She opened the flap with care, easing it up instead of ripping it. The first thing inside was a piece of heavy card, with lines of calligraphy:

> *A token opens into lines below,*
> *Which traveled wisely lead to hidden space,*
> *Where following the track can only show*
> *The choice the chosen candidate may face.*
>
> *Two locks, but only one will meet this key,*
> *Because once turned, unturning can't be done.*
> *The choice is given, and your will is free—*
> *Uncertainty in choice is half the fun.*
>
> *And what's the other half? The mystery:*
> *The door unopened, prize that's never known,*
> *The longing for what you will never see,*
> *The flower from the seed that's never sown.*
>
> *You've always felt alone and ill at ease;*
> *Accept this invitation if you please.*

CHADBOURNE

Her breath quickened. The final two lines sent a shiver across her skin. It was like sensing a gaze on the back of her neck, like being seen by someone unseen. Except she liked it.

Digging into the envelope again, she found one of the old subway tokens, still valid but increasingly rare, and a much older style of key—the long kind that was ornate at the top, but looked too simple at the business end to either lock or unlock anything. Also, a final card with a hand-drawn map showing only an intersection of streets, and a note that said, "Tonight. Promptly at 11."

Addison checked her phone: 8:03. The sun would set late, but eventually this event would involve walking after dark. Not ideal, when she wasn't sure how to get there or what she'd find upon arrival. Could she use an app to find an intersection, with no address? It took a few tries, but she figured it out and soon started walking, wiping her face with a wadded-up tissue from her bag. No money for a ride, no place to sleep, but she had an invitation. Someone wanted her. She had somewhere to go.

Inhaling the scent of the envelope periodically, Addison flowed along with the shifting crowds on the sidewalks, giddiness rising as the sky faded far above and the lights brightened on tall and taller buildings. This was it; she was really in the city, having the adventures she came for. So different from the girl who never knew what to wear or what to say or when to stop drawing embarrassing pictures. The girl who tried to ignore kids taunting, "Loser! Loser! Mom's a sloppy boozer!" Addison walked on as vivid scenes from high school unfolded into waking dreams. Colors of lit signs along the streets triggered memories: the green of the gym uniform she wore all day after someone stole her clothes: the red of paint someone poured across her drawing in art class; the neon yellow poster glued to her locker, hand-lettered "Everyone Hates You, Freak!!!" It was like being there, but more colorful each time another memory replaced the last. A part of her mind monitored her progress and location. Another part marveled at how her feet did not hurt and her stomach did not growl. She noted increasing thirst, but felt that was better than needing to pee. Through the whole sequence, Addison also recalled the inner transformation that had come at the end of high school, as her urges to go to the city strengthened until she *damn well went*. With a few hundred dollars, two suitcases, and all the clothes she could stuff into them. Willing to work at a strip club if she had to. It hadn't come to that yet, but she had a feeling it would within a day or two after this night, whatever it would become. Dreamily, she inhaled the envelope's mix of scents one more time, which were becoming more distinct and numerous the more she smelled it. She remembered how the clown had pulled it out of his suit. Had it been up against his skin? Was this what clown skin smelled like? If so, she wondered how it would taste. If she unbuttoned those big red buttons and licked the clown flesh underneath…. She laughed out loud to think of the clown having marshmallow white skin all the way down.

I'm thinking funny, she mused. It was a relief to let go of all the stress and float along like a balloon tied to her own wrist. She laughed again, because just after having that thought she saw a bunch of balloons, tied to a wrought-iron fence, under a street light. It was the guardrail around a subway entrance, at the intersection of streets from the map in her invitation. She had arrived.

Addison checked her phone and frowned. 10:37? How had so much time passed? Yet it was *only* 10:37, so she wasn't late. That was good. She dismissed the question of where the time had gone. It didn't matter. The sleepy neighborhood of cozy brick apartment buildings offered nothing that might hurry her away, and there was even a tiny park next to the subway entrance. The only worrisome element was the chain stretched across the stairs below the balloons, with a sign dangling from the middle: CLOSED. But she was early. Addison sat in the wee park and waited, watching as the balmy air shifted the balloons back and forth.

A young black woman approached along the street. She walked with a swaying, intoxicated relaxation, her hair in a stunning natural halo around her face. Addison envied that hair from her position beneath ashy, stringy locks that she kept long because there was no point in trying to make any other style happen. Another dark-haired woman wandered toward the intersection from the cross street, also clearly feeling high and good, in contrast to the usual defensive tension women in the city wore when they walked alone. And then Addison spotted another, farther away, coming from the opposite direction of the first. Within moments there were four; Addison waved her invitation at them, blushing until they smiled and showed theirs, too. A club of five.

Her phone showed 10:59. Then a clown came up from the subway stairs and unhooked the chain. Addison might have thought it was *her* clown, except that this one's hair was cobalt blue. Nonetheless, she tingled at the thought of powdery clown skin, white like clouds, white like snow, paper white. Hunger finally set in. The clown beckoned, and the women all passed him on the stairs, heading downward as he clinked the chain back across the entrance again.

They all knew the drill. The tokens went in, and they passed through the turnstile. Walked onward to the subway platform. The blue-haired clown joined them, capering in place and then bowing extravagantly to each, kissing their hands. They giggled as he exaggerated a flustered response to their proximity.

The rumble of a train approached; it arrived with a roar and blast of wind. Their escort gave a game-show hostess gesture, inclining his head toward the train's open door and waiting until Addison and the others entered before he followed them into the otherwise empty car.

They clustered in seats close together, companions instead of strangers after introducing themselves: Addison, Isabella, Hailey, Juliana, Olivia. The clown coyly mimed zipping his lips, locking them and throwing away the key. The women chattered gaily, talking around the situation as if they all knew each other and were going to a party together, so Addison rolled with that, too. Words flowed out of her mouth and into her ears, but beyond the names she didn't remember a thing she said or heard.

At last a recorded voice announced, "End of the line. Please leave the train and follow the signs to the exits." The clown shook his head, so the group stayed on the train as it passed three dark and lonely stations, and then stopped at a fourth. The clown bounced and cavorted, blowing kisses to each of the women and pointing at the open door of the train car. There was nothing to do but file out.

Flickering lanterns of blue and green glass, placed along the wall, lit the arched ceiling of the abandoned station, reflecting glints from tile mosaics. In her weeks of using the subway system, Addison had never seen a station so ornate; she strained her neck to gaze upward at the abstract patterns set within carved stone swirls which were surprisingly visible in the low, erratic light. Peripheral motion caught her eye—another clown, cartwheeling along the subway platform, herding them after the one from the train, who had already moved ahead toward an installation at the far end. Following,

Addison mused that this was all weird, and probably illegal in multiple ways, but the thoughts didn't bother her. In fact, despite the long-delayed appetite growing in her belly, her energy increased with every step.

Glancing back, she saw the pursuing clown casually doing complicated flips, without ever losing his pointy hat; behind him a third clown went along the wall, smothering the flames in the lanterns. He left full darkness in his wake. Not even an emergency light glowed at that end of the station. Both clowns caught her looking and shooed her forward. Addison hurried to catch up with the others.

At the farthest, lit end of the platform, before the train tracks vanished into a tunnel to who-knew-where, Addison saw her orange-haired clown again. Behind him stood something like a five-sided study carrel, with each of the other women already placed around it at individual stations with dividers between them. Addison's clown blinked his bright blue eyes at her in happy recognition, and then gestured to the last section of the carrel. She stood at the empty counter-height desk and waited. The last light behind her dimmed until only a small flame burned in the lantern sitting atop the carrel's center, where the dividers met. Excitement rose within Addison. What would come next? A moment later, her clown came up close behind her back—his breath warming her neck, his familiar scent flowing around her—and placed two black boxes on the desk. Each box had a lock. She remembered the key, and took it from the envelope she'd carried for the last few hours. The clown closed his hand around the invitation and gently pulled it from her fingers. Addison gasped softly at the loss. She minded less when he eased her purse away. He patted her shoulder, and retreated.

She was alone with the two boxes and the key. She could choose only one lock. At first glance they were identical, but were they really? They couldn't be. One was right, the other wrong. She caressed each box, but they felt the same. She lifted one to her ear, and then the other, shaking gently. Nothing caught her attention. But didn't one seem a bit brighter than the other? Didn't it smell a tad more delicious? Yes and yes—she stabbed with the key, and twisted. The lid sprang open. It was right, it was right! Inside, a gift-wrapped cube, two inches on a side, sat on top of another envelope. She lifted the exquisite little gold-wrapped prize and set it aside, wanting to read the note first.

That craving, never sated, now is fed!
Devour this tiny taste, and more could come.
Your path away from home has turned and led
To where you may awaken what's been numb.

Forget the past, when you did not belong:
Surrounded, yet so rarely understood,
And treated as if you were always wrong,
Convinced your life would never come to good.
Feel that? A true awakening begins.
Within you stirs the will to soon compete,
And strength to do so. For whoever wins
Will find herself at home at last, and eat!

Disturbing as the changes will soon grow,
Attend to instinct. That's what you should know.

The poem sank into Addison's mind as she unwrapped the gift. The gold paper peeled away to reveal an inner layer of foil, which covered a waxy, pale chunk that squished under the pressure of her fingers. Despite its appearance, with all the repulsiveness of mushrooms and all the appeal of tofu, the sight of the spongy cube filled her mouth with saliva. A whiff of its scent made her stomach clench with need. It was in her mouth before Addison could consciously register the moaning that arose nearby. As she chewed ecstatically, she took notice of the building ruckus:

"No, no! Let me try again! Please? Please? Oh please, I'm so hungry! I smell it! Please? No no no, don't, I promise! I swear! I'll do anything you say, but please just let me have it. I'm so hungry! Please! Please! No, don't take me away, oh please!"

The delicious, delightful food melted down Addison's throat even as someone—was it Hailey? whined and begged. The voice retreated back into the dark distance behind her as Addison experienced the greatest satisfaction of her life…briefly. The food was so good. The bite was so small. Addison needed more. She knew she would do anything for more.

Excess saliva began to drip from the corners of her mouth. Her clown was again at her side, tenderly wiping her chin with a ruffle of his collar, gazing into her eyes. She wanted to lean in and nibble on his lip. But then her stomach cramped, hard enough to make her whimper. He nodded sympathetically and took her hand, tugging Addison toward the tunnel opening where the others, again, were already ahead. Anger flared—who did they think they were? Acting like she was too slow! She took longer, faster strides, even as her legs began to ache. The stomach cramps continued, but she only wanted to show them. She was no one to leave behind.

Her clown gave the most adorable squeak of delight, almost enough to distract Addison, but she was in the grip of a compulsion to chase the others down, to pass them, to prove herself. The need pushed claws from her fingertips, hard pointy black ones that left her pale thin fingernails pattering down to the train tracks in the tunnel. Clown held her hand but avoided the claws. They were nearly upon a rival couple as they reached the side tunnel that veered away from the tracks. Walls of pale stone glowed just enough to guide their way.

Addison's impatience peaked. She reached with her free hand to grab a fistful of Isabella's long black hair and yank her head back. The hair pulled free. Addison shoved her into the stone wall. Isabella went down and her companion crouched to tend to her. Addison pulled her own dear Clown along faster, stuffing Isabella's hair into her mouth to push the hunger back.

The others were too far ahead for her liking. Her belly felt so strange, though, her lower abdomen so bloated but her stomach so empty, the clump of hair so unsatisfying. As her legs grew longer and thicker they became heavy and hard to control. Her shoes and leggings, even her elastic-waist skirt, became too tight. She kicked off the shoes. The leggings and her underwear ripped and fell away, followed by the skirt. She wasn't used to such long steps, or such aching, burning pain. Her arms, too, the building weight of her arms and shoulders made everything more difficult, and destroyed her blouse and bra. Her skin thickened. Sobbing, she pushed herself harder. Addison couldn't bear to lose, even if she had to bite the poor Clown to make the hunger stop. Later, she could save that for later if it became unavoidable. First, more effort. The new sharp teeth filling her mouth gave her confidence. She spat out the old ones, and Clown giggled. His voice filled her with desire and she knew she would try so hard not to eat him.

They burst from the tunnel into the most dazzling cave. Candles burned by the hundreds, suspended from above in massive chandeliers; more of the green and blue lanterns hung from great hooks around the walls. Calliope music began to play as the ringmaster called out, "Ladies and gentlemen! Your attention please! Our third finalist has entered the ring, and the show is about to begin!"

Applause and cheers rose from the crowd—so many people! seated around the ring. In a front row of red velvet theater seats, Addison spotted a famous blonde movie actress sitting beside the mayor. His wife was not present. Other wealthily dressed men and women, and someone she thought was a famous football player, all gazed avidly at the ring. Behind them, rows of people in shiny nightclub attire filled wooden bleachers. Closer by, Olivia and Juliana—accompanied by their clowns with purple and yellow hair—lumbered fitfully around the ringmaster's central platform in the ring. Addison couldn't help admiring their size, much as she needed to destroy them. They had grown and grown, in all directions. But then she noticed Olivia's stunted upper right half, her lopsided face and arm that now looked tiny, having failed to match the rest of her body's development. The right arm looked dry and dark, as though—yes! it had begun to fall off.

Addison itched to end someone. Juliana would be a true challenge, but Olivia? No. Addison looked into Clown's eyes, smiled, and then ran at full speed across the ring, driving her new bulk into Olivia and knocking that preposterous weakling arm right off. She toppled Olivia and tore into her neck with her new teeth, so sharp, so good! The flesh filled her mouth with echoes of the food-gift she craved. She wanted more of it in great delicious mounds. The warm rich blood, tasting like dreams and wishes fulfilled, would be so perfect poured over the top like syrup over ice cream. Olivia's clown collapsed beside her, and Addison burned to eat him up, but there was Juliana, so angry to have her kill stolen! So ready to fight!

Addison dragged herself up, abdomen swelling, skin hardening, and spikes forming on her arms. Feverish. The music sped up. The mayor was on his feet, the actress draped against his side. Addison preened, validated by their attention in her moment. She faced a rival who was everything desirable: strong, beautiful, thriving, adapting. Addison too was all of those things. An unsettling thought of her recent past nearly broke her vibe. She rejected that humiliating, weak old version of herself, flexed massive new muscles and pushed away the past.

The fight took her down to instinct, primal wordless action, reflex. Slamming impacts, shoving, twisting, biting, clawing, leaping. The smell of rival crotch and armpits ignited unbearable fury. Only *one* could win the prize. Images rose from her transforming mind, memories from ancestral queens winning back and back, taking their turns to feast and mate and push out the eggs and raise the circus young: baby strongmen, clowns and ring-master, artists and queens and all. To send the baby rival queens to human homes as changeling parasites, until their time to find new colonies and fight. Drawn to the cities to be found and gathered. Addison strained, kicked, ripped with her claws. Wheezed air into her lungs after a fall. Rebounded. It was so good to be herself, to be here! She bit off Juliana's thumb; the crowd roared. Strength surged up. She tackled Juliana, knocked her down and landed on her chest and ripped her throat right out.

The audience lost it! Their cheers burst into vibrations in her bones. Spangled acrobats built triumphant formations. The ringmaster's voice boomed with congratulatory pronouncements. Addison understood the gist, but had other things on her mind. A carriage had arrived from the far tunnel, coming up from the queen's lair in the great tradition. Six black horses pulled the gilded, topless carriage, conveying the old queen on her bed of silken cushions. After years of tender care and luxury, her expansive white flesh glowed in great, softened, curving, jiggling piles; she drowsed in her well-fed splendor, glistening with unguents, well-prepared for her final glory.

Addison achieved suitable gravitas. She stood dignified under her mantle of rival's blood, awaiting delivery of her prize. Clown joined her again, as her partner in the feast. It would take some time, but they would savor every morsel. Then would come their love, deep in the queen's lair—her lair! and the cycle would begin again. The old feeding the new. The circus reborn.

The Black Ferris
by Ray Bradbury

The carnival had come to town like an October wind, like a dark bat flying over the cold lake, bones rattling in the night, mourning, sighing, whispering up the tents in the dark rain. It stayed on for a month by the gray, restless lake of October, in the black weather and increasing storms and leaden skies.

During the third week, at twilight on a Thursday, the two small boys walked along the lake shore in the cold wind.

"Aw, I don't believe you," said Peter.

"Come on, and I'll show you," said Hank.

They left wads of spit behind them all along the moist brown sand of the crashing shore. They ran to the lonely carnival grounds. It had been raining. The carnival lay by the sounding lake with nobody buying tickets from the flaky black booths, nobody hoping to get the salted hams from the whining roulette wheels, and none of the thin-fat freaks on the big platforms. The midway was silent, all the gray tents hissing on the wind like gigantic prehistoric wings. At eight o'clock perhaps, ghastly lights would flash on, voices would shout, music would go out over the lake. Now there was only a blind hunchback sitting in a black booth, feeling of the cracked china cup from which he was drinking some perfumed brew.

"There," said Hank, pointing.

The black Ferris wheel rose like an immense light-bulbed constellation against the cloudy sky, silent.

"I still don't believe what you said about it," said Peter.

"You wait, I saw it happen. I don't know how, but it did. You know how carnivals are; all funny. Okay; this one's even funnier."

Peter let himself be led to the high green hiding place of a tree.

Suddenly, Hank stiffened. "*Hist!* There's Mr. Cooger, the carnival man, now!" Hidden, they watched.

Mr. Cooger, a man of some thirty-five years, dressed in sharp bright clothes, a lapel carnation, hair greased with oil, drifted under the tree, a brown derby hat on his head. He had arrived in town three weeks before, shaking his brown derby hat at people on the street from inside his shiny red Ford, tooting the horn.

Now Mr. Cooger nodded at the little blind hunchback, spoke a word. The hunchback blindly, fumbling, locked Mr. Cooger into a black seat and sent him whirling up into the ominous twilight sky. Machinery hummed.

"See!" whispered Hank. "The Ferris wheel's going the wrong way. Backwards instead of forwards!"

"So what?" said Peter.

"Watch!"

The black Ferris wheel whirled twenty-five times around. Then the blind hunchback put out his pale hands and halted the machinery. The Ferris wheel stopped, gently swaying, at a certain black seat.

A ten-year-old boy stepped out. He walked off across the whispering carnival ground, in the shadows.

Peter almost fell from his limb. He searched the Ferris wheel with his eyes. "Where's Mr. Cooger!"

Hank poked him. "You wouldn't believe! Now see!"

"Where's Mr. Cooger at!"

"Come on, quick, run!" Hank dropped and was sprinting before he hit the ground.

UNDER GIANT chestnut trees, next to the ravine, the lights were burning in Mrs. Foley's white mansion. Piano music tinkled. Within the warm windows, people moved. Outside, it began to rain, despondently, irrevocably, forever and ever.

"I'm *so* wet," grieved Peter, crouching in the bushes. "Like someone squirted me with a hose. How much longer do we wait?"

"Ssh!" said Hank, cloaked in wet mystery.

They had followed the little boy from the Ferris wheel up through town, down dark streets to Mrs. Foley's ravine house. Now, inside the warm dining room of the house the strange little boy sat at dinner, forking and spooning rich lamb chops and mashed potatoes.

"I know his name," whispered Hank, quickly. "My mom told me about him the other day. She said, 'Hank, you hear about the li'l orphan boy moved in Mrs. Foley's? Well, his name is Joseph Pikes and he just came to Mrs. Foley's one day about two weeks ago and said how he was an orphan run away and could he have something to eat, and him and Mrs. Foley been getting on like hot apple pie ever since.' That's what my mom said," finished Hank, peering through the steamy Foley window. Water dripped from his nose. He held on to Peter who was twitching with cold. "Pete, I didn't like his looks from the first, I didn't. He looked—mean."

"I'm scared," said Peter, frankly wailing. "I'm cold and hungry and I don't know what this's all about."

"Gosh, you're dumb!" Hank shook his head, eyes shut in disgust. "Don't you see, three weeks ago the carnival came. And about the same time this little ole orphan shows up at Mrs. Foley's. And Mrs. Foley's son died a long time ago one night one winter, and she's never been the same, so here's this little ole orphan boy who butters her all around."

"Oh," said Peter, shaking.

"Come on," said Hank. They marched to the front door and banged the lion knocker.

After a while the door opened and Mrs. Foley looked out.

"You're all wet, come in," she said. "My land." She herded them into the hall. "What do you want?" she said, bending over them, a tall lady with lace on her full bosom and a pale thin face with white hair over it. "You're Henry Walterson, aren't you?"

Hank nodded, glancing fearfully at the dining room where the strange little boy looked up from his eating. "Can we see you alone, ma'am?" And when the old lady looked palely surprised, Hank crept over and shut the hall door and whispered at her. "We got to warn you about something, it's about that boy come to live with you, that orphan?"

The hall grew suddenly cold. Mrs. Foley drew herself high and stiff. "Well?"

"He's from the carnival, and he ain't a boy, he's a man, and he's planning on living here with you until he finds where your money is and then run off with it some night, and people will look for him but because they'll be looking for a little ten-year-old boy they won't recognize him when he walks by a thirty-five-year-old man, named Mr. Cooger!" cried Hank.

"What are you talking about?" declared Mrs. Foley.

"The carnival and the Ferris wheel and this strange man, Mr. Cooger, the Ferris wheel going backward and making him younger, I don't know how, and him coming here as a boy, and you can't trust him, because when he has your money he'll get on the Ferris wheel and it'll go *forward*, and he'll be thirty-five years old again, and the boy'll be gone forever!"

"Good night, Henry Walterson, don't *ever* come back!" shouted Mrs. Foley.

The door slammed. Peter and Hank found themselves in the rain once more. It soaked into them, cold and complete.

"Smart guy," snorted Peter. "Now you fixed it. Suppose he heard us, suppose he comes and *kills* us in our beds tonight, to shut us all up for keeps!"

"He wouldn't do that," said Hank.

"Wouldn't he?" Peter seized Hank's arm. "Look."

In the big bay window of the dining room now the mesh curtain pulled aside. Standing there in the pink light, his hand made into a menacing fist, was the little orphan boy. His face was horrible to see, the teeth bared, the eyes hateful, the lips mouthing out terrible words. That was all. The orphan boy was there only a second, then gone. The curtain fell into place. The rain poured down upon the house. Hank and Peter walked slowly home in the storm.

DURING SUPPER, Father looked at Hank and said, "If you don't catch pneumonia, I'll be surprised. Soaked, you were, by God! What's this about the carnival?"

Hank fussed at his mashed potatoes, occasionally looking at the rattling windows. "You know Mr. Cooger, the carnival man, Dad?"

"The one with the pink carnation in his lapel?" asked Father.

"Yes!" Hank sat up. "You've seen him around?"

"He stays down the street at Mrs. O'Leary's boarding house, got a room in back. Why?"

"Nothing," said Hank, his face glowing.

After supper Hank put through a call to Peter on the phone. At the other end of the line, Peter sounded miserable with coughing.

"Listen, Pete!" said Hank. "I see it all now. When that li'l ole orphan boy, Joseph Pikes, gets Mrs. Foley's money, he's got a good plan."

"What?"

"He'll stick around town as the carnival man, living in a room at Mrs. O'Leary's. That way nobody'll get suspicious of him. Everybody'll be looking for that nasty little boy and he'll be gone. And he'll be walking around, all disguised as the carnival man. That way, nobody'll suspect the carnival at all. It would look funny if the carnival suddenly pulled up stakes."

"Oh," said Peter, sniffling.

"So we got to act fast," said Hank.

"Nobody'll believe us, I tried to tell my folks but they said hogwash!" moaned Peter.

"We got to act tonight, anyway. Because why? Because he's gonna try to kill us! We're the only ones that know and if we tell the police to keep an eye on him, he's the one who stole Mrs. Foley's money in cahoots with the orphan boy, he won't live peaceful. I bet he just tries something tonight. So, I tell you, meet me at Mrs. Foley's in half an hour."

"Aw," said Peter.

"You wanna die?"

"No." Thoughtfully.

"Well, then. Meet me there and I bet we see that orphan boy sneaking out with the money, tonight, and running back down to the carnival grounds with it, when Mrs. Foley's asleep. I'll see you there. So long, Pete!"

"Young man," said Father, standing behind him as he hung up the phone. "You're not going anywhere. You're going straight up to bed. Here." He marched Hank upstairs. "Now hand me out everything you got on." Hank undressed. "There're no other clothes in your room are there?" asked Father.

"No, sir, they're all in the hall closet," said Hank, disconsolately.

"Good," said Dad and shut and locked the door.

Hank stood there, naked. "Holy cow," he said.

"Go to bed," said Father.

PETER ARRIVED at Mrs. Foley's house at about nine-thirty, sneezing, lost in a vast raincoat and mariner's cap. He stood like a small water hydrant on the street, mourning softly over his fate. The lights in the Foley house were warmly on upstairs. Peter waited for a half an hour, looking at the rain-drenched slick streets of night.

Finally, there was a darting paleness, a rustle in wet bushes.

"Hank?" Peter questioned the bushes.

"Yeah." Hank stepped out.

"Gosh," said Peter, staring. "You're—you're *naked!*"

"I ran all the way," said Hank. "Dad wouldn't let me out."

"You'll get pneumonia," said Peter. The lights in the house went out.

"Duck," cried Hank, bounding behind some bushes. They waited. "Pete," said Hank. "You're wearing pants, aren't you?"

"Sure," said Pete.

"Well, you're wearing a raincoat, and nobody'll know, so lend me your pants," said Hank.

A reluctant transaction was made. Hank pulled the pants on.

The rain let up. The clouds began to break apart.

In about ten minutes a small figure emerged from the house, bearing a large paper sack filled with some enormous loot or other.

"There he is," whispered Hank.

"There he goes!" cried Peter.

The orphan boy ran swiftly.

"Get after him!" cried Hank.

They gave chase through the chestnut trees, but the orphan boy was swift, up the hill, through the night streets of town, down past the rail yards, past the factories, to the midway of the deserted carnival. Hank and Peter were poor seconds, Peter weighted as he was with the heavy raincoat, and Hank frozen with cold. The thumping of Hank's bare feet sounded through the town.

"Hurry, Pete! We can't let him get to that Ferris wheel before we do, if he changes back into a man we'll never prove anything!"

"I'm hurrying!" But Pete was left behind as Hank thudded on alone in the clearing weather.

"Yah!" mocked the orphan boy, darting away, no more than a shadow ahead, now. Now vanishing into the carnival yard.

Hank stopped at the edge of the carnival lot. The Ferris wheel was going up and up into the sky, a big nebula of stars caught on the dark earth and turning forward and forward, instead of backward, and there sat Joseph Pikes in a black-painted bucket-seat, laughing up and around and down and up and around and down at little old Hank standing there, and the little blind hunchback had his hand on the roaring, oily black machine that made the Ferris wheel go ahead and ahead. The midway was deserted because of the rain. The merry-go-round was still, but its music played and crashed in the open spaces. And Joseph Pikes rode up into the cloudy sky and came down and each time he went around he was a year older, his laughing changed, grew deep, his face changed, the bones of it, the mean eyes of it, the wild hair of it, sitting there in the black bucket-seat whirling, whirling swiftly, laughing into the bleak heavens where now and again a last split of lightning showed itself.

Hank ran forward at the hunchback by the machine. On the way he picked up a tent spike. "Here now!" yelled the hunchback. The black Ferris wheel whirled around. "You!" stormed the hunchback, fumbling out. Hank hit him in the kneecap and danced away. "Ouch!" screamed the man, falling forward. He tried to reach the machine brake to stop the Ferris wheel. When he put his hand on the brake, Hank ran in and slammed the tent spike against the fingers, mashing them. He hit them twice. The man held his hand in his other hand, howling. He kicked at Hank. Hank grabbed the foot, pulled, the man slipped in the mud and fell. Hank hit him on the head, shouting.

The Ferris wheel went around and around and around.

"Stop, stop the wheel!" cried Joseph Pikes-Mr. Cooger, flung up in a stormy cold sky in the bubbled constellation of whirl and rush and wind.

"I can't move," groaned the hunchback. Hank jumped on his chest and they thrashed, biting, kicking.

"Stop, stop the wheel!" cried Mr. Cooger, a man, a different man and voice this time, coming around in panic, going up into the roaring hissing sky of the Ferris wheel. The wind blew through the high dark wheel spokes. "Stop, stop, oh, please stop the wheel!"

Hank leaped up from the sprawled hunchback. He started in on the brake mechanism, hitting it, jamming it, putting chunks of metal in it, tying it with rope, now and again hitting at the crawling weeping hunchback.

"Stop, stop, stop the wheel!" wailed a voice high in the night where the windy moon was coming out of the vaporous white clouds now. "Stop…" The voice faded.

Now the carnival was ablaze with sudden light. Men sprang out of tents, came running. Hank felt himself jerked into the air with oaths and beatings rained on him. From a distance there was a sound of Peter's voice and behind Peter, at full tilt, a police officer with pistol drawn.

"Stop, stop the wheel!" In the wind the voice sighed away.

The voice repeated and repeated.

The dark carnival men tried to apply the brake. Nothing happened. The machine hummed and turned the wheel around and around. The mechanism was jammed.

"Stop!" cried the voice one last time.

Silence.

WITHOUT A word the Ferris wheel flew in a circle, a high system of electric stars and metal and seats. There was no sound now but the sound of the motor which died and stopped. The Ferris wheel coasted for a minute, all the carnival people looking up at it, the policeman looking up at it, Hank and Peter looking up at it.

The Ferris wheel stopped. A crowd had gathered at the noise. A few fishermen from the wharfhouse, a few switchmen from the rail yards. The Ferris wheel stood whining and stretching in the wind.

"Look," everybody said.

The policeman turned and the carnival people turned and the fishermen turned and they all looked at the occupant in the black-painted seat at the bottom of the ride. The wind touched and moved the black wooden seat in a gentle rocking rhythm, crooning over the occupant in the dim carnival light.

A skeleton sat there, a paper bag of money in its hands, a brown derby hat on its head.

Intermission:

Poetry

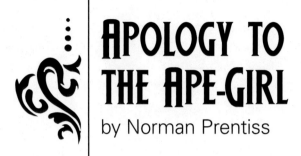

Apology to the Ape-Girl

by Norman Prentiss

Words on the painted banner
flapping above the tent
spoke to me in your voice,
more melodic than the gruff barker
distorted through tin loudspeakers
inviting me to

SEE an amazing transformation
SEE a beautiful native woman
change into a savage beast.

Those days, my friends and I watched movies
cringing at the bad effects. "How fake!" we'd say
to wires clearly visible above flying heroes, fuzzy blue
outlines around travelers flat as stamps
pasted into miniature jungles with rubber lizards.
When the troubled man reverted into
Hyde or a werewolf, we mocked the obvious
dissolves between changes to his makeup.

You promised more. An authentic
transformation, the real thing
that inspired movie scenes.

Inside that dark tent, I stand
behind a rail, facing iron bars.

I am the youngest in the crowd,
a boy among men who
stare at you in your leopard-skin
bikini, arms above your head,
chained to the wall. They want you
to struggle in your chains,
shake in your revealing costume.
The announcer sets the scene,
whispers about deeper mysteries,
then the lights snap out, and you scream.

I hear the faint sound of a sliding panel.
The lights return, reveal a man
in an ape suit, chained in your place
making angry monkey noises. It's fake,
the whole damn thing, and then a cheap scare
when the ape breaks free,
runs toward the bars protecting
the audience, pulls off the door to the cage.
A drawn curtain is enough to stop
the raging animal. The show's over.

Afterwards, I sought out books
explaining movie effects, worked my own
magic with a super-8 camera and clay figures,
experimented with masks and makeup.
I learned to decode even the best effects,
find the seam of joined images, notice
where the painting blurs into a real mountain,
where the human in the rear-projection
switches to an animated puppet.
I know, I know how it's all done.
The beauty of future cities
painted on glass, flying cars,
and a second moon in the evening sky.

The drab truths of the world covered over
with something fake.

Please understand,
it's not that you weren't beautiful.
For me, it wasn't about sex. I wanted you
to be a miracle.

I'm sorry it's not worth my time
to give you another chance,
to let my younger self
sneak back to the circus
after closing time, peer
between tent flaps, see
the head of an ape
atop a plastic chair,
and your cohort, a bald man
costumed and furry from the neck down,
a parody of evolution,
smoking a cigarette, and laughing.

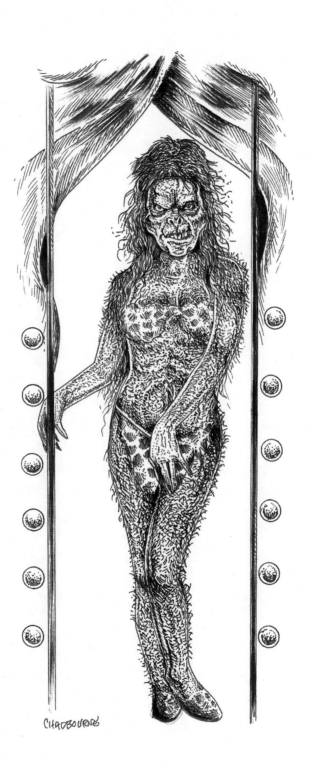

CHADBOURNE

HITCHHIKER

by G. O. Clark

A hitchhiking clown late for
his next appearance, balloon strings
clutched in his white gloved left hand,
thumb on right hand extended towards
the speeding traffic, beckoning to
the weekend travelers.

Your kids want you to stop
and pick him up, multi-colored
balloons reflected in their bright eyes.
Your wife wants you to pass him by,
already mad at you for not leaving
on time for the movie.

As for you? You're conflicted.

Ignore your wife, which will
have consequences later in bed; please
the kids, which will be construed as more
spoiling on your part; or heed the memory
of *Killer Klowns From Outer Space*
and Stephen King's *It*.
Erring on the side of caution,
you speed on by, the clown framed
in your rearview mirror lowering his

thumb and raising his middle finger,
sun glinting off the tip of a blood-
stained butcher knife poking out
of his baggy, red sleeve.

THE OLD CLOWN REFLECTS

by G. O. Clark

The old clown
rests between shows,
red nose on table, movie
contact lenses in box,
clown shoes kicked off
exposing his webbed toes,
a glass of bourbon in
his white-gloved hand.

He's tired of the
old routines; the pratfalls,
pie throws and seltzer bottle
water fights, the young clowns
in the troupe humiliating
him at every turn.

He still aches from
the last clown-car routine,
the other clowns' elbows and
knees bruising without mercy,
the audience's laughter still
ringing in his oversized ears.
The darkness in his
heart never goes away.
The insane voices in his head
urging him each show to wipe

the smiles off the innocent kids
in the front row, and replace
them with tortured ones
like his own.

Running away to join
the circus was his best option
as a teen. At least he didn't
end up in some freak show,
cast as The Amazing Lizard Boy.
His true nature is now hidden
by gaudy face paint and standard
baggy clown costume.

He reminds himself each day
that the show must go on,
another new town and audience,
another challenge to stay the
clown course and control
those sadistic urges that set him
on the road in the first place;
the road of nightmares past,
and terrors still to come.

CHADBOURNE

CARNIVAL OF GHOSTS

by Marge Simon

So there was an argument
about something, you forget what.
Wife took the car, fled to her mother,
or maybe you dropped her off,
you can't be sure, but never mind.

Now here you are, a free man
with nothing planned
on a warm summer night
pulsing with excitement,
a carnival down the street.

You enter the gate expecting
the rush of joy you knew as a boy,
but you're met instead with
a discordant roar in your ears.

Beneath the cacophony, there is
a sense of isolation stabbed by time,
defaming Bradbury's gestalt;
a magic dark and unsettling,
nostalgia by proxy.
A carousel of skeletal horses
revolves, strobe lights flicker
on the palsied faces of the riders,
pale hands clutching the poles,

bobbing up and down
in blissful madness.

You are captivated by
music from a glittering organ
charming the night, while
faceless vendors vie for attention;
a charade of tempting games—
hit the baby elephants and swans.

Around and around they parade
before the sights of your gun.
You think you hit them all
because the shill hands you
a blood-soaked Teddy Bear.

In the Tunnel of Love, your wife
is waiting for you in the little boat, but
something is wrong with her neck.
There is blood on her dress, in her hair.
She kisses your hand.

You stagger past the wreck of a car—
a very familiar car, crumpled outside
the entrance to The Hall of Mirrors where
you find reflections of yourself in multiples—
body under a sheet, toe tag with your name.
The raucous laughter isn't yours.

There is no exit,
this is your last stop,
you're just another prisoner
in the Carnival of Ghosts.

CHADBOURNE

THE DAILY FREAK SHOW

by Bruce Boston

When I was a lad
and little more
a circus came to town,
with lions and bears,
aerialists and clowns,
and a carnival besides,
where a clever barker
caught my ear with
his spiel of horrific
oddities guaranteed,
right before my eyes.

So I spent the money
I had saved and saw
the freaks upon display:
the dog-headed boy
who drank from a bowl,
a woman buried deep
in shelves of flesh,
a seal man sprouting
flippers for hands,
a two-headed lamb,
a dog with six legs,
and other monstrosities,
both foul and fearsome,
no sane god would design.

BRUCE BOSTON

And I dreamed them long,
nightmared them hard,
hard as their suffering lives.
They filled my thoughts
and weighed on my mind.

Now I am a man
and so much more,
I walk the city streets.
I see the passing crowds,
the carnival flowing by:
the beaten who shuffle
with heads turned down
and shoulders hunched,
the dreamers who wander
with thoughts in the sky,
visions of unreal times,
the arrogant, the meek,
the dazed, the drunkards,
the poseurs and the takers,
and the other lost souls
no kind god would consign.

And I dream them long,
nightmare them hard,
hard as forsaken lives.
They fill my thoughts
and weigh on my mind.

Normal is a word
and not much more,
a mean, an average,
a dot upon a graph,
a calculated ideal that
can rarely be applied.

CLOWNS

by Robert Payne Cabeen

I envy those who live a life
Where nothing strange takes place.
The lucky ones whose days and nights
Slip by without a trace.

At one time I was one of them.
I never really knew
That horror waits at every turn
And nightmares can come true.

By random chance or dark design,
My ordered life was thrown
Into a state of dread and fear
That I had never known.

It happened three short years ago,
October thirty-first.
Of all the nights that I've lived through,
That night alone was cursed.

I'd finished up a business trip,
And I was heading home.
I'd finalized a contract with
the Houston Astrodome.

My company makes souvenirs—
T-shirts, pins and hats.
The Astros bought our brand-new line—
Collector baseball bats.

I told my wife that I'd be home
In Denver late that night.
I sped across the Panhandle.
The autumn moon was bright.

The interstate was long and flat.
The night was warm and dry.
The restful rhythm of the road
Was like a lullaby.

I nodded off, then jerked awake.
I'd driven much too long.
So, I pulled off the interstate,
Where I did not belong.

I made a turn, then turned again
Down dusty, dark dirt roads—
Saw armadillos, bats and snakes,
Heard crickets, owls, and toads.

Beside the road, an old hotel,
Ten miles from any town,
Lay rotting in the grim landscape—
That's where I saw the clown.

I thought that I was seeing things.
He ran in front of me.

I swerved in time to miss the fool
And almost hit a tree.

My headlights stopped him in his tracks,
Just like a startled deer.
He stood there—big shoes, bald-cap wig,
And evil greasepaint sneer.

His eyes were round and red and wild.
He pointed to the sky.
The clown began to hop around—
Pretending he could fly.

He flapped his big arms up and down,
Then tapped my window hard.
He honked his red nose several times
And handed me his card.

His name was Bouncing Benny Brown
From Twin Falls, Idaho.
He pointed to the old hotel
And said, "Come on, let's go."

Reluctantly, I let him in
And drove across a field.
We neared the crumbling edifice—
He clapped and laughed and squealed.

We pulled up to the hotel door.
He thanked me for the ride,
Then handed me a bright green wig
And said, "Come on inside."

The reason why I followed him
Is still unclear to me.
I felt a strange euphoria—
A dark and haunting glee.

A clown on stilts stood by the door,
His face was broad and fat.
He greeted us, then waved us in
And tipped his doorman's hat.

My senses were assaulted by
A deafening, giddy din,
The sickening smell of pungent sweat,
And garish painted skin.

As I skulked across the lobby,
A skull-faced, little clown
Was leering at my normal clothes.
He looked me up and down.

I quickly put my green wig on
And fluffed the nylon hair.
I forced a phony, nervous smile
And wished I wasn't there.

The hotel had an atmosphere
Of danger, dread and doom;
And even though I needed rest,
I didn't want a room.

We pushed our way through crowds of clowns
Of every shape and size,

And though they all were quite unique,
They all had crazy eyes.

Above the yawning ballroom door
I saw a sign that read:
Psycho-Killer Cannibal Clowns
Convention Straight Ahead.

I laughed and turned to Benny Brown,
The sign seemed like a joke.
He looked confused and grinned at me,
Then licked his lips and spoke.

"Just think of us as hunters, friend,"
His voice gave me a chill.
"We never waste a single life.
We always eat our kill.

We stalk our prey at carnivals,
The circus and the fair.
At children's parties, look around,
You'll often find us there.

If they believe you're one of us,
You might leave here alive.
You'd better play along, my friend
Or you will not survive."

He dragged me to the ballroom floor,
Where psycho killer clowns
Assembled by the hundreds from
Their sleepy little towns.

They beamed with ghoulish greasepaint grins
As terror tales were told.
Their gory stories were insane,
Malicious, cruel, and cold.

A blue-haired, brutish, drunk buffoon
Was boasting to the crowd
That once he ate some high school kids.
The clowns all laughed out loud.

He passed around some Polaroids.
The prints were smeared with blood.
One half-devoured victim's corpse
Was face down in the mud.

I feigned that I was interested
As I thumbed through the stack
Of picture trophies showing him
Slash and stab and hack.

One grisly photo clearly showed
A young girl with a crown.
The pretty prom queen's severed head
Was chopped off by the clown.

Then Benny slapped him on the back
And gave a knowing nod.
He cleared his throat, and then he spoke.
His voice was low and odd,

"Dear clowns and colleagues, can I have
Your full attention, please?

These pictures are magnificent,
But take a look at these."

He winked and started taking off
His circus-colored vest,
Then opened up his baggy blouse,
And bared his hairy chest.

A strange thing hung around his neck.
It dangled in a loop.
The other clowns all oohed and aahed,
As Benny charmed the group.

A closer look at what he wore
Confirmed my deepest fears.
What looked like dried up apricots
Were really shriveled ears.

He'd made a necklace out of them
With bones and beads and teeth.
He twirled around so all could see
The decomposing wreath.

He bowed and fingered them with pride,
Then turned to me and said,
"I cut my victims' right ear off
Before I make them dead.

It comforts me to keep them close.
Each one's a patient friend.
I talk to them when I'm alone—
They listen without end."

ROBERT PAYNE CABEEN

The savage clowns were all impressed.
I thought that I might scream.
Their rowdy cheers and jealous sneers
Made Bouncing Benny beam.

A paunchy Punchinello yelled,
"Attention, one and all,
Our gourmet dinner's being served
Inside the banquet hall."

Then Bouncing Benny grabbed my arm
And pulled me off my feet,
"Come on get movin'," Benny said,
"I'm hungry—let's go eat!"

I'm sure the hall was elegant—
A century ago.
But now it reeked of foul debris
That rotted down below.

Their decorations were grotesque.
Intestines draped the hall.
A rude collage of body parts
Was hung on every wall.

A string of severed human hands
Swung from a chandelier.
They cast a ghastly shadow show
Of light and dark and fear.

The tablecloths were tattooed skin,
Arranged in odd designs.

The knives and forks were carved from bones.
The candlesticks were spines.

An army of tuxedoed clowns
Brought hors d'oeuvres on a tray.
The severed tongues in a blood clot sauce
Made quite a foul display.

A heavy hunchbacked harlequin,
With teeth filed razor sharp,
Played eerie dinner music on
A human rib cage harp.

The clowns were waiting in a line
For bloody smorgasbord.
They'd butchered up the hotel staff
To feed their hungry hoard.

The steaming bins of half-cooked meat
Were disappearing quick.
The way they gnawed the thick, red flesh
Was making me feel sick.

They gorged themselves and passed foul gas,
Spit gristle, bone, and hair.
They belched and drooled, then ate some more—
The gore was everywhere.

A bowl of steaming hearts arrived.
The ghastly clowns dug in.
But when they munched on baby toes
My head began to spin.

I fainted like a debutante
And slid down to the floor.
When I woke up, I looked around
And saw an open door.

I hid beneath the tabletop
While Bouncing Benny ate
And gossiped with his fiendish friends.
I knew I couldn't wait.

I inched toward the door outside
Through table-legs and feet.
They didn't see me slip away.
Their eyes were on their meat.

But as I crawled, I kicked a skull—
A candle burned inside.
The fire danced across the floor—
The planks were old and dried.

The fire crept up tablecloths
And leaped from chair to chair.
The bloated clowns burst into flames
And wailed in wild despair.

I bounded through the open door
As flames engulfed the hall.
The sizzling clowns were trapped inside.
The fire cooked them all.

I stumbled through the open field.
The hotel belched out smoke.

The stench from those cremated clowns
Caused me to gag and choke.

Some waddled from the old hotel,
Their costumes in a blaze.
They broiled and screamed out in the dark.
I stood there in a daze.

Then, from the fierce inferno ran
A clown consumed in flame.
He made his way to where I stood
And called me by my name.

He lunged at me as I backed up,
Then tumbled to the ground
And curled up in a smoking heap.
He shrieked and writhed around.

I knew that it was Benny Brown—
I can't imagine how.
There wasn't much of Benny left.
I still can see him now.

The fire seared and charred his flesh.
His burned and blackened bones
Protruded through his blistered meat.
His eyes were sightless stones.

With all the strength that he had left,
He raised a glowing hand.
He coughed, then he began to speak.
I tried to understand.

He sighed, "The hunger…" then he paused.
Black smoke was in his breath.
"The hunger made me do bad things."
The clown was close to death.

"Don't give in to the hunger, friend."
His lips cracked off like coal.
"The hunger gets inside of you,
And eats away your soul."

He said, "Thanks for the fire, friend,"
And simmered like a roast.
His embers swirled around my feet
As he gave up the ghost.

I waited there a long, long time,
Until the clowns were dead.
Each twisted brain lay smoldering
Inside a haunted head.

The darkness of the desert night
Snuffed out the dying flames.
The fire had destroyed the clowns
And only left their names:

Joe Jigs the Clown and Benny Brown
And Topsy from Saint Paul,
Rags Malone and Jolly Joan
Are all I can recall.

I made my way through smoking piles
Of soot and bones and shoes.

I couldn't help but think about
Those stories on the news.

The ones where people disappear
And never can be found.
How many were the victims of
Those ashes on the ground?

I suddenly felt numb and ill.
The air was dry and cold.
The morning sun lit up the sky
With blue and pink and gold.

My face and hands were covered with
A smoky, oily grime—
The evil, reeking residue
Of homicidal slime.

It soaked into my skin and bones
And everything between.
I knew that if I washed for days—
I never would get clean.

I found my car and drove away
But I was not secure.
I knew I'd left with memories
That I could not endure.

Since then, there hasn't been a day
I've felt completely right.
I always think about those clowns
And what I saw that night.

ROBERT PAYNE CABEEN

Sometimes I wake up in the night
From dreams about that place—
The barren Texas wasteland
And Benny's burning face.

His charred lips whisper obscene things
That make me feel afraid.
And, even after I wake up
My fears refuse to fade.

At sundown every Halloween,
The moon is low and big,
I go down to the basement and
Put on my bright green wig.

I nail the doors and windows shut
While trick-or-treaters play—
And crouch behind the furnace till
The hunger goes away.

THE MURDER OF GREAT PIETER

by David E. Cowen

Jo Jo stroked his beard and hairy ears
smiled at the little man
in the napoleon suit
Isabel
long whiskers down to her chest
nodded her complicity

Pieter's muscles rippled
as he set his body for his leap
noose tight on his neck
the crowd knew what he would do
75 feet he would fall
whip the elastic rope elliptical
to release the pressure off his throat
land breathing and smiling
the throngs would cheer the man
with the strongest neck in the world

always as he exited triumphant
he would sneer at the sideshow freaks
pulling Jo Jo's dog-faced hair
dragging bearded Isabel to a dark corner
to release the tension in his taut frame
then kicking Tom Thumb
as he sat waiting for his turn in the ring

DAVID E. COWEN

The Great Pieter
the brute who did not read
but knew the mathematics of ropes
the sine curve of avoiding death

even a freak can study ropes
to know just where
to stretch them beyond bending
so the curve of survival
becomes a discordant snap

the crowd stared in silence
at the dangling carcass
wondering
if they should demand refunds
as clowns tried to ascend
on bending ladders
to cut him down

Jo Jo raised a flask
of cheap whiskey
passed it round
to the newly promoted
center ring attractions

THE CAGE

by Alessandro Manzetti

When the show begins
a man is locked in a cage
next to the red-and-white striped skirt
of a suburban stinky circus,
one of those where hungry dogs
can't stop barking.

The knife-thrower is doing his job
with eyes shut, in a top hat painted with blood,
while the wooden wheel is turning
together with its beautiful fleshed skeleton:
a naked woman tied with ropes
—Dorina, the wife of the King of Knives—
with her breasts filled with poisoned milk.

She must be punished for her sins,
She's hatching a monster!
the knife-thrower thinks, humming a song
—I See a Darkness—
like a drunk ghost of Johnny Cash.
What people are seeing, sprayed on Dorina's skin
is not tomato, or paint; no tricks this time.
No encore.
The man in the cage,
the nameless King of the Crazy

with his baggy pants
and the old Charlie Chaplin's shoes
hears the cries of the woman,
while the audience yells "Go for her throat!"
He knows that the motherfucker, after the show,
will cut her belly open to pull out the monster,
fishing in Dorina's paradise.
—A monster with his same funny red nose—

A little girl with a lollipop clutched in one hand
is approaching the cage
and the huddled shadow of the man.
She likes clowns, and the blue-eyed tigers
like the one, inside there
which is awakening, powering up
its predator engine.
Today it must be its birthday:
the dinner walks on two legs, wow,
and smells good, like freedom
like some orange mirage of India.

When the tiger snaps forward,
pouncing on the King of Crazy,
the little girl drops her lollipop
jumping back like a doll, a puppet
when the master, back there
the King of Dead, masquerading as a butcher,
pulls her thin strings.

She was never born, actually
so she disappears from the scene
flying away like a fake angel.
Dorina, her only warm house
was buried beneath a new shopping mall
with a soft human meatballs rosary

around her so white fingers.
—what's left of the King of Crazy—
The knife-thrower, with his handlebar moustache,
is chased by the barking dogs
and by the ghost of Johnny Cash dressed in black;
he runs around the imaginary tent
—a giant wheel which never stops turning—
of the Circus of the Dead,
over there…you can see it
if you get out of your colorful cage.

THE CARNIE'S CONFESSION

by Terri Adamczyk

Perhaps it's their arms, their pinwheel
through the midway that prickles
the crib of my mind. I suspect
it despises itself, or the light,
or these tiny palms everywhere, stinging
my eyes. Perhaps I have marbles
for eyes, but they ache
in their furious sockets. They follow
each child seen tugging the larval
cyst of a sister confined
to a stroller. There can be mouths
drowned in the clatter, crowing
"Look, look, look,"
but what do they know?
These are dwarves
no one stole and the changeling
brought up on the fairground's
equation can't bear
the weight of their small smiles
pressed against glass. I was raised
with the decimal of faces
repeating the tune of the peddler's spiel
coaxing kaleidoscope faces to answer
again, "How much?" But I always awake

TERRI ADAMCZYK

to the sideshow where children are
everywhere. Waving their arms
in my eyes as they enter
the merry-go-round corral and their horses
proceed, these unborrowed children
won't tell where they've hidden
my room. I remember
a room where night light hushes
the dark, and some sister cradled
against me stirs. Now

there are too many lights
on the midway. The night disappears
and I envy the curled hand
led home to be tucked
under bed quilts too clean to be won
for a quarter at Spin the Wheel. Listen,
if I could return,
plucking the crumbs you have left
to your slow baking July of lost
kickballs and splayed hands,
the merry-go-round would be yours,
and the changeling
would visit for keeps.

CHADBOURNE

MAGIC SHOW

by Christina Sng

They cut that poor woman in half
Yet she is still smiling.
What else can I conclude but that
Humans enjoy being dismembered?

Yet the crowd screams in terror
When I cut up members of their own.
Their innards hold no clues
To this strange contradiction.

I search from body to body
Hoping to find out the reason.
One will eventually reveal it
As other species have proved.

THE CLOWN

by Christina Sng

When the clown
Started following me,
I feared the worst

For what else
Does one associate clowns with
But terror and horror and death?

So I sped into
The haunted house
Where I was mauled and robbed

Then into
The mirror maze
Where I was lost for hours,

Till he found me there,
Ushering me out
Despite my screams,

Where a crowd
Gathered about,
And he said, "It's alright…"
"It's me, your ex
In his weekend job,
Did you forget?"

I stared at him.
"No, you're not.
He died here last spring.

"Here, at the circus,
So frightened that
His heart just stopped."

The clown smiled.
A knowing grin.
"Yes, indeed he did."

He waved his hand.
The crowd vanished. I ran.
And he began

To chase me again.

LUCIFER AT THE CARNIVAL

by Christina Sng

snake man
hello
my old friend

contortionist
I've broken bones
trying this

fortune teller
I read hers
instead

so many screaming
seeing my handsome face
in the mirror maze

haunted house
I've already seen
everything

tunnel of love
they messed my hair
so no love there

rollercoaster
finally something
screamworthy

fairy floss
first sticking to my chin
then my horns

corn dogs
why's there no corn
and no dogs

no kid
I'm not wearing
a mask

perfect aim
in the carnival games
carrying all my stuffed toys home

CAGES

by Christina Sng

The old circus bear
Stared at me through its cage,
Its eyes luminous and wide

For it recognized
A kinship between us,
Only it and I would know.

An arm grabbed me
And a voice bellowed,
"Where've you been all day?"

I bowed my head
And released the bolt,
Freeing one of us from our cage.

The bear charged out
And tore him to shreds.
I helped with a nearby rake.

When it had eaten its fill,
We left the circus and town
And into the forest we went.

CHRISTINA SNG

There we vanished
Into the embrace of the trees,
The only place we'd be safe.

Never again
To be chained and whipped
Or locked in a cage again.

CHADBOURNE

THE ADMISSION PRICE TO CARNEVIL

by Stephanie M. Wytovich

The aftershock of blood balloons spattered
on funhouse mirrors shook the peppermint swirl
of draped fabric, the tent like a straitjacket,
each crease a woven scream, the kiss of a whip
against an elephant's bare back.

There, on your neck. Can you feel the breath
of The Wolf Boy? He growls in the corner,
his silver-bullet cage a glowing marvel
against the moon, his teeth as sharp
as the fish hooks stolen from The Human
Mermaid's tank, her siren call still singing,
the crunch of bone meal riding in the waves.

Listen now to the accordion player's machine:
watch how the burn of freshly swallowed flames
eats the lice off The Bearded Lady's face,
the laughter of children ringing like serrated knives,
each plunged into the skin of ladies trapped in boxes,
their lower halves running like mannequins
under twinkling lights, their escape
a private ventriloquist act.
I wonder, have The Twins found you yet?
They watch with two sets of eyes,
their shared heart beating, their cheeks
a deeper shade of rouge, this the longing

of monstrosity, each a peeping tom
when the other starts to pant, licks shaved ice
off The Living Torso's chest.

Yes, it hurts to walk on these fields made of glass,
but the trapeze artists hang like stars,
their bodies covered in sequins and silk nooses,
the ringmaster cheering, the clowns smiling,
their faces the stitched-on mouths of last
season's guests.

Tell me, do you find yourself bleeding? Your insides
turning to insulation, a cotton-candy parade
where each ticket is a poison apple, every trick
its own sawed-off limb? By the time you realize
the crunched glass in your tongue, we'll be feasting
on your flesh, your body forever in the circus,
this the admission price to see the freaks of CarnEvil.

TICKETS, GAMES, FREAKS

by Stephanie M. Wytovich

The sound of knives cutting through air,
the Wheel of Death spinning, bodies like
stigmata hanging in technicolor, their blood
blossoming like fresh roses handed out
to ladies after the act.

It's a song box of magic tricks, this the
yellow brick road to the Devil's mouth,
the water rising, the popcorn popping;
yet there's a quiet hush through the audience,
each lung crying as it holds its breath, watches
The Pinheads laughing, The Snake Woman writhing,
the uncanny stares of caged freaks swinging
above screams, their wails like slaughterhouse victims
chopped and ground to feed monsters and Fat Ladies,
each corpse a kissing booth, a lick of cherry ice.

Now taste the perfume in the air, the bells ringing,
the feathers falling, we're this season's biggest
show, each night a howl, a gasp, a different sword
to swallow, and like contortionists we twist and turn,
we fold to you, our meat-sack saviors, who buy tickets
to behold wonders and are instead sold their own deaths.

What Is a Body?
by Stephanie M. Wytovich

The ingrown hairs of ladies with teeth
grow next to tattooed pictures of two-headed
men draped in velvet with the promise of
orgy on their lips.

There's a flat-bellied woman hiding in the crease
of a hedonist's thighs, her gluttony the rival
to feathered flesh that begs to be tarred, the giggle
of armless women hanging like smoke under
a strong woman's jaw.

If you push one of three legs aside, you will see
the blood from the pin-cushioned face of
a man with tired eyes, the Siamese wonders
trapped in bodies shaped like hoops, spinning,
twirling, the glare of two reflections trapped
in mirrors made for one.

Yet with bat wings and forked tongues, the man
with three eyes holds claws with a lobster,
his flesh pincers no matter to invincible skin
painted with bullet holes and wounds, each chest
a caravan of possibilities, this gene pool of mutation,
every body a miracle, a madness, a true test of who,
or what, lies down with God in the dark.

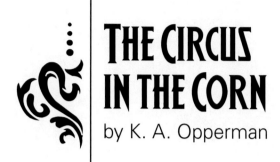

THE CIRCUS IN THE CORN

by K. A. Opperman

Amid the corn-maze lies a secret circus,
A scarlet tent where cryptic games are played.
The spectral clowns in ruff and dunce-cap shirk us—
This desolation is a strange charade.

The harlequins at night appear and caper,
Tumbling amid the hay-bales, watched by toads;
Beyond the glow of bamboo witch's taper,
A great gray owl will sing nocturnal odes.

Beneath the harvest moon, so near the Veil,
When twilight falls, the ghost-white clowns await;
Beneath the Big-Top, past the haunted trail,
A pretty seeress reads the cards of fate….

But now my fancies fade—the sun is setting.
A faint calliope begins to play.
And so we hasten on our way, forgetting
The grinning Fool card found amid the hay.

THE CLOWN WITCH

by K. A. Opperman

With pointed cap of patterned crepe,
And ruffled collar round her neck,
She twirls her skirts where pumpkins gape,
Through rooms that bats and goblins deck.

I follow her throughout the rooms,
Through smoke and weirdly mirrored halls,
Befuddled by the incense fumes,
And watched by blank white stares of dolls.

I pass through black and orange beads,
And find myself in open space;
A path of lamps and lollies leads
Through autumn woods with winding grace.

A horse from some lost carousel
Regards me with a tarnished gleam;
Just where I wander, who can tell—
Some haunted carnival of dream.

A music box, half buried, plays
Its melancholy melody;
I meet the tiny dancer's gaze—
But hurry past her desperate plea.

At last I find a circus tent,
And through the flaps, I step inside—
And there, above her crystal bent,
The clown witch winks, with grin so wide.

She bids me gaze into the glass,
And with my image I am faced—
But from the crystal's dim morass,
In fragile china fast encased,

There stares a clown of porcelain,
A pierrot with small cap complete—
I am become a manikin,
And 'mid the dolls I take my seat.

BENEATH THE FULLEST MOON

by Ashley Dioses

Amid the star-filled moonlit night,
A carnival stands near,
With contortionists in firelight,
And dancing clowns who sneer.

The lioness, with agile bounds,
Leaps through the hoops with care;
While fire-eaters make their rounds
Throughout the aisles for flair.

The mimes portray such dreadful acts
To harlequins who swoon
Beneath the reddest candle wax,
Beneath the fullest moon.

The howls from fields of corn nearby
Are masked by all the sounds
Of music, laughter, and the cries
Of guests upon the grounds.

The fortune tellers hide their smirks
As they foresee what comes.
Incense and smoke all mask what lurks
In fields till prey succumbs.

ASHLEY DIOSES

The Moon is picked from out the deck
Of Tarot cards face down;
Then Death is pulled for just one peck,
One kiss for all the town.

The werewolves come, a fearsome pack,
And feast on all the guests,
Till blood rains down on every back,
And hearts lie still 'neath breasts.

The carnival then takes it down,
The tent and all, till noon.
They will arrive at a new town,
Beneath the fullest moon.

ACTTwo

THE GREAT WHITE WAY

by Robert McCammon

They travel by night.

Along the roads that cut through massive fields of wheat and sunflowers as high as a man's head, beneath the silent stars and the watchful moon, the caravan of horse-drawn wagons and gypsy trailers creak and groan on their way from here to there. They pass through towns, villages and even-smaller hamlets that have been asleep since sundown, and the dust they raise glitters in the moonlight like diamonds before it returns to the Russian earth. They go on until the circus master, the white-bearded Gromelko, decides to pull his leading wagon to a halt at the centerpoint of two or more rustic towns that have likely never seen a circus since a Cossack first sharpened his saber on a blood-red stone, and there Gromelko uses his hooked nose to smell the summer wind. Then, if the wind is right, he says with satisfaction to his long-suffering wife, *This is our home for tonight.*

The wagons and the trailers form a small village of their own. Torches are lighted and placed on poles. The main tent goes up first. Then the smaller tents, and the canvas signs announcing the attractions. One of the signs says how many coins are needed for entry, or how many chickens. The work animals are kept in a corral. The show animals—one young mule that can count up to twenty, two aged snow-white horses and a bandy-legged zebra all sleepy and dusty from their trip—are herded into a green tent to eat their hay and await their moments. The black leopard with one eye is kept in its own cage, because it has been known to bite the hand that feeds it. The wolf, too, is kept caged apart, because the wildness can't be whipped out of it. The ancient toothless bear lumbers around freely until it wants to return to its cage as protection from the leopard, the wolf and mean little children who taunt it.

Then there comes the birth of the Great White Way.

This is Gromelko's huge pleasure in life, now that he's nearly seventy-five years old and he can neither drink, smoke, nor screw. He stands watchful as ever, expectant of miracles, and it *is* somewhat miraculous that from the dirt and the sawdust rises within hours the village of the travelling circus, and then—miracle of miracles—that the Great White Way blinks several times like an old man waking up from a solemn snooze, and suddenly there is an electric odor like a passing thunderstorm and all the dozens of bulbs light up in simultaneous splendor along the midway's length. As long as someone pedals the stationary bicycle that powers the generator, the bulbs will glow. The bulbs not very bright nor the midway very long, but as the saying goes: A sparrow in the hand is better than a cock on the roof.

In the morning, the towns awaken and the farmwork begins with its routine and drudgery, and then someone in the fields sees the tents. Not long after that, the wagons come through with the circus banners rippling on their sides, and in the backs of the wagons stand—or wobble, if they've been early with their vodka—some of the star attractions. There are the catlike Boldachenko sisters, Vana and Velika, who perform jaw-dropping feats of acrobatics and contortions atop a forty-foot pole; the Lady Tatiana, who with her daughter Zolli gallop the horses and the zebra at full speed around and around a terribly small bigtop; Yuri the clown and his miniature clown-doll Luka, who always seems to get the better of his befuddled master; Arman the handsome, who walks a wire in his black tuxedo and throws a paper rose to a lucky farmer's wife at every show; and Gavrel the fire-eater from whose mouth flares ropes of flame and showers of sparks that whirl around the tent like the eyes of demons in the dark.

And also to mention the stars of the midway! For after the big show has ended, the audience is encouraged to walk in the glow along the Great White Way, to spend more coins or trade more chickens to visit Eva the bearded lady, Motka the man with skin so hard a hammer bends a nail upon his breastbone, Irisa the wrinkled dwarf who also plays superb classical Tchaikovsky on her pink toy piano, Natalia the emaciated spider woman, and last but not least the massive wrestler Octavius Zloy, who wears a purple cloak and a Roman helmet and stands with treetrunk arms crossed over his traincar chest and, his slab of a chin upraised and his small eyes narrowed, dares any son of Russia to pin his shoulders for the count of three.

Though many have tried, no one ever has. And Octavius Zloy has no mercy for any son of Russia who climbs into the ring. Many have been removed, senseless and bloody, while his young and beautiful wife Devora raises his sweat-streaked arm and accompanies him as he parades back and forth like the superhuman species he believes himself to be.

The sons of Russia do not know that Devora, for all of her dark gypsy beauty and nineteen supple years, is missing several teeth and used to have a straighter nose. They don't know about the broken arm of last summer, and the black bruise across her lower back that caused her to hobble like an old woman through the month of June. But it is late August now, in this year of 1927, and as the saying goes: When Anger and Revenge are married, their daughter is called Cruelty.

It is the vodka, Devora thinks. Always the vodka. He lets it own him. And then when he has had more than enough to blaze his bonfire and not yet quite enough to topple him into sleep, Octavius Zloy rises up ragged and enraged within his own skin and he will not rest until someone has been hurt.

That someone being herself.

Oh, how he can use his hands. His hands were made for the punishment of other people. They are as strong as shovels, as brutal as bricks. They suit his soul.

So on a night like this one, after the big show is over and all the people have gone, after the coins and chickens have been put away, after the midway has closed down and everyone departed to their little wooden trailers and bolted their shutters and the Great White Way has faded to dark, Devora wipes the blood from her nostrils with a cloth and walks past the drunken bulk of Octavius Zloy snoring on the bed. She checks her face in the oval mirror behind the door. Her ebony eyes are puffy from tears and pain. Her nose is swollen. Her lips look crushed. Her thick black hair is streaked with henna, because he likes the appearance of fire in his fists when he grips her head. She realizes she looks like a slim hard girl who has come many miles from where she began, yet she is still so far from anything.

It is time to go, if she is going tonight.

She has slipped into a patched gray dress, like the other few she owns. Octavius Zloy says he prefers her naked, anyway, and spread out upon the bed beneath him in helpless abandon. She puts upon her bruised lips a fingertip's worth of color, a deep red. Octavius Zloy would not like this, if he were to see. But soon it will be worn off. When she leaves the trailer she has a key with her, but she does not lock the door.

It is silent in the village of the circus.

Well, not quite silent…for as Devora walks her path she hears the distant note of someone's fiddle, a soft sad playing, and then the plinking of a toy piano. She can't understand the kind of music that Irisa plays, it's too far over the head of a country girl, but she appreciates how swift and sure the small hands are.

She goes along the darkened Great White Way. The night's breeze stirs tent folds. Moonshadows lie at her feet. Her heart is beginning to beat harder, it seems, with each step. She is going to see the boy who takes care of the animals. Her lover. Her desire and her freedom, if just for a little while.

As the saying goes: There is no winter in the land of hope.

He is waiting for her, as always, in the green tent.

He is a strange boy. He stays by himself most of the time. He seems to prefer his own company and the company of animals. Seventeen years old, he's told her. His first name Mikhail. He hasn't offered his family name, nor does she ask. He arrived at the circus little more than a month ago, with no belongings, wearing baggy clothes that might have been stolen from a fence where they were drying in the sun. Had he ever owned shoes? He never wears any. He is lean and sun-browned, and she can count his ribs. He has an untidy mop of shaggy black hair that always seems to have straw in it, and when he stares at her calmly and fixedly as he does with his luminous green eyes something in her soul thaws and warms and melts. At the same time, something lower than her soul moistens and tightens and readies itself like a creature over which she has no control. It was such the first time she saw him, and has been every time, and is now.

He has lighted a few candles for them, in his private space of hay where he sleeps. He has put down a wheat-colored blanket and smoothed a place for her. But first, before she can enter his domain, he turns and picks up something folded upon a piece of clean canvas, and turning toward her again he smiles and lets unfold the beautiful dark blue dress he has brought for her, and Devora catches her breath because no one has offered her such a gift for a very long time. Of course there were the wildflowers he had for her last week…but *this*…

He tells her to try it on, so that he can take it off.

Over from the far side of the tent, Devora hears the wolf pacing in its cage.

She does what he asks, with great happiness. The dress makes her feel sleek. It makes her feel...what is the word, when one feels uncommon? Well...*uncommon*. She won't ask where Mikhail stole it from, because now it belongs to her. She owns so few pretty things. She tells him she loves it. Loves, loves, loves it. The woman who gave her birth told her to say *loves* a lot to a certain kind of man, because they liked to hear it. Devora is very sure Mikhail is that kind of man. Boy. Whatever he is.

But she knows she must have him, for the need for him is rising in her and as he advances and begins to slowly and gently remove her new dress she puts her arms around his neck and he kisses her mouth so softly it is like a feather tracing the outline of her crushed red lips. An angel's feather, Devora thinks. For truly this boy has come to her from Heaven.

He blows out every candle but one.

The wolf paces faster, back and forth. The leopard sits watching, its single eye catching a glint of light. The bear sleeps, and shivers a little in some dream of honey. Apart from the caged animals, the horses and the zebra doze but the ears of the intelligent mule twitch to catch the sounds of human passion.

Devora interrupts their deep kisses to remove her lover's clothes. Then they sink down together upon the blanket in the hay, and she puts a hand in his thick hair and guides his head between her thighs because this is what she craves most tonight, and he is so good at it, he is so wonderful at this, and so she moves against his tongue faster and harder and he is patient and content to give her everything she needs.

She will not ask who his teachers were. She will not ask who else he has loved in this way. But she loves, loves, loves this, and it is a sensation the selfish Octavius Zloy has never given her.

When she is wrung out and trembling and the sweat of heat and exertion glistens on her body, she tells Mikhail what she needs now to do for him, and he turns over and says he is all hers, which sounds to her ears even better than music.

She has a little trouble with this, though, and he understands why because she's told him about the force of Octavius Zloy's thrusts into her mouth, and how he seemed to want to choke her and though Octavius Zloy is not very large he uses himself like a battering-ram in her throat. So Mikhail quietly says, as he always does, that all else of life might be pain but love should be pleasure, and so he moves her back upon the blanket and lets her wait for a moment as his tongue plays with her navel and downward. Then he slowly presses into her, and they are one.

As the boy moves within her, Devora looks up into his handsome face and green eyes. A light sheen of sweat glows on his cheeks and forehead. She thinks she could live with him forever. She thinks she could follow him wherever he went. But, alas, he has no money. He is a pauper, whereas Octavius Zloy has a boxful of money hidden somewhere in the trailer. She dares not search for it, but she believes it's there because her husband has never lost a bout and so never had to return any coins.

Mikhail's rhythm is stronger. He is ardent and powerful and somehow older than he seems.

She has told him, over the many nights, how her husband has beaten her. And he has seen the marks, too. She has told Mikhail how the brutish wrestler took her from her home when she was sixteen because she was the prettiest girl in the village, and he was a bully passing through and no one could stand up to him. So the thirty-year-old Octavius Zloy, which was not his real name but suited him as much as his hurtful hands suited his selfish soul, threw her into the back of a wagon and told her she belonged to him. He was so huge and so terrible, she had told Mikhail, that fighting him was like trying to fight a whirlwind. So she had simply waited for her moment to escape, and yet…the moment never seemed to come. Where would she go if she tried to run away? Who would help her? And if he caught her—*when* he caught her—it would be more blood on her face and on his fist. It was as if, she'd said, he was trying to make her look as ugly as he was inside.

Mikhail and Devora kiss and bite and cling to each other as they thrust together, and the wolf and leopard are both very interested in this performance.

At last, when the spasms have shaken both of them and Devora has squeezed her eyes shut and cried out and Mikhail has pulled out of her and left his white signature upon the damp hair between her thighs, she rests her head against his shoulder and in the golden light he listens to her speak.

She tells him that Octavius Zloy has vowed he is going to kill her when he awakens. She tells him that her husband may be insane, and that he cannot be stopped.

Mikhail listens. The wolf is pacing again.

She tells him that if she were free from Octavius Zloy she would find a way back to her village. But how to be free from him? How to be free from such a mad whirlwind as that?

Mikhail is silent for awhile. Then he says he will go to the trailer and talk to Octavius Zloy.

Devora shakes her head and tells him that talking will not do. She tells him that Octavius Zloy only understands violence, and so if Mikhail wants to help her he must go into that trailer where the bad man is sleeping and knock his brains out with whatever is at hand.

Then, she says, she can be rid of him. The *world* can be rid of him. And she will be free. But, she says, he has vowed to kill her when he wakes up… so what shall happen next?

And she presses her head against Mikhail's shoulder and cries a little bit, until Mikhail stands up, his face grim and his lips tight. He puts on his clothes and says he will go and talk to Octavius Zloy.

This time, Devora does not speak.

Mikhail says he will return and, without a weapon but his own slim frame and fists, he strides out of the tent on his urgent mission.

Devora waits for a while.

Then she puts on her drab gray dress, made ugly with the patches that hold it together, and she looks with contempt at the blue dress the traitor has brought her.

He will learn a lesson tonight, she thinks. The lesson will be: do not stand and let Zolli take your hand, when you belong to me. Do not smile and laugh and talk with Zolli, the little bitch, and think that I don't see what you're doing. I could put a knife into Zolli's heart and twist it a hundred times, but instead I will stab you in the heart with a blade called Octavius Zloy.

Yes, she thinks. Her eyes are slitted, her face crimped with ugly rage because her jealousy is and always has been a crippling disease. Go talk to him. He will be awake by now. Go talk to his fists, because I have told him you steal things and beware that you come to steal the moneybox in the dark of night.

I will survive as I always have, she thinks. I will take my blows from him, because I know that when he beats me it is out of the purest love and sweetest possession.

She knows that the boy and Zolli have been here, right here, in this same place. She knows that they must have laughed at her stupidity, for letting herself believe that the boy cared only for her.

No one cares for her but Octavius Zloy.

He has told her so himself.

Devora stands up and leaves the tent, and she walks slowly and gracefully, as if in a dream, back the way she has come, back along the dark and moonshadowed Great White Way, back to the gypsy trailer where by now her husband has delivered justice to a very evil boy.

As the saying goes: A stranger's soul is like a dark forest.

And Devora is very certain the strange boy carries within him an unknown wilderness. But it is not one that any other woman in this circus will share, and for sure it will not be the simpering and smiling and oh-so-pretty Zolli.

The trailer's door is open. Wide open. There is only blackness within.

Devora goes up the steps and then inside. She speaks softly, calling for her husband. She hears breathing in the dark. It is a harsh rushing of breath. She smells the caged wolf on her skin. She spends a few seconds fumbling for matches and the candle on the table near the door, as she continues to call for her husband. He should be right there, the bed is right in front of her. The match flares and the candle's wick is lighted and she holds the flame out and then she sees the blood.

Well, she thinks, justice has been delivered. Perhaps *too* harshly, but still…

And she smiles a little, not thinking yet of what she's going to say to her husband to explain where she's been, except out walking in the moonlight as she sometimes tells him when he is contrite and weeps like a little child after he awakens.

Then by the candlelight she sees the red mass on the floor at her feet and in it is something that might be a beefy arm torn from its socket, and there a leg with a massive thigh clawed to the crimson muscle and white bone.

On the floor are blood-spattered clothes. She has seen those clothes tonight. She has removed those clothes tonight.

She calls in a weak and trembling whisper for Octavius Zloy, her husband and her protector, the tyrant of her heart.

The candlelight finds a head upon the bloody planks. It has a slab of a chin and small eyes and bears an expression of open-mouthed wonder and horror. On the end of an arm that has an elbow but no shoulder is a clenched fist, the scarred knuckles already turning blue.

Devora is about to scream when something shifts just beyond the range of the light.

He speaks from the dark. What he says she can't understand, because it sounds like a growl. It sounds like an animal's rage put to nearly-human voice. Then he speaks again and this time his voice is almost his own.

"You're free," he says.

And he repeats it: "You're free."

Devora shakes her head and spittle drools from her mouth. Because she doesn't want to be free. She doesn't know how to be free. She knows only that he beats her because he loves loves loves her so very much. He wants her to be the perfect wife for a great man like himself. And the film that is to be based on his life...she was to star in it also, and they would be stars together on the cinema screen, and both of them so uncommon the dolts and whores in her village couldn't stand to look upon the savage sun of their faces. He had promised about the film. Just as soon as he raised enough money. Then all life would be pleasure, and so many people would be jealous. But now...*now*...

A hand moves into the light, reaching for her. It is not quite human, and seems alive with moving, shifting bands of hair.

"I love you," the boy whispers.

A word comes from Devora's bruised lips.

That word is *Murder*.

She speaks it again, louder: *Murder*.

And now her eyes widen into terrified circles and she lets the scream go that will awaken the entire village of the circus and have the first of them here within seconds: *Murder*.

A figure leaps from the darkness. It is strangely shaped, glimpsed from a nightmare. As Devora staggers backward, the figure throws itself into the bolted window shutter and crashes through. Devora screams *Murder* again but now she is alone in the trailer with the torn meat, broken bones and smeared guts of a wrestler.

They take her away to a place to sleep, but she cannot sleep and they cannot get the extinguished candle out of her hand. She lies in the bed with her eyes open and stares at the ceiling, and she doesn't respond when Lady Tatiana and her daughter Zolli, both of them so kind to everyone, come to sit at her bedside. It is soon clear to all that Devora has embarked on a journey that has no destination.

The hunt for a murderer goes out across the countryside, but the boy has vanished. How the boy did what he did, to a formidable man like Octavius Zloy, is a mystery with no solution. Why did the boy take off his clothes? And another very odd thing: why did the boy leave a puddle of piss on the trailer's floor? It would be talked about in the village of the circus, and under the glowing bulbs of the Great White Way, for the rest of this dwindling season and surely into the next, as well.

But, as with everything, life—and the show—must go on.

Over several bottles of vodka and with men sitting around a table in the last twilight of August, old white-bearded Gromelko sums it up best.

Beware the quiet ones, he says. Beware the ones who would rather live with animals than in the company of humans.

For as the saying goes: Make a friend of the wolf, but better keep your axe ready.

BURIED TALENTS

by Richard Matheson

A man in a wrinkled, black suit entered the fairgrounds. He was tall and lean, his skin the color of drying leather. He wore a faded sport shirt underneath his suit coat, white with yellow stripes. His hair was black and greasy, parted in the middle and brushed back flat on each side. His eyes were pale blue. There was no expression on his face. It was a hundred and two degrees in the sun but he was not perspiring.

He walked to one of the booths and stood there watching people try to toss ping-pong balls into dozens of little fish bowls on a table. A fat man wearing a straw hat and waving a bamboo cane in his right hand kept telling everyone how easy it was. "Try your luck!" he told them. "Win a prize! There's nothing to it!" He had an unlit, half-smoked cigar between his lips which he shifted from side to side as he spoke.

For a while, the tall man in the wrinkled, black suit stood watching. Not one person managed a ping-pong ball into a fish bowl. Some of them tried to throw the balls in. Others tried to bounce them off the table. None of them had any luck.

At the end of seven minutes, the man in the black suit pushed between the people until he was standing by the booth. He took a quarter from his right-hand trouser pocket and laid it on the counter. "Yes, sir!" said the fat man. "Try your luck!" He tossed the quarter into a metal box beneath the counter. Reaching down, he picked three grimy ping-pong balls from a basket. He clapped them on the counter and the tall man picked them up.

"Toss a ball in the fish bowl!" said the fat man. "Win a prize! There's nothing to it!" Sweat was trickling down his florid face. He took a quarter from a teenage boy and set three ping-pong balls in front of him.

The man in the black suit looked at the three ping-pong balls on his left palm. He hefted them, his face immobile. The man in the straw hat turned away. He tapped at the fish bowls with his cane. He shifted the stump of cigar in his mouth. "Toss a ball in the fish bowl!" he said. "A prize for everybody! Nothing to it!"

Behind him, a ping-pong ball clinked into one of the bowls. He turned and looked at the bowl. He looked at the man in the black suit. "There you are!" he said. "See that? Nothing to it! Easiest game on the fairgrounds!"

The tall man threw another ping-pong ball. It arced across the booth and landed in the same bowl. All the other people trying missed.

"Yes, sir!" the fat man said. "A prize for everybody! Nothing to it!" He picked up two quarters and set six ping-pong balls before a man and wife.

He turned and saw the third ping-pong ball dropping into the fish bowl. It didn't touch the neck of the bowl. It didn't bounce. It landed on the other two balls and lay there.

"See?" the man in the straw hat said. "A prize on his very first turn! Easiest game on the fairgrounds!" Reaching over to a set of wooden shelves, he picked up an ashtray and set it on the counter. "Yes, sir! Nothing to it!" he said. He took a quarter from a man in overalls and set three ping-pong balls in front of him.

The man in the black suit pushed away the ashtray. He laid another quarter on the counter. "Three more ping-pong balls," he said.

The fat man grinned. "Three more ping-pong balls it is!" he said. He reached below the counter, picked up three more balls and set them on the counter in front of the man. "Step right up!" he said. He caught a ping-pong ball which someone had bounced off the table. He kept an eye on the tall man while he stooped to retrieve some ping-pong balls on the ground.

The man in the black suit raised his right hand, holding one of the ping-pong balls. He threw it overhand, his face expressionless. The ball curved through the air and fell into the fish bowl with the other three balls. It didn't bounce.

The man in the straw hat stood with a grunt. He dumped a handful of ping-pong balls into the basket underneath the counter. "Try your luck and win a prize!" he said. "Easy as pie!" He set three ping-pong balls in front of a boy and took his quarter. His eyes grew narrow as he watched the tall man raise his hand to throw the second ball. "No leaning in," he told the man.

The man in the black suit glanced at him. "I'm not," he said.

The fat man nodded. "Go ahead," he said.

The tall man threw the second ping-pong ball. It seemed to float across the booth. It fell through the neck of the bowl and landed on top of the other four balls.

"Wait a second," said the fat man, holding up his hand.

The other people who were throwing stopped. The fat man leaned across the table. Sweat was running down beneath the collar of his long-sleeved shirt. He shifted the soggy cigar in his mouth as he scooped the five balls from the bowl. He straightened up and looked at them. He hooked the bamboo cane over his left forearm and rolled the balls between his palms.

"Okay, folks!" he said. He cleared his throat. "Keep throwing! Win a prize!" He dropped the balls into the basket underneath the counter. Taking another quarter from the man in overalls, he set three ping-pong balls in front of him.

The man in the black suit raised his hand and threw the sixth ball. The fat man watched it arc through the air. It fell into the bowl he'd emptied. It didn't roll around inside. It landed on the bottom, bounced once, straight up, then lay motionless.

The fat man grabbed the ashtray, stuck it on the shelf and picked up a fish bowl like the ones on the table. It was filled with pink-colored water and had a goldfish fluttering around in it. "There you go!" he said. He turned away and tapped on the empty fish bowls with his cane. "Step right up!" he said. "Toss a ball in the fish bowl! Win a prize! There's nothing to it!"

Turning back, he saw the man in the wrinkled suit had pushed away the goldfish in the bowl and placed another quarter on the counter. "Three more ping-pong balls," he said.

The fat man looked at him. He shifted the damp cigar in his mouth.

"Three more ping-pong balls," the tall man said.

The man in the straw hat hesitated. Suddenly, he noticed people looking at him and, without a word, he took the quarter and set three ping-pong balls on the counter. He turned around and tapped the fish bowls with his cane. "Step right up and try your luck!" he said. "Easiest game on the fairgrounds!" He removed his straw hat and rubbed the left sleeve of his shirt across his forehead. He was almost bald. The small amount of hair on his head was plastered to his scalp by sweat. He put his straw hat back on and set three ping-pong balls in front of a boy. He put the quarter in the metal box underneath the counter.

A number of people were watching the tall man now. When he threw the first of the three ping-pong balls into the fish bowl some of them applauded and a small boy cheered. The fat man watched suspiciously. His small eyes shifted as the man in the black suit threw his second ping-pong ball into the fish bowl with the other two balls. He scowled and seemed about to speak. The scatter of applause appeared to irritate him.

The man in the wrinkled suit tossed the third ping-pong ball. It landed on top of the other three. Several people cheered and all of them clapped.

The fat man's cheeks were redder now. He put the fish bowl with the goldfish back on its shelf. He gestured toward a higher shelf. "What'll it be?" he asked.

The tall man put a quarter on the counter. "Three more ping-pong balls," he said in a brisk voice.

He picked up three more ping-pong balls from the basket and rolled them between his palms.

"Don't give him the bad ones now," someone said in a mocking voice.

"No bad ones!" the fat man said. "They're all the same!" He set the balls on the counter and picked up the quarter. He tossed it into the metal box underneath the counter. The man in the black suit raised his hand.

"Wait a second," the fat man said. He turned and reached across the table. Picking up the fish bowl, he turned it over and dumped the four ping-pong balls into the basket. He seemed to hesitate before he put the empty fish bowl back in place.

Nobody else was throwing now. They watched the tall man curiously as he raised his hand and threw the first of his three ping-pong balls. It curved through the air and landed in the same fish bowl, dropping straight down through the neck. It bounced once, then was still. The people cheered and applauded. The fat man rubbed his left hand across his eyebrows and flicked the sweat from his fingertips with an angry gesture.

The man in the black suit threw his second ping-pong ball. It landed on the same fish bowl.

"Hold it," said the fat man.

The tall man looked at him.

"What are you doing?" the fat man asked.

"Throwing ping-pong balls," the tall man answered. Everybody laughed.

The fat man's face got redder. "I know that!" he said.

"It's done with mirrors," someone said and everybody laughed again.

"*Funny*," said the fat man. He shifted the wet cigar in his mouth and gestured curtly. "Go on," he said.

The tall man in the black suit raised his hand and threw the third ping-pong ball. It arced across the booth as though it were being carried by an invisible hand. It landed in the fish bowl on top of the other two balls. Everybody cheered and clapped their hands.

The fat man in the straw hat grabbed a casserole dish and dumped it on the counter. The man in the black suit didn't look at it. He put another quarter down. "Three more ping-pong balls," he said.

The fat man turned away from him. "Step right up and win a prize!" he called. "Toss a ping-pong ball—!"

The noise of disapproval everybody made drowned him out. He turned back, bristling. "Four rounds to a customer!" he shouted.

"Where does it say that?" someone asked.

"That's the rule!" the fat man said. He turned his back on the man and tapped the fish bowls with his cane. "Step right up and win a prize!" he said.

"I came here yesterday and played *five* rounds!" a man said loudly.

"That's because you didn't win!" a teenage boy replied. Most of the people laughed and clapped but some of them booed. "Let him play!" a man's voice ordered. Everybody took it up immediately. "Let him play!" they demanded.

The man in the straw hat swallowed nervously. He looked around, a truculent expression on his face. Suddenly, he threw his hands up. "All right!" he said. "Don't get so excited!" He glared at the tall man as he picked up the quarter. Bending over, he grabbed three ping-pong balls and slammed them on the counter. He leaned in close to the man and muttered, "If you're pulling something fast, you'd better cut it out. This is an honest game."

The tall man stared at him. His face was blank. His eyes looked very pale in the leathery tan of his face. "What do you mean?" he asked.

"*No one can throw that many balls in succession into those bowls*," the fat man said.

The man in the black suit looked at him without expression. "*I* can," he said.

The fat man felt a coldness on his body. Stepping back, he watched the tall man throw the ping-pong balls. As each of them landed in the same fish bowl, the people cheered and clapped their hands.

The fat man took a set of steak knives from the top prize shelf and set it on the counter. He turned away quickly. "Step right up!" he said. "Toss a ball in the fish bowl! Win a prize!" His voice was trembling.

"He wants to play again," somebody said.

The man in the straw hat turned around. He saw the quarter on the counter in front of the tall man. "No more prizes," he said.

The man in the black suit pointed at the items on top of the wooden shelves—a four-slice electric toaster, a shortwave radio, a drill set and a portable typewriter. "What about them?" he asked.

The fat man cleared his throat. "They're only for display," he said. He looked around for help.

"Where does it say *that?*" someone demanded.

"That's what they are, so just take my word for it!" the man in the straw hat said. His face was dripping with sweat.

"I'll play for them," the tall man said.

"Now *look*!" The fat man's face was very red. "They're only for display, I said! Now get the hell—!"

He broke off with a wheezing gasp and staggered back against the table, dropping his cane. The faces of the people swam before his eyes. He heard their angry voices as though from a distance. He saw the blurred figure of the man in the black suit turn away and push through the crowd. He straightened up and blinked his eyes. The steak knives were gone.

Almost everybody left the booth. A few of them remained. The fat man tried to ignore their threatening grumbles. He picked a quarter off the counter and set three ping-pong balls in front of a boy. "Try your luck," he said. His voice was faint. He tossed the quarter into the metal box underneath the counter. He leaned against a corner post and pressed both hands against his stomach. The cigar fell out of his mouth. "God," he said.

It felt as though he were bleeding inside.

THE CARNIVAL

by Richard Chizmar

Ronnie Parker couldn't believe his luck.

When he glimpsed the flicker of bright lights glowing on the horizon, his first thought was: it's either a baseball stadium or one of those gigantic used car lots he'd seen on television (COME ON IN! LET'S MAKE A DEAL! the red-white-and-blue banner screamed).

Neither of which made a whole lot of sense considering he was currently cruising a back road in the middle-of-nowhere Iowa countryside.

But what else could it be?

Find out soon enough, he thought, pressing down on the gas pedal. Not too fast, though, checking his rearview. Last thing he wanted was to be pulled over by a copper. Not after he'd *borrowed* his Uncle Manny's brand-new, two-toned, silver and blue Plymouth Belmont the night before.

The year was 1954. The month was August, but just barely, with September already peeking its nose around the corner. Ronnie Parker was eighteen years old and madly in love, which explained why he'd swiped the set of keys from the foyer table and taken off in the dead of night in his favorite uncle's fresh-off-the-lot prize possession. Ronnie knew he was in for a heap of trouble whenever he made his way back home—and not just the "you're grounded for a week" kind of trouble, either—but sometimes, true love called for desperate measures.

Home (for both Ronnie and Uncle Manny) was Florence, Nebraska, a postage-stamp-sized town just north of Scottsbluff. Ronnie had been born in Florence and lived there his entire life. It was where he had fallen in love with Caroline Cavanaugh—blonde, vivacious, smart, and two years younger than Ronnie—and it was where they would one day be married.

He was sure of it. He just had to make it to Cleveland and convince her parents of that outcome.

Edward and Patsy Cavanaugh didn't much care for Ronnie. He knew it, and so did Caroline. Ronnie tried his best to be polite and friendly in front of the two of them, but no matter what he did—flowers for her mom on Mother's Day, baseball small talk with her dad, offers to mow the lawn and wash their cars—nothing seemed to make a positive impression. Caroline promised him repeatedly that it was nothing to worry about, they would come around eventually, and if they didn't, what did it matter? She turned eighteen and a legal adult in just under two years. Then they no longer had any say as to what she could and couldn't do with her life.

At some point, Ronnie decided he could live with that version of the future, and that's exactly what he'd done—right up until her parents had pulled a fast one, packing up their Buick Skylark one morning and whisking Caroline away for the second half of the summer to a relative's lakeside home near Cleveland.

At first, Ronnie and Caroline had both been miserable. They'd swapped daily letters for the first month, and their love had seemed to blossom even stronger. Absence really did make the heart grow fonder, it seemed.

But then, a couple weeks ago, something had changed. Caroline's letters began to arrive less frequently. And where before, Ronnie could count on three or four pages, front and back, of her neat, perfume-scented handwriting, now he barely got a single, one-sided page, and no more perfume, either. He knew it couldn't be Caroline losing interest—or God forbid, he hated to even think it, Caroline falling out of love with him—so his suspicions fell squarely on her parents. After all this time, they had somehow managed to get inside her head.

He pictured Patsy, with that Cheshire cat grin of hers, introducing Caroline to a wealthy, tanned, sunglass-wearing, convertible-driving life-guard at the lake—the stud would inevitably be named Chad or Brad or Biff—and Ronnie didn't know whether to scream or cry or break things.

Instead, he'd decided to take matters into his own hands and head off to Cleveland. The only roadblock had been: *how was he going to get there?*

He knew his father's Chevrolet pick-up was out of the question. There wasn't a chance in hell he would let Ronnie borrow it, and as for taking it without his father's permission, that, too, was a dead-end. For whatever reason, Ronnie's old man guarded those truck keys like a stack of gold bars in Fort Knox, probably because it had taken him the better part of a decade of working factory overtime to afford the bright green Chevrolet.

Uncle Manny was a different story. His father's younger brother was a salesman of questionable moral fiber (Ronnie's mother's favorite words to describe the man). He liked the ladies and he liked his bourbon (those were her second favorite words to describe Uncle Manny). He was also immensely likable and trusting to a fault when it came to his favorite nephew. Ronnie genuinely felt bad about what he'd done, but borrowing his uncle's Belmont had been about as difficult as swiping a lollipop from a sticky-faced toddler.

After all that, Ronnie still didn't know what he was going to say or do once he reached the lake and confronted Caroline and her parents, but he had plenty of time to figure it out.

He'd crossed the state line into Iowa earlier in the afternoon and had made good time, leaving Des Moines in the dust some three hours earlier. Next up was the Illinois border and then Indiana and into Ohio.

There was only one problem: Ronnie was almost broke.

He didn't make much working at the gas station back in Florence, and any extra cash he was able to stash away usually didn't last for very long. He'd end up digging it out of his sock drawer a week or two later and spending it on Caroline. Movies and popcorn didn't come cheap.

He wasn't worried about a place to sleep. Even if he'd had the dough, he wouldn't have given it up for a hotel room. The back seat and an empty parking lot off the beaten path suited him just fine. He also wasn't worried about eating. His stomach was a knotted mess of worry, so he didn't have much of an appetite.

He needed the money for gas. The Plymouth ate fuel like a fat kid eats ice cream.

Ronnie took his eyes off the horizon, where the mysterious flickering lights were growing brighter with each passing mile, and glanced at the gas gauge: it hovered a notch above a quarter-tank. Ronnie reached down and smoothed a hand over his front pants pocket. He knew he had just over twelve dollars tucked away there. He'd counted it twice to make sure. Once it was gone, he didn't know what he was going to do.

So when he steered around the long, winding bend of the country road he was traveling, and the carnival appeared out of the vast cornfield, like a mirage surfacing in the desert, Ronnie knew once and for all that Fate was on his side.

HE TAPPED the brake pedal and swung the car off the road into a plowed-over section of cornfield that was serving as a makeshift parking lot. A barrel-chested man wearing a watch-cap and dirty overalls stood by the entrance and waved him in with a lantern. The field's boundaries were marked on three sides by strings of colorful lights that had been stretched between thin wooden poles about ten feet off the ground. The lot was nearly full.

Ronnie slowly drove to the back of the field, braking several times for hurrying pedestrians, and found an empty spot in the last row next to a Buick Roadmaster. He turned off the engine.

The place was packed, especially for eight forty-five on a Thursday night in the middle of nowhere Iowa. Thick rows of head-high corn stood between Ronnie and the carnival, obscuring his sightline, but the night sky beyond was afire with the dazzling lights of the midway. His car window was rolled down and the sound of the calliope and the squeals of delighted patrons drifted toward him. He could hear the steady cry of the pitchmen and smell the rich scent of roasting peanuts and grilled onions and hamburgers and hot dogs. His stomach growled, surprising him.

He cranked up the window and climbed out of his uncle's Plymouth, locking the door behind him. A wide swath of corn had been cleared up ahead, connecting the parking lot with the carnival grounds. A pair of huge red WELCOME flags marked the opening.

Ronnie waited for a pair of cars to pass—waving at a group of giggling teen-aged girls in the back seat of the second car—and made his way into the tunnel of cornstalks. In front of him, an older couple, holding hands and dressed in their Sunday best, walked with their heads together, talking in hushed, excited tones. The woman clutched a small black handbag at her side.

Staring at the purse, Ronnie thought once again of Fate's fickle nature and how stumbling upon the carnival had to be a sign of good things to come.

As he emerged from the corn and entered the bustling midway, he brushed those thoughts aside. There would be plenty of time for that later.

He had work to do.

SOME TEENAGERS took naturally to solving difficult math problems or hitting a curveball. Others grew up with an innate understanding of how to craft an evocative poem or repair a faulty carburetor. Still others reached adulthood with the seemingly inborn ability to paint vivid canvases or play sophisticated melodies on a musical instrument.

Ronnie Parker wasn't one of those teenagers.

From a very early age, Ronnie's parents—as well as Ronnie himself—understood that he was a boy of limited talents and abilities. To their credit, they all seemed to accept this and move on with their lives accordingly.

There was, however, one natural gift that had been bestowed on Ronnie few people knew about—two, to be exact. Ronnie and his best friend back at home in Florence, Harry Marshall.

So why you may wonder would a young man of such limited prospects keep his one and only real talent a secret from everyone?

The answer was simple: because his talent was of the highly illegal variety.

Ronnie Parker was a pickpocket.

He'd discovered this gift for the first time when he was in the fifth grade. His father had given him a folding pocketknife for his eleventh birthday, and Ronnie had brought it into school that Monday morning to show it off to his friends. When Frankie Johnstone—otherwise known as Frankenstein and the class bully—caught sight of the knife, it didn't take long for it to be wrestled out of Ronnie's skinny hands and stuffed into the back pocket of Frankie's hand-me-down dungarees.

Ronnie knew that fighting Frankie to get the knife back was a losing proposition, downright suicide. The kid was six inches taller than most of his classmates and thirty pounds heavier. He also had the faintest hint of a mustache. So Ronnie decided to try a less direct route.

He'd waited until Frankie was standing in the lunch line, holding his tray with both hands, shooting the bull with the kids in front of him. He'd quickly cut in line and positioned himself two places behind the bully. When it was Frankie's turn to pay the cashier his dime, Ronnie had bent down and pretended to tie his shoe. Instead, he had snaked his hand around the kid in front of him, reached up and simply slid the pocketknife out of Frankie's back pocket. The big, dumb gorilla had been none the wiser.

As the years passed, Ronnie realized that not only was he good at picking pockets, the very act itself seemed to fill him up in a way few others things did. It made him happy in a weird sort of way, proud in another, and made him feel alive, almost like he had a purpose.

And so from the ages of eleven to sixteen, Ronnie Parker picked pockets around Florence with a reckless abandon and efficiency usually reserved for career criminals. He lifted wallets from pants pockets and from inside purses. Pocket watches from suit jackets and fountain pens from dress shirts. He even took pocket change and school supplies from fellow students when the mood served him.

But all of this activity came to a screeching halt around the time he turned seventeen—and met Caroline Cavanaugh.

Caroline was a good girl from a good family. At a time when many kids her age were rebelling and acting out, she was completely comfortable in her own skin and always strived to do the right thing. She saw and believed in the best of Ronnie, and as he fell deeper and deeper in love with Caroline, his number one fear was that he would somehow disappoint her and she would leave him.

So he'd put a stop to the stealing and gotten a job filling gas tanks and checking oil at the local gas station.

The urge to pick pockets didn't magically evaporate as their relationship blossomed—if anything, it grew; once again, absence making the heart grow fonder—but Ronnie simply wasn't willing to risk it. Caroline had become the most important thing in his life.

But now, strolling down the middle of the carnival midway as people hummed with excitement around him, many of them juggling handfuls of change or clutching loose dollar bills, Ronnie reminded himself that Caroline was far, far away—not writing him letters and doing God-knows-what with God-knows-who.

He frowned and waded in.

CARNIVALS, FAIRS, and circuses—they were all like a gift from the heavens when it came to picking pockets.

All those people together in one place, rubes as far as the eye could see. Happy. Distracted. Excited. Often intoxicated—and even if they weren't, sky-high on sugar and caffeine, loud music and bright lights.

Ronnie started the night slowly. First, he lifted a change purse from a giddy teenage girl waiting in line with her friends at the Mirror Maze, and then he went for a pair of wrinkled dollar bills sticking out of a bearded, older man's back pocket.

It was almost too easy.

Careful to stay on the move, he gradually worked his way across the carnival grounds—past the Spook House and Rocket Thrill and Ferris Wheel—to a roped-off area where the kiddie rides were set up. There, just beyond the Petting Zoo, he eyed a flustered young couple struggling to keep up with their three wide-eyed children. The mom threw her arms up in frustration and went one way, chasing two little girls, ribbons bobbing in their long brown hair and identical blue puppy dogs sitting up and begging on the front of their pink blouses. The father shook his head, fighting back a smile, and remained in line at the Space Spin with a little boy who looked around five years old.

Ronnie stood in the background and watched the man and his son for several minutes before making his move. Once the ride had ended and passengers began to exit the miniature space ships, the line in front of the ticket booth shuffled forward. That's when Ronnie sprung into action.

He craned his head in the direction of the row of portable toilets lined up along the far edge of the cornfield, and waved to an imaginary friend as he started cutting through the line.

"Excuse me, I'm sorry, excuse me," he said, still waving, and bumped into the young father. "Pardon me, sir." And then he was on his way without a backward glance.

A short time later, he ducked behind the Win-A-Goldfish tent and looked over his catch. The man's wallet was old and made of worn leather. His driver's license read JOHNATHON ROBBINS of Rising Sun, Iowa. There were creased photographs tucked inside, mostly of his wife and three kids, and one of the dad holding up a largemouth bass and smiling at the camera. The billfold section held eleven dollars and two loose quarters. *Not bad,* Ronnie thought, pushing away the faces of three disappointed kids when Dad announced they had to go home early.

Ronnie pocketed the money and returned to the midway, casually dumping the wallet in a nearby garbage can. *A couple more, and it's time to hit the road,* he thought, slowing his pace and blending into the crowd.

Based on years of experience, he searched the throng of people for a well-dressed couple, preferably in their late twenties or early thirties, and clearly new to each other. The man would be wearing a nice suit and tie and shiny black shoes. He would look a little nervous. The woman, a moderately expensive dress with a short-sleeved sweater on top. No capris or sandals. She would look a little excited. It would be a first or second date, and they'd both be trying their darnedest to impress. The man's wallet would be as full as his ambitions for the night.

He was about to head for the Shootin' Gallery—winning your date a stuffed giraffe or bear was definitely a first date standard—when a large man stepped in front of him, blocking his way.

"You dropped something," the man said in a deep tone. He was wearing a tan suit and slacks and matching bowler cap. His fingers were the size of sausages and he was smiling, but the smile didn't even come close to reaching his eyes, which were squinty and questioning.

Ronnie, heart thumping wildly in his chest, turned around and scanned the ground behind him. A piece of paper the size of a business card lay in the dirt. He bent over and picked it up. Examined it with shaking fingers. It was an advertisement for color televisions.

"Thanks, but it's not mine," he said.

The man wrinkled his nose, like he smelled something rotten, and frowned at the paper in Ronnie's hand. "Then I apologize for the intrusion," he said and went on his way.

Ronnie watched the man disappear into the crowd—there was something odd about him, but Ronnie couldn't quite put his finger on what it was—and released a deep, rattled breath. For a moment there, he was sure he'd been nabbed.

He stuffed the piece of paper in his pocket and continued on his way. Accepting the strange incident as a warning, he decided to grab a snack—the night air had done wonders for his upset stomach—and then do one last job before scramming.

He spotted a tent up ahead selling candy apples and cotton candy and headed in that direction. As he got closer, the sweet aroma assaulted him, making his stomach rumble. He licked his lips in anticipation.

The line out front was at least twenty customers deep, so he slipped into the shadowy space between two tents and approached from the rear. *Might as well save my nickel,* he thought.

Once he was certain he was alone, he eased close to the back of the tent, carefully pulled aside the canvas, and peeked inside. There was a narrow table set up along the back and several crates of candy apples laid out across it. A trio of thick-bodied, gray-haired ladies at the front of the tent was doing their best to keep up with the surge of customers. They had their backs to him, so Ronnie reached in and snagged one of the apples.

Even as he was making his way out of the dark alley between tents, unable to wait even one second longer, Ronnie took a big bite of the apple—

—and gagged in disgust.

"*Uggh,*" he said, spitting a hard, flavorless chunk onto the ground. He reached the brightly lit midway and looked down at the caramel-covered apple in his hand.

It was made of wax.

The apple, the caramel—all of it was wax.

"What the hell?" he said, thinking of the fake fruit his mom sometimes put in a basket and used as a decoration on the dining room table. He spit the waxy taste from his mouth and glanced at the tent where the apples were being sold. A woman walked in front of him with a pink cloud of cotton candy in one hand and an apple in the other. She took a big bite of candy apple and moaned in obvious pleasure. Ronnie watched as she licked a stray dab of caramel from her lips. *Okay, if they're selling real apples, what are the boxes of fake ones for?* He stared at the tent again, trying to make sense of it. *Was one of the old ladies glaring at him or was that his imagination?*

He didn't wait around to find out.

Tossing the wax apple to the ground (half expecting the man in the tan suit to show up, calling after him, "You dropped something!"), he worked his way toward the front of the carnival—and the big red exit flag flapping in the breeze. Now more than ever, he was determined to do one last lift and get the heck out of there. His good feelings about the night had vanished.

He cruised past the Dart Throw and Ring Toss, scanning the midway. He winced as he walked by the Dodgem Cars, the loud music and flashing lights making his head throb. Francesca, a dark-skinned Gypsy of indeterminate age, grinned with a mouthful of tobacco-stained teeth and winked at him as he passed the dimly-lit entrance to Francesca's Fortunes. He ignored her and kept walking.

Until he heard the chain-driven rumble of the Rocket Thrill and saw the robust crowd gathered in front of the mini-coaster. "Bingo," he said, slowing to a halt.

Standing at the edge of the horde was a well-dressed couple. The woman's arms hung down at her side, and the fingers of her right hand fidgeted with the hem of her dress. She wanted to hold the man's hand, but he wasn't getting the hint. Typical first or second date behavior.

Ronnie waded into the crowd and maneuvered behind the couple for a better view, quickly spotted the bulge of the man's wallet in his back pocket. There was only one problem: the pocket was buttoned.

Never one to shy away from a challenge—well, of the pick-pocketing variety, anyway—Ronnie edged closer, keeping his eyes glued to the man's back. Thirty seconds later, he was standing directly behind him and working up the courage to make his move.

He slowly reached his hand out—

—and as his fingertips grazed the man's pocket, the lights of the midway dimmed and the carnival grounds were transformed into a spider-web of shadows. A nervous murmur went through the crowd, but before anyone could voice their concern, a brilliant shower of blue-green fireworks lit up the night sky above them. The crowd oohed and aahed.

The well-dressed couple gazed upward. "Oh, Jeffrey, it's beautiful," the woman gushed, and Jeffrey finally took her hand in his.

While this was happening, Ronnie unbuttoned the man's back pocket with his right hand and carefully slipped the wallet free with his left. And then he was gone.

CRADLING THE wallet against his belt buckle, moving quickly while the lights remained dimmed, Ronnie worked his way out of the crowd and slipped behind a nearby tent. The wallet felt unusually thick, and he was anxious to get a look inside.

Once again, checking first to make sure no one was watching, he unclenched his hands and opened the wallet.

Or tried to, anyway.

The wallet wouldn't open.

He stared at it in confusion.

A spiraling burst of red-white-and-blue flashed high above in the sky, giving him a better view.

By all accounts, it looked and felt like a real wallet. It was made of a dark material that resembled leather, but the texture was slicker than any leather Ronnie had ever seen before, and when he held it up to his nose, there was no odor at all. Ronnie had once held a movie-prop gun that his buddy Harry Marshall's father had been given as a gag gift; the wallet reminded him now of that fake gun. It looked and felt real—right down to the worn crease where the wallet was folded in half—but it wasn't. It was a pretend wallet.

Before he could think about it further or decide what it meant, there came a rustling noise from somewhere nearby in the darkness. And then whispering:

"He weighs a ton. Where we putting him?"

"There's still room in my tent."

"Jesus, no more fatties after this one."

Ronnie froze, afraid to move, afraid to breathe.

The muffled sound of footfalls soon faded.

Ronnie didn't know what was going on, but he knew enough to realize he wanted nothing to do with it. To make matters worse, he was almost certain the second man who had spoken in the darkness had been the man in the tan suit he'd met earlier on the midway.

RONNIE WAITED in the dark for another couple of minutes to make sure the men weren't coming back, and then he slinked out of his hiding place and headed to the midway, his heart thumping so hard he was convinced people would be able to hear it.

Just as he rejoined the crowd, the carnival lights flickered back to life and brightened. Everyone cheered—except for a handful of bratty kids who whined to their parents for more fireworks—and then people began to scatter, anxious to get back to having fun.

After a brief scan of the crowd, Ronnie spotted the same well-dressed couple waiting in line at the Rocket Thrill and zig-zagged his way through a pack of rowdy teenagers to get closer. It was a dangerous move, approaching a mark just minutes after emptying his pocket, but he knew he had to try.

Once he reached the couple, it took no time at all for Ronnie to get the answers he was looking for. The silver clasp at the top of the woman's purse was all one piece and clearly not functional. The purse itself was made of the same slippery material as the wallet. There was no question in Ronnie's mind: it was a pretend purse.

He walked away in a daze and found an empty wooden bench next to the Funhouse. He sat down and rubbed his temple. Ronnie knew he wasn't the smartest stick in the stack, but he was bright enough to know something strange was going on.

But what?

Wax apples. Fake wallets and purses. Mysterious whispering in the shadows. Sure, it was weird, but what did it all add up to? Then there was the man in the tan suit.

Ronnie was convinced the man stopping and talking to him hadn't merely been a coincidence. *So what did it mean—*

And then just like that, sitting there on the bench listening to the screams echoing from inside the Funhouse, it came to him in a flash of clarity—what had been wrong with the man in the tan suit.

It had been his ears.

At a glance, they'd appeared to be perfectly normal. Maybe a tad on the large side, but big guys had big ears, didn't they? Nothing wrong with that.

But as the man had turned and headed back into the crowd, Ronnie's subconscious had picked up one small, irregular detail and filed it away for later: the man didn't have ear canals. The flesh there in the center was all closed up, like a swirl of melted wax. They were pretend ears.

"Son of a bitch," he whispered.

Ronnie felt an icy finger slowly trace its way along his spine and shuddered.

He got up from the bench, unsure of what to do next, and noticed something else—something that troubled him every bit as much as fake ears and wallets and fruit, something that immediately caused his skin to break out in a cold, clammy sweat: *the crowd had gotten smaller.*

The midway had been bursting at the seams when the fireworks had begun. He'd hardly been able to move without bumping into someone. *So where had everyone gone? Had that many people left during the light show? Or had something else happened to them?*

Doing his best to remain calm, Ronnie strode toward the carnival exit, his mind working at a frantic pace. He glanced at the cheap wristwatch his Aunt Nadine had given him the year before as a graduation gift. It was later than he'd thought: twenty minutes after ten. *Maybe people really* had *left during the fireworks. Maybe…hopefully…there was a reasonable explanation for all of this.*

He entered the tunnel of corn that served as the carnival's only entrance and exit. Alone now, he could hear the brittle snap of dead stalks crunching beneath his feet. He shivered and glanced over his shoulder at the midway. Nothing appeared out of the ordinary. No one was lurking in the shadows.

Maybe I made a big deal out of a whole lot of nothing.

But as he neared the end of the tunnel, Ronnie was able to survey more and more of the parking lot—and he wasn't the least bit surprised to discover it was still jam-packed with cars. Almost as full as when he'd first arrived.

So where did all the people go? a small voice whispered inside his head.

The cold sweat returned. He started to walk faster.

Run, the voice warned. *Before it's too late!*

But before he could even consider listening, a man appeared out of the darkness ahead of him. The man stood at the mouth of the tunnel with his back to Ronnie and barked instructions to someone else unseen. Ronnie couldn't understand a word of what the man was saying, but he could see just enough details to know exactly who it was: the man in the tan suit.

He spun on his heels and headed back into the carnival.

RONNIE CROUCHED in the darkness behind the Beverage Booth and studied the twenty-or-so-yard-wide strip of midway he was able to see. People came and went, strolling in all directions, many of them smiling and laughing, sipping soda pop and eating ice cream cones or sticky towers of cotton candy.

But only a handful headed for the exit.

Ronnie was waiting for a sizeable group he could join as they made their way to the parking lot, a group large enough for him to blend in with and sneak safely past the man in the tan suit. Ronnie didn't know why he was so frightened of him, but he was.

His stomach growled and he realized he still hadn't eaten a bite. He was starving. He swallowed and his throat felt like he had just gargled with sawdust from his father's workshop.

He scooted closer to the corner of the booth and peeked inside. A man and woman were serving tall glasses of lemonade to a pair of red-faced kids. From where Ronnie was kneeling, he couldn't see well enough to determine if any of them had fake ears or not—but he *was* able reach the glasses of lemonade sitting on the countertop right in front of him, so that's exactly what he did. He carefully snaked his hand in between the network of two-by-four support beams, grabbed one of the icy plastic cups, and maneuvered it back to safety.

He chugged half of it right on the spot and sucked an ice cube into his mouth. The lemonade tasted like perfection, but it also reminded him of Caroline and all the times they had sat out on the front porch, watching the deer run in the meadow and the clouds floating by, holding hands and sneaking kisses, sipping frosty glasses of his mom's lemonade. He drained the rest of it and dropped the cup to the ground, squeezed his eyes shut and tried to think of something else. Anything else.

His eyes were still closed when he heard the voices coming from directly in front of him.

He snapped them open and saw two workers he didn't recognize dragging by their arms the young mom (Mrs. Robbins of Rising Sun, Iowa) he'd seen earlier near the kiddie rides and one of her daughters, still wearing the pink blouse with the blue puppy on the front of it.

Ronnie scrambled backward on all fours and hugged the rear wall of the booth, praying they wouldn't notice him there in the shadows. They walked within five feet of him, close enough for Ronnie to hear their heavy footsteps and ragged breathing—and glimpse their waxy, fake ears.

The mom and little girl were gagged. They twisted their heads from side to side and grunted against the strips of cloth. The men pulled them roughly along until they reached the back of a tent some twenty yards away. Ronnie saw a wedge of bright light as they lifted the tent flap—and there was a sudden loud *slap* of beefy palm meeting tender flesh—and then they were inside and everything was dark and still again.

RONNIE PARKER was a lot of things—not too bright, a lousy driver, and a petty thief among them—but he had never thought of himself as a coward.

Until tonight.

He stood behind the tent in which he had watched the two workers stash the woman and little girl not five minutes earlier, and listened to the inner dialogue playing out inside his head:

"They could be cops or working security for the carnival. Maybe the mom and her daughter did something wrong."

"Yeah, sure, maybe they stuck up the Crazy Cups or stole a prize pig from the Petting Zoo. Or, hey, maybe they got caught pick-pocketing someone."

"I'm just saying, smart aleck, you can't go busting in without knowing the whole story."

"Carnival cops don't gag people, Einstein. And you heard the slap as clearly as I did. They don't hit 'em, either, at least not the women."

Ronnie knew what he had to do, what Caroline would have wanted and expected him to do. It was time to shut down the voices in his head and stop stalling.

He took a deep breath, eased aside the tent flap, and peered inside.

The woman and her daughter were locked in cages.

And they weren't alone.

There were a half-dozen additional cages lined up against the far side of the tent. Ronnie quickly counted four other adults and two children held captive inside. Three male and three female. All of them gagged and terrified. The woman's (Mrs. Robbins of Rising Sun, Iowa) left eye was beginning to swell shut and her lip was split and bleeding.

Ronnie's vision blurred and he was rocked by a sudden wave of nausea. *Please God*, he thought. *Don't let me faint now.*

He could only see one of the workers inside the tent, pacing back and forth in front of the cages, muttering angrily to himself. Ronnie couldn't make out what the man was saying, but it sounded a lot like the same odd language the man in the tan suit had been speaking at the exit tunnel.

Each time the man pivoted and walked with his left side facing the cages, it gave Ronnie a perfect view of the right half of the man's face—and the fingernail grooves the woman must have gouged into his cheek. The slashes were ragged and deep but lacked the angry red color you would have expected from such a vicious wound. In fact, there was no color at all. There was also no blood.

It was the lack of blood on the worker's waxy face that finally woke up Ronnie enough to get him moving. Instead of charging into the tent, he slowly pulled his fingers back, letting the canvas flap slide closed again, and retreated. He moved stealthily through the darkness, careful to make as little noise as possible, but once he reached the well-lit midway and fixed his eyes on the exit flag, his pace quickened.

This isn't cowardice, he thought, thinking of Caroline again. *It's common fucking sense.*

He craned his head to see if the man in the tan suit was still blocking the exit, but it was too far away. His vision blurred again. The carnival swam in and out of focus, and he was forced to slow down.

He was staggering past the merry-go-round when the boy in front of him collapsed. One minute, the teenager, dressed in faded dungarees and a black T-shirt, a cigarette dangling from his mouth, was walking with his circle of friends, and the next, he was flat on his back on the ground, his eyes rolled back in his head.

Ronnie barely gave the boy a sideways glance as he lurched past him and his friends. He squeezed his eyes open and closed, trying to refocus them and control his suddenly shallow breathing.

The Crazy Cups grinded to a stop up ahead, and Ronnie watched as not a single passenger exited the ride. They were all slumped in their seats unconscious.

Off to his left, next to the Rocket Thrill ticket booth, a family of four lay, writhing and moaning, in a tangled heap in the dirt, discarded soft drink cups scattered around them.

A group of carnival workers appeared and, with practiced efficiency, quickly dragged the family away. Ronnie watched them disappear into the darkness beyond the tents and remembered the glass of lemonade he had drunk.

They drugged us.

He tried to make a run for it then, but he couldn't even get started. He could barely see now, barely draw a breath. It took everything he had left inside of him just to keep his feet moving.

A bald man he had never seen before suddenly appeared at Ronnie's side, his mouth foaming and his nose gushing blood. He gazed at Ronnie and croaked, "We have to get out of here," and just as they reached the mouth of the exit tunnel, the man collapsed hard to the ground, his arms pin-wheeling behind him. "Please don't leave me," he begged, reaching up with a trembling hand.

Ronnie groaned and kept moving. His stomach lurched and he vomited a thick stream of blood-speckled bile onto his shoes. He was too weak to reach up and wipe his chin.

As he made his way deeper into the tunnel of corn, he risked a look behind him—and watched in terror as a stiff-shouldered carnival worker emerged from the field and dragged the now unconscious bald man deep into the corn. The cornstalks rustled behind them and went still again.

Where was he taking him?

Ronnie Parker might not have been the brightest stick in the stack, but the answer came to him then, crystal clear and fully formed:

They're collecting us.

I don't know who they are or what they are or where they came from, but they're collecting us.

And then with the same level of clarity and certainty, in his final hazy moment of consciousness, Ronnie Parker realized what was coming next:

Feeding time.

MR. BONES' WILD RIDE

by Billy Chizmar

Every autumn, for three days and three nights during the month of October, the Peddler Brothers' Carnival came to Jericho, Maryland. For as long as I could remember, the carnival arrived a weekend or two before Halloween, opening its gates for business on Friday afternoon and packing up its tents and rides and leaving in a long, dusty caravan of big trucks on Sunday night. My parents once told me they'd taken me every year since I'd been born.

The carnival was a big deal in Jericho, especially for kids. There's not an awful lot to do around here besides going to the movies or high school football games. My older brother played on the team, or at least I think he did. I'm not sure anymore. He always came to the carnival with us, too, usually with some of his older friends. Heck, pretty much the whole town showed up. It was one of the only times people around here came together like people are supposed to.

Each year, the carnival set up in the same spot, a big grassy clearing called Runnals Field, right behind the Baptist church. On opening night, my family walked around the whole field, getting "the lay of the land," Dad always said, which really meant checking out which rides we wanted to go on so we knew how many tickets to buy. The best rides usually came back year after year, including my all-time favorite, *The Whirly Dirly*. It looked like a big metal Frisbee that you sat down in, and once you were belted in, it started spinning really fast and tilting up and down. I think I saw something like it once in that old movie *The Sandlot* that my brother likes so much, but unlike the guys in the movie, I never puked on it. Actually, I'm pretty brave when it comes to rides. I like them all, even *The Zipper*, which my dad refuses to go on.

There *is* one ride I never liked and made a point to avoid: the mirror maze. Not that there's anything scary about mirrors, I mean I have one back home in my bedroom and every bathroom in the house, but I never liked the big sign that welcomed customers near the entrance to the maze. All the attractions had hand-painted billboards up front, right next to the ticket collector booth, and most of the signs featured really cute animals or cartoon characters—but not the mirror maze.

Instead of a fluffy, pink bunny wearing a top hat or a goofy old man riding a unicycle, the mirror maze sign was painted black and had a big skeleton on it. It didn't look anything like the posters in the nurse's office at school or at my doctor's office. It was too weird for that. The bones on the skeleton's body were tiny and skinny, and there were fingers and toes missing as if someone had forgotten to paint them on. The bones weren't even white, but closer to brown or gray.

The skeleton wasn't doing anything either. Most of the cartoons were riding a carnival ride or playing a game, but the skeleton was just standing there, looking really creepy. If all that wasn't bad enough, what was even worse, what I *hated* most of all, was its head.

The skull was at least three times larger than it should've been. And while it was the same icky, not-quite-white color the rest of the skeleton was, there was a thin red outline around it, and it was glowing like someone had stuffed a lava lamp inside the skull. Its teeth glowed, too, and there were too many of them. Dozens and dozens of small teeth lined up in rows in its open, hanging mouth. My brother always said that someone probably painted the first couple of teeth too small and then the others had to match. I don't know if I believe him.

But, for me, the worst part of all was the skull's *eyes*. Where the empty eye sockets should have been, there were red flowers instead. Big, bright, blood-red flowers, like roses, except I never saw any thorns. The flower petals curled in a weird way, too. They folded inward and made it look like there were *real* eyes in the thornless roses, eyes made out of red petals. I hated it, everything about it. It just looked *bad*. Like how you can always tell who the bad guy in a movie is going to be, that kind of bad.

Finally, right above the skeleton, in big white, drippy letters: *Welcome to Mr. Bones' Wild Ride*. The same horrible sign had hung over the mirror maze

entrance every year. Some of the signs for the other rides changed from year to year. New paint, new characters, but the mirror maze was always the same. I never went in, never wanted to, because of that sign, because of Mr. Bones.

But that never stopped my older brother, or his friends, or even some of my friends, from ponying up three tickets and going inside the maze. Every year, they tried to talk me into it, but I never gave in. I waited outside, and when they came out, usually laughing and pushing each other around, we moved on to the next ride, and the mirror maze and Mr. Bones were forgotten for another year.

All that changed this October, when the Peddler Brothers' Carnival rolled into town one autumn-crisp Friday morning, and my brother insisted I do the mirror maze with him and his friends. I had just turned ten years old the week before, and my brother told me now that my age was in double digits, I was finally old enough to stop being afraid of Mr. Bones. I wouldn't answer him at first, but after he kept begging, I took a deep breath and said okay, pretending to be brave.

I closed my eyes the entire time we stood in line, never once sneaking a peek at the abominable, flower-eyed skull towering above me.

In fact, I didn't open them again until my brother poked me in the shoulder and told me we were inside. I immediately looked around and felt a little better. The actual mirror maze didn't seem very scary at the time. The plywood floor and ceiling and dirty lightbulbs hanging down on pieces of wire were a little creepy, but nothing I couldn't handle, nothing like Mr. Bones.

My brother's friends ran ahead, laughing and yelling, but he waited for me and asked if I wanted to race. I think he did it because he knew I didn't want to stay inside very long. He was a great big brother.

Of course, I said yes. A race to escape—and we were off!

I followed him for the first couple minutes, zigging left when he zigged left, and zagging right when he zagged right. But then we went our separate ways. The last time I saw him was at a split in the maze. He went left this time, and I went right.

That was the last time I saw *anybody*.

Well, except for myself. I always see myself—hundreds and hundreds of times. Sometimes it seems like the mirrors go on forever. I really believe they do.

I don't know how long I've been in here. I've gotten taller, I can tell that. And my shoes stopped fitting a while ago. The dirty light bulbs never turn off. Sometimes I see them swinging back and forth and think it's from the wind, from a nearby exit. But it never is.

A while ago I started bleeding in my pants. I think it's called a period. My mom told me about it when I was back home. I don't remember most of what she said. It's hard to remember things in here. I know periods are supposed to come once a month, but I've lost count of them.

Sometimes I get splinters from walking without shoes. In the beginning, I curled up and cried a lot, but now I usually walk until I get tired and need to sleep.

Sometimes I find plates of food waiting for me, as if someone knows I'm trapped in here. The food—usually chicken or some kind of fish and a vegetable—doesn't taste very good, even though it looks like it comes from a restaurant. It all tastes the same, like nothing. There's never any flavor. But it fills me up and keeps me going. It gives me enough energy to keep walking, to keep searching for a way out.

Sometimes I find other things. Usually nothing special. A screw, an acorn, a cheap pen, a toothbrush. Just random things. Sometimes I find scary things, though. Once I found a big black box, the kind that a magician would use, and it was marked with one of those label guns that my grandpa has. It read: *Box Of Rain*. I don't know who put it there, but when I held the box close to my face, I heard thunder coming from inside it. I heard a storm. I couldn't open it, though. It was locked. Maybe someday I'll find the key.

The roses are the worst. I find those on bad days. The days where I feel like I can't walk anymore, where I just want to give up and cry. Those are the days I walk slower, and when I walk slower I almost always find a rose. A thornless, blood-red rose, petals curled inward in the shape of an eye. It means *he* is getting closer. It means I need to stop feeling sorry for myself and start moving faster.

I used to think about home a lot, especially during the first few days (weeks? months?) I was in here, but as the weeks (years?) dragged on, it got harder and harder to remember. At first it was just the little stuff: the posters on the walls in my bedroom, the kind of cars my parents drove, classmates' nicknames, addresses, and phone numbers. Then it was the school I went to and what my house looked like. And then it got worse: the faces of my friends, my parents, and finally, my brother. His name starts with a B, that's all I can still grasp of him. Sometimes I focus really hard and try to remember what they looked like, but the only faces I see are the ones I see in the mirrors: Me and Mr. Bones.

Sometimes, if I sleep too long, I can hear *him*. The *click click clicking* of his fleshless feet marching towards me. Those are the days I find a lot of roses, those are the days I end up running, but running isn't easy in the mirrors.

I've only seen him once. I woke up after a bad walking day, and there he was—Mr. Bones. Standing as still as a statue in the mirrors. Dozens of huge, deformed skulls, dozens of rose-petal eyes, hundreds of tiny, sharp teeth. His jaw hung wide open like he was meant to be screaming, but the maze was silent, the quietest place I'd ever been. The only sound came from the red glow of his skull. I could hear it whispering, taunting. I wanted to run but I couldn't tell where he was actually standing, what was real and what was mirror. A crooked trail of flower petals followed me as I walked deeper into the maze. Eventually, I saw less of Mr. Bones and the red glow grew dimmer. I didn't stop walking for a long time after that.

I don't think there's an exit. I think the maze goes on forever. I think I left the carnival and Jericho and my family a long time ago and traveled to wherever Mr. Bones calls home.

So, I walk and I eat and I sleep. And I do my best to stay away from him. I don't know what will happen if he catches me, but sometimes, I can't help but wonder if I should let him. I'm so tired. I still dream of home, but it's only a word now. I remember nothing.

I stare at myself in the mirrors.

My clothes are too small for me.

I look like a stranger.

I want to get out of Mr. Bones' Wild Ride.

I want to get out of Mr. Bones' Wild Ride.

I want to get out of Mr. Bones' Wild Ride.

FAIR TREATS

by Jeff Strand

There were so many delicious foods available at the state fair that twelve-year-old Bobby didn't know where to begin. A funnel cake covered in chocolate sauce and powdered sugar? Deep-fried pickles? Some kind of meat on a stick? He planned to spend the afternoon going on rides, so he didn't want to make himself *too* queasy, but he'd been saving up his lawn-mowing money for months to get this opportunity to pig out.

The booth straight ahead had a colorful sign that read "Candy Apples." Yes! That was a perfect place to begin, and there was no line! In fact, the whole area around it was deserted. Bobby hurried over to the booth.

"Hello, young man," said a gray-haired man, sliding open the window. "What delectable treat can I get you today?"

"Candy apple."

"You literally could not have made a better choice. Some places are stingy with the candy coating or they use soft apples with brown spots, but not here. I'm about to hand you the largest, crispest apple with the stickiest, most sugary candy you've ever encountered. That'll be three dollars."

Bobby took three dollars out of his pocket and handed it to the man.

"Thank you, thank you, thank you. I'll have your apple in a jiffy. Less than a jiffy, even." The man stepped out of sight, then returned to the window a moment later and extended the candy apple to Bobby. "There you go, my good friend. Enjoy."

Bobby took the apple. Without hesitation, he bit deep into it.

The candy coating was indeed pure sugary deliciousness.

But he couldn't finish the bite. His teeth were stuck.

He tried to bite down harder. It didn't work. He tried to reverse course and open his mouth, but that didn't work, either.

He waved at the man and frantically gestured to the apple.

"What's the problem, young man? Teeth stuck?"

Bobby nodded.

"Pull them free! I'm sure you've got strong jaws!"

Bobby tried to open his mouth. His teeth would not come free of the candy coating. He tried to explain this to the man, but his words were completely muffled.

"Why, it's as if you've never eaten a candy apple before. You have to work at it. If you'd like, I can cut away at the apple with my sharpest knife, but the knife is so very sharp that I can't promise it won't take a flap of your cheek with it. Are you willing to risk having a generous flap of your cheek sliced away to free yourself of that candy apple?"

Bobby shook his head.

"Smart lad. People gape at you when you're missing part of your face. I suppose you could find your mom and dad and have them take you to the emergency room, but that would end your day at the fair far too soon. There are still so many attractions left to see. Do you agree?"

Bobby nodded.

"Then all I can say is: tug! Tug your hardest! Show that apple that it can't get the best of you! Grab the stick with both hands and give it a great big twist!"

Bobby followed the man's advice. The candy apple popped free, taking three broken teeth with it. He stared at the apple for a moment, feeling the panic rise, then let out a wail as blood squirted from his mouth.

"Calm down, calm down, you don't want everybody staring at you, do you?" asked the man, waving him closer to the window. "When a child breaks his front teeth on a candy apple, the shame can follow him for the rest of his life. Trust me, you don't want any of those apple-related nicknames."

Bobby forced himself to stop wailing. He put his hand over his mouth and blood trickled between his fingers.

"Those were just your baby teeth, right?"

Bobby shook his head.

"Oh. Pity. Well, dentists can do remarkable things. False teeth don't get cavities. I think you're going to be just fine, young man. Just fine. First let's clean out that ghastly wound. Have some of my delicious refreshing lemonade, compliments of the house!"

The man held out a large cup of lemonade. Bobby hesitantly took it.

"Go on, take a great big drink! I'd never give out free lemonade unless you broke your teeth on my candy apple, so seize the opportunity!"

Bobby took a drink.

"Tasty, isn't it? My lemonade is the sourest in the whole county!"

The pain was unbelievable. Bobby let out a yelp and spat out the liquid.

"Don't spit it out! Swish it around! It's cauterizing your wounds!"

"It hurts!"

"Are you a pre-teen or are you a tiny little baby? Man up! I'll wager that there's a five-year-old girl watching you right now who is shaking her head in disgust. You've got a problem and you need to fix it. Do you know how many people die each year from over-bleeding due to broken teeth?"

"No."

"Thousands. You never hear about them because the media buries their stories to protect the families from ridicule. You could bleed out in the next thirty or forty seconds if you don't drink that whole cup of lemonade."

"I don't want to die!"

"And I don't want you to die, so we're on common ground. Do you think I want my customers to bleed to death? Do you think I like giving out free beverages when my profit margin is already paper-thin? Drink the lemonade!"

Bobby ignored the excruciating pain and gulped down the lemonade, drinking so quickly that pink liquid (yellow plus red) dribbled down the sides of his mouth. When he finished, he had to admit that his entire mouth was numb.

"Feel better?" the man asked.

"Yes," said Bobby, slurring the word.

"I feel guilty about your unpleasant experience at my booth. You came to the carnival for a wonderful time and instead you've suffered almost unbearable pain. You enjoy things that are deep-fried, right?"

Bobby nodded.

"How about a deep-fried chocolate bar? Oh, what an indulgence they are! So decadent. And I won't charge you one red cent for it."

"But my teeth are broken."

"All of them? Every single one? Because I only count three on that apple. You had thirty-two teeth when you arrived, so now you have twenty-nine.

Are you telling me that you can't eat a deep-fried chocolate bar with twenty-nine teeth? You should be able to eat that with only gums. You truly are one of the least ambitious young men I've ever encountered."

"Okay, I'll eat it," said Bobby.

"That's the spirit." The man handed him a paper basket with three deep-fried blobs in it.

Bobby shoved one of the blobs into his mouth, then howled in pain as it sizzled his tongue and the inside of his cheeks.

"You fool!" the man said. "You didn't blow on it first! Everybody knows that you blow on a freshly made deep-fried snack before you shove it into your mouth! Goodness, but you're a simpleton. I regret selling you a candy apple in the first place."

Bobby spat out the deep-fried chocolate and dropped the other two pieces onto the ground.

"And you're a wasteful simpleton as well! What kind of boy flings perfectly good deep-fried chocolate onto the filthy ground? Are you even a real boy at all?"

"My whole mouth is burning!"

"Yes, because of your carelessness. I don't understand how you even lived long enough to part with your three dollars today."

Bobby looked around the fair for help, but there were no other people. How was that possible? The rest of the fair was crowded. How could this area be completely empty? Why was nobody coming to help a little boy screaming in agony?

"I apologize for the insult," said the man. "That was unkind and unprofessional. You're doing the best you can with the genes you received."

"Thank you."

"I hate to see a displeased customer. How about some popcorn?" He held up a red and white striped bag and rattled the contents. "Freshly popped. Fluffy. No salt or butter, so it won't irritate your injuries."

"No."

"No? No? You're saying no to freshly popped popcorn? Who would do such a thing? Young man, you've made some questionable decisions in the short time we've been acquainted but nothing comes close to this. When somebody offers you popcorn, you accept without hesitation. To do otherwise is odd."

"I don't want any popcorn. I just want my mom!"

"What can your mother do for you? Take you to the hospital? Do you know what the doctor there is going to say? He's going to say that the entire bottom half of your face should be removed. Does that sound like fun? Oh, I'm sure they'll use Novocain and use precise surgical tools, but still, you're going to wake up with no face between your nose and your neck."

"I hate this fair!"

"Do you know what would make you feel better about it? Popcorn."

Bobby took the bag of popcorn from him, but he wasn't going to eat it.

"You know to watch out for unpopped kernels, right?" the man asked.

A kernel popped, sending a hot piece of popcorn right into Bobby's eye. He shrieked and dropped the popcorn. He put his hand over his eye and fled from the booth as fast as he could, but since his depth perception was all messed up he just smacked into the booth and fell to the ground.

"Careful there!" said the man. "I don't want to have to repaint."

Bobby got back up. He moved his hand away from his face but couldn't get his injured eye to open.

"You get that you're in Hell, right?" the man asked. "I figured it was obvious by now, but wanted to state it upfront so that we're both on the same page."

"I'm...dead?"

"Yeah. You choked on a candy apple."

"You're the devil?"

"That's me. You were probably expecting the red skin and the horns and the pitchfork, but if I took that form, you would've been disinclined to buy a treat from me. Would you like some cotton candy?"

"No!"

The man held up a large pink ball of cotton candy. "What can go wrong with this? It's as harmless as you can get."

"I could poke my eye out with the holder."

"Fair enough, fair enough." The man pulled the cotton candy off the paper cone. "Now it's totally safe. Go on, take it. You deserve a treat after all you've been through this morning."

"I don't want it."

"Is it because of the urban legend? You know, the one where there were millions of spider eggs in some cotton candy, and they all hatched as this kid was eating it? Don't worry about that. Everybody knows that spiders don't exist."

"Uh, yeah they do."

"Very well. You're too clever for me. There are indeed millions of spider eggs in this cotton candy, and if you ate it they'd hatch and millions of spiders would scurry around inside of your stomach." The man tossed the cotton candy aside. "Would you like a corn dog?"

"No!"

"It doesn't contain real dog."

"No!"

"Actually, it does contain real dog, but not *your* dog. That would be ghastly."

"I want to go home!"

"Well, you can't. Your parents are kind people and don't deserve a Monkey's Paw scenario with their dead kid. I've got to have something here that would appeal to you. What about spiral-cut French fries? What could go wrong with those?"

"I don't want any."

"You're right, you're right. Too much starch is unhealthy. Especially for a growing boy, not that you'll be growing anymore. How about some hummus and pita chips?"

"Why am I in Hell?" Bobby demanded. "What did I do that was bad?"

"I don't know. Were you a Holocaust denier?"

"No."

"Then I can't explain it. Actually, I can explain it. This isn't Hell. This is Heaven."

"What?"

"I invented a drug that saved hundreds of thousands of lives. Many kids just like you will get to grow up because of me. In terms of getting into the afterlife, that amazing amount of good that I brought to the world out-weighed the fact that I'm a sadist who loves to torment young boys. If I molested them, I'd probably be skewered on a pitchfork right now, but caus-ing them misery for my amusement is okay. So I'm here in Heaven, where I get to spend my days doing what I love the most."

"But…what about me? This isn't how Heaven is supposed to be."

"You make a good point. Honestly, I think you can just chalk it up to bad timing. If you'd choked to death one bite later, some other kid might be in your place and you'd be sitting on a cloud with your PlayStation 42. I'd register a complaint if I were you. When we're done here I'm sure I can direct you to somebody with the proper forms."

"Okay," said Bobby. "Will my teeth grow back?"

"Before you died, did you say a prayer for your teeth to grow back?"

"They were fine then."

"Yeah, I know. Bit of a conundrum there. This place has been around for quite a while but they still haven't worked out all the kinks. I'm sure there's a form for that. Anyway, we're in Heaven, and my idea of Hell is discussing bureaucracy, so I'd like to get back to offering you fair treats if I may."

"Yes, sir."

The man looked around the booth. "Ooh! Ooh! Everybody's favorite! How about a delicious skewer of flaming marshmallows on a rusty sword delivered to you between the jaws of a live alligator?"

Bobby nodded. "That sounds good."

Smoke & Mirrors

by Amanda Downum

The circus was in town.

Not just any circus, either, but Carson & Kindred's Circus Fabulatoris and Menagerie of Mystical Marvels. The circus Jerusalem Morrow ran away to join when she was nineteen years old. Her family for seven years.

She laid the orange flyer on the kitchen table beside a tangle of beads and wire and finished putting away her groceries. Her smile stretched, bittersweet. She hadn't seen the troupe in five years, though she still dreamt of them. Another world, another life, before she came back to this quiet house.

Cats drifted through the shadows in the backyard as she put out food. The bottle tree—her grandmother's tree—chimed in the October breeze: no ghosts tonight. Glass gleamed cobalt and emerald, diamond and amber, jewel-bright colors amid autumn-brown leaves. Awfully quiet this year, so close to Halloween.

Salem glanced at the flyer again as she boiled water for tea. Brother Ezra, Madame Aurora, Luna and Sol the acrobats—familiar names, and a few she didn't know. She wondered if Jack still had the parrots and that cantankerous monkey. The show was here until the end of the month…

It's the past. Over and done. She buried the paper under a stack of mail until only one orange corner showed.

Salem woke that night to the violent rattle of glass and wind keening over narrow mouths. The bottle tree had caught another ghost.

She flipped her pillow to the cool side and tried to go back to sleep, but the angry ringing wouldn't let her rest. With a sigh she rolled out of bed and tugged on a pair of jeans. Floorboards creaked a familiar rhythm as she walked to the back door.

Stars were milky pinpricks against the velvet predawn darkness. Grass crunched cool and dry beneath her feet. A cat shrieked across the yard—they never came too near when the bottles were full. The shadows smelled of ash and bitter smoke. Goosebumps crawled up her arms, tightened her breasts.

"Stay away, witch."

Salem spun, searching for the voice. Something gleamed ghost-pale on her roof. A bird.

"Get away!" White wings flapped furiously.

The wind gusted hot and harsh; glass clashed. Salem turned, reaching for the dancing bottles.

A bottle shattered and the wind hit her like a sandstorm, like the breath of hell. Glass stung her outstretched palm. Smoke seared her lungs. She staggered back, stumbled and fell, blind against the scouring heat.

Then it was over. Salem gasped, tears trickling down her stinging cheeks. The tree shivered in the stillness, shedding singed leaves.

Cursing, she staggered to her feet. She cursed again as glass bit deep into her heel; blood dripped hot and sticky down her instep. The burning thing was gone, and so was the bird.

Salem limped back to the house as quickly as she could.

FOR TWO days she watched and listened but caught no sign of ghosts or anything else. She picked up the broken glass and replaced the shattered bottle, brushed away the soot and charred leaves. The tree was old and strong; it would survive.

At night she dreamed.

She dreamed of a lake of tears, of fire that ate the moon. She dreamed of ropes that bit her flesh, of shining chains. She dreamed of trains. She dreamed of a snake who gnawed the roots of the world.

On the third day, a bird landed on the kitchen windowsill. It watched her through the screen with one colorless round eye and fluffed ragged feathers.

Salem paused, soapsuds clinging to her hands, and met its gaze. Her shoulder blades prickled.

It held a piece of orange paper crumpled in one pale talon.

"Be careful," she said after a moment. "There are a lot of cats out there."

The bird stared at her and let out a low, chuckling caw. "The circus is in town. Come see the show." White wings unfurled and it flapped away. The paper fluttered like an orange leaf as it fell.

Salem turned to see her big marmalade tomcat sitting on the kitchen table, fur all on end. He bared his teeth for a long steam-kettle hiss before circling three times and settling down with his head on his paws. She glanced through the screen door, but the bird was gone and the bottles rattled empty in the sticky-cool October breeze.

That night she dreamed of thunder, of blood leaking through white cloth, shining black in the moonlight. No portent, just an old nightmare. She woke trembling, tears cold on her cheeks.

The next morning she wove spells and chains. She threaded links of copper and silver and bronze and hung them with shimmering glass, each bead a bottlesnare. They hung cool around her neck, a comforting weight that chimed when she moved.

As the sun vanished behind the ceiling of afternoon clouds, Salem went to see the circus.

THE CIRCUS Fabulatoris sprawled across the county fairgrounds, a glittering confusion of lights and tents and spinning rides. The wind smelled of grease and popcorn and sugar—Salem bit her lip to stop her eyes from stinging.

It had been five years; it shouldn't feel like coming home.

She didn't recognize any faces along the midway, smiled and ignored the shouts to *play a game, win a prize, step right up only a dollar*. Ezra would be preaching by now, calling unsuspecting rubes to Heaven. Jack would be in the big top—which wasn't very big at all—announcing the acrobats and sword-swallowers. He'd have a parrot or a monkey on his shoulder. It was Tuesday, so probably the monkey.

She found a little blue tent, painted with shimmering stripes of color like the northern lights. *Madame Aurora*, the sign read, *fortunes told, futures revealed*.

Candlelight rippled across the walls inside, shimmered on beaded curtains and sequined scarves. Incense hung thick in the air, dragon's blood and patchouli.

"Come in, child," a woman's French-accented voice called, hidden behind sheer draperies, "come closer. I see the future and the past. I have the answers you seek."

Salem smiled. "That accent still ain't fooling anyone."

Silence filled the tent.

"Salem?" Shadows shifted behind the curtain, and a blonde head peered around the edge. Blue eyes widened. "Salem!"

Madame Aurora rushed toward her in a flurry of scarves and bangles and crushed Salem in a tea-rose-scented hug.

"Oh my god, Jerusalem! Goddamnit, honey, you said you'd write me, you said you'd call." Paris gave way to Savannah as Raylene Meadows caught Salem by the shoulders and shook her. She stopped shaking and hugged again, tight enough that her corset stays dug into Salem's ribs.

"Are you back?" Ray asked, finally letting go. "Are you going on with us?"

Salem's heart sat cold as glass in her chest. "No, sweetie. I'm just visiting. A little bird thought I should stop by." She looked around the tent, glanced at Ray out of the corner of one eye. "Has Jack started using a white crow?"

Ray stilled for an instant, eyes narrowing. "No. No, that's Jacob's bird."

"Jacob?"

"He's a conjure man. We picked him up outside of Memphis." Her lips curled in that little smile that meant she was sleeping with someone, and still enjoying it.

"Maybe I should meet him."

"Have you come back to steal another man from me?"

Salem cocked an eyebrow. "If I do, will you help me bury the body?"

Ray flinched, like she was the one who had nightmares about it. Maybe she did. Then she met Salem's eyes and smiled. "I will if you need me to."

"Where can I find Jacob?"

Ray's jaw tightened. "In his trailer, most likely. He's between acts right now. It's the red one on the far end of the row."

"Thanks. And…don't tell Jack or Ezra I'm here, okay? Not yet."

"You gonna see them before you disappear again?"

"Yeah. I'll try." Laughing voices approached outside. "Better put that bad accent back on."

The wind shifted as she left the cluster of tents and booths, and she caught the tang of lightning. Magic. The real thing, not the little spells and charms she'd taught Ray so many years ago.

Jack had always wanted a real magician. But what did a carnival conjurer have to do with her dreams, or the angry thing that so easily broke free of a spelled bottle?

She followed the tire-rutted path to a trailer painted in shades of blood and rust. A pale shadow flitted through the clouds and drifted down to perch on the roof. The crow watched Salem approach, but stayed silent.

Careless humming inside broke off as Salem knocked. A second later the door swung open to frame a man's shadowed face and shirtless shoulder.

"Hello." He ran a hand through a shock of salt and cinnamon curls. "What can I do for you?" His voice was smoke and whiskey, rocks being worn to sand. But not the crow's voice.

"Are you Jacob?"

"Jacob Grim, magician, conjurer, and prestidigitator, at your service."

"That's an interesting bird you have there."

His stubbled face creased in a coyote's smile. "That she is. Why don't you step inside, Miss…"

"Jerusalem." He offered a hand and she shook it. His grip was strong, palm dry and callused. She climbed the metal stairs and stepped into the narrow warmth of the trailer.

Jacob turned away and the lamplight fell across his back. Ink covered his skin, black gone greenish with age. A tree rose against his spine, branches spreading across his shoulders and neck, roots disappearing below the waist of his pants.

He caught her staring and grinned. "Excuse my *dishabille*. I'm just getting ready for my next act." He shrugged on a white shirt and did up the buttons with nimble fingers. The hair on his chest was nearly black, spotted with red and gray—calico colors. Ray usually liked them younger and prettier, but Salem could see the appeal.

"How may I help you, Miss Jerusalem?"

She cocked her head, studied him with *otherwise* eyes. His left eye gleamed with witchlight and magic sparked through the swirling dark colors of his aura. The real thing, all right.

"Your bird invited me to see the show."

"And see it you certainly should. It's a marvelous display of magic and legerdemain, if I do say so myself." He put on a black vest and jacket, slipping cards and scarves into pockets and sleeves.

"Actually, I was hoping you might have an answer or two for me."

He smiled. Not a coyote—something bigger. A wolf's smile. "I have as many answers as you have questions, my dear. Some of them may even be true." He smoothed back his curls and pulled on a black hat with a red feather in the band.

The door swung open on a cold draft before Salem could press. A young girl stood outside, maybe nine or ten. Albino-pale in the gray afternoon light, the hair streaming over her shoulders nearly as white as her dress. Salem shivered as the breeze rushed past her, much colder than the day had been.

"Time to go," she said to Jacob. Her voice was low for a child's and rough. She turned and walked away before he could answer.

"Your daughter?" Salem asked.

"Not mine in blood or flesh, but I look after her. Memory is my assistant." He laid a hand on her arm, steering her gently toward the door. "Come watch the show, Jerusalem, and afterwards perhaps I'll invent some answers for you."

SHE SAT in the front row in the big top and watched Jacob's show. He pulled scarves from his sleeves and birds from his hat—Jack's parrots, not the white crow. He conjured flowers for the ladies, read men's minds. He pulled a blooming rose from behind Salem's ear and presented it with a wink and a flourish. Velvet-soft and fragrant when she took it, but when she looked again it was made of bronze, tight-whorled petals warming slowly to her hand.

He tossed knives at Memory and sawed her in half. She never spoke, never blinked. It was hard to tell in the dizzying lights, but Salem was fairly sure the girl didn't cast a shadow.

She watched the crowd, saw the delight on their faces. Jack had wanted an act like this for years.

But not all the spectators were so amused. A man lingered in the shadows, face hidden beneath the brim of a battered hat. Salem tried to read his aura, but a rush of heat made her eyes water, leaking tears down tingling cheeks. The smell of char filled her nose, ashes and hot metal. When her vision cleared, he was gone.

AFTER THE show, she caught up with Jacob at his trailer. Ray was with him, giggling and leaning on his arm. She sobered when she saw Salem. The two of them had given up on jealousy a long time ago; Salem wondered what made the other woman's eyes narrow so warily.

"Excuse me, my dear," Jacob said to Ray, detaching himself gently from her grip. "I promised Jerusalem a conversation."

Ray paused to brush a kiss across Salem's cheek before she opened the trailer door. "Try not to shoot this one," she whispered.

"I'm not making any promises," Salem replied with a smile.

She and Jacob walked in silence, away from the lights and noise to the edge of the fairgrounds, where the ground sloped down through a tangle of brush and trees toward the shore of White Bear Lake. The water sprawled toward the horizon, a black mirror in the darkness. She made out a bone-pale spire on the edge of the water—a ruined church, the only building left of the ghost town the lake had swallowed.

Jacob pulled out a cigarette case and offered Salem one. She took it, though she hadn't smoked in years. Circuses, cigarettes, strange men—she was relearning all sorts of bad habits today. He cupped his hands around a match and she leaned close; he smelled of musk and clean salt sweat. Orange light traced the bones of his face as he lit his own.

"So, witch, ask your questions."

She took a drag and watched the paper sear. "Who is the burning man?"

"Ah." Smoke shimmered as he exhaled. "An excellent question, and one deserving of an interesting answer." He turned away, broken-nosed profile silhouetted against the fairground lights.

"These days he's a train man—conductor and fireman and engineer, all in one. He runs an underground railroad, but not the kind that sets men free." His left eye glinted as he glanced at her. "Have you, perchance, noticed a dearth of spirits in these parts?"

Salem shivered, wished she'd thought to wear a coat. Jacob shrugged his jacket off and handed it to her. "This train man is taking the ghosts? Taking them where?"

"Below. Some he'll use to stoke the furnace, others to quench his thirst. And any that are left when he reaches the station he'll give to his masters."

"What are they?"

"Nothing pleasant, my dear, nothing pleasant at all."

"What do you have to do with this?"

"I've been tracking him. I nearly had him in Mississippi, but our paths parted—he follows the rails, and the Circus keeps to the freeways."

"So it was just bad luck he got caught in my bottle tree?"

"Your good luck that he left you in peace. He hunts ghosts, but I doubt he'd scruple to make one if he could."

"So why the invitation?"

He smiled. "A witch whose spells can trap the Conductor, even for a moment, is a powerful witch indeed. You could be of no little help to me."

"I'm not in the business of hunting demons, or ghosts."

"You keep a bottle tree."

"It was my grandmother's. And it keeps them away. I like my privacy."

"He'll be going back soon with his load. The end of the month."

"Halloween."

He nodded. "That's all the time those souls have left, before they're lost."

"I'm sorry for them." She dropped her cigarette, crushed the ember beneath her boot. "I really am. And I wish you luck. But it's not my business."

"He takes children."

Salem laughed, short and sharp, and tossed his jacket back to him. "You don't know my buttons to press them."

He grinned and stepped closer, his warmth lapping against her. "I'd like to find them."

"I bet you would. Good night, Jacob. I enjoyed the show." She turned and walked away.

THAT NIGHT Salem drifted in and out of restless sleep. No dreams to keep her up tonight, only the wind through the window, light as a thief, and the hollowness behind her chest. A dog howled somewhere in the distance while she tossed in her cold bed.

Six years this winter since she'd come back to nurse her grandmother through the illnesses of age that not even their witchery could cure, until Eliza finally died, leaving Salem her house, her bottle tree, and all the spells she knew. Years of sleeping alone, of selling bottles and beads and charms and seeing living folk once a week at best.

We'll always work best alone, her grandmother had said. Salem had been willing to believe it. She'd had her fill of people—circus lights and card tricks, grifting and busking. The treachery of the living, the pleas and the threats of the dead. Dangerous men and their smiles. Living alone seemed so much easier, if it meant she never had to scrub blood and gunpowder from her hands again, never had to dig a shallow grave at the edge of town.

But she wasn't sure she wanted to spend another six years alone.

OCTOBER WORE on and the leaves of the bottle tree rattled and drifted across the yard. Salem carved pumpkins and set them to guard her porch, though no children ever came so far trick-or-treating. She wove metal and glass and silk to sell in town. She wove spells.

The moon swelled, and by its milksilver light she scried the rain barrel. The water showed her smoke and flame and church bells and her own pale reflection.

A week after she'd visited the circus, someone knocked on her door. Salem looked up from her beads and spools of wire and shook her head.

Jacob stood on her front step, holding his hat in his hands. His boots were dusty, jacket slung over one shoulder. He grinned his wolf's grin. "Good afternoon, ma'am. I wondered if I might trouble you for a drink of water."

Salem's eyes narrowed as she fought a smile. "Did you walk all this way?"

"I was in the mood for a stroll, and a little bird told me you lived hereabouts." He raised ginger brows. "Does your privacy preclude hospitality, or are you going to ask me in?"

She sighed. "Come inside."

The bone charm over the door shivered just a little as he stepped inside, but that might have been the wind. She led him to the kitchen, aware of his eyes on her back as they crossed the dim and creaking hall.

The cat stood up on the table as they entered, orange hackles rising. Salem tensed, wondered if she'd made a mistake after all. But Jacob held out one hand and the tom walked toward him, pausing at the edge of the table to sniff the outstretched fingers. After a moment his fur settled and he deigned to let the man scratch his ears.

"What's his name?" Jacob asked.

"Vengeance Is Mine Sayeth the Lord. You can call him Vengeance, though I'm pretty sure he thinks of himself as the Lord."

Jacob smiled, creasing the corners of autumn-gray eyes; his smile made her shiver, not unpleasantly.

"Sit down," she said. "Would you like some coffee, or tea?"

"No, thank you. Water is fine."

She filled a glass and set the pitcher on the table amidst all her bottles and beads. Vengeance sniffed it and decided he'd rather have what was in his bowl. Jacob drained half the glass in one swallow.

"Nice tree." He tilted his stubbled chin toward the back yard, where glass gleamed in the tarnished light. He picked up a strand of opalite beads from the table; they shimmered like tears between his blunt fingers. "Very pretty. Are you a jeweler too?"

She shrugged, leaning one hip against the counter. "I like to make things. Pretty things, useful things."

"Things that are pretty and useful are best." He ran a hand down the curve of the sweating pitcher and traced a design on the nicked tabletop. Salem shuddered at a cold touch on the small of her back.

Her lips tightened. Vengeance looked up from his bowl and rumbled like an engine. He leapt back on the table, light for his size, and sauntered toward Jacob. Big orange paws walked right through the damp design and Salem felt the charm break.

"Did you think you could come into my house and 'witch' me?"

"I could try."

"You'll have to try harder than that."

"I will, won't I."

He stood and stepped toward her. Salem stiffened, palms tingling, but she didn't move, even when he leaned into her, hands braced against the counter on either side. His lips brushed hers, cold at first but warming fast. The salt-sweet taste of him flooded her mouth and her skin tightened.

After a long moment he pulled away, but Salem still felt his pulse in her lips. Her own blood pounded like surf in her ears.

His scarred hands brushed the bottom of her shirt. "You said something about buttons…"

"WILL YOU help me?" he asked later, in the darkness of her bedroom. The smell of him clung to her skin, her sheets, filled her head till it was hard to think of anything else.

Salem chuckled, her head pillowed on his shoulder. "You think that's all it takes to change my mind?"

"All? You want more?"

She ran her fingers over his stomach; scars spiderwebbed across his abdomen, back and front, like something had torn him open. Older, fainter scars crosshatched his arms. Nearly every inch of him was covered in ink and cicatrices.

"Is prestidigitation such dangerous work?"

"It is indeed." He slid a hand down the curve of her hip, tracing idle patterns on her thigh. "But not unrewarding."

"What will you do if you catch this demon of yours?"

He shrugged. "Find another one. The world is full of thieves and predators and dangerous things."

"Things like you?"

"Yes." His arms tightened around her, pressing her close. "And like you, my dear." She stiffened, but his fingers brushed her mouth before she could speak. "Tell me you're not a grifter, Jerusalem."

"I gave it up," she said at last.

"And you miss it. You're alone out here, cold and empty as those bottles."

She snorted. "And you think you're the one to fill me?"

His chuckle rumbled through her. "I wouldn't presume. Raylene misses you, you know. The others do too. Wouldn't you be happier if you came back to the show?"

The glass in her chest cracked, a razorline fracture of pain. "You don't know what would make me happy," she whispered.

Callused fingers trailed up the inside of her thigh. "I can learn."

HE ROSE from her bed at the first bruise of dawn. "Will you think about it, if nothing else?" Cloth rustled and rasped in the darkness as he dressed.

"I'll think about it." She doubted she'd be able to do anything else.

"We're here through Sunday. The circus and the train." He stamped his boots on and leaned over the bed, a darker shadow in the gloom.

"I know." She stretched up to kiss him, stubble scratching her already-raw lips.

Her bed was cold when he was gone. She lay in the dark, listening to hollow chimes.

SALEM SPENT the day setting the house in order, sweeping and dusting and checking all the wards. Trying not to think about her choices.

She'd promised her grandmother that she'd stay, settle down and look after the house. No more running off chasing midway lights, no more trouble. It had been an easy promise as Eliza lay dying, Salem's heart still sore with guns and graves, with the daughter she'd lost in a rush of blood on a motel bathroom floor.

She didn't want to go through that again. But she didn't want to live alone and empty, either.

The bird came after sundown, drifting silent from the darkening sky. The cat stared and hissed as she settled on the back step, his ears flat against his skull.

"Come with me, witch. We need you."

"Hello, Memory. I thought I had until Sunday."

"We were wrong." The girl lifted a bone-white hand, but couldn't cross the threshold. "We're out of time."

Salem stared at the ghost girl. Older than her daughter would have been. Probably a blessing for the lost child anyway—she had a witch's heart, not a mother's.

The child vanished, replaced by a fluttering crow. "There's no time, witch. Please."

Vengeance pressed against her leg, rumbling deep in his chest. Salem leaned down to scratch his ears. "Stay here and watch the house."

As she stepped through the door, the world shivered and slipped sideways. She walked down the steps under a seething black sky. The tree glowed against the shadows, a shining thing of ghostlight and jewels. Beyond the edge of her yard the hills rolled sere and red.

"Where are we going?" she asked Memory.

"Into the Badlands. Follow me, and mind you don't get lost." The bird took to the sky, flying low against heavy clouds. Salem fought the urge to look back, kept her eyes on the white-feathered shape as it led her north.

The wind keened across the hills and Salem shivered through her light coat. The trees swayed and clattered, stunted bone-pale things shedding leaves like ashes.

The moon rose slowly behind the clouds, swollen and rust-colored. Something strange about its light tonight, too heavy and almost sharp as it poured over Salem's skin. Then she saw the shadow nibbling at one edge and understood—an eclipse. She lengthened her stride across the dry red rock.

TIME PASSED strange in the deadlands, and they reached the end of the desert well before Salem could ever have walked to town. She paused on the crest of a ridge, the ground sloping into shadow below her. On the far side of the valley she saw the circus, shimmering bright enough to bridge the divide.

"No," Memory cawed as she started toward the lights. "We go down."

Salem followed the bird down the steep slope, boots slipping in red dust. A third of the moon had been eaten by the rust-colored shadow.

Halfway down she saw the buildings, whitewashed walls like ivory in the darkness. A church bell tolled the hour as they reached the edge of town. Memory croaked along with the sour notes.

Shutters rattled over blind windows and paint peeled in shriveled strips. The bird led her to a nameless bar beside the train tracks. Jacob waited inside, leaning against the dust-shrouded counter.

Salem crossed her arms below her breasts. "You said Sunday."

"I was wrong. It's the burning moon he wants, not Hallow's Eve." Witchlight glowed cold in the lamps, glittering against cobwebbed glass. His eyes were diffcrent colors in the unsteady glow.

"Where is he now?"

"On his last hunt. He'll be back soon."

"What do you need me for?"

He touched the chain around her throat; links rattled softly. "Distraction. Bait. Whatever's needed."

She snorted. "That's what Memory's for too, isn't she? That's why he was watching your act. You're a real bastard, aren't you?"

"You have no idea."

She reached up and brushed the faint web of scars on his left cheek. "How'd you lose your eye?"

He grinned. "I didn't lose it. I know exactly where it is."

Memory drifted through the door. "He's coming."

Jacob's smile fell away and he nodded. "Wait by the train station. Be sure he sees you."

"What's the plan?"

"I had a plan, when I thought we had until Sunday. It was a good plan, I'm sure you would have appreciated it. Now I have something more akin to a half-assed idea."

Salem fought a smile and lost. "So what's the half-assed idea?"

"Memory distracts him at the train station. We ambush him, tie him up, and set the trapped ghosts free."

"Except for the part where my charms won't hold him for more than a few minutes, that's a great idea."

"We won't mention that part. Come on."

A TRAIN sprawled beside the station platform, quiet as a sleeping snake. Its cars were black and tarnished silver, streaked with corrosion, and the cowcatcher gleamed fang-sharp.

Jacob and Salem waited in the shadows of the empty platform. She could barely make out the words White Bear on the cracked and mildewed sign.

"They built this town for the train," she whispered, her face close enough to Jacob's to feel his breath. "But the Texas and Pacific never came, and the town dried up and blew away."

"This is a hard country. Even gods go begging here."

Footsteps echoed through the silent station. A moment later Salem heard a child's sniffling tears. Then the Conductor came into view.

A tall man, dressed like his name, black hat pulled low over his face. Even across the platform Salem felt the angry heat of him, smelled ash and coal. A sack was slung over one broad shoulder; his other hand prisoned Memory's tiny wrist.

Salem swallowed, her throat gone dry, and undid the clasp around her neck. The chain slithered cold into her hand. Jacob's hand tightened on her shoulder once. He stepped into the moonlight.

"Trading in dead children now?" His growl carried through the still air. "You called yourself a warrior once."

The Conductor whirled, swinging Memory around like a doll. His face was dark in the shadow of his hat, but his eyes gleamed red.

Jacob took a step closer, bootheels thumping on warped boards. "You fought gods once, and heroes. Now you steal the unworthy dead." He cocked his head. "And didn't you used to be taller?"

"You!" The Conductor's voice was a dry-bone rasp; Salem shuddered at the sound. "You died! I saw you fall. The wolf ripped you open."

Jacob laughed. "It's harder than that to kill me."

"We'll see about that." He released Memory and dropped the bag as he lunged for Jacob.

Memory crawled away, cradling her wrist to her chest. The chain rattled in Salem's hand as she moved. Jacob and the Conductor grappled near the edge of the platform and she had no clear shot.

Then Jacob fell, sprawling hard on the floor. The Conductor laughed as he stood over him. "I'll take you and the witch as well as the dead. The things below will be more than pleased."

Salem darted in, the chain lashing like a whip. It coiled around his throat and he gasped. His heat engulfed her, but she hung on.

"You can't trap me in a bottle, little witch." His eyes burned red as embers. Char-black skin cracked as he moved, flashing molten gold beneath. A glass bead shattered against his skin; another melted and ran like a tear.

She pulled the chain tighter—it wouldn't hold much longer. The Conductor caught her arm in one huge black hand and she screamed as her flesh seared.

"Didn't the old man tell you, woman? His companions always die. Crows will eat your eyes—if I don't boil them first."

A fury of white feathers struck him, knocking off his hat as talons raked his face. The Conductor cursed, batting the bird aside, and Salem drove a boot into his knee.

He staggered on the edge for one dizzying instant, then fell, taking Salem with him. Breath rushed out of her as they landed, his molten heat burning through her clothes. Her vision blurred and White Bear Valley spun around in a chiaroscuro swirl.

"Jerusalem!" She glanced up, still clinging to the chain. Jacob leapt off the platform, landing lightly in a puff of dust. "Hold your breath!"

She realized what was coming as he stuck his fingers into the ground and pulled the world open.

White Bear Lake crashed in to fill the void.

"**WAKE UP,** witch. You're no use to me drowned."

She came to with a shudder, Jacob's mouth pressed over hers, his breath inside her. She gasped, choked, rolled over in time to vomit up a bellyful of bitter lake water. Her vision swam red and black as she collapsed onto weed-choked mud. Cold saturated her, icy needles tingling through her fingers.

"Did he drown?" she asked, voice cracking.

"His kind don't like to swim." He turned her over, propping her head on his soaking knees. "I could say it destroyed him, if that's how you'd like this to end." Above them the shadow eased, the moon washing clean and white again.

"What could you say if I wanted the truth?"

Jacob's glass eye gleamed as he smiled. "That it weakened him, shattered that shape. He lost the train and its cargo. That's enough for me tonight."

"Not too bad, for a half-assed idea." She tried to sit up and thought better of it. The cold retreated, letting her feel the burns on her arm and hands. "Are you going to thank me?"

He laughed and scooped her into his arms. "I might." He carried her up the hill, toward the circus lights.

HALLOWEEN DAWNED cool and gray. Glass chimed in the breeze as Salem untied the bottles one by one, wrapping them in silk and laying them in boxes. The tree looked naked without them.

The wind gusted over the empty hills, whistled past the eaves of the house. The tree shook, and the only sound was the scrape and rustle of dry leaves.

"Sorry, Grandma," she whispered as she wrapped the last bottle. Light and hollow, cold in her hands. "I'll come back to visit."

When she was done, Jerusalem Morrow packed a bag and packed her cat, and ran away to join the circus.

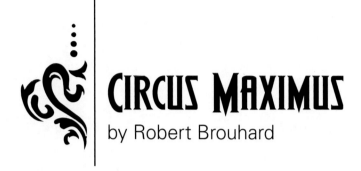

CIRCUS MAXIMUS

by Robert Brouhard

The dust motes whirl before Timothy's fascinated eyes as the pendulum swing of the trapeze hypnotizes him. The ringmaster's words make no purchase in his ears as the calliope-filled circus-world around him slips away. He hopes she won't fall, and he clenches his father's arm tighter.

TIMOTHY IS unsure about the darkness inside the colorful circus tent, but his father seems excited. So, he follows. "I haven't been to one of these since I was your age," he tells the boy when they slip into the dimly lit tent. The only light seems to come from the open flaps. "You weren't old enough to go the last time the circus came to Goldville, but I'm glad we can share this together now." He musses his son's black hair, and the boy quickly smooths it back into place while giving his dad a reproachful look. "I'm just glad that Oregon's liquid sunshine stopped before the circus arrived." Timothy's father laughs at his own joke and looks around the tent.

They find a seat easily in the back row, and Timothy looks back at the trail their feet made in the hay and dirt. His eyes follow it toward the entrance of the tent where the flaps are shut by two tough-looking men. He watches as the sunbeams, enhanced by swirling dust, disappear as if they never existed in the first place. Darkness swallows the world. Then a spotlight blinds him. Timothy snaps his head away and spots swim in front of his eyes. He blinks and sees the spotlight move. It stops on a man dressed in a bright-blue tailcoat with flashy gold trim like a light cavalry man in his picture books. He expected a red tailcoat, but he still finds it fascinating. Blackness surrounds the audience and all that can be seen is in the spotlight.

The seven-year-old boy holds his father's hand tightly in anticipation as the ringmaster begins.

"Ladies and gentlemen, boys and girls, welcome to Circus Maximus. The most prodigious of its kind in the entire world." The dazzling man gestures wildly as he speaks.

Timothy tugs at his father's shirtsleeve and asks, "What's prod...*prodjus*, Daddy?"

"*Biggest*, but please be quiet," his father whispers as he gives the boy a stern but friendly look.

Timothy looks up and sees that the ringmaster is looking right at him. The tall man smiles and winks. Timothy smiles weakly back, but a chill runs up his back. Something isn't right about the man's eyes and smile. They seem...*crooked?* No. Something else.

"And now the clowns!"

Timothy perks up and squints. He watches as the clowns come out. The ringmaster makes exaggerated comments about their training and their outfits' materials including silks from the "deepest darkest Orient." Timothy tries to ignore the ringmaster's long-winded speeches as he wishes they were closer to the action. He gets mesmerized by the clowns running around, smiles, and lets go of his father's hand.

BEHIND TIMOTHY and his father, Ammon moves in the dark between the last row and the back of the tent. He hasn't been with the circus for long, but he knows what he wants.

No one sees or hears him as he silently moves closer to Timothy and his father.

"WATCH NOW ladies and gentlemen, boys and girls, as the Amazing Egyptian goddess Berenike makes her way up to the deadly flying trapeze!" The ringmaster's white-gloved hand gestures to the oscillating bar and the high platform that Berenike is climbing her way up to. "The daredevil Berenike has trained tirelessly to master this acrobatic art. Just as Jules Léotard performed in the Cirque Napoleon in the 1860s, observe as this daring young lady 'flies through the air with the greatest of ease.'" The ringmaster's wide white smile breaks through. Timothy's eyes stare at the ringmaster's mouth.

Pointy? Is that it? thinks Timothy. He looks away and he stares back at Berenike. She looks naked—golden brown and shining in the spotlight at the top of her platform.

Ammon moves closer.

"Is she really gonna do it, Daddy?" Timothy whispers. His father lifts a finger to his lips to shush him.

"As you can see, we have no net. For we are a humble and diminutive circus," the ringmaster continues. Timothy gasps when he realizes that Berenike could fall—and he's about to ask what diminutive means—when he looks at his father, who has a strange smile on his face. Why would his father smile at her peril? Timothy's question is lost as he looks back at the swinging trapeze.

Ammon knows his time to strike is about to happen.

Berenike steps to the ledge. The horizontal bar swings toward her and away, toward her and away. Finally, she jumps.

She misses.

The crowd gasps and many stand staring in shock as Berenike crashes to the ground. Her brown body unmoving.

Ammon strikes Timothy's neck. His face spreads monstrously as two saw-like appendages spring from his mouth and tear open Timothy's skin. Two hideous needle-like tubes extend and pierce into the hole and Ammon begins his feeding on the blood he's been craving to his inner core.

"Ladies and gentlemen! I am so sorry. This has never happened before. A medical team has been called and will arrive shortly. Please exit slowly and safely."

The crowd murmurs and leads their children out.

Timothy's father looks at his son. Timothy is still. His eyes are unblinking as they stare at Berenike. A tear rolls down and splashes on his shirt collar.

Then Berenike hops up and exits as if nothing happened. Timothy blinks in astonishment and a smile creeps up his face and becomes an excited grin.

"Look! She's all right, Dad!"

"That she is. Who'd of thunk it."

The ringmaster appears next to them making them both jump. He towers over them and looks down at Timothy. "Of course she's all right, my boy.

ROBERT BROUHARD

It's all part of our spectacular show, but don't tell your friends the secret. Now run along."

TIMOTHY AND his father exit following the 10 other spectators that had filled the four bench seats in the small tent. Many are scratching the backs of their necks as they pass a brightly painted sandwich-board sign:

CIRCUS MAXIMUS: THE FLEA CIRCUS
Come one and all!
See our astounding collection of exotic
Oriental Xenopsylla cheopis as they
perform death-defying acts of bravery
and amuse you with their zany antics!
Bring the whole family!
NO PETS ALLOWED!

Inside the tent, the ringmaster smiles as Ammon and his eleven brothers hop back to him. "Well done. Now, get ready for the second show." He opens a wooden box filled with diseased rats, and the fleas hop in with excitement. The bubonic plague has come to Goldville and the ringmaster's manager will be happy.

LAUGHABLE

by Dominick Cancilla

L ee couldn't kill someone, even if he wanted to, which he did. It wasn't for lack of trying. He'd bought a gun, he'd sweated in his car for days waiting for the right moment, and when it came he'd sat there, frozen, watching it pass him by. If Falco was going to die, Lee was going to have to get someone else to do it.

That Falco was a stain in need of bleaching was a fact not up for debate. Lee's grandfather had started his own business in a new country back when Chinese laundries were a thing, passing it to son to daughter to son until it was the little empire that ran smoothly and efficiently in Lee's hands. At least, it had run that way until Falco stuck his grimy finger in those well-oiled gears.

Then there had been unrest among employees who'd never had anything to complain about. There'd been a ridiculous investigation into waste disposal based on anonymous tips. There'd been a sudden rash of angry online reviews. Repair persons had begun "forgetting" to show up. Cash had gone missing.

And Falco had been there, every few weeks, offering to buy the whole lot "before things got too bad."

Fucking Falco. His every move was calculated to keep him free from provable blame, but Falco was a problem that a bullet could solve, even if the law couldn't.

So Lee had turned to professionals.

Hollywood implies there's a killer for hire in the shadowed corners of every bar, but in the real world it's incredibly difficult to find a hitman or mercenary. There are places on the dark web you can put out feelers, but if you know about them, it's a sure bet that the authorities know about them too. Seven times Lee had thought he'd made contact with someone promising, and seven times he'd backed out when the questions became too close to the mark or the supposed trigger man started to sound too eager. "Just to be clear, you're hiring me to kill someone, right?" "I'll meet you anywhere, no problem." "Sure, I've got rocket grenades." That had to be the cops, pretending, fishing, building a case. Lee just knew it.

Lee must have been doing an even worse job keeping under the radar than he thought he'd been, because one day he received a text from an obviously faked number instructing him to download an app and message a certain address. The app was one of those things that allowed you to send encrypted messages but wouldn't let you keep them. It wouldn't even allow you to take screenshots of them. When a message was sent, you had two minutes to read it, then it was gone for good.

Curious, Lee did as instructed. Less than a minute later, he had a message from someone calling himself "ThreeRing" offering to "hook him up" with a "major player" and promising "no gags, no bozos."

For once, this felt legitimate. In his bones, Lee knew this was the real thing, and what did he have to lose? Well, aside from his business, freedom, and maybe his life. He took the bait.

Soon, Lee was messaging through the app with someone who called himself Bangles. He claimed to have done jobs big and small all over the country as part of what he not-even-slightly humbly claimed to be the greatest band of mercenaries on Earth. Bangles proposed that they meet somewhere public for a face-to-face.

"You know THE Steak House?" Bangles asked. "2880 South Las Vegas Boulevard, near the end of the Strip."

Lee didn't know it but was sure he could find it. Vegas was less than a day's drive from L.A. He could do that.

"Friday then," Bangles confirmed. "Just you and me. No company. No shadows. No tricks. No guns. Be there at 4 and ask for me. Then wait."

"I should walk into a restaurant and ask for Bangles?" Lee asked, feeling that that might make him sound a little silly. He didn't get a response.

TWO DAYS later, Lee walked into a steak house inside a cheap casino hotel and asked the man at the front for Bangles. Expecting a smirk, confusion, or outright ridicule, Lee was surprised when the man simply maintained his frozen, professional smile and showed him to a booth in an empty private room in the back of the restaurant.

Lee waited about 20 minutes. Then in walked Bangles.

Bangles was a big man, at least six-foot four and dressed in a way that completely hid the true shape of his body. The one-piece outfit was of a loose, shiny material—silk, maybe?—all white with red and blue trim and three huge, red pompoms down the front like fuzzy buttons. The waist had some kind of hoop built in, making the man look ridiculously, misshapenly fat.

His hands were hidden by white gloves; his feet had been swallowed by garish red-and-yellow shoes big enough to have a side gig as flippers. His face was covered in white makeup aside from a broad red smile painted around an expressionless mouth, black lines highlighting his eyes and replacing his eyebrows, and a big, red, foam nose. Atop his bald head sat a conical party hat so small it must have been made for a doll.

"I'm Bangles," said the man, sounding like James Earl Jones trying to do a Betty Boop impression. "You 'The Cleaners?'"

That was indeed the name Lee had been using online, but he found that he'd temporarily misplaced the ability to speak. Was this a trick? A joke? What was going on here? There were too many possibilities for him to settle on a course of action.

"If you're chickening out, I'm gone," Bangles said. "Say the word."

That was enough to snap Lee out of it. "No, no," he said. "Not chickening." He started to stand up and extend his hand in greeting, but Bangles waved him back and went around the table. It took a couple of minutes for Bangles to wedge his tall self and giant hoop into the booth, and Lee couldn't decide if it really was that big a problem or if the man was making a production out of it.

When Bangles finally dropped into the seat, the moment was punctuated by the loud honk of a horn secreted somewhere Lee dared not guess. After the honk, there was silence. Lee attempted to fill it. "So," he said, but Bangles cut him off with a wave of the hand and a shake of his head.

A few silent minutes later, a waiter came in, bringing menus and taking drink orders. Wanting to keep his head clear, Lee ordered a Coke. Bangles ordered a piña colada in a coconut.

"After we order, then we talk," said Bangles when the waiter was out of earshot.

Lee decided on the prime rib with all the trimmings. Bangles got six orders of king crab legs and a shrimp cocktail. Apparently, he assumed Lee was paying.

Food ordered, Bangles got down to business. "So, what you got for me?" he asked.

The voice, the outfit, were impossible to take seriously, but the man's eyes—they were so cold and lifeless that Lee didn't dare even crack a smile. The thought that something was very wrong still nagged at Lee, though, and he was afraid to say anything incriminating until that was assuaged. Bangles could be hiding a whole 1960s-era police surveillance suite in that outfit.

"Well," Lee said, "before we get too far into this, I want to make sure there aren't any, you know, misunderstandings."

"You want someone dead," Bangles said, forced falsetto pushed into a half whisper. "Isn't that what we understand?"

"Yes, yes," Lee said.

"Then what? You want references?"

"Well—"

"This isn't a job where you get letters of recommendation."

"I know, but—"

"You hire me, the job gets done, you don't see me again. That's better for everyone, right?"

"Of course. I just—" He let his eyes flicker down to the bright pom-poms. "I want to make sure you're serious about this."

Bangles' glare somehow made his not responding seem like a cold slap with a wet fish. "Do I not look serious?" he said, pokerfaced aside from the broad, painted-on grin.

"Of course. Yes." Lee stammered. "Yes."

"Well then," Bangles said, retracting the glare, leaning back in his seat and honking once again. He made a little welcoming gesture. "What you got for me?"

Lee sighed and just let it out. "There's a man named Falco. He's been trying to weasel his way into my—"

"No, no, no," Bangles said. "I don't need no backstory. I just need to know how many, where, and what's in the way."

"Oh, of course." Lee reached into his pocket and pulled out a little envelope. He slid it across the table. "Here's his name and address. There's a picture of him and his house that I took, for reference."

"You shouldn't do that," Bangles said.

"Do what?"

"Hang 'round the house of some guy you're going to drop the bucket on. You don't want to be associated with that."

"Right. Of course."

Lee sat quietly while Bangles looked at what he'd been given and then squirreled it away somewhere in his voluminous clothes.

"I can do that," Bangles said after a little consideration. "It'll take planning to get into the house, though."

"I thought you could wait for him to come out. Do it on the street or something."

Bangles shook his head, making the little tassel atop his hat wiggle. "Nah. Too many chances for some rube seeing somethin' he shouldn't. That happens and you get into dusting witnesses—which is an extra charge, by the way. You don't want that."

"I don't want that," Lee parroted.

The food arrived.

Lee tried to continue their conversation, but Bangles made clear a very strict no-business-while-eating policy.

How the man managed to put away so much food without smearing his makeup Lee would never know.

Near the end of his steak, Lee dared break the silence. "If you don't mind my asking. I mean, if it isn't inappropriate. What's with the, you know, the—" he wiggled a finger at his own face.

"The scar?" Bangles asked, the coldness coming back into his eyes.

"No, no!" Lee hurried to say. "The makeup." He hadn't even noticed any scar.

"Right. That," Bangles said. "The face." He stuck a piece of crab in his mouth and chewed thoughtfully. "I'm comfortable this way," he said. "It gives me character. Lets the real me out, you know? Besides, if you saw me without it, would you recognize me? No, you would not. That's big in this business. Now I'm finishing and ordering a sundae. When I'm done, we settle up. Good?"

Lee agreed that it was.

When Lee's pie and Bangles' banana split with extra whipped cream and sprinkles was done and cleared away, coffee was served. Bangles asked, "Mind if I smoke?"

"I guess not," Lee said. "Does the restaurant allow that?"

"They don't care," Bangles said. He reached somewhere below the table and his hand came up with a cigar as long as Lee's forearm and as thick around in the middle as his wrist. Bangles stuck it in his mouth, left it unlit and, for the rest of the conversation, kept his teeth clenched so he could talk around it without it falling. "Let's get down to brass here."

Bangles pushed his cup and saucer to the side and leaned forward, getting as much in Lee's face as he could with the table between them. "This is a big job. You understand that, right?"

Lee nodded agreement.

"This guy's got security. You can see it from the pictures. There's a guard at the gate, which means guards inside. There's cameras on the walls. This isn't a baby elephant walk, right?"

Lee nodded agreement again, although without really knowing what he was agreeing to.

"That being the case, I know and you know that it's a buyer's market right now, there being kind of a glut on my side since the circus went belly up."

Lee laughed at that. It was a sudden burst, like a guffaw that had been suppressed and then forced out by a gut punch.

Bangles' hand shot across the table and grabbed a fistful of Lee's shirt front. "You laugh at that? You think my trying to make a living doing what I do is a joke? You think I'm trying to be funny?"

Lee was so, so, so close to saying yes. It was hard, it was so hard staring right into the face of a man in clown makeup and saying he didn't think he was trying to be funny. In the sudden heightened stress of the moment Lee didn't think he could do it, so he just shook his head vehemently.

"Good then," Bangles said, releasing the shirt to settle into a ball of wrinkles on Lee's chest.

"Like I was saying," Bangles continued, "it's a big job, but all things considered, I'm gonna cut you a deal."

Lee nodded, feeling a knot form in his stomach. "How much are we talking about?"

He really had no idea how much this was going to cost. In all his online conversations, he'd never gotten that far.

Bangles looked left and right as if checking to make sure nobody had snuck into their little room while he wasn't looking. Then he put a hand under the table and produced a little coin purse. He unzipped it, looked inside, frowned, turned it inside-out to show how empty it was, then turned it outside-in again. With thumb and forefinger, Bangles reached into the purse and pulled out a red handkerchief. Which was tied to a blue one. Which was tied to a yellow one. Then a green one, an orange one, a purple one, a pink one, and on, and on, and on, and on, for almost thirty seconds until there was a pile of handkerchief on the table beside him. It all ended in a black-and-white checkerboard handkerchief at the end of which was taped a piece of paper. Bangles detached the paper and slide it across the table to Lee.

On the paper was written a sum of money. A very large sum.

"That's, well—is that typical?" Lee asked.

"See it from my side," Bangles said. "This isn't a one-man blowoff some geek could toss out between chickens. I gotta take a troupe with me, and all those guys are going to need a little piece of the cake. And it's not just your guy we have to get, neither. Those guards aren't going to write their own punchlines. That's an all-inclusive number you got there."

Lee nodded. "In advance?" he asked.

"Nah," Bangles said. "Here's the thing. You're not hard to find. You try to stiff me, and we can run you down no problem and have a lot of laughs at your expense. That's why I can make it easy for you and let you pay afterward. Besides, there's another thing. You know Chuck E. Cheese's?"

Lee said he did. He'd gone to a nephew's birthday party at one once. Bad food, lame games, too much cake, insufferable noise—everything a six-year-old loves.

"Good," Bangles continued. "I don't want cash. I want it all in Chuck E. Cheese tokens. It's easier to launder."

Lee didn't know if that was a joke. Was that a joke? He hoped it was a joke.

"That going to be a problem?" Bangles asked.

Lee shook his head. Apparently, it wasn't a joke. He'd figure it out. Somehow.

"Good. So, how soon you want this done?"

"How soon can you do it?"

Bangles shrugged. "I say I need eight guys for this. I can get a crew in three days. We set up near the house, tap the phone, and wait for 'em to order pizza or something. Once they're expecting company, we head over there and when they open the gate, kaboom! We got 'em."

That didn't sound right to Lee. "How are you going to get them to open the gate?"

"I just said. They order a pizza or something and we pretend to be the delivery guy."

"In what? A van? Won't that look fishy?"

"What van? I've got an old VW Bug. It looks lame as hell. Nobody will suspect a thing."

"A Bug? For eight guys?"

"Yeah. No problem. Room to spare."

Lee decided to just let that go. One final practical matter still nagged at him. "What do I do if they connect you to me? Like, what if his business associates or the police figure out I hired you."

Bangles gave him a genuine smile. "You got nothing to worry about with the police. I run a strong show; the fix is in. Sure, you got to worry about getting it back in your face if someone figures out this was from you, but that's always the breaks. All I can tell you is that if someone comes after you, it won't be one of mine. Professional courtesy and all that. Okay?"

"Okay," Lee said. "We have a deal. What happens next?"

"What happens next," Bangles said, "is you go home and wait. When it's done, I'll contact you and give you a password along with info on where to deliver the coin. Got that?"

"I got it," Lee said, and after he settled the bill they went their separate ways.

ALMOST A week later, Lee was sitting on his couch reading the news on his iPad. Apparently, there'd been some kind of mass murder at a mansion in a nearby city the previous night. Police were baffled by the killings—almost a dozen dead, some suffocated by balloons pulled over their heads, some apparently bludgeoned to death with giant hammers, and some found lying on dry land but drowned by what the coroner identified as lungs full of seltzer.

Lee's business problems evaporated almost instantly. After receiving a brief message with the password ("Swordfish"), he made the payment to Bangles by way of a big-rig truck filled to the walls with fresh-minted arcade tokens.

Lee slept well that night and the night after, but a week after Falco had been wiped away Lee came home to find a little envelope on his entry floor, apparently slipped beneath the door. Inside was a small card with just two words written on it: "We know."

He'd been made. Falco's people knew what he'd done and they were coming after him. What could he do? Where could he turn?

Lee could only think of one possible solution. Grabbing his phone, he touched the secure message app and sent a message: "Do you have a bodyguard available?"

A minute later a response appeared. "Sure," ThreeRing said. "How do you feel about lions?"

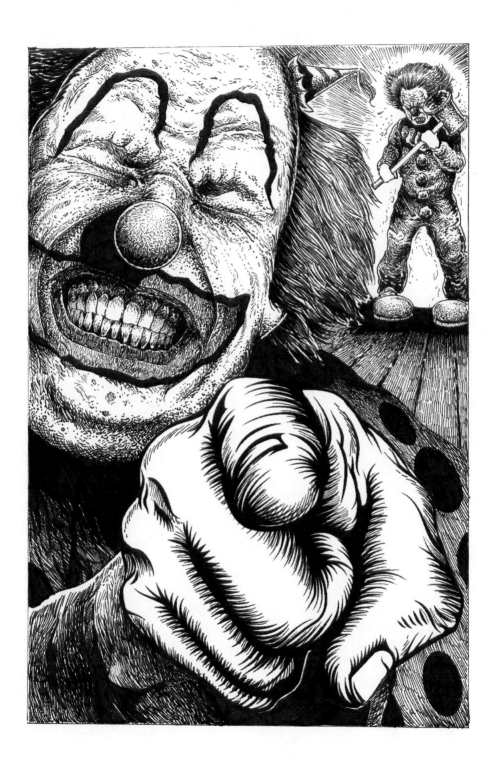

Count Zardov's Circus and Museum of Terrifying Grotesques

by Heather Graham

1980
The Middle of Nowhere, America

Shelley

"And now! A feat of death-defying showmanship that will leave you breathless!" Count Zardov, resplendent in his hat and red ringmaster's jacket made the announcement.

And then...

Zack flew.

Yes.

He flew through the air with the greatest of ease.

And Shelley sighed inwardly, aware that she was madly in love with the daring young man on the flying trapeze.

She was equally aware that there was no hope for her.

Handsome, virile young men like Zack Gregor didn't fall in love with young women like her. In fact, if he were to fall in love with anyone, it would be Zelda—the amazing blonde beauty who worked the trapeze along with him.

The woman was now flying through the air as well, to be caught by Zack's incredibly strong hands.

Shelley could only imagine being touched by hands like that.

The night's show was almost over. Still, she clung to the curtain watching as Zack and Zelda finished up the evening's last act.

Shelley turned away before they spectacularly ended with one of their triple-exchanges—something that brought the audience to their feet. The two would hold hands and bow.

Shelley didn't need to see it.

Jerry—the big cat trainer and incredible performer—would be feeding his two tigers and bedding them down for the night. Jerry was fantastic with the creatures—the tigers adored him. There were just two of them, and Jerry never needed any help.

But Mort would need help bedding the six horses down for the night; and while she wasn't required to help him in any way, she was happy to do so. Mort was kind to her—and the horses loved her in a way people never would.

They didn't care about the thick hair that covered her lower cheeks and jaw.

To be fair, she was only surviving because of the hair on her face. She'd been left in the hay at "Count Zardov's Circus and Museum of Terrifying Grotesques" when she'd been just a baby. Nordica, the old gypsy telling fortunes back then, had taken her in.

Nordica was gone now; she'd foreseen her own death at the age of eighty, and when the time had come, Shelley had held her tenderly in her arms while she had breathed her last.

And now...

While Zack and Zelda were applauded for their talent and grace, it was the "Terrifying Grotesques" who had made the show so incredibly popular.

A "grotesque" herself, Shelley wasn't sure she'd ever understand the fascination people seemed to have for those who were *odd* or *different*. Of course, there were those in the world who decried the freak shows, and Shelley felt a pride and warmth in her heart for those members of humanity.

And then again...

Without the freak shows, what would she, and others, do for a living—for survival?

Shelley walked on out of the great tent and headed toward one of the secondary tents—where Mort tended to the horses. He was just removing the harness from Great Zeus, the giant silver percheron gelding that carried General Washington—their obligatory "little person"—through the ring as the show opened.

"I'll brush him down!" Shelley offered, hurrying forward.

"Ah, Shelley, you don't have to be doing that—you worked your shift beautifully before the show began—people love you, you know. Zardov did a good thing, letting old Nordica raise you. Hey, lots of shows have bearded ladies—but how many have bearded ladies who dance and do acrobatics for the crowd while singing Irish ditties?"

"I like helping you, Mort—and I love the horses," she said.

She was, she knew, a popular "attraction." Nordica had woven a tale about her birth. Her mother had been an Irish princess who had fallen in love with a wolfman—and because their love had been forbidden, they had left her with Nordica who would care for her tenderly.

The story was rot—she was certain. But because of it, she'd learned old Irish tavern songs, and how to act out a few old tales along with a bit of dancing and singing while she did so. She was popular, yes.

She was still a freak—not the kind of girl a golden god like Zack might love.

She knew; she understood. She still loved from afar.

Great Zeus nudged her; he knew she carried apple bits for him and the other horses. She laughed and let him have his treat, and then she set to work.

It was just about time to head to her tent to get some sleep.

She was, of course, quartered with the rest of the "freaks." They included Harry, their wolfman, plagued by an abundance of hair over his entire body; Victoria, their vampire queen, born with a pair of canine teeth that could put any fanged serpent to shame; Frank, their monster, a man simply so huge and hideous that he could terrify the most stalwart man; Mom, their mummy, a poor woman so wretchedly burned in a fire that her skin now resembled ancient wrapping; Swampman, Larry, a good seven feet in height and afflicted with a disease that had left his skin with a scale-like appearance; and General George Washington, a young man whose growth pattern had allowed him to be a bare two-feet plus.

There had been others through the years—many whose strange defects had also brought about premature death. But these days, she, Harry, Victoria, Frank, Mom, Larry, and General George Washington were the "terrifying grotesques." Shelley didn't see herself as particularly terrifying—nor could that be said of General George. But the others had acts in which they pretended to try to break through the bars separating them from the crowds who came to ooh and aah—and jump back in terror. Often Victoria, playing a great vampire, would hypnotize someone planted in the audience, drawing them nearer and nearer until Count Zardov—really Lou Goldstein from Milwaukee—would intercede with a cross and a stake sending her cowering to a corner—simply hissing.

Frank was tamed with a fiery torch, as was Mom. Alligator guns were kept in order to keep Larry under control, and the wolfman was tamed with the threat of a sliver bullet.

While self-styled Count Zardov thought the freaks belonged together, "entertainers" were in slightly finer surroundings—although just how "fine" you could be in one of his cheap tents she wasn't sure—he did have the tents separated. She had also heard him say all the freaks were so disgusting he couldn't imagine any of them wanting to sleep with any one of them!

Her bunk was next to Victoria's. When she came in, Victoria was lying awake staring at the darkness.

"You smell like horses," Victoria said.

Shelley never had a chance to reply. Because that was when they heard the bone-chilling scream, coming from the big tent.

"What the hell?" Victoria was out of her bed. From the canvas sheet that separated the men from the women, Shelley heard commotion and exclamations as the others rose.

It then seemed as if, in a single body, they went racing out of the tent, nearly tripping over one another to reach the big tent.

And that's when they saw him.

Or what was left of him.

Or the pieces of him.

Count Zardov—Lou Goldstein of Milwaukee, Wisconsin—lay in pieces around the tent, only recognizable as himself because his head sat atop the balance beam to the right of the center.

His torso, clad in the red ringmaster's jacket he wore for performances, was in the center of the arena—most of it, anyway.

Limbs were scattered here and there.

Along with pieces of his insides.

It appeared that Zardov had been ripped apart by a giant hand, haphazardly tossed about, here and there and everywhere. Blood stained the balance beam, the ground, the little stands for the dog shows, the few props that the clowns had left behind.

And it was Mort who had been doing the screaming. So terrified by the sight he had come upon that he was still screaming, his voice as shrill and high-pitched as a woman's.

The great tent was filled with numerous voices as some people screamed, some moaned and cried, and everyone shouted that someone needed to call the cops.

"Cops? What cops? We're in the middle-of-nowhere America. People came to see us from all around the surrounding counties. For this town, there are no cops! No deputies! Is the sheriff in town?"

Shelley knew the voice that had spoken. It was that of her secret true-love, Zack. He stood in the center of the ring then, consternation knitting his beautiful brow.

Zelda rushed up to be at his side, gently touching his shoulder. "Who would do this?" she asked. "Who *could* do this?" she demanded, and she turned to look at the freaks who had gathered in a semi-circle together staring at the scene in horror.

"Which one of you *freaks* did this to Lou?" she demanded angrily.

Accusing faces turned toward Shelley's group.

Mort finally stopped screaming; he wasn't a freak or an entertainer. He, like a few others, was just there to attend to all the animals in the show.

"Hey, there's no way to know—" he began.

Something about the way Mort was willing to stand up for them gave Shelley courage. She stepped forward and said with clear assertion, "Excuse me, Zelda, but there's no way to know without an investigation just who did this thing!"

"Hey, we have a wolfman and a vampire and God-knows-what-else among you? Who else?" Zelda demanded angrily.

"I have freakishly long canine teeth—but I'm not a monster!" Victoria cried angrily. She appeared very beautiful and dignified as she spoke, Shelley thought, and she was proud of her friend. "I don't even eat meat—I'm a vegetarian!"

"And I'm a pescatarian," Harry, the "wolfman," announced.

Julie, the lion-tamer's assistant, let out a snickering sound. "You don't have to eat meat to rip a man to shreds. Lou's guts are everywhere. Not eaten—just ripped to shreds."

"You people are the monsters!" Mom declared, stepping forward and pointing a finger at the entertainers. "I heard you whispering behind the tent, Julie Smith! I don't know who you were whispering to, but it was about breaking a contract! You were hoping the circus would fall apart, or that, or that... something would happen. To Lou. And something happened all right!"

Julie gasped, stepping back and looking around at everyone who had gathered, the performers, the freaks, and the animal caretakers and set-up workers.

"I—I, yes, I wanted out of my contract. But—I didn't want anything to happen to Lou. I never said that, I swear. I got an offer from a magician who has an act in Vegas. It's such a good offer. But I didn't want anything to happen to our circus—or to Lou, I swear it."

As they stood there arguing, Lou's decapitated head began to fall to the side.

Shelley shivered and winced with the macabre horror of it and tried stepping forward, trying to be assertive again. "People, people, please! We are all decent human beings—be we those that others gawk at, or those who amaze them with talent, or those who take care of us all. Please, let's have some respect for Lou. If the sheriff is in the town, he can call in the state police. None of us did this—some human monster from the area stayed behind—someone truly sick. Please, we need to band together now, not tear each other apart."

There was silence beneath the big top.

Perhaps her last words had been ill-chosen. Silence followed them. She became aware that everyone in the big tent was staring at her.

Including Zack.

Then Zelda walked over to her and before Shelley could stop her, Zelda tugged lightly at the edge of her beard.

"Well, we know you didn't do it, right? I mean, it's obvious that the man didn't die by being chaffed to death!"

"Hey!" It was Zack who protested.

Shelley didn't need to be defended. She gently moved Zelda's hand away, determined to take the high road.

Lou was dead. His body parts were dripping all over the big tent.

"I loved our Count Zardov. He gave me a living," she said quietly. "We need to find out the truth—it's more than possible that an old enemy got in here tonight. We need the police."

"I used the old two-way radio and explained the situation. Sheriff Jones has called in the state criminal investigation unit; he was in the area and he'll be here soon," Tito, one of the old clowns, said breathlessly from running back from the ticket booth.

Even as he spoke, they could hear a siren.

"He's here," Mort said, leading the way out of the tent. It occurred to them all that they shouldn't have been in the tent—it was a crime scene. Shelley knew they were thinking the same by the way they looked at one another as they exited and waited.

Shelley had met Sheriff Jones when they had first started their run in this out-of-the-way field. He seemed to be a good man. There was a country twang to his voice, but she didn't think of him as any kind of a hick; he was a bright man who spoke slowly and thoughtfully and had a great smile.

And he didn't treat the freaks like—freaks.

He stood there staring at them all, eyes going from one to another. He was an imposing figure, six feet with maybe two or three more inches on him, dark hair, dark eyes, and a way of standing very straight when he looked at you, as if his very manner demanded the truth.

"What the hell happened here?" he demanded.

"He's dead—Lou is dead. Torn to shreds!" Zelda cried dramatically.

"We have no idea," Zack said.

"We have plenty of ideas," Zelda murmured.

Shelley was glad to see Zack elbowed her in the ribs.

Sheriff Jones stared straight at Zelda. "Never make assumptions," he told her. "Our state criminal investigation unit will be out shortly. For now—you all stay out here. Outside of the big tent. You can come and talk to me, one by one. Mort—you discovered the body. We'll start with you."

Mort's eyes were wide. He nodded his assent.

"The rest of you—stay together and stay out of the big tent. Investigators will be here shortly—then the process will move a great deal more quickly."

At that moment, Delilah, their current "gypsy" fortune-teller, turned away gagging violently. Her reaction was a little delayed, but it was actually surprising that none of them had as yet given up their last meal.

It seemed the accusations had stopped for the time being. They all stood waiting, while Sheriff Jones led Mort into the ticket-seller's booth.

Conversation had run dry.

Zack was called next, and then Zelda, and then Shelley. And as she sat in one of the flimsy metal chairs where the sheriff had indicated she should sit, she wondered if Zelda had already told him that she couldn't be the murderer—the man hadn't been "chaffed" to death.

"When did you last see Lou?" he asked her, his notepad out, pencil in hand, ready to set her answer down for the record.

"When he was announcing the trapeze artists," Shelley said. "That's the last act. I stayed through part of it, but then went back to help Mort with the horses. When they were all bedded down for the night, I headed to the…" She paused for a moment, and then continued, "to the 'freaks' tent for the night. I had barely gotten there when we all heard Mort's horrible screams."

"Who was with you?" Sheriff Jones asked.

"Victoria—our 'vampire'—was already in bed. Naturally, she hopped up. Mort's screams were the most horrible thing I've ever heard," Shelley said softly. "But Mom was there—mummy—she'd been talking to the guys—General George, midget, Swampman, and Frank—disease has wrecked him and he's a big man, and Harry—wolfman."

"You saw all of them—together—after the screams?" Jones asked.

"I did. I swear it." She hesitated. "I know everyone thinks we are monsters—because we're horrible to look at. Victoria is the sweetest young woman in the world, and Frank…he'd cut off his own right arm before hurting anyone. And we survive because of Lou—or survived because of him. We'd have no reason to kill him."

Sheriff Jones eased back, relaxed despite the wretched folding chair.

"You don't know, do you?"

"Know what?"

"About the will."

She shook her head, confused. "What will?"

Jones leaned forward once again, folding his hands as he rested his elbows on his knees, coming closer to her. "Shelley, Lou left the circus to you."

"What?"

To her great humiliation, the news was so startling that she nearly fell off her chair. Jones reached out to steady her, his arms strong and his slow, slightly grim smile, just as steadying.

"Mort told me no one knew—including you. It was important to him that no one know the truth. I guess several people involved think they should inherit, but...Lou told Mort you were the one who would be equitable and fair and...I guess he saw you as his own child, since you were raised right by his side, in the circus."

Shelley swallowed hard. "Does...does anyone else know? Some of them are so certain one of the 'terrifying grotesques' did this that...I hope they don't think any of us...I'm babbling. I don't mean to be. You must understand—the others can live outside the circus. We—we need the circus. We earn a living—we're almost useful citizens."

"Mort thought he was the only one Lou had confided in, but...I don't know. Anyway, is there anything else at all you can tell me? Did you see anyone do anything?"

"I know Zelda wanted out of her contract, but that doesn't mean anything," Shelley said, and then hesitated. "But I admit, she tends to be very disparaging of us, so I can't say I'm particularly fond of her. And others have wanted out of their contracts. Still, I can't believe any of the circus performers, freaks, or maintenance people could have done this. We were honestly like a family. One that squabbled, yes. But still..."

"Sadly, we never want to believe those we care about can be—evil. In any way. Shelley, we're done for tonight. Of course, none of you is to leave the general area of the circus. You understand that, right?"

"Of course."

"A crime scene unit has arrived. They may get something."

Shelley nodded and stood. He would go down his list.

"Thank you, Sheriff Jones," she said.

He stood as well. "Michael. My name is Michael. And for what it's worth, I know you're innocent. And I don't believe any of you other...freaks can be guilty either. But that all remains to be seen. Someone here is guilty." He hesitated. "Don't worry. I've been at this a long time—even in this no man's land. I started out in the city. I learned that those we see as monsters are often the most beautiful people, really. And I've learned that beauty can hide the heart of a monster."

Beautiful people. Like Zack and Zelda.

Zack. Never.

Zelda?

She nodded again and hurried out, all but crashing into Zack. He steadied her, smiling as he did so.

He'd always been kind. He was no monster.

"Hey, I'm up next. Wish me luck."

"Luck?"

He flexed a muscle playfully. "Strong, you know. Capable of ripping people up."

"Oh, Zack!" she said, and she smiled in return, hoping he could see that she was sincere beneath the hair on her face. "You're fine—no fangs. I mean you could pull a man apart, but..." She broke off, wincing. "Oh, my God. Lou is dead!"

He gave her a hug. She was glad that her face pressed to his chest—and his jacket.

No danger of her chaffing his face.

He went on in.

As he did so, the whole of the circus area was suddenly plunged into darkness. Shelley froze where she stood. For a moment, it seemed that all was very black. Then she realized she could see around the area at least. A full moon rode high in the night sky—casting down a gentle, hazy kind of light.

All kinds of light began to emit from the big tent—the crime scene people apparently came equipped with all manner of flashlights. She could hear them all talking—someone saying to keep working.

Other lights, flashlights, pen lights, began to appear.

There was safety in numbers, and they were surrounded by cops.

Shelley stood where she was for several minutes.

"Scared?"

Shelley jumped at the sound of the voice and turned quickly. She didn't want to be afraid.

She wanted to believe a stranger had come and killed Lou and just as quickly disappeared, but her heart was racing.

She realized she just wanted to reach her tent—and the comfort and security of her fellow freaks.

"Shelley, sorry, so sorry!"

It was Jerry, the big cat trainer, and he had a sorrowful expression on his face as he set his hands on her shoulders.

"I didn't mean to frighten you!" he said.

"No, I shouldn't have jumped. It's just…"

"It's just that Lou has been ripped to shreds. I understand. Have you spoken with the sheriff or the crime unit yet?"

She nodded.

"Are they scary?" he asked, smiling awkwardly then. Jerry, too, was a good-looking man. Tall and dark with well-honed muscles. She figured that was how one dealt with big cats.

"No, no. I mean, they want to find out what happened to Lou. Jerry, we all *must* know what happened to Lou. He was our—everything."

He glanced away, nodding grimly. When he looked at her again, she realized that he didn't think she was guilty.

But he was suspecting one of her number.

Victoria or Harry—vampire or wolfman—she thought.

"I guess I should try to get some sleep. Who am I kidding? I'll never sleep. But…"

"Yes, get with your friends," he told her.

He started to head for the ticket booth where the sheriff was questioning people. As she looked, she saw Zack come out. She almost walked over to him. But Zelda came running out of the shadows and right to him—almost into his arms.

"Stay safe, Jerry," she told the cat-tamer earnestly, even though she knew he meant that her only real friends could be her fellow freaks.

As she started off once more with determination, a cloud apparently swept across the sky—covering the moon.

Once again, the world seemed dark. Pitch dark. But now, of course, there was still light from the big tent.

Her own tent seemed covered in the deepest shadow.

Safety in numbers!

She did want to be with her friends. And, yes, they were her friends.

She started to walk resolutely toward her tent.

MICHAEL

IT WAS happening again, Michael thought wearily.

Because it had happened before. Once in this state, and if he were right in his assumptions, it happened once before in the bordering state to the south. Here, before, two counties away, it had been two nurses who had been ripped to shreds as if a giant garbage disposal had embraced them in a continuous hug.

"I know my job and I intend to do it well," Lieutenant Joe Casey of the state police said wearily. "But—no pun really intended—this circus is a zoo. Some of them are so damned weird…like rats eating other rats."

Michael stared at Casey. The man was about fifty, wearied by years in public service and seeing the worse of man's inhumanity to man.

"Are you forgetting a few years back—the nurses found in much the same shape as we just found Lou?"

The police had never found the killer. And Casey, an investigator with the state, had the grace to turn red. Michael knew, of course, the man had dealt with a great deal of frustration when it had appeared that a similar crime had been committed nearby—but under a different jurisdiction.

While the police in the next state had chosen not to share their files—calling it an open case with details being withheld for the investigation—it was known that the two killed had been a young woman named Dorothy Barnes, a fashion model, and Bryan Harper, an architect. They had been dating, but they had not been killed together. She'd been attacked in a dressing room—*just off stage, with hundreds of people in the audience and dozens working the show.*

Bryan Harper had been killed late at night—in his own office. That murder hadn't been discovered until the following morning.

Michael hadn't been an investigator on either case. He was local, the *only* law enforcement for this tiny county where nothing ever happened, and where the circus coming to town was the greatest excitement for miles around.

He looked at Casey—sure, the man was getting worn out. But his attitude was atrocious—and when you forgot you were dealing with human lives—and human deaths—it was time to get out of the business.

"I knew Lou," Michael said firmly. "He was a friend of mine. I have known many of these people over the years—oh, yes, Detective Casey—they are people."

Casey stared back at him, irritated. "Are they—just people? Lou was torn to shreds—like something out of a monster movie. And you've got some gorgeous, talented performers. But you have a *wolfman*. A *vampire*. Who is to say that one of them didn't take being a monster seriously?"

Michael hesitated.

When the call had come tonight, he looked back into the research he had done. And checking into everything that had gone on with both situations, he had seen that the Count Zardov's Circus and Museum of Terrifying Grotesques had been set up nearby both in this state—and in the neighboring state—where the previous horrendous, *unsolved*, murders had taken place.

He hadn't drawn the conclusion someone in the circus was guilty—assumptions could mean a man tried to make facts and evidence fall into a story he had created himself.

No. He had simply noted the killings had occurred when the circus was near, but the circus came every year, following the same route, pitching tents in areas of nothing—yet areas with large surrounding populations that were just not quite large enough to really attract the big time.

He had known Zardov—and he had liked Zardov. He had at least met many of the performers, freaks, and workers. Some he had talked to often.

Shelley. The bearded woman. Despite the hair on her face, she had a fantastic smile. While she was a "freak" in a cage, he'd seen her little act—seen her dance and sing and delight the children. He had told Zardov once she would have been loved with or without her beard. Zardov didn't really want to hear it, but he admitted to really caring for his bearded lady.

"Closest I ever came to raising a kid myself," Zardov had told him. "Even if the old gypsy did most of the caring. Still...good kid. Really good kid. And smart as a whip. Animal lover, team player—a good girl."

That was when Zardov had confided in him that he had left his circus to Shelley in his will.

"Who else? I have great people—but I know Shelley will be fair. Keep it good for everyone," Zardov had said, before making a face. "She even stands back when some of my uppity stars are on a rampage; she ignores them with a look that would make an observer laugh. She doesn't say anything—that look just shows their bad behavior."

Michael didn't realize how reflective he had become until Casey slammed both hands on the old folding desk he sat behind. "These freaks are dangerous!" he said. "And this should have proven it! Keep an eye on the freaks. I say we divide when questioning them. You're too soft where they're concerned."

"I'm too logical, Casey. A skin disease doesn't create a murderer."

"Fifty-fifty on the freaks and all the others, performers, and so on. Hey—I'm a state official—"

"And you're here to assist—not take over," Michael said firmly.

"I'm telling you—"

"What? The one 'freak' was the victim of a horrible fire. And a midget—how the hell could a midget have even reached anyone to rip them up?"

"They aren't the only freaks."

"No, and I won't assume that none of them could be guilty—as long as you don't assume one of them has to be. So, I say we get on it—sure. You're welcome to a fifty-fifty split on all. It's going to be a hell of a long night."

SHELLEY

Shelley was nearing the freaks' tent when she heard the whisper.

Soft and slithering, a sound that seemed to slip beneath her skin and chill her very bones.

"Shelllllley..."

She stopped, spinning around. There was no one there. She was halfway between the ticket booth and the freaks' tent.

Her imagination?

She determined she was not going to be afraid. And still, she remembered then that Lou had left the circus to her.

This was now hers.

Because someone had killed Lou.

And now...

She owned the circus!

That fact hadn't really come home to her at all. How could it? Lou was dead. That hadn't even sunk in yet, though she had seen him...

Seen the pieces of him, guts scattered, blood...everywhere.

"Shelllllleeeey!"

Again, the awful sound. And darkness all around, except for the strange haze glowing from the main tent—and leaving the rest of the little world of the circus in deepest shadow.

She was closer to her own tent, and she was also sure there was a tiny beacon of light coming from the freaks' tent. She ran there, suddenly moving as fast as she could go.

But when she reached the tent, the little beacon of light against the darkness was gone.

She hesitated and opened the flap.

There was nothing but gaping, stygian darkness.

"Victoria...Mom?" she called. No answer.

She stepped in and almost immediately, a reek assailed her. She didn't know what it was—and then she did.

Death.

Blood. Blood and...

She was stepping on something. It squished beneath her. And she knew what—if she didn't know *who*.

Flesh...an organ...something that had once been part of someone human, no matter how distorted or mangled that human might have appeared.

She never had a chance to scream. Someone came bursting out toward her, letting loose with a horrible sound even more bone-chilling than that emitted by Mort earlier.

It was hairy. He toppled over her, bringing them both to the ground. He looked at her with wide, terrified eyes, barely aware that he had tackled her. "Oh, my God, oh, my God…"

"Harry, Harry, stop, please, up. We have to get to Sheriff Jones and the crime scene people—what is it, what happened, who…who did I step on?"

He pushed himself up, still staring at her—still in shock. She wasn't sure what to do, but he was on top of her and something was in their tent or had been in their tent. She'd seen people slap people in the movies, so she slapped Harry—hard. He wouldn't feel much of it beneath the dense fur-like hair on his face, but it might work.

It did; he leapt up, drawing her to her feet as well. He looked back at the tent and grabbed her arm and together, they ran.

"Sheriff Jones, Sheriff Jones, please, for the love of God!"

Sheriff Michael Jones came hurrying out of the ticket-taking booth, followed by one of the state men. The crime scene people—some techs, some deputies—came hurrying from the big tent.

Performers and freaks and workers all appeared as well, coming from different areas of the circus spread, the different tents, the stables and cages.

Harry was shaking. "He struck again…he…she…the killer. In our tent. I…heard something. I'd gone to bed. Then I heard…it was terrible. She never had a chance to scream. Mom never had a chance to scream. She…she's in there. What's left of her!"

Suddenly, the circus lights came back on—with glaring brutality. The whole of the acreage where the big tent and all the supporting tents had been pitched seemed to be illuminated.

And looking toward the freaks' tent, they could all see that blood stained the flap…that it was interspersed with flecks of white.

Brain matter? Vital organs…Mom's skin?

Shelley didn't know.

Sheriff Jones started walking that way. The state investigator—Casey, Shelley thought his name was—followed behind him.

Keeping a distance.

Harry nervously stepped forward and caught Sheriff Jones' arm. "No… the killer…the killer could still be there."

Jones stopped and looked at Harry.

"I hope so; I hope we'll get him," he said grimly, drawing his gun as he continued walking, purpose in his steps.

Shelley thought the other deputies from the state were hesitant—even Casey—but they had to follow him.

And en masse, everyone followed slowly behind until Sheriff Jones stopped and looked back. "Stay here; don't move. We'll check. No one goes anywhere from this spot."

He was ready to go into the tent—and find the killer. But at that moment, Shelley realized with certainty the killer wasn't still in the tent.

The killer had struck and left—*and whispered her name in the darkness.*

She stood where she was, looking around at the others—as the others all looked around at one another, too.

Suspicion lay as heavily in the air as a wet fog.

Sheriff Jones carried his own light. What he illuminated was horrible. Shelley caught a glance just before turning away.

Mom, sweet Mom, more tragically torn apart than Lou.

Her head left at the entry like a strange stone sentinel, clearly visible in the spotlight glow of the sheriff's flashlight.

Jones didn't walk in; he backed out staring at the scene for a moment, as if he, too, were horrified beyond measure—no matter what he had seen before.

He shouted to one of the officers hovering behind him that they needed to call for even more reinforcements. He faced the group in the center of the circus compound and shouted evenly, having found control, "No one moves. We stay here, in the field. Who is missing?"

Again they all looked around. Everyone was there, from the performers, to the animal keepers, the workers—and the freaks.

Except for Mom. And they all knew where Mom was.

"Take seats—right where you are, on the ground, it's going to be a long, long night!" Sheriff Michael Jones said.

And it was—a hell of a long night.

More investigators from the state joined in the questioning while the crime scene people tried desperately to find some kind of a clue.

One of the investigators brought water around as the night passed.

Sitting eventually became—no matter what their position—curling into little balls in the grass and dirt, exhausted no matter how horrified.

One by one they were questioned—but the group was never left alone, and sometimes they were pulled out to be questioned twice.

Such was Shelley's case. The second time she wasn't questioned by Sheriff Jones, but by Detective Casey, the state detective, one who was very suspicious of Harry.

"You saw the wolfman in the tent—he was there. And no one else—when the mummy was murdered."

"Harry isn't a wolfman—that's what he plays on stage," Shelley said. "And when I came to the tent and saw what had happened, he was terrified," she assured the man. Casey had a narrow face and his expression never altered from grim.

"He burst out from the back," Shelley continued. "He was screaming his head off—he was so frightened he almost ran over me and tackled me outside of the tent."

"What was he doing there?" Detective Casey leaned close to her face.

Then he moved back. His distaste for her evident.

"I repeat, what was he doing there?"

"He lives there."

"But what was he doing there?"

"Trying to sleep, probably! It's a very long day for us!"

"Think about it. He's a wolfman. She was torn apart."

"He's a man inflicted with a disease!"

Just like she was.

"What do wolfmen do? They tear people to shreds."

"Harry didn't kill Mom—he loved her. She was supposedly our mummy, but she was really a mom to everyone. She tended to colds and little wounds and she...she was wonderful." Tears suddenly filled Shelley's eyes. Mom had been wonderful. As had Lou. And they were gone—and this man was accusing Harry. It suddenly seemed to be too much. Tears streamed down her face—soaking her beard.

"That doesn't work with me—freak!" Detective Casey announced.

Shelley didn't care; she sat there and cried.

"Get out, get out, get out!" he told her. "God help me, I don't want to touch that hair on your face, but I'm doubting that, bad as it is, you could tear anyone up with it! Besides, I saw you with Sheriff Jones and walking back while the mummy was being killed. I know you're in the clear."

She left him. He'd taken over the concession stand to do his questioning. Another man had garnered the performers' tent while Sheriff Jones was still in the ticket booth.

It was as she was leaving—escorted by one officer—and Zelda was being led in—escorted by another officer—that they all heard the strange cackling.

"What the hell?" the officer demanded.

The night suddenly seemed to be alive with that sound and those who had been sleeping awoke in panic. Leaping to their feet were deputies, detectives, crime scene folk. Everyone either jumped out or came tearing from the tents where they had been working.

It was that time now when night was just ending—and the sun was trying to crawl up on the horizon. Something seemed to be flying through the night, a shadow, a cloud of darkness, and the cackling seemed to be coming from the cloud.

It whipped around in the air, lowering, rising, lowering again.

Freaks and performers, all were out watching. Everyone was stunned and amazed.

So incredulous, in fact, that they didn't see the danger in it at first.

Shelley, looking across the field, saw many of the performers—hanging together naturally, perhaps just standing there—staring up.

Then she saw the thing. It was suddenly soaring downward, coming straight at Zelda.

Shelley would never be sure why she did what she did. She certainly didn't think she had any great care for Zelda.

But she could see it was swooping straight for the trapeze artist.

She didn't know she could run so fast. She was at Zelda's side in seconds, knocking her down to the ground, bringing her flat against the earth just as the *thing*, the cackling *shadow*, swept over them both so close Shelley could feel something like the whisper of wings touching her.

Then it was gone.

Zelda looked up at her, eyes wide. Shelley waited for the young beauty to berate her—yell that she'd hurt her, or made her filthy, or...

"Thank you!" Zelda whispered. "Oh, Shelley, thank you!"

"I—I—I—of course!" Shelley whispered.

"Vampire!" Someone cried. "It's a vampire. It's that damned freak...vampire queen!"

But Victoria was standing with her group—the freaks.

"I'm right here!" she cried. "Damn you all!"

But the word *vampire* rang in Shelley's head. Sheriff Jones had stepped out in the group, his gun drawn. He shot at the thing in the air.

Detective Casey joined him. They both shot at the creature and others joined them until the sound of the shots being fired became thunderous.

The cackling continued, the thing wasn't affected in the least by the shots. *Vampire…*

One thing the freaks had always done was read. They'd read everything, they'd tried out their "monster" acts on one another.

"Stake!" Shelley cried.

"Stake!" Harry repeated, looking at her.

"Yes, yes!" Victoria said.

Monsters hadn't been real before. Monsters were the creatures they performed as—for survival.

But it seemed that they were real.

And there was one way to kill a vampire—stake it through the heart and lop off the head!

They worked in unison, Harry helping Shelley to rip out one of the stakes tying down a tent. Victoria and Frank went for a heavier stake. Swampman ripped out a few of the nails on the ropes binding the stakes, helping them all.

It was coming again, the shadow, swooping around and around, deciding where it would zero in. It seemed to be taking form—the form of a bat.

This time, it suddenly honed-in on Detective Casey. Harry and Shelley looked at one another and nodded.

Casey was shooting into the air. Michael Jones was shooting into the air, rushing forward—always the true cop, ready to fight for anyone.

"Get him out of the way!" Shelley whispered to Harry.

Harry did so, slamming against the sheriff as Shelley carried the stake.

Shots did nothing…it kept coming and coming, cackling…

And just as it started to make a beeline for the desperately shooting Detective Casey, Shelley made her move. She sprang forward with the support pole with its razor-honed point.

The thing—shadow, bat, vampire—couldn't stop. Shelley gripped the stake with every ounce of her strength. The power of the thing was terrible, but in seconds, the others were with her—massive Frank with his strength, Harry, Swampman and Victoria.

The cackling became a different sound, something that shrieked of both fury and pain.

There was a minute when it seemed even the five of them couldn't bear the terrible power of the thing flapping and screaming and struggling with such rage and strength to escape them.

Then, suddenly, it was over.

The size of the thing diminished.

The wings were gone, and they had nothing at all impaled on the stake except for...

A man.

It was Jerry. Jerry, the handsome performer, beloved of his cats...

Jerry, the big-cat tamer, master of the tigers.

Dead now; eyes open and glaring up at the sky. He was impaled through the chest, and still held up by the five of them, an image straight out of history books about the dreaded Romanian count who had so viciously impaled his enemies.

And for a moment, despite the agony in their arms and limbs, they stood just as they were—too stunned to move. The night was filled with silence.

Because no one believed what they had seen.

Then there were cheers from the others, and the beautiful performers came forward, still disbelieving what they saw, but aware that they had been saved—by the freaks.

The monsters.

To Shelley's amazement, she found herself being hugged again by Zelda, beautiful Zelda, and Zelda was babbling her thanks, and everyone was hailing the freaks, the monsters...

Shelley saw Sheriff Jones was looking at her, and his look of approval meant the world to her.

Then, of course, the arguing began. Vampires couldn't really exist. Yes, of course, Jerry had been the killer, but what they had seen...

Mass hysteria, illusion!

Shelley saw the detectives gathered together. They were discussing what would be in their reports.

No one would believe them, of course. Even though the crowds loved it when the freaks played monsters, they couldn't really believe in a vampire.

Couldn't believe a handsome charmer like Jerry could have been the real monster.

The talk went on so long that, by the next day, Shelley was wondering herself what she had really seen, what had really gone on.

Then, of course, they all had to pick up the pieces.

People still needed to work...to survive. Magazines and newspapers offered different members of the circus nice payments for their stories.

In every one of those stories, it all became Jerry being a cold-blooded and vicious killer—and a master of illusion.

Life fell back into place. They mourned Lou and Mom.

Shelley took over the circus, but she handed the management and ring-master jobs over to Mort. She gave her own time over to the animals.

She might be the bearded lady, but she no longer wanted to play the bearded lady.

It was almost a year later when she looked up from the books one day to see Sheriff Michael Jones was looking at her, smiling.

She smiled back. "Everything okay?"

"Sure. You need a break. Want to go to dinner and a movie? There is one theater—a couple of miles from here."

She'd never in her life been invited to dinner and a show. And by a man like Michael Jones...

Fear suddenly filled her. Fear of what could never be.

"I—uh—" she began awkwardly. "I uh...there's a show tomorrow."

"And Mort handles it all nicely. Come on—I'll have you back early."

She winced. And then she decided, what the hell?

Dinner and the movie were great.

All the things they did in the following months were great. And she was able to see him often enough—the circus was very popular, but the route they followed covered about three hundred circular miles and Michael had little trouble finding the days to come out and see her.

But when he did finally kiss her—really kiss her, such a deep, rich, wet, sloppy, wonderful kiss—he wound up with a terrible rash.

And then she tried to hide from him.

But he wouldn't let her.

"Okay, we have a few challenges!" he said. "But, what couple doesn't? And if it's all right with you, I think I have an amazing way to deal with our challenge! If you'll trust me."

She did trust him; she loved him. She was *in love* with him. It was something deeper and far richer than the silly hero-worship she'd once had for Zack.

So when he came for her the next day, his intention mysterious but bringing a smile to his lips, she laughed and went right along.

MICHAEL

SHELLEY WAS beautiful.

He'd always known, of course, that she was beautiful inside. But now…
Who would have imagined?

The wavy auburn hair that fell around her shoulders framed a finely shaped face. And her eyes, a crystal hazel, seemed huge and amazing.

There might be women who were more beautiful in the world.

But not for Michael.

Of course, when the others saw her, they were amazed, whistling and whispering. And it was fun, too, because Zack was suddenly aware of her in a way he had never been before.

Zelda admired her, too. Zelda had learned her lessons well. She'd been saved by a freak—and she knew it.

Except that the freak was no longer a freak.

"Electrolysis!" Shelley explained happily to the circus crew who all flocked around her. "A long process—sometimes a bit painful—but it worked!"

The others gushed and Victoria wondered if she shouldn't just try to see a really good dentist.

Swampman just shook his head.

Michael set a hand on his shoulder. "Hey, I didn't care about the beard. It was the rash that was so bad. I loved her no matter what. And you're a great guy."

Swampman nodded and turned to him. "Yeah," he said. "I am a great guy! And I'm going to believe it now and find my own happiness."

By the time of the massive party they had when Shelley finally said, "I do" and she and Michael were duly married, Swampman and Victoria had become a thing.

And later that night—much later, after an amazing time of really knowing one another—Michael lay awake, staring at the night, and thinking. She moved in his arms, and he knew he'd never imagined such happiness.

But then, he was a lucky man. He'd known that monsters often wore the most amazing masks of beauty...

And that what might appear to be monstrous often concealed the greatest strength and beauty.

DANDY
By Josh Malerman

I

Dandy digs.

He tucks his disobedient black hair behind his ears and wipes the sweat from his forehead. The walls are getting wider down here. No doubt about that. But it hasn't gotten any cooler. Even at night. The crappy fan he's got plugged into the generator doesn't do much more than send the dust spiraling up into his nose and mouth and no matter how much room he makes, no matter how big it gets, it still feels like a grave.

Underground, what else could it feel like?

Momma, Dandy knows, would love this.

Jabbed into the eastern wall is the handle from the shovel he'd started with. Dandy still used it for two days after the head cracked in half, before he found the guts to crawl out of the hole and steal a new one from Logan's Lumber on Agnes Street. He lost a fingernail in those two days, felt a physical pain he hadn't known existed. And yet, shoveling, sometimes by hand—in a way, those were the days.

Momma used phrases like those.

Those were the days.

Can't win 'em all.

Nobody really wants to be scared, even those who say they do.

Dandy digs.

This *was* once the size of a grave. Had to be. Six feet by three. But only because a hole must have been all sizes until it reaches the size it was meant to become.

This hole is meant to become the size of a carnival house of horrors. And it's close.

He began digging in spring, but now it's summer. Dandelion Andrews hasn't seen daylight in three months.

His sleeveless jean jacket lies more than a hundred feet from where he works. His hands are calloused, long past blistered, and his eyes hurt from the lanterns. Down here, below Samhattan's Holly Park, the ceiling is eight feet high, more than two feet taller than Dandy stands. He planned it this way, modeled the place after the first floor of the house he's been squatting in. The place he'd mapped it all out. The place he'd done the numbers.

Dandy knows he will need all the space he's making.

"Eight feet high," he says, digging. "One hundred feet across. Two hundred feet deep." He looks up, as though through the dirt above him. Are there people up there? Burnouts in the park? "Momma," he says, "it's what you'd call a downright *lair*."

It's way early Monday morning, four AM. The Hoke County Carnival won't open its gates until Saturday morning, but they'll be arriving Thursday night to set up. Dandy knows this because he knows everything there is to know about the HCC. Some of that is from experience. Holly Park, Samhattan's prized, manicured fairgrounds where any and all manner of public events take place, has hosted the Hoke County Carnival for seventeen years, the exact number of years Dandy has been alive. Thanks to Momma, he's been to every one. She'd carried her baby from stand to stand, booth to booth, rarely engaging in the activities, always playing the part she loved to play, the thing she knew they called her when she wasn't around: the creepiest woman in Samhattan.

The tattered black dress helped. So did the bare feet. So did the look in her eyes.

Momma liked to scare.

And Dandy knows people were afraid of Momma. Not because they thought she rode a broomstick through the sky but because they wondered what kind of woman would want to unnerve, quake, and rattle the world around her.

Dandy smiles.

"You were the best," he says. But he feels like he's talking too much. It ruins things, even for him. Ruins the idea of the madman who's built his

own house of horrors beneath where the Hoke County Carnival House of Horrors will stand come Thursday night.

Dandy knows; the less sound he makes, the scarier he is.

He sets the splintered shovel handle (third shovel now, third shovel he's used) against the dirt wall and crosses the enormous subterranean space. The lanterns only reach so far and most of the corners down here are in shadow. But the sky above is always easy to find.

The stars and moon provide a small beam at the far northeastern corner of the space. It's what Dandy thinks of as his front door. While it's not the spot the victim will eventually enter the lair by, it's how Dandy comes and goes. Digging a subterranean attraction, many halls of many horrors, is a complex task, of course, but certain aspects are simpler than he'd originally conceived. You sneak into the park after dark. You go to the thickest cluster of bushes. You get on your knees and crawl through said bushes to the front door. You uncover the front door. You lower yourself down into the abhorrence you've created. At first, you only work at night. Once the lair is big enough to stand up in, you can work all day. But you only go out again at night.

You dig the front door in the bushes because nobody in all of Samhattan (or Hoke County for that matter) is going to spend any time in there at all. It doesn't even look like someone could fit. But Dandy knows someone can. He can.

A bona fide lair. Right under the rosy nose of Samhattan.

Dandy grabs his jean jacket and exits by way of the front door. Climbs the same brand of rungs he's already installed on the other side of the space. The rungs the victim will eventually climb down. Once out, he crawls through the spider webs and pointed branches of the bushes. Then he gets up, inhales the air of the otherwise empty park, and looks up at the moon.

He feels like howling. He knows he shouldn't.

But the horror fanatic in him can't repress the urge.

Dandy howls at the moon.

Momma said, if a man can't howl like a wolf when he feels like it, he's standing in the wrong spot.

Dandy's in the right spot.

He stands there some minutes, eying the darkness of the park. Nobody here now. But come Thursday, tons.

Who's gonna go down below? Who's gonna pay for phony scares and experience the real thing instead?

Momma didn't like phony scares. Didn't like them one bit. Liked to show people what the real thing felt like.

Dandy, using his mental map of the carnival layout, knowing exactly where each and every attraction would be stationed in the park, thinks of how much Momma hated that particular attraction.

The House of Horrors at the Hoke County Carnival.

No matter. Dandy was making up for it.

He puts on his jean jacket and steps out from the extra shadows provided by the bushes that hide the front door. He crosses the park, thinking, who? Who's gonna experience the real thing?

A head appears in his mind's eye, a head with ever-changing faces, no two the same. Man, woman, boy, girl. It doesn't matter. And he doesn't pick one, but opts instead to watch the many possibilities whir by, face after face, as he exits the park and heads for the all-night store, in need of a fourth shovel.

AT FOUR in the morning, this same Monday morning, Susan wakes from a scary dream. In it, she's forced to perform in front of other people. She isn't sure *what* she's supposed to perform, but that doesn't matter; she's shoved onto a stage. People wait. She doesn't know what to do. People look the other way.

She sweats.

People ignore her.

She wakes.

She gets up out of bed and crosses the ranch-style home, all the way to the kitchen. She fixes a glass of apple juice. Through the kitchen window she sees the street is empty. The sky is black. She likes this. No crowd out there. Nobody waiting. These are her favorite hours. The early hours when Dad and Mom are asleep and nobody at Holly High has had a chance yet today to ignore her.

She frowns.

Dad tells her all the time she's silly for thinking on this at all. Not gonna matter down the road. Not one bit. Who cares that she's all but invisible to the rest of the school? Who cares that nobody friends her online, nobody likes the photos she posts? Who cares that the girls *she*'s always considered to be anonymous get more attention than she does?

Silly, Dad says. And maybe he's right. Here's Susan, jealous of Beth Berman for being a little less ignored than her.

Susan looks at herself reflected in the kitchen window. The night-light on the counter illuminates just enough of her so that she can make out her incredible height and weight.

At six feet tall, and what feels like the same distance wide, shouldn't it be impossible for everyone to miss her?

She drinks the apple juice, staring out into the dark. Dad's voice comes to her, his dismissive tone:

High school sucks. Ten years from now you'll be embarrassed you ever cared at all. I sure as shit am.

Susan loves herself. She's not worried about that. But she doesn't think there's a person alive who can't use a little positive attention.

She checks her phone. Sees no new likes. No new requests. In the kitchen window she looks sad.

She turns away, doesn't want to see that face on her own head.

Outside, movement, barely perceptible through the dark of her own reflection. Susan is scared for a second, then recognizes the shape as a deer.

The momentary thrill, her beating heart, reminds her that the Hoke County Carnival is coming this week.

"Great," she says. "Maybe I'll go alone."

She finishes the juice and puts the glass in the sink. She thinks of the other unfortunate souls who have gone unnoticed in the halls of Holly High. She can hardly believe she's ended up being one of them. You wanna talk books? Susan can talk books. Art? Movies? Even math? She can do it. Take Nan Crane for example. With a name like that, the poor girl never stood a chance. She practically slithers along the school halls, avoiding the light, as her huge curly hair covers her face like a helmet. Half the student body probably doesn't know what Nan Crane looks like. But Susan does. Because Susan takes the same shadowed paths. Passes Nan in places other kids don't know exist.

"There are more than four corners in every room in Holly High," she whispers, still alone in the kitchen. "I stand in the fifth."

So does Nan Crane.

Like knows like, she'd once heard her mom say about something unrelated to Susan. But the phrase stuck.

Marla Handel knows Susan. Susan knows her. They didn't have to talk about it to know it was true.

Like knows like.

Adam King. Sherry Stewart. Nan Crane. They all know Susan and Susan knows them all because the way you really know someone is to live in their shoes.

How the *fuck* did she end up in these shoes?

"You're nothing like them!" she says, loud enough to wake her parents. But she doesn't.

Standing still in the kitchen, shaking her head, as the blood boils within, she tells herself the same thing she'd told herself a hundred thousand times: that this would all work itself out. That one day the universe would see the mistake it had made. Some celestial force would come swoop her out of the same company as Adam King, Sherry Stewart, and Nan Crane, and apologize for thinking she was ever anything like them!

Take Dandelion Andrews, for example. Jesus, take him. An entire semester passed before she even noticed he was gone. Susan, who had walked the same paths and stood in the same fifth corners as him. They'd never talked, she can't even imagine now what they might've said, but she should've noticed he'd dropped out.

Susan sighs. A legitimate seventeen-year-old's sigh.

She feels bad for that guy. Did anybody notice? If not her, who?

No rumor. No story. No care.

One day here, next day gone.

Her phone lights up and Susan looks at it, sensing a tiny surge of hope within. But it's just the news.

She crosses the ranch home, enters her bedroom, and wonders if she could do that. If she could drop out. Of course Mom and Dad wouldn't let her, but that's not the point. She wonders if she could, in theory, turn her back on the world, *her* world (which isn't actually her world at all!), too.

She crawls into bed. On her back, she thinks of Nan Crane and Adam King. Does she seem as sad to them as they do to her? She hopes not. She hopes they aren't sad at all.

Is she sad herself?

She doesn't know.

She closes her eyes.

Her thoughts get wavy before an image of the Hoke County Carnival rises to her mind's eye. She wants to go. She *really* wants to go. But who is there to go with? She doesn't have a best friend. Doesn't even have a first person in mind to call, to text, to ask.

Susan falls asleep to this image, herself alone at the HCC. The vision effortlessly becomes a dream and the colors of the carnival become breathing living things with enormous watery eyes that track her from booth to booth, stand to stand, asking her if she is alone, is she really so alone? The Ferris Wheel watches her like the biggest eye of all, its mouth across the park on the façade of the funhouse, its lips parted wide to let people in, people who walk in twos and threes, but parted also to ask her, in front of all of Samhattan, everyone at the HCC,

Are you really alone, Susan? Are you really so all alone?

DANDY SETS up the walls.

He's already got the metal tracks in place; seven of them, spaced eight feet apart, giving him the bases for six halls. Because this is not enough, because the victim must feel as though he or she is taking infinite halls deeper and deeper into the Earth, the walls must be movable, to create disorientation, the idea that the victim is never in the same place twice. There was a wall here before, now there isn't. The last wall was covered in picture frames, this one has none.

There ain't nothing more frightening than the unknown, Momma taught him. *And almost nothing scarier than "where am I?" 'Cause if you don't know where you are, how do you know how far you are from safety?*

Thin cedar planks are stacked against the south dirt wall of Dandy's lair. Dandy tested the many materials in that house on First Street, recorded the sound of many potential walls sliding along many potential tracks until he determined cedar on Glasgow closet-door tracks moved soundlessly. He'd studied the making of Alfred Hitchcock's *Rope* and how Hitch wanted to shoot the whole thing in one shot but ended up doing it in eight or nine.

The way the walls were moved the moment they were out of frame struck him as particularly brilliant. Why, his own victim could keep walking forever so long as he kept pace, guiding him or her to the next hall that would take them to the next room, a room they'd already stood in, with no way of knowing so.

Dandy smiles.

He carries the first cedar plank to the first track in the dirt. He lines up the ball bearings and easily slips the wall into place. Having sawed the boards himself, he isn't surprised by how well it fits. Yet, there is pride in it.

He thinks of Momma.

Momma hated a lot of things. But there was nothing, *nothing* Momma hated more than a phony.

And a phony scare most of all.

Lifting the second plank, Dandy thinks of the haunted hayride that Momma took him to out at Goblin Farms. He can still see her boney finger pointing out the couples that held on to one another as men in wolf masks leapt from the woods. She whispered in six-year-old Dandy's ear:

What they're having is fun, Dandy. Fear ain't fun.

Look at them, Momma said, her hands boney as the phony skeletons in the hay. Dandy saw teenagers laughing as fog filled the rows of corn, as men and women dressed as vampires growled from the grass.

Momma taught him.

You can't be afraid of something you know is coming.

Dandy slides the wall on the track. He gets up and tests both planks. They slide easily, silently; they work.

He feels the first rush of being close to finished.

He thinks of how Momma scared that girl on the hayride. Scared her for real.

She'd pulled her lips from his young ear, ceased whispering, and started staring.

Dandy could tell who Momma was staring at but it took a second for the blonde teenager to figure it out for herself. When she did, her face went through a series of quick expressions. Dandy saw her lips melt from a polite smile to a thin line of worry.

Why is that woman staring at me?

She said it just like that. *That woman.* It was the first time Dandy heard her called anything but Momma.

What? the girl asked Momma. She sounded strong but Dandy could tell she was nervous. *What are you looking at me for?*

Momma only stared. Kept staring. Wouldn't stop.

But her anger got smaller the longer Momma stared. Even when the men in lizard masks screamed boo and the speakers in the trees screamed witch-cackle thunder, Momma didn't flinch.

Stop it, the girl finally said. Then her boyfriend said it, too.

What's wrong with you, lady? he said, removing his arm from around the girl's shoulders. Dandy can still see the colors of the Samhattan varsity jacket now.

"Boy made a fist like he was gonna hit you, Momma," Dandy laughs now.

If you don't quit staring at Diane I'm gonna make you stop, the boy said.

Momma didn't stop staring at Diane.

She's scaring me, the girl said. Dandy remembers that now. A girl on a haunted hayride but the last thing in the world she wanted was to be scared.

Either way, Momma hadn't begun scaring her yet.

Without taking her eyes off the girl, without *blinking* as far as Dandy could tell, Momma stuck her hand into her dress pouch and pulled out a knife.

It was chaos from there.

The boyfriend got up. A creature banged against the side of the wagon. The boyfriend fell back down to sitting.

Momma sliced her own finger with the knife. When the moonlight showed the blood, even Dandy cried out.

The driver stopped the ride. Made Momma and Dandy get off. Yelled things at her. Told her he was gonna call the cops. Looked to Dandy like he was worried for him. Looked like he wanted to take Dandy and leave Momma behind.

Momma didn't mind.

Dandy thinks she wanted that time, walking through the cornhusks alone, to teach him phony from fear.

There ain't nothing more embarrassing than false bravery, she told him, sucking her finger, passing men and women in masks that only watched them walk by. *And you can't be brave if there ain't something to be afraid of first. Do you understand?*

Yes, Momma.

A teenager in a skull mask half-heartedly emerged from the corn. Like he wasn't sure if he was supposed to be playing along anymore.

You see people laughing and hollering when they're supposed to be afraid, you know those people aren't true.

Yes, Momma.

You can't ask to be afraid. Do you understand?

Yes, Momma.

Rounding a bend, Dandy could see the wagon that left them, far ahead, the passengers unloading. They looked back into the corn like they were afraid. Really afraid. And Dandy knew it wasn't the werewolves and rattling bones that had done it.

I want you to promise me something, Dandelion.

Yes, Momma.

That you won't never pretend to be scared. That you won't never pretend to be anything at all but what you are at that moment in time.

She stopped and Dandy stopped, too. Then Momma bent at the waist and placed her palms against Dandy's cheeks. Her eyes reflected the moonlight and, for this, they shined.

Dandy felt her blood on his face.

Don't play games with fear, Dandelion. Be true to it and it'll be true to you.

Yes, Momma.

You promise me?

Yes.

She smiled. And her smile was cornstalks crackling, a teenager changed.

Now, underground, Dandy hears thunder from above. Real thunder, not like the phony stuff in the tree-speakers at Goblin Farms. He crosses the lair and fixes it so the tarp is covering the front door.

Rain falls steady against it.

"Momma," Dandy says, facing the lair and the three raised walls. "I promise."

SUSAN WAKES to thunder crushing the sky outside the house. The carnival is still a few days away but she had dreams of walking from stall to stall alone. She gets out of bed and goes to the window, watches the rain come hard. Mom and Dad are up and talking down the hall in bed, their voices muffled. Dad appears at Susan's bedroom door.

"You alright?" he asks.

"Me? Yeah. Pretty neat, huh?"

"It is." He watches from the door for a while. "You're like me, Susan. We've always loved thunderstorms."

"Yeah."

"But I don't love it more than I love sleep. Goodnight, honey."

"Goodnight, Dad."

He leaves her and Susan continues to watch the rain. When she's sure Mom and Dad are sleeping again, Susan gets out of bed, leaves her bedroom and soundlessly goes to the foyer. At the closet, she considers grabbing her red raincoat but decides not to.

Very quiet, she opens the front door. She slips outside. The night air is crisp, feels fantastic against her body. Because she's only wearing a T-shirt and shorts, this is the most nude Susan has been outside her bedroom in years.

She breathes deep and steps out from under the cover of the front door's awning.

She raises her hands high. Palms up. She looks to the sky, sees the pellets coming fast. She opens her mouth and lets the rainwater pour in.

It's easy to laugh like this, not thinking about school, not thinking about her height or her weight or how she has so few friends or how cruel and embarrassing the pecking order of youth can be.

For now, she smiles. And gets soaking wet, as the black sky dumps down upon her, washing her bad carnival dreams away.

Dandy tests the props. The effects. The weapons.

The walls are up. They move in so many directions, in so many ways, that even he forgets exactly where he is.

But he doesn't lose track of time.

The time has come.

It's early in the morning, Thursday. The Hoke County Carnival will arrive later this afternoon; the trucks carrying the rides, the booths, and the makeshift attractions that will be erected on the spot; rickety fold-up walls, cheap plastic façades, chipped paintings of clowns and mermaids, the megaphones by which the barkers will draw the people in.

Dandy tests his own megaphone. He walks the length of the lair, through passages now realized. He adjusts the speakers wedged into the dirt. Sound will be very important down here. Just as powerful as the darkness.

Crouching by the eastern wall, the lantern delivering monster-lighting up the sweating features of his face, he unzips the black backpack in the dirt. He doesn't reach inside. Too dangerous. The needles are in there.

Behind him are the metal arms that will hold these needles, the arms that will move, as Dandy wants them to, by remote control.

He tests them now, pressing buttons on the black console that hangs by a shoelace around his neck. This console will govern a lot of what happens down here.

The animal growls from the shadows where the eastern and southern walls meet. Dandy looks but can only make out the front bars of its cage.

He thought the thing was sleeping, but no matter. He removes the flashlight from his utility belt and shines it on the open pack. The needle tips glisten and Dandy is very careful as he pulls them out. Even more cautious as he fits them to the steel grips at each end of the metal arms. He tests them again.

The needles plunge forward, a quick jab, before retracting.

Another growl from the shadows.

"Hush up," Dandy says, standing up again. His black hair hangs to his naked shoulders. It's warm down here. Always.

Dandy raises a palm to where the needle should strike. He presses the corresponding button.

Pulls his hand back just in time.

"Wow," he says, smiling. He scared himself a little with that one.

He hears breathing from the unseen cage. Thinks of Momma. Momma breathed like that. Like something ready to pounce.

He remembers Momma sitting on the edge of the couch cushion. Thin as a sick woman. Her hair in pigtails, a sight that never fit together for Dandy; old leathery Momma as a little girl.

 DANDY

Come here, Dandelion.

Momma looked stoned that night. Dandy knew the word.

He went to her, seated on the couch like she was balancing, like she could fall off the edge of the cushion if she leaned forward too far, hit the wood coffee table, crack into a dozen dusty fragments.

She beckoned him closer, using her yellowed fingertips like casting a spell. Dandy went to her.

You know your daddy's a dead man, don't you?

Dandy hadn't met his father.

Yes, Momma.

Uh huh. And did you know he comes back from the dead if you want him to?

No, Momma. Daddy doesn't come back from the dead.

She cackle-laughed, the veins and wrinkles of her neck strong under the lamplight.

You see that door there, Dandy? She lifted a drink from the coffee table. Spilled some on her hand as she pointed. *The basement door?*

Uh huh.

Dandy was trembling now. A little bit.

Go and knock on it.

Dandy looked to the stained and faded green carpet.

I don't wanna.

Another cackle. Sounded like plastic breaking, the ice machine turning on.

Don't wanna? Sipping her drink. *I'm not asking what you* wanna *do, Dandelion. I'm telling you what you're going to do. Now go knock on that basement door.*

Sometimes, to Dandy, her eyes looked wetter than tears could make them.

Dandy crossed the living room; his small sneakers squeaked when he reached the cracked tile.

At the basement door, he raised a closed fist.

I don't wanna.

Go on now.

I don't wanna.

Go on.

Dandy breathed deep.

He knocked.

Then he turned quick with a mind to run to the couch.

But Momma was standing right there behind him.

Dandy cried out and Momma laughed again and spilled more of her drink. It made a thick splashing sound on the tile. Sounded like falling blood.

Face the door, Momma said. *Face your dead daddy.*

Dandy, shaking, shook his head no.

Daddy ain't coming through that door.

Not yet he ain't, Momma said. *We have to ask him to first.*

She laughed and her laugh was the cracking of glass, the splintering of a basement door. She put her arm around Dandy's shoulders.

But we don't have to ask him today.

They never did ask him. But Dandy never saw that door the same way again.

Momma knew how to scare someone. Momma knew horror.

Now, in his lair, Dandy's blood is hot. He feels the old familiar heat, rising within, the heckling madness of knowing that all these people in all these places pretend to be scared with their movies and their stories and their hayrides and their ghost hunts and their cemetery break-ins and Goddammit *nobody* would do any of these things if there were actually *something to be scared of.*

He takes a deep breath. He's got to. Getting too hot.

Because this is where Dandy comes in.

He's gonna give someone what they ask for. He's gonna scare someone for real.

Right here in Samhattan. Right here at the Hoke County Carnival.

He's breathing as hard as his pigtailed momma did that day outside the basement door. He closes his eyes. If he thinks about this too much he can go crazy with memories of the kids at Holly High, frothing in the halls about how *scared* they'd been.

At Niagara Falls, Gardner Nolan said to Kelly Rhine in the hall before math class, *there's a haunted house where you gotta follow this little red dot through darkness. By the end you don't even know what's coming from where!*

They laughed that day. Gardner and Kelly. Shared a laugh in the hall.

Dandy punches the dirt wall. Didn't they *know* that the only reason they entered that fucking tourist attraction was because they knew that it was *safe?* Didn't they *KNOW THAT?*

Dandy tries to calm down. But it's not working.

The carnival will be here in hours. They'll set up their rides so the people of Samhattan can pretend to be brave.

The animal in the cage growls. Dandy doesn't even look its way, just growls with it. Then he closes his eyes, releases a chilling howl, and digs his fingertips into the dirt walls. The anger is electrifying; his anger is not phony.

A memory comes unannounced, a stretch three months ago when he was following the carnival on its southern course. Hell, he'd *dropped out* so he could study the damn thing. Spent time in Memphis, Little Rock, Jackson, and Baton Rouge. And every small town between. Dandy bought a ticket for each, but didn't ride the rides, didn't toss the rings. Rather, he studied. From what felt like deep within his jean jacket and raven hair, he observed the faces of the people; the people Momma could've scared to death.

He learned the layout, too. The exact dimensions of the carnival. Where everything would stand. Including the House of Horrors, and where to dig beneath it.

Dandy opens his eyes. His fingertips are bleeding. The lantern light makes his blood look black. Like he's got something very dark inside him and it's just begun to leak.

The caged beast growls. This time Dandy responds directly.

"*Not yet!*"

THURSDAY EVENING, Susan tells Dad and Mom that she's going to the Carnival on Saturday afternoon.

"Who with?" Dad asks.

"Nobody."

The word just slips out. Susan doesn't like the sound of it. *Nobody.*

Dad doesn't like it either.

"Really?"

"Come on," Mom says, looking up from the book she's reading. "Surely one of your…"

She can't even say the word, Susan thinks. Can't even say *friends.* There aren't any of those.

"*Nobody?*" Dad echoes.

"Don't worry, Dad," Susan says, a tremor in her voice. But what can she do? Why should she be denied the Hoke County Carnival? "I'm not asking you to come along."

Dad looks to Mom. Susan can read it in their eyes. Do we let her go? Do we try to stop her? She's certainly old enough. Seventeen is old enough to do just about anything.

"It's not a big deal," Susan says, playing with the ends of her blonde hair. She means to look comfortable but it's actually making her look nervous. She stops. "Everyone from town will be there. And the Carnival lasts three days. I'm sure I'm not the only person going alone."

But she's not sure. And the feeling hurts.

Another look between Mom and Dad.

"You'll need to borrow my car," Dad says.

Susan nods. "Okay. Thanks. I was going to walk but—"

"No. Holly Park is three miles away."

It's supposed to be a touching moment: Dad helping her out in a different way. Not going with her to the Carnival like he would've even a year or two ago, but still…helping.

Still, it comes off flat. For Susan, it all feels flat.

But she won't let it stop her from going to the Carnival.

"Thank you," Susan says, believing that one day she'll look back at this conversation as the time Mom and Dad officially accepted that there were some things their daughter had to do alone, if she were going to do anything at all. It's incredibly empowering. She doesn't need to know what anybody is doing, or who might attend the HCC with whom. For a moment, she doesn't care.

But by Friday evening, she's online, checking social media.

She shouldn't be doing this. She knows she shouldn't. But sometimes she slips into what she calls "The Pit." It's the place she goes when she's feeling especially self-aware. The Pit is her own place, where she reads posts from other students at Holly High, reads about their exciting lives, sees the photos of parties she knows nothing about, trips to the beaches, nights out at the movies, and, yes, right here, plans to attend the Hoke County Carnival. How is it possible, Susan seethes, that here she has so much in common with all these people yet not one of them is a friend?

Jesus. Take Melissa Underwood. Here her page says she's trying to wrap up all her homework tonight so that she can spend all three days at the HCC. All three days. Isn't Susan preparing for the carnival, too? Just look how many comments there are on Melissa's post!

Susan sees the number is fourteen. Not to mention the ninety-one likes. Jesus Christ, if Susan posted the same thing she'd get none of any of it, except Aunt Pam, who always posts encouragements even if Susan says she's having a great day.

I love Michigan summers, Susan has posted in the past.

Chin up, Susan! Aunt Pam has responded.

"Nobody can believe somebody like you is happy."

Susan shouldn't say these things, shouldn't think this way. She stares at her own page and considers writing the same thing Melissa did. Verbatim.

She types it in. Then she changes it to something more her own.

Plan: get homework done, then Carnival it for three days.

"This is ridiculous," she says. She gets up from her desk and crosses the room. Dad and Mom have taught her that what matters are the actual people you surround yourself with, your family and your friends. And if you haven't made friends yet? You will. She will. Susan will. At college and beyond college and dammit there's somebody out there who feels the same way she does about it all and maybe Susan will meet him or her in line at a grocery store in California or maybe they'll meet on a plane to New York. But to worry about something so trivial right now...the amount of likes...

Her computer dings. She hurries to the desk again.

Who from? She checks.

"Dammit."

Aunt Pam.

Homework is good for you, Susan! Don't worry! You can do it.

Because *that's* what Susan meant with her post.

Susan deletes the post.

She takes her backpack to her desk and pulls out her homework.

The Pit, she thinks. So easy to fall into.

So hard to climb back out.

"Well, it's your own fault," she says. "You dug it yourself."

WITH THE exception of two things, Dandy is done.

His lair is what he wants it to be. And with the lights off, it's even more. Still, work to be done. Fun work. Final touches.

For starters, there's the mask.

It's just an oval mirror, taken from the first floor bathroom of the house he'd squatted in for six months. But it's not really just a mirror anymore. Two holes drilled for the eyes and a leather belt he'd found in a box of dead Dad's things many years ago. The belt hurt the back of his head when he tightened it, but that didn't matter because he wasn't going to wear it for very long.

He wears it now.

With the lights on, he can see enough of the lair through the holes to know where he stands, to avoid knocking anything over. But he wonders. How well will it work in the dark?

From his backpack he removes a second, much smaller mirror. He holds it up.

The effect is magnificent, though nobody is going to see it this way; the tunnel of reflections, his own mirrored face forming that tunnel, traveling deeper into a reflective infinity.

He removes the mask.

He only has one more dig to do. The most important dig yet. But he can't take care of *that* until the Carnival is set up.

They will arrive in minutes.

Dandy crosses the lair and gets his jean jacket from the dirt. He turns off the lights. Because he was very careful not to put the light switch anywhere near the entrance to his lair (lest someone looks for it), Dandy has to pass through his creation the same way his victim will.

Blind.

It's a chilling experience and Dandy finds himself scared, though, of course, he can't be truly horrified by something he himself has built. When he reaches the point of entry, he climbs the metal rungs, slides the tarp aside, and sticks his head out from underground.

He hears a rumbling. Cars in the parking lot? Maybe. Maybe it's the carnival trucks, arriving minutes earlier than Dandy has anticipated. The sun is on its way up and Dandy squints as he emerges from his lair. Through the bushes, he eyes the empty park. The next time he sees this place, it will be completely changed.

He makes sure the front door is covered, then makes sure again.

By the time he reaches the parking lot, a red pickup truck is pulling in. The timing is incredible. The men in the cabin look the part: unshaven, groggy, probably hung over, too. The night before was Pinckney, Michigan. Less than a hundred miles from Samhattan. Dandy knows this because he knows everything there is to know about the HCC.

"So close, Momma," he says.

The men don't see him as he exits the parking lot and turns right on May Street, heading toward town on foot. But he sees them.

And that, he knows, is how it's going to be.

SUSAN WALKS the dog. She must make the same decision every time she walks Bonnie; either she follows Darryl Road left, tracing a mile and a half circle through subdivision streets that will bring her back home, or she follows May Street to Old Town.

Tonight, she chooses masochism. Tonight, she chooses downtown.

Ahead, the lights are plenty. The restaurants and shops, the ice-cream parlor, the theaters, the offices, the stores. Other people walk their dogs, couples hold hands, middle schoolers skateboard the brick stretch of road known as Old Town, though it is all mostly new.

Bonnie tugs on the leash. She's interested in the garden lining the front walk of the very last house before Old Town. The street lamps illuminate the mutt as she lifts her legs and pees on the flowers.

"Bonnie," Susan tugs. "Do you have to do it in the light?"

But Bonnie's not finished. Susan watches the couples ahead. The teenagers. Hears the laughter. The music coming from the restaurants. She thinks there's a live band. Isn't sure. Altogether, with the lights, the music, the people, Old Town looks like its own little carnival.

Susan realizes, suddenly, that she is growing older. And just like the day came when she gave up trick-or-treating, her carnivals are ultimately numbered.

"This will be the last," she tells Bonnie. The dog rubs her side against Susan's leg, letting her know she's finished. Susan looks down. "Did you hear that, Bonnie? I'm growing up."

She walks Bonnie toward the lights. The high squealing laughter of a young woman sails from a restaurant patio and Susan pauses.

It's Juan's Place, Samhattan's Mexican restaurant, and Susan's favorite food in the world. The customer who laughed, the young woman, the one Susan recognizes as Lisa Marigold, is wearing a sombrero.

"Come on, Bonnie."

Susan looks up the street to the lights of the movie theater. She thinks she spots Dandelion Andrews entering the building. Was that him? Whoever it was seemed to emerge from the blur of bodies and cars on May Street. Could've been him. She hopes it was. Hopes he's out there somewhere, living a better life than the one he led at Holly High.

She considers the movies herself. Why not? A night out. Alone. Why not take in a movie tonight, the Carnival tomorrow? She's seventeen years old. She can do anything she wants to. Like Dandelion Andrews, if that was him, she can emerge from the blur of every day life with a purpose. A plan.

"Come on, Bonnie. Let's head home."

No movies tonight. Not for her. But the carnival. Soon.

DANDY IS at the movies. The movie is called *Blood*. The magazines told him it was a good one, a modern classic, but Dandy can't quit thinking about the man behind the camera, the fact that someone is running the lights. The idea that one or more of the actors or actresses has a list of demands that have nothing to do with the characters they play and it's completely ruining any possibility of a scare for him.

And there's more. There's a group of four teenagers four rows up. The guys snicker, the girls half-cover their eyes. After a woman covered in blood rolls out of a fallen garbage can on the screen, one of the boys lightly punches the other's shoulder. The girls shake their heads then bury them further into their boyfriends' shoulders.

Dandy is feeling the heat.

This, he knows, is the apex of phony fear.

The movies.

Sitting alone, no drink or snacks, he watches the backs of their heads.

A scare on screen. The girls scream. The boys laugh. Then the girls laugh, too.

Blood.

The girls, one blonde, one brunette, look so straight out of an Archie comic that they represent all of phony America for Dandy. As if the whole country is laughing at the scares.

The blonde whispers something to the boy beside her. The boy, adjusting the collar of his Holly High varsity jacket, shakes his head.

Nothing to be afraid of, he must be saying. *Gotta be brave.*

So brave.

So brave.

Another scare, a telephone ringing at just the wrong moment, and the girls shriek berserk. The boys laugh at them. One of the girls, the brunette, pony-tailed, looks over her shoulder, wearing a smile of relief, and sees Dandy is staring at her.

She stops smiling.

Looks ahead again.

On the screen, an old man is telling a young girl about the temperature of blood. How it gets hotter with fear, with excitement, with anger.

Dandy is feeling the heat.

The brunette, anxious, looks over her shoulder again. The images play out huge beyond her but Dandy can make out some of her face. Can she make out his?

She taps her boyfriend on the shoulder.

He half turns, shrugs.

Don't worry about it, baby. Be brave.

But the girl looks worried.

These are exactly the kind of Holly High kids Dandy needs to scare.

Momma's way.

As the dark colors of the movie, the deep reds, dance upon his eyes, the tip of his nose, his fingers upon the arm rests, Dandy imagines any of these four in his lair.

Oh man.

Oh *man.*

The brunette turns again. Yeah, she's worried. Yeah.

Dandy knows now she's more afraid of him than she is of the movie.

That's because she paid for the movie.

Dandy doesn't move a muscle, still as a snake. Stares back.

She seems transfixed. Deep down she knows the pictures on the screen can't hurt her. But the man behind her in the theater…

She almost seems to be shaking her head no. And Dandy agrees. *No. That's not real. But yes. This is.*

Another jump scare, screeching violins, crashing drums, and the blonde is still in it, still gripping her boyfriend's Holly High varsity jacket, still lifting her bare knees up to her chin, hiding from the terrible, violent scenes on the screen.

But the brunette is different now. Doesn't react at all to the movie.

She's scared of something else.

Dandy's blood boils. It feels good: the heat, the claustrophobia, the proximity to real fear. He wants to take all four of them into the lair, teach them. Give them a lesson on horror. Teach them the truth about scares.

But the brunette alone would do.

By the end of the movie, the boyfriends have laughed so much it's almost become part of the soundtrack. And when the four teenagers get up to leave, as the white credits scroll, Dandy watches them walk the aisle. He keeps a steady eye on the brunette who anxiously looks, once, twice, in his direction.

When they're out of the theater, Dandy gets up and follows them.

But the Holly High teenagers aren't done with the movies yet. Of course not. They're not exiting the theater, not stepping out into the well-lit wonders of Old Town. Instead, one of the boys stands guard, plays lookout (so brave) as the others sneak into a second movie. Then lookout follows them in.

Dandy follows them in, too.

It's a comedy and it's already begun. The Holly High kids are sitting near the front. Dandy slips up the carpeted stairs, hands deep in the pockets of his jean jacket; a phantom, a vampire, a strangler along the theater wall.

He sits two rows behind them.

When the very first joke is made, when the bearded fat actor trips over a tricycle and the theater erupts into laughter, Dandy screams.

It's an awful sound. Pained, porous, pure.

The sound of a man who has seen the face of fear.

Everybody turns to face him. The scream is so violent that something terrible must have happened, and yet…

Just Dandy. Just a guy watching a movie screen.

The quartet faces him.

"Hey, man," one of the brave boys says. "What the hell was *that?*"

But Dandy stares at the screen. Watching the movie, after all. And with the next joke, comes the second scream.

It's even more honest than the first.

Dandy thinks he hears the brunette say, "That's him." But her voice is trembling. She is more scared here, in this comedy, than she was in *Blood*.

People whisper. Some ask him to be quiet.

Dandy isn't listening.

Another joke. Another scream.

Then hands upon him, the ushers drag him, screaming still, bug-eyed, out of the theater, through the lobby, to the front doors. They yell at him, tell him he's done something wrong, ask if he's been drinking. Dandy isn't listening. Once they've got him outside, Dandy makes a phony lunge toward the bigger of the two, then turns and walks away.

Buried in the shadows of his black hair, Dandy smiles, recalling the expression on the face of the big usher.

Real fear.

The unknown.

Dandy heads to Holly Park.

Where more smiles await him.

SUSAN SLEEPS. Bonnie is at the foot of her bed. Mom and Dad are watching a movie downstairs. It's Friday night, but Susan is already in bed, already dreaming. In her dream she is forced to give a speech, or a performance, she isn't sure. Either way, she's waiting to take the stage, waiting to get up and make a fool of herself in front of everybody ignoring her. She tries to find a friend to help her out, someone to tell her she's going to be okay, but there's nobody backstage with her. Not even someone to tell her when to go on.

There is no friend.

And she will have to endure this moment alone.

DANDY IS below. He's taking care of the final dig. Upon returning to Holly Park he saw that the carnival had indeed been set up exactly as his map told him it would be. Sneaking past the night watchman was easy; the carny was drunk and snoring in the cabin of his Dodge truck.

Now, Dandy digs up, creating a hole, a new point of entry. Not a second front door, no, but the friend door, the door by which he'll invite someone in.

When he's dug through, he has to saw a hole in the floor of the House of Horrors. It's the most important step in the whole process. Connects the two lairs. One paid for. One not.

Once he's sawed, the lair no longer stands alone. Now an extension of what the carnies have erected above.

Dandy screws hinges into the circle he's sawed.

Susan sleeps.

Dandy tests the sawed circle, making sure it opens and closes. Closes securely. Adds the lock. Locks from below.

Susan sleeps.

Dandy, done, sleeps, too.

And tomorrow, at last, is the Hoke County Carnival for both.

AT THE gate, on foot now, Susan pats her pockets and makes sure she's got her phone and wallet. She's checked for both many times since she got behind the wheel of Dad's car and drove the three miles to Holly Park. The key is in a holder connected to the back of her phone.

"One?"

"Yep."

The small old lady behind the yellow wooden booth reminds Susan how big she is. And while Susan is smarter than this, she remembers something Dad said:

Just because you know what's right and what's wrong doesn't mean you always believe it.

The lady hands her a red ticket and Susan enters Holly Park through an aisle of plastic yellow flags that split the evergreens on both side. Then, past the last of the trees, she sees, finally, the carnival in all its kaleidoscopic splendor.

She smiles, but the smile doesn't last long. Yes, it's as colorful as she recalls, a memory as recent as last year. Yes, the music is right, the hollering little kids are right, the couples laughing and playing games, the groups of boys and girls. It's all right, she doesn't doubt that, but at the same time, this time, she also notices the dirt beneath her shoes. The dirt beneath the stalls and attractions. The garbage cans. The fact that the façades on most the rides are cheap plastic and not forged in some carnival netherworld, risen to be ridden. She notices the smells, not all of them elephant ears, some of them cringe-worthy, like passing the Samhattan dump in June. The paint on the Ferris Wheel is chipped. The tattoos on the arms of the carnies are faded (and don't necessarily suggest fantastical realms, like her much younger self assumed). The air is stuffy, the lines are long, and even the big hideous eyes above the door to the House of Horrors are two slightly different colors.

Has she changed? Is it her? Has the HCC always looked this way and now, for Susan, nothing will look the same ever again?

"Okay," she says. "Loosen the heck up."

Yes. Time to have fun. Because going to the carnival alone doesn't mean standing at its outer edge, watching everybody else get involved. Susan's decided to experience the HCC no matter what. So she better get to experiencing.

The very second she starts walking, a man eyes her, looks her up and down, head to shoe. At first, Susan thinks the older man is going to ask her a question, then realizes he's actually interested in her. She blushes. It feels, today, like a silent compliment. One she'll take.

She's taller than most people she passes, boy or girl, man or woman, almost every carny, too.

To her right a mustachioed barker cries out through a megaphone, begging newcomers to try their hand at a game of basketball. Susan was once courted by the Holly High coaches. She tried out, did alright for never having played in her life, and never went back again.

"Three shots for a dollar," the man says. His ponytail looks phony, like it's a part of his hat. Susan fishes a dollar out of her shorts and hands it over. He hands her the ball.

"You any good?" he asks.

Good. The word sounds nice. She hasn't thought it all day.

"Yeah, I'm any good."

She shoots, misses badly.

"Make one and you get a prize."

"Just one?"

She shoots. Makes it.

"Well, I'll be," the man says.

"What happens if I make two?"

"You get a bigger prize."

Susan eyes the stuffed animals. There's one of Sylvester the Cat from Looney Tunes that she likes.

"They're all the same size," she says.

She shoots and misses, then asks for the black and white Sylvester Cat, which is bigger than it looks hanging from the fence. She notices the fence is old, all bent up.

She feels good, carrying the cat. Like she needed something to do with her hands and hadn't realized as much. As soon as she's past him, the barker's voice blends in with three-dozen others, and Susan finally feels carried away by the carnival. The creaking of the big steel rides, the flapping of the plastic flags, the sign boards painted with prices, the smells of candy and fried foods, the people.

"I'm glad you came," she tells herself. She holds Sylvester close to her side, smiles at the kids who ogle the stuffed animal with envy.

She sees a little girl trying to catch a wooden fish with a magnet attached to a fishing line. Her parents cheer her on.

Susan imagines the girl grown up.

Who will be her friends? Who will notice her when she's all grown up?

"None of that," she tells herself.

"Tall Blonde! Miss Tall Blonde!" a wiry woman calls. "Come throw a dart! Could change your life!"

"How much?"

"A dollar for three tries."

Susan eyes the prizes. Rubber snakes and rubber rats. She thinks these strange.

She fishes a dollar out of her pocket and hands it over. Sylvester in the dirt at her feet, she tosses the first dart, the second, the third.

"I'm sorry," the lady says. "You looked like someone with good aim."

Susan shrugs, thanks the lady, moves on.

Ahead, the words: *FUNNEST HOUSE!* Susan recognizes some students from Holly High in line.

"You!" A thin, bearded man, red carnival apron, "Test your strength?"

Susan smiles kindly at the man. She's in it now, the HCC; it feels like she's floating on her own disc, tossed by an unseen hand, still heading toward the bottles. Will she land a winner?

"You look like you could beat most of the men here."

The bearded man again. Kind of paying a compliment but also kind of not. Susan eyes the sledgehammer in his hand. He winks at her.

"Try it?"

Some oohs and ahs. People watching. It feels like the start of one of her bad dreams.

Susan reaches into her pocket.

"Hell yeah," the man says, holding out the sledgehammer. He steps aside, revealing the object Susan is supposed to strike. It looks like a flattened doorknob.

"I'm one of those tall people who's also really weak," Susan jokes. Nobody laughs.

"The high today is Not Bad," the man says, pointing to a low appellation on the strength meter.

Susan nods. "Okay."

"One strike and—"

But Susan is already hefting the hammer, already bringing it down. She's used everything she's got, given all her anger and isolation to that oblong metal target.

Above, the word WEAKLING blinks red and yellow.

"Aw," the man says. "Try again?"

"I think that's all I had."

The man winks again. "Naw, you've got more. I wouldn't be surprised if I saw it come out today."

Susan nods, not sure what he means. But she likes the sound of it. The truth is, she feels good. Suddenly glad to be alone. It's as if she's experiencing the Hoke County Carnival for what it actually is for the first time.

There's truth in being alone, she thinks. Just as there's truth in light.

Susan picks up the Sylvester stuffed animal and continues, past the feats of strength. Kids sit for caricature drawings. Couples order corn dogs. Dads admonish their kids. Moms do it even better.

Directly above her, people howl from the Ferris Wheel. Next to her, a sudden voice:

"Hey you, can I guess your weight?"

He's an older man. In his sixties, Susan thinks. He's tiny, wears a plaid suit, and clearly knows a good show when he sees one.

It's not that Susan is unhappy with herself. She's not. But she knows what the people near the All Knowing Scale are thinking. To prove she doesn't care, and to, perhaps, continue the free feeling she has, the unfamiliar joy at being alone, she says yes.

She hands the man a dollar.

"And we've got one, ladies and gentlemen!"

A cluster of boys watch. Couples. Little girls. Susan winks at one of the girls.

"Step on the All Knowing Scale," the man says. Suddenly Susan imagines him as a father, like her own dad, worried about his own daughter being out on her own somewhere right now.

Why does it feel like the truth of everything is showing itself today? And why is it not so bad?

"Step on the scale so they can all see your weight. I'll be facing them as I guess."

He turns his back to her, covers his eyes with one hand.

Susan steps up onto the wobbly metal disc. She reads the meter.

There are some gasps from those gathered, but Susan doesn't mind. She notices a small mirror in the hand covering the man's eyes.

"I looked at you, miss," he calls over his shoulder. "And I added up the numbers. And I *know* that you must be…" a pause, anticipation.

When he guesses her weight correctly, the people clap. It's all a dismal little display, Susan thinks. Something she'll tell friends about one day, rolling her eyes.

Yes, she thinks, friends.

Because suddenly she knows she'll have them one day. Suddenly she knows the exact amount of influence this moment will have on the rest of her life.It's not much.

The man is looking at her, smiling. He takes a bow.

"I'm rarely wrong," he says. "It's why they gave me this particular gig."

Susan reaches across a yellow rope and takes a prize boomerang from the fence. Sticks it in her back pocket.

"Hey hey," the man says, coming closer. "Those are for the winners. For the ones I guess wrong."

Susan smiles. Nods. "Or I can tell everyone about the mirror you hold up to your eyes when you pretend not to be looking. Up to you."

The man in plaid looks over his shoulder. Nods to Susan.

"Scram," he says.

Susan scrams. Sylvester doll, boomerang, and all.

Ahead, the big eyes of the House of Horrors. She's in line before she's decided to do it.

The line moves quicker than it looks like it should and Susan notices speakers above the entrance. It's not for music but rather the screams of the people inside.

"You can only go with the people you came with!" the barker tells the line. His face is painted green. "No teaming up!"

Susan wonders if this means she's going to have to do this alone.

A few feet from a witch painted on a sign, she receives a text from Mom.

You get there okay?

Susan writes back.

Yep. I'm good. About to enter the scary house.

"You," the barker says. "You alone?"

Screams come through the speakers. Then laughter, too.

"Yes."

"You're very brave!"

"I guess so. Today anyway."

She climbs the wooden steps.

"You can only go in with who you came with," the man repeats, just for her. "That okay?"

"That's fine."

"Alright," the man says. "You're on. And remember…you can keep telling yourself it's only a ride…but that doesn't mean the monsters know that."

He winks.

The wooden doors open. They're teeth, Susan realizes. The mouth belonging to the big eyes, the mouth spreading open.

Susan steps inside.

AFTER THE first jump-scare, it's not too bad. Susan isn't as scared as she thought she'd be. So many rubber faces, most behind glass, lit from below, green skulls, bleeding eyes, claws and jaws. Random and recurring smoking gunshots make her jump and there must be air holes by her feet because every few steps she feels a brief hard-blowing wind. Ahead is darkness, and Susan knows something must be waiting.

She's right.

But it's not too bad.

Down one hall, then another. A strobe light is triggered, showing her a werewolf, taller than her, arms raised, teeth bared.

Susan smiles because, while it gives her a start, she knows there's a man who's touring with a carnival and whose job it is to stand in that mask and wait for her. She likes the costume and so she lifts her phone to snap a photo of it.

But the werewolf fans a hand.

"No phones," he says.

Susan has time to see a text from Mom.

Be careful in there. Dad's making tacos later. Love you.

A scream ahead. Fog. Fake webbing on the walls. Giant plastic spiders in purple light. To her right, a coffin door creaks open. A half-rotted man sits up.

Susan thinks they did a good job with the makeup. Wants to tell them so, but keeps walking.

Howls in the distance. Howls nearby. She bumps into a wall, realizes she has to turn left.

Ahead, darkness.

"I'm alone," she says, as if these two words might bring whoever's ahead to take it easy on her.

She ducks under something gooey and is blinded by another strobe. This time it shows her an old woman in a rocking chair. Darkness again. A flash of green light. An evil elf against the wall. The sound of knives sharpening. A chainsaw starting up.

She enters a dimly lit room. A metal fence separates her from men and women in lab coats, a writhing patient on a slab.

"Just in time," one doctor says. He steps aside, revealing that the patient has been sawed in half. Then, darkness again. Another wall. Howling. A legitimate shriek. A strobe revealing a graveyard. Green turf and dirt. Organ music. The foam stones read:

Rest in Pieces
Here lies you
A skeleton falls from the ceiling, rattles inches from her.
To her right a rat scurries. Something bigger to her left.
A mummy down the hall, seen in strobe. There, gone. There.
Gone.

Total darkness ahead. Susan goes to it. Walks with her arms out, feels a wooden wall, has to turn, but no, she's in a corner. How? She feels with her feet, feels an opening by her knees. She has to crawl.

She gets on her knees and worries she won't fit through the opening.
She fits. She crawls.

Hands reach out and grip her ankles. Cackling laughter from close speakers.

Through it, she gets up. Takes a hall to the right. Sees a dead family, rubber, behind glass. A left hall. A giant spider. Darkness. Wood. Has to turn.

Ahead, a sight.

She can't say exactly why, but it's the scariest thing in here.

It's not rubber. It's not a creature she recognizes from a movie. Not a vampire, a zombie, a mummy. No ghost.

It's a man. She can tell by the way he moves.

His back is arched, he's pointing down, pointing to the ground.

Susan walks toward him because there's no other way to go. Is it blood on the ground? A grave? What's he pointing to? What is she supposed to see?

Arms out, her fingertips graze the wood walls. She thinks of Dad making tacos. Thinks of herself out of this place; imagines the hot sun again.

"I'm alone," she says again. Maybe he'll go easy on her. But he's not doing anything but pointing to the ground.

Inches from him, she recoils.

Where his face should be, she sees her own.

"Jesus," she says. A mask made of mirrors. Or just one. Like someone strapped the bathroom mirror to his head.

Susan makes to pass him but the man holds out an arm and points to the fog at his feet with the other one.

In the glass, she looks confused.

At her feet, through the fog, she sees ladder rungs. A hole in the floor.

"Really?" Susan says. Far away someone screams.

The mirror does not move. Nor does the arm in her way. Nor does the finger pointing down.

Susan stares into her own eyes.

Are you going to do this? she seems to ask herself.

But what else is there to do? This is the next step in the House of Horrors at the Hoke County Carnival. A walk through the basement.

"Okay," she finally says. "I get it. I'm supposed to go down."

Her head nods but she's not nodding her head. He is.

A question flies bat-like and quick through her mind, too fast to catch.

A basement in Holly Park?

She looks in the mirror. Shakes her head.

"Okay. You guys are crazy."

She turns, plants a foot on the first rung. Climbs down. Looks up to see the mirror is facing her, sees herself up to her waist in cellar shadow.

Another few rungs and she feels dirt beneath her shoes.

A lighted green arrow tells her where to go next. Otherwise, a darkness darker than that above.

She takes a few steps, spots a second green arrow, hears the unmistakable sound of a wood door closing. A latch. A lock.

She turns around.

A glowing green arrow. Pointing at her.

Did someone close the door to the basement?

She turns and walks. If she's going to do this, she's going to do this.

Above, thuds. Screaming. Low voices.

A scratching behind her, long nails splintering wood. Susan turns. For a second she thinks she sees the outline of a coat. A jacket. A jean jacket.

She pulls her phone from her pocket and turns on the flashlight.

He's there, the man with the mirror mask, crouched on the rungs, facing her.

She turns. Feels a little hot. She's going to walk through this basement, then walk back up, then exit this place.

From the darkness to her right, fingers, a hand snatches her phone.

The green arrows go dark.

"Hey! What are you doing? That's mine!"

She waits, palm open, expecting to feel her phone returned.

When it isn't, she turns around, heads back toward the rungs, walks hard into a flat wooden wall that wasn't there when she used her light.

She feels a little hot. A little shut-in.

"Hello?"

Susan turns to face the darkness.

Her nightmare has begun.

II

IT'S THE sounds coming from above that are the worst of it. The darks halls don't help, the seemingly undecorated walls, the fact that nobody and nothing has leapt out at her in what feels like too long a time, none of that is any good. But the sounds…upstairs…muffled shrieks and screams, the creaking ceiling, even laughter from far away. It's as if she's not only in a different part of the House of Horrors than anybody else, but it's like she's actually completely alone.

It's one thing to be alone in life, and Susan has worked hard to come to grips with where she's at, she's in a good place, she sees a good future, but it's a different thing to feel alone *here*.

"Hey," she says, arms out, walking slow so she doesn't run into another wall. "Someone took my phone. Are they going to give that back?"

Her voice doesn't carry the way she thinks it should. It stops mere inches from her lips, doesn't sound powerful enough to reach anybody, if anybody else is down here.

She thinks of the man in the mask.

It's no good, thinking of him, the way he was crouched in the rungs, the reflection of her own flashlight in the mirror. In her right hand is Sylvester the Cat, still, the stuffed animal like a buffer between herself and whatever is waiting ahead. But it doesn't feel like enough. Sylvester versus the man in the mirror mask. Doesn't feel like enough.

"Hello?"

Her voice isn't enough either. She sounds tiny. Muffled. Scared.

Is she scared? She doesn't want to be. But isn't that what she's asked for? To be scared?

Maybe, she thinks, just maybe this is the best carnival horror house she's ever walked through. Maybe, just maybe, what she's experiencing right now is what the students at school would call "next level shit." There's no question the halls she walks now are much freakier than the ones she walked upstairs. Is it possible the HCC has had a breakthrough? Are all haunted house attractions scarier now, all over the country?

She remembers Dad saying something like this to her. Warning her that the world keeps growing whether or not you do. That was why a person needed to accept who they were, what they looked like, how much money they had, how funny they were, so that they could make the changes they wanted to make before the world spun so fast that everything whirred out of reach.

Besides, she thinks, if this *isn't* a really good advancement in the House of Horrors, then what is it?

"Hello? Am I alone down here?"

It feels that way. Christ, it feels like she's been alone since the green arrows went dark. She hasn't heard so much as a shuffle from behind, ahead, from the side. And the halls just keep coming, one after another. She must have walked twenty of them by now. How far could it go? Could it stretch farther than the boundaries of Holly Park? Could she be blindly walking all the way home?

Susan looks up.

Is she that far away? Is she all the way home?

"No," she says, keeping her voice down. The ceiling creaks, or rather, she hears the floor creak up there. The ceiling down here is dirt.

She stops walking. This is too much. Someone must be watching her, someone must know where she is. The man in the mirror mask works for the HCC and he saw her come down and he knows she's still down here. Nothing to worry about. Or, she shouldn't *let* it worry her because if she starts freaking out, for real, down here, in the dark, overhearing the sounds of a world she believes she should be a part of, a world away, if she loses it right now, she's going to *really* lose it down here.

She breathes. Steady. She's never been an anxious person and she doesn't plan on becoming one now. She believes that if she keeps walking ahead, she'll eventually come to a door that leads to some steps that bring her back upstairs. This? This right now? This is the royal treatment is what this is.

"You're alone."

Okay, she can work with this. She recalls the line she stood in to enter the House of Horrors. She sees the big eyes. The doors she hadn't known were teeth until she got close enough to tell. Was anybody else alone in line? Anybody at all?

The ticket-taker's face, the way he winked at her. Ah. Okay. He must have decided, then, to give her the royal treatment. *This one*, he must've told someone, by way of a small gesture. *This one goes down to the basement.*

There's that word again. *Basement.* How in the world does Holly Park have a basement?

This must be one of those scenarios in which the answer to a seemingly impossible question is actually very simple. Something she hasn't thought of at all. Must be. Has to be. Is. Because if it's not, if the question she's asking can't be answered with an easy explanation, then Susan must be, has to be, is, in some trouble.

Is she in trouble?

"You can't just take someone's phone," she says. "You're not even supposed to touch people."

No answer. Not even the sound of someone breathing. Shit, she would never have imagined, on her own, how much scarier the House of Horrors could be if you walked through it when, say, it was closed. Nobody to jump out at you. No thumping music. No air-pressure gunshots. No games. Just you and the empty space. You and the shitty wood walls. The stuffy smell. The sense of being closed in.

In the dark.

She walks again. Has to. If she doesn't, if she stands still for too long it starts to feel like something worse than a man with fangs is going to get her. No lights down here. Not even the solitary red dot she'd heard of in other houses of horrors across America. She'd love to follow a red dot right now. She'd love someone to scream in her ear. Anything to prove she hasn't been forgotten. Hasn't been ignored.

Susan wants to stop again, wants to yell, hey hey, this isn't right. This sucks is what this does. Do you know I'm down here? Did the guy in the mirror mask forget I was down here? Does he still have my phone?

Is he down here with me?

She closes her eyes, opens them, closes them again. She can't tell which is worse. At the end of another hall, she turns right, continues, hands out, using Sylvester like a blind woman's support cane, let him take the brunt of a wood wall, let him get splinters in his paws. She needs to move faster. Wants to. It's the smell of it now. Before it was the sounds from above but now it's the smell. If she's honest with herself, if she really lays it out there, she has to admit that these basement halls don't smell like the halls upstairs did.

Down here it all smells like dirt. Fresh dirt. Like when Mom gets motivated and digs up half the back yard or when Dad pots the plants. Fresh dirt, yes, but not like the kind you buy to fill a hole. More like the kind that's exposed when you dig one.

Susan stops because Sylvester tells her there's a wall in front of her. She hopes she's reached the end. Now, finally, a strobe light is going to go off and she'll see a skeleton to the right or left and it'll become clear that she's gotta turn around and head back the exact way she came. Because the halls can't go on forever down here. Because there must be some kind of scare down here. And when she gets all the way back to the rungs she used to climb down here, when her phone is handed back to her, she'll look at the time and laugh at how brief a time it actually was.

But there's an opening to her left. And when she turns around to head back anyway, as she's lifting Sylvester to use him, she scrapes her fingers against a wood wall.

"Come on."

She feels disoriented, no doubt. Enclosed. Entombed. She takes one step into the hall veering left, then another. One step. Another. It's all she can do. It's what she must do. Someone is watching her, some carny in a booth, giggling at how good this really is, how scared the big blonde girl looks walking the empty halls, waiting for the scare, waiting, waiting, oh mercilessly waiting. Yes, there's some asshole who's loving this, sitting in a booth or standing out there in the dark, arms crossed, waiting for just the right moment to scare the living shit out of Susan.

Susan stops. She doesn't want to but the truth is, she's not liking this. At all. The idea of the carny isn't sitting well. Because to see her would mean to be near her. Night goggles on. Close enough to know when she's had enough; close enough to know when the big scare should come.

She swings Sylvester behind her, one solid windmill, expecting the stuffed animal to strike the very goggles she's imagining, sure to hear someone cry out. But Sylvester connects with nothing, *nothing*, and Susan loses her balance, stumbles forward, imagines falling into the arms of whoever must be down here with her, the tattooed arms of a carny whose entire job it is to scare her.

"Oh!" she cries out, nearly falling all the way over. But she stabilizes herself and stands, one leg out, Sylvester raised again in both hands, facing the darkness she'd just passed through, feeling the pressure of the darkness she has yet to endure.

She stays this way. If someone's gonna come, let them come. In fact, she considers staying this way until someone does. It's not a bad idea. If they're watching her, they'll know. They want her to keep going. What's a house of horrors without someone passing through it?

Yes. It's a revenge of sorts. As Susan comes to a standing position again, she imagines the frustration of the carnies. Come on, girl. Take the halls. Don't stand still. Come on. We've got something for you. We've got a big surprise for you. Don't rob us of our big surprise. Don't—

She thinks of the words she saw printed on the black wall behind the ticket taker outside. Something about "safe words"? Something about if you couldn't "take it"? Shit. She should've read that stuff. She shouldn't have assumed that the House of Horrors at the Hoke County Carnival would be exactly the same as it was every year.

The world moves fast, Dad often said, a look of having been blindsided every time he did. *Sometimes it'll sit still for what feels like forever and then it's turning so fast you miss the handrails.*

Okay. The HCC is turning too fast for Susan. That's fine. She'll stand still for what feels like forever. She'll stand still until they have no choice but to come get her.

That is, of course, if they're watching.

And which is worse? She wonders. The idea of the carnies in night goggles, stifling their laughter? Or nobody down here with her at all?

Doesn't matter. Not now. That's fine. She's fine. She'll wait.

Wait for them to come get her.

NOBODY'S COME. Nobody's coming.

Susan can't believe it. She alternates between anxiety and anger. The anger feels better, of course, but the situation is so shocking that she can't sustain any one emotion. She looks back the way she came, ahead the way she's supposed to go. How long has she been standing still? And are the sounds from above coming less frequently?

Yes. Yes they are. There are more spaces between the cries, the creaks, the shrieks. Susan tries not to think too much on this. It's enough to drive someone who feels like they may have been overlooked berserk.

She thinks of that movie where the people were left out in the ocean. How can she not? The boat counted wrong, forgot that couple. They had to fend for themselves. In the middle of the ocean. The lady made it. Didn't she? Did they both? She can't remember. Was it based on a true story? If so... couldn't she make it, too?

She's gotta stop thinking this way. But how else to think in the dark, alone, beneath the park?

She's gotta move. Whether or not someone's coming, there is most definitely a way out. There was a way in, there is a way out. It's not like a cement truck has come and closed the hole she entered by. She's gotta find it. Get back to those rungs.

She reaches out, feels along the walls, feeling for those green arrows. If she could find those she might find her way back. The arrows pointed deeper *into* the basement. She wants to get back out. Go the opposite way of the arrows. Right?

Nothing to it.

Only, the walls are bare. Or mostly. They're smoother than they should be, she thinks. No splinters here. She imagines them covered in fake carnival blood.

She pulls her hands away.

"Onward," she says, loud enough for the carny to hear, if a carny is actually near. Is one? Has to be. Because if there's not…

She looks up. When was the last time the ceiling creaked? What time did she come down here and how long has it been?

Susan walks. Into the darkness she walks, Sylvester the Cat like a shield, there to bear the brunt of the worst of what's to come. Because something has to come. Has to. A woman can't be told to climb down into a hole, told by someone who works for the carnival, and expect to never come out.

A bad thought comes to her. So bad that she actually winces, makes the face and all.

Does this particular carny work for the carnival? The man in the mirror mask, last seen crouched on the rungs. Didn't he look different to her than the other carnies? Didn't he move differently? Younger? Stronger? More like he had a plan?

She walks faster. Sylvester scrapes against one wall, another wall. Susan is starting to freak out a little bit. It's true. She doesn't want it to be true, but it is. It's not that it's so hot down here, it's not, it's cool like a basement is cool. But that's not helping. In fact, this particular cold is making her skin feel like rubber. Like she's the one in a monster costume. Like she's the one who's supposed to jump out when the man or woman comes traipsing through the dark, couples holding on to one another, whispering each other's names. The Tall Blonde Susan is supposed to come out, to make a sound, to scare them.

She wishes someone would make a sound. The anticipation is maddening. It has to happen. So happen already. Flash some lights. Send in the clowns. The scary ones. Send in anything that moves, anything with ears and eyes and a mouth behind a mask so she can ask it what's going on, how far to the end, how much longer till I'm out of here?

"Please," she says.

But that doesn't sound good. Saying that word makes her feel like she's in an even worse situation than the one that's scaring her. Saying please is like begging. It is begging. Please, end this for me, okay? Please?

"Hey, anyone down here?"

Down here. Why is she down here?

"Just let me know. Make a sound. You know? It's okay. I'm not mad. Just a little confused is all."

She can't even laugh nervously. Feels totally wrong.

"Okay," she says. She's getting angry again, walking faster. "Just make a sound, okay? Say something or do something. I'm worried I was left down here? Do I gotta start yelling for help? Am I gonna have to—"

"*BE CAREFUL IN THERE.*"

The words are so loud, so suddenly, brazenly loud, that Susan must bring her hands to her ears. The sounds from above are eclipsed. Her skin feels hot, too hot, like the lips the words passed over cannot be real, cannot be man or woman, cannot be of this world.

"*DAD'S MAKING TACOS LATER.*"

"Jesus!" Susan calls out. "What the fuck is going on?"

Because this doesn't feel right at all. It's not just the volume, the unbearable crackling of the words. It's the content. Someone is bullying her. Someone is reading the last text from Mom.

But it's not just the content either.

It's the voice, she thinks. *I never wanna hear that voice again.*

But she does. Right away.

"*LOVE YOU.*"

Despite the crippling volume of the words, despite the darkness, Susan is borderline running. Sylvester before her, she bangs into one wall, then another, then actually pounds on the walls with her fists, asking to be let out, demanding to be let out, talking about suing, about the law, about how much trouble the Hoke County Carnival is going to be in when people find out. The words sound weak, not to mention the muted aspect to her voice.

Incredibly, Susan has been in a recording studio before. Her Uncle Mitt, Dad's brother, plays guitar in a band of older guys and one afternoon Dad took Susan to the studio where Mitt and his band were making an album. Susan sat in the control room for hours, listening to the men bicker about seemingly small things and laugh together over mistakes. She read and looked on her phone and every now and again someone beyond the glass would ask her what she thought. Their voices were flat, no embellishments at all, as they came through the control room speakers. Dad took her into the live room for a few minutes and her own voice sounded just like theirs in that room.

See the foam? Dad said. *That's to dull the extra noise. This is a controlled environment.*

Her voice, her pleas, sound like that now. Flat. Meek. Like she could give a speech to rival Martin Luther King Jr. and the words would have no power here.

Controlled environment. Well, isn't all of the carnival a controlled environment? Isn't the House of Horrors a series of set-ups? Lead the people this way, leap at them, lead them that way, leap again?

Okay, but this is different. It sounds different, smells different, it even looks different. Where are the lights? Where are the teenagers who found work for a summer wearing rubber masks in old wooden attractions?

It's soundproof, she thinks. And it's just about the darkest thought she can have, now, here, because it means nobody above can hear her.

She moves fast; there must be a way out, an easy way out. And if anybody steps out *now*, if anybody says, *Rawr, I got you!*, Susan is going to punch them straight in the nose, no questions asked, no apologies accepted.

She slams into a wall. Another. She turns, waves Sylvester frantically before her, hits another wall, turns, hits another wall. Feels like she's gotta be a mile from Holly Park. The Hoke County Carnival feels very small to her now, a blip behind her, an island on a world map. Getting back there (or getting out at all, she's just gotta get out at all) feels like an enormous task, one she isn't prepared for, one nobody ever told her she'd have to do.

Susan stops. She has to. She's moving too fast in the dark, someone else's dark, with scratches up and down her arms and legs. She thinks the knuckles on her left hand must be bleeding. A little bit. She feels them with the fingers of her right hand.

Bleeding.

She doesn't want it to feel like a profound moment, a very bad thing, but how can it not? She woke up today, borrowed Dad's car to go to the carnival and now…now she's bleeding.

"Hey," she says, "you gotta get me out of here. Come on. This isn't fun anymore."

It never was. But what else to say? She's surprised by how much she's actually said already. Did she threaten to sue them? She's never done something like that in her life, never been in any position to threaten at all.

Love you.

Mom's text, bastardized by whoever (the man in the mirror mask?) is down here with her, or is watching her, or is listening in a control room like the producer of Uncle Mitt's album, sitting behind a large console, controlling not just the timbre and tone of the sounds she produces, but producing her whole existence it seems.

Susan is moving again, not running, but moving well. She's fueled by anger, reminding herself that whoever this is (the man in the mirror mask?) he's just a man who works for the carnival, an employee who has taken the House of Horrors too far.

Why? Why would someone do this? It feels like an important question to ask. And while the possible answers are endless, one of them might help her get out of here.

Does this person mean to hurt her? Is she going to get killed down here?

"No," she says, less of a response to herself and more of a command to quit thinking about being killed. But it's real easy to imagine herself on the cover of *The Samhattan News*, her senior picture beneath a chilling headline like: LAST SEEN AT THE CARNIVAL.

Oh my God, the guy used her Mom's text, read it in a voice that now, in her memory, sounds more like the crackling of a Hollywood demon than a carny who is too into his job. Fuck, it's not cool. Fuck, it's scary down here. Fuck, Susan keeps moving because (again) if there was a way in, there must be a way out.

Where?

Back?

She shakes her head. Ha. There's no *way back*. She would've had to leave ten thousand breadcrumbs and Jesus how would she see them anyway?

"Hey, come on," she says, somewhat calmed by the strength in her voice. She sounds mad, not afraid. Direct, not desperate.

Not yet.

How long has she been down here?

Winded, she moves. She remembers herself in line, thinks again how maybe, just maybe, this is the ride for the solo artists, the people who came to the carnival alone.

Doesn't sound fair. Sounds like punishment. But maybe, just maybe, someone else would like this?

This is encouraging. Yes, this could still be the House of Horrors, of course, the way it's supposed to go. The world spins and sometimes it spins too fast for you and suddenly the innocuous old carnival isn't so easy to stomach anymore. The roller coasters get taller, the Tilt-a-Whirl turns faster, the games are harder to win. And the House of Horrors? That's gotten harder, too. More advanced. Could scare the shit out of a dead body.

Susan tries to shake off these last two words, too easy to imagine herself MISSING again on the cover of the newspaper. Oh, Christ, what would Mom and Dad do? Surely they'd come to the carnival, check everywhere, check the House of Horrors, find the door leading to the hole in the ground, take the rungs, take the halls.

But with light, they'd have light, something Susan so badly wishes she had.

And while this fantasy is enticing, she can't help but imagine her parents lost down here, too, swallowed up by the same darkness that won't let her go.

Susan moves, turns, moves, turns, takes another hall, feels picture frames along a wall.

She stops.

This wall isn't devoid of decoration. This is a new wall. A good sign? Progress? Is she closer to the end?

She sets Sylvester at her feet, feels along the wall. Picture frames suggest life, someone to put pictures in the frames, someone to hang those pictures. Her head still echoes with the impossibly loud voice that came through the speakers and she imagines that man in this hall. Maybe there's a door? The man must have a way in, a way out. He spoke into a microphone. Had to. Where is it? Where are the speakers?

Creaking from above. When's the last time she heard it? How many people are up there still? And is it still the House of Horrors above her?

Can't be. She's been walking forever. She could be beneath anyplace in Samhattan. The movie theater. The mall. Home.

She almost shouts for her parents and stops herself. It feels like she almost lost it there for a second. Almost did something she knows would be useless to do.

A light flashes.

Bright white.

A single strobe, so strong that she recoils from it, squints, brings her hands to her eyes. And in her head an image remains. A picture on the wall, the closest one, the one she happened to be facing in the dark when the light flashed.

"Hey!" she calls out. "I know you're down here!"

Because she does. Or she thinks she does. Whoever flashed that light knows where she is. Right? She could've triggered something. A tripwire. She touches the wall, this wall, and a light flashes. To show her a picture. A picture of an empty carnival. The Hoke County Carnival without the people, the suckers like her, no lines, no couples, nobody.

How long has she been down here?

The image is wedged into her mind, it's all she can see, as if she's in it, like she's the only person standing in Holly Park. There's dirt beneath her feet and colored flags framing the park's border. She's alone.

She closes her eyes but the image remains. The light did that to her, pressed the picture deep into her head. She bends her knees, feels for Sylvester at her feet. But the stuffed cat is gone.

"Oh, come on."

She's on her knees now, feeling around the hall. It's all dirt, cold and (she thinks) fresh. How can she not think of a grave? How can anybody beneath the ground for so long, in a place where nobody good can hear her, not think of a grave?

"Where is it?" she asks, still feeling. Because if the cat is gone, that means somebody took it. And she didn't hear anybody take him. She didn't hear anybody at all.

She looks left. Looks right.

The image of the empty carnival is mercifully fading, but in its stead is the darkness of this subterranean house of horrors all over again. She wonders if the sun is still up outside. If there's anybody at the carnival. How recently that photo was taken.

Crouched as she is, she's more aware of the boomerang in her back pocket. The shitty prize she took from the All-Knowing Scale. She takes it out. Jams it into the dirt. The middle of the hall. It's the first breadcrumb she's left herself. And the only one she has.

She gets up.

She walks. Deeper into the basement. One hall, then another, without the cat.

Her fingertips scrape wood and she turns. Scrape wood and she turns. Then, as if she's made it to what feels like a second tier, the next level of this horrid scenario, her fingers don't touch anything at all.

Susan reaches out as far as she can, both arms extended. She steps to the right, stumbles to the left. But she feels no walls.

Is she in a new room? A big room? And what else is in this room with her?

"I can see you," she says.

She isn't sure why she's said it. Her own words scare her.

"I can see you," she repeats, staring at a singular space in the darkness. "Standing right there. You don't think I can see you but I can."

Silence. No movement. No breathing. And she doesn't actually see anything at all. Yet, it feels like the right thing to do. To fight back. To tell him he's not hidden like he thinks he is. Even if the carny (*I don't think this is a carny, Susan, and I think it's time you admit that*) has to think about it for one second, has to look up, check for light, a mistake on his part, if she can just get him to second guess himself, it would be a start.

But a start to what?

"You're right there," she says, eying that same spot in what she believes is an open room, not a hall. "You're wearing night goggles and you're looking right at me. You've got a stupid smile on your face and you think you're so tough, scaring the shit out of a woman by herself, but you're just a man standing in the dark, too scared to make yourself known."

Is this working? What is this doing for her? She doesn't know, but she can't stop.

"Turn the lights on. Come on. Let me out. Get me out of here. You scared me. You did it. Good for you. But I can see you and you're just a man standing in the dark just like I'm standing in the dark, too."

She feels someone behind her, a shifting of the air perhaps, the swelling of something, and she turns so fast she almost stumbles over.

"Who—" she manages to say but whatever else would have followed is interrupted by a growl, a sound she knows, instinctively, is not prerecorded, does not come from the throat of a man.

"Oh my God," she says. Because it's growling again, because there is an animal down here with her, a living thing that might not be trained, might not belong to this man at all.

She can hear it breathing. How far away? Feet? Ten feet? Her mind's eye shows her a tiger. Shows her a big cat. Show's her, incredibly, Sylvester the Cat, but bad now, big teeth, watery eyes, hungry.

Susan runs. She doesn't care that she can't see, doesn't even hold up her hands, doesn't think.

Behind her, no sound. No growl, no quick feet on dirt, no pounce. But she sees it anyway. Sees herself mauled by a monster in the dark below the carnival. Sees her photo on the cover of *The Samhattan News*. These days papers show more than they used to. Dad told her that. Where's Dad now? Is Mom out looking for her? How long has she been gone?

She hears a creaking above. People. Life. But where? She can't possibly be below the House of Horrors anymore. Somehow that idea makes her sick. Makes her feel like she's made of rubber, as she runs, through the dark, screaming, she realizes, actual words.

"Don't touch me! Keep it away from me!"

A big cat. A hyena. A bear.

What's down here with her?

She's still looking up when she crashes hard, too hard, into another wall. Her chin strikes first, causes her head to cock back. Feels like she broke something in her face. Feels like the wall was made of steel.

She falls to the dirt, on her side. Can't get her head right. What's up? What's down? Which way is the animal?

Susan looks into the darkness but doesn't know which direction she's looking. She knows she's on the ground, but this information is fleeting, quick as that earlier flash of light. And as she goes under, as she passes out from the hit her chin took, she sees the same image she saw by way of that very light.

An empty carnival. Nobody left. Nobody there to notice her. Nobody left to say hey, there was a blonde girl, tall girl, here all alone. Where did she go? Where did the tall blonde girl go?

When she comes to, Susan doesn't take long to remember where she is.

The smell of this place is unmistakable. She thinks she dreamt of it, as it doesn't feel like her mind's taken any time off from the darkness.

She gets up.

Her chin hurts. Her chest hurts. Feels like there might be a splinter in her right wrist. She checks. Then she checks to make sure her shorts are still on. Her clothes. She was knocked out. How long? Did he touch her while she was out? Did he?

She thinks the answer is no. She's sure of it now. She wasn't violated. She also wasn't killed.

Why not?

What's the aim of the person keeping her down here?

Because there's absolutely no doubt about that anymore. No carnival in the known universe would allow customers to knock themselves out against a wood wall and leave them there until they woke. No way. As Susan faces the darkness once again, she's now convinced she's being held prisoner beneath the ground of Holly Park.

The thought should be scarier than it is, and maybe it will take its correct form soon, but for now she's glad for any knowledge at all. Okay. Someone is doing this to her on purpose. This is not the exciting upper-level experience for those who travel alone. Someone is trying to scare her. Someone is.

The man in the mirror mask.

What does she know about him?

"Nothing," she says. And the sound of her voice reminds her of the sound of the animal. The growl that sent her running.

She goes quiet.

She stares into the darkness and actually tries to hear better. For the first time in her life she's setting out to hear more of a room she's standing in.

But when the lights come on, she sees (sees!) she's not in a room at all. It's a hall. And the man did touch her. She's been moved.

"Oh God," she says, looking ahead to the long row of mirrors that line both walls. Behind her, a solid red wall. Ahead, beyond the many mirrors, what looks like another red wall. But she can't be sure.

Susan breathes deep. She straightens her orange shirt, her white shorts. The light shows her she's got dirt all over her legs and arms. But she doesn't spend much time taking stock of herself.

There's a reason for this hall. There must be. She can't help but think it's the reason the man trapped her down here in the first place.

For the first time since taking the rungs to the dirt she now stands on, she feels a wave of embarrassment for having agreed to descend. But how could she have known? When one enters a House of Horrors at a county carnival they rightly assume all the inevitable moments ahead have been tested, practiced, and that they're in the hands of those who know better. Would anybody else have stepped around the man? Anybody else who was alone?

"Walk," she tells herself. Because she can't stand here forever. And if she's going to get to the end of this nightmare, she's going to have to move her body to do it.

She enters the hall of mirrors. Mirrors hung the way they are in homes, oval mirrors on hooks on the red walls. The state of the walls tells her that the place she's in is possibly even worse than she imagined. Splintered and poorly painted. Thick red streaks of red coursing from dirt ceiling to dirt floor. Where is the light coming from? She looks but she can't tell. At the first mirror, she fails at refusing to look at herself.

She doesn't look good. Her chin is bruised; a discoloration that fans up along her cheeks and almost reaches her eyes. There is dirt in her hair. The collar of her shirt sits uneven on her neckline. The orange looks more red in the glass.

She looks ahead, continues.

Because the way she entered this experience was by way of the front door to a house of horrors, she expects to see terrible things in the glass she passes. There is no music, no screaming ahead, nothing to suggest she's back in what anybody would consider a traditional carnival attraction.

At the second glass, to her left now, she doesn't eye herself but everything else it shows. It's impossible not to expect a hand to erupt from the other side, her face to melt into that of a waxen witch, images to be distorted, reality changed. But the anatomically correct reflection she sees frightens her more than any of that could.

Does he know this? The man who has her here? Does he know that a series of oval house mirrors that show nothing but the truth is more disturbing than ceiling to floor funhouse mirrors of deceit?

She continues. Looks right. Sees herself. Looks left. Just her, all her. Maybe she should run. The end of the hall ahead is still difficult to determine but she thinks, yes, it's red. A mirror image, it seems, of the end at which she started.

She continues, passes two mirrors, pauses, then steps back between them. She faces left but her eyes are on the glass reflected, the glass on the red wall behind her. That mirror is oval, not much larger than the size of a human head. She pretends to examine the mirror she faces, touches the frame, the wire behind it. But her eyes are on the twin holes she believes have been drilled into the glass hanging behind her.

Eye level, is someone looking through?

Susan tries to breathe steady. It's impossible. Unfair to think she might. What else can she pretend to look at? What else can she do but turn to face the glass behind her? To get closer to the tiny holes she sees there?

She doesn't do this yet. Too scared. Is the man who's trapped her on the other side of the wall? Is he watching her now? Is he waiting to see what she does? And when she does it, whatever it is, will he be prepared?

Susan turns. The wall around the oval appears particularly red, as if the light is coming from above it. She doesn't look up to check.

There are eyes through those holes.

She knows this now.

Heart thundering, she imagines herself pretending to check out the frame before quickly removing it from the wall. Then, infused with a strength she didn't know she possessed, she moves fast, not checking, grabs the oval, lifts it and tears it from the wall.

A smell strong enough to choke her erupts from a cut hole in the wall.

It's a dead body. A dead face. Susan drops the mirror. She backs up, shaking her head no. No, this is no makeup job. No, there is no rubber involved, no latex. This is no mask.

The lights go out.

Susan hears violent movement from the hole. The sound of something trying to get out, to crawl its way through.

She screams because she has to. And the scream acts as a thread, keeping the sides of her mind together.

She runs from the hole, from the smell, from the sound. She keeps her arms extended, she has to, can't risk knocking herself to the ground again.

The thing behind her, the thing she saw through the hole, it's in the hall now. She hears its feet on the dirt.

Is it him? Blind, running, she knows it must be. But she can't stop herself from believing in horror right now, can't do anything to corrupt the idea that a dead man might crawl through a wall, might follow her down a hall. A hall with no openings, right? A flat red surface like the other end? Right?

Susan crashes against one side of the hall, hears a mirror drop. Hears feet in dirt behind her.

She continues, she must. She bangs against the left wall, hears a second mirror drop. She reaches the end of the hall, feels thick paint on a flat surface, turn left, nothing, turn right.

A door.

She's touching a doorknob.

She turns it, opens it. See the same darkness ahead.

Behind her, glass cracking. A foot upon one of the fallen mirrors.

But Susan's already moving through the open door, trembling so badly she can hardly pull it closed behind her.

She does. She closes the door. She hears a creak from above. Muffled voices?

"*HELP!*" she yells.

MOM HAS a way of distilling enormous philosophical questions down to simple sentences, a thing that has always impressed Susan. Whether or not Mom means to do this is up for debate and usually after one of Mom's spot-on quips, Susan and Dad exchange a look across the room, a look that says, *She did it again.*

Many of Mom's pocket-revelations swirl through Susan's mind now, but none so much as this: *Everything has a point A and a point B. Point A, you got the job. Point B, you can't stand it. Quit the job.*

Dad argued there were nuances and Mom said those nuances didn't matter, only the points A and B.

Susan can't quit thinking that as she jumps to knock on the dirt ceiling (as if this will be heard, in any capacity, above, at any volume at all; and what is she beneath now? The random muffled screams suggest it's still the House of Horrors, but is this possible? Are the screams she hears now actual screams? Does the man in the mirror mask own a house above, where other people are held captive in the dark?). For Susan, right now, point A is going to the carnival.

Point B is yelling for help.

She can hardly believe she's doing it. But the most surprising thing is how good she is at it. There's power in her voice. Urgency. The one word is strong, bright, and she knows she can't blame herself if it isn't heard.

Should she be making so much noise? If she'd been silent since entering, would the man in the mirror mask know where she is? She thinks he would, but she doesn't *know.* All the victims in stories get to a point where they get smart about their scenarios. Either they placate their captor, or steal some object that will be their eventual triumph, or they get methodical and pick apart the situation until they're free. Susan isn't feeling methodical, Christ no. She just wants out.

So she cries for help.

The reality of this event is sinking in, way in, and she realizes she didn't catch it when she thought the word *victim* seconds ago. Is she using that word now? Is that what she is?

Is Susan a victim?

She opens her mouth to yell once more but doesn't do it. It's that word. She doesn't want it near her at all. She wants to believe this is still somehow part of the Hoke County Carnival, the annual event that, for the first time, looked different to her this year.

"This isn't the carnival," she says, remaining still in the dark.

She has to get out of here.

So she walks, okay, she can do this. She can walk. She can find her way out. This is a game for the man in the mirror mask. Let it be that. For him. For her? She has to go. And she can because she has to. Because she can't keep using the word victim or it's going to turn to wet mud and she's going to sink into it until she can't breathe, until she dies.

She reaches another wall, imagines it's red, now, in the dark. Imagines all the walls down here are red walls with thick streaks of fatty strokes, snakes painted over, painted red, suffocating like Susan is going to suffocate if she doesn't get out of here now.

She hears a barrel tip over. There's no other image that comes to mind and she believes it has to be that, a barrel, falling to its side. She hears the contents as they pour out. Is this ahead or behind? To the side? Which side?

It's gasoline.

Oh, God. Susan can smell it. Oh, God. The man in the mirror mask just dumped gasoline out on the floor. Why would we he do that if not to hurt her? Why would he do that? *Why?*

"Stop it," she says. "Just stop this."

Sounds like victim-speak to her.

She walks, hands out, missing Sylvester the Cat in an almost ridiculous way, and worries she's going toward the gasoline and not away from it. He's going to burn her. He is. He's going to burn the whole basement with her in it.

Susan cries out for help. Because now she has to. This man is one match away from killing her. One simple strike of a match. And it's like she can hear it, can hear the sound before he does it. Was that it? Did he just light a match? No. That was her elbow against the (red, dripping red) wall. Go, Susan, go. Find a way out of here. This isn't the carnival, Susan. This is a psycho. A sick man is doing this to you, and you alone, on purpose. This is planned. He fooled you, tricked you into climbing down into the basement.

How could she have done it? How could she have allowed herself to be tricked so easily? There's no basement in Holly Park! There are no cellars on public land!

There are graves, she thinks.

She's got to get out of here. Got to keep walking. Got to—

Susan slips.

It's awful the way it happens. The way the tip of her right shoe is taken by the substance on the ground, the way she's almost forced to do the splits. She makes a meek sound, *oh*, and is falling, awkwardly, in a bad way, the splits, until she connects with the dirt and falls to her side and realizes immediately that now her clothes and arms and legs (*your hair, too, Susan, your hair!*) are covered in gasoline.

Susan tries to get up, flails, falls to her already banged-up chin. Now she has gasoline on her face.

She tries to get up again, does it, gets to a standing position in the dark, eyes wide, her face and hair slick with it.

What about the animal? What if the animal comes?

There's too much to worry about. She's got to calm down.

Gasoline, though.

Gasoline.

Susan starts to head back the way she came, turns again, heads toward the gasoline, stops. She doesn't know which way to go. She must be miles from the carnival. She looks up.

Creaking? Distant screaming?

Nothing.

Since coming down to this basement, the sounds she's heard from above, while walking, have painted, for her, an awful picture of Samhattan and its neighbors, a hellish walk beneath small town America, where the only place you can hear everybody's anguish, their shocks and screams, is from below. It's a series of locations for her now, places she hasn't seen, the world above, all of them sad and scared, all of them alone and out of reach.

Is this what she wants so badly to get back to?

"Yes," she says, walking toward the gasoline, walking slower now, noting that the smell of it has lessened. For this she is grateful. A smell like that could've filled the basement, choked her with fingers of its own. Fumes.

Susan walks carefully, one shoe planted, her hands flat to the splintered wall to her right. She finds her balance and, *carefully*, places her other shoe ahead. Okay. She's taken a step. She takes another.

How long until she reaches the end of the slick substance? How long before the man in the mirror mask strikes a match? How long before she hears, again, the growl of the animal down here with her?

Her stomach feels twisted, like it's physically folded over itself. She's sweating, she's hurt, she's covered in flammable fluid. She takes another step, hands flat to the wall.

She slips.

Doesn't fall. Almost does. Splinters her palms.

"Come the fuck *on*," she says.

But she doesn't want to talk. Not only because she's afraid of hearing anything close to defeat in her voice, and not because she actually believes the man is only tracking her by the sounds she makes, but because she doesn't want to give him the satisfaction of hearing her at all. Christ, the piece of shit is probably smiling, now, here in the dark, watching her struggle upon gasoline spread across the dirt in a subterranean lair. The fucking asshole is probably inches from her, nodding along, yes, yes, all going according to plan, all happening now, yes, yes, I've got her right where—

The lights come on. One light. An overhead bulb.

There's a woman sitting in a chair, facing Susan.

She's old. She's very old. She's not moving, but she's looking right at Susan. Looking Susan in the eye.

Within seconds, Susan takes stock of the room. The dimensions. The door beyond the woman, on the other side of this blue painted room.

"Help," Susan says. "Can you help me?"

In the woman's hand, a cigarette smolders.

Susan eyes the ash. Looks down to the slick floor her chair is situated upon.

"Oh, miss, miss, you can't—"

But Susan is moving, moving toward the woman, slowly, too slowly, as the ash hangs from the smoke, as the woman doesn't seem to know she's about to light herself and Susan on fire.

"Miss," Susan says without meaning to. One step, then another. Faster now. Too fast.

Susan slips. Falls to her hip. Gets back up.

"Miss…"

The woman is a doll, a mannequin, can't be real, no longer looking Susan in the eye but looking where Susan stood seconds ago. She can't be real, just like nothing in a carnival house of horrors is real. Rubber and latex. Fake hair. Fake teeth. Those aren't real eyes. That isn't saliva on her lips. Someone pinched the false skin to make wrinkles in her face, her neck, her hands, her fingers that hold the cigarette that's about to fall.

Susan moves fast. Too fast. She has to.

The cigarette falls. Susan dives. Catches it. Closes her fingers over the hot part as her face (lips and nose) connect with the gasoline and dirt.

She feels the burn in her palm. Tastes syrup on her lips.

Susan looks to the dirt. Syrup?

She looks up. The woman's head is turned. The woman is looking directly at her.

Susan gets to her knees, fast, grabs the woman with her free hand, grabs her shoulder, says, "Help me get out of here. There's a way out, I know there is, there's—"

She's not real.

Susan knows that now. Can feel the rubbery shoulder. Plastic beneath.

But somehow that head turned. Somehow those eyes moved.

Susan gets up and stands before the woman. The woman still stares to where Susan was on the ground.

Susan reaches out a finger, touches the woman's eyelid, then her eye.

She brings her hand back quickly.

Fake. She's fake. And there's syrup on the ground.

Susan moves past the woman, to the door on the other side of the room. She takes hold of the knob, looks over her shoulder.

The woman is looking over her own shoulder. Looking at Susan.

The woman starts to rise.

And the lights go out.

IT WAS him, Susan tells herself, moving so fast through the hall, not caring if she hurts herself, not caring if she runs into another wall. *He was in a costume. Dressed as an old woman. It was him.*

She should turn around, rush back to the room, face the woman, the man in the mirror mask, the man in the old woman mask.

But she isn't sure. She isn't sure of anything. Blind, darting, she can't stop thinking of the movies with entirely evil families, dad and the boys, mom and dad and the kids, brothers, sisters, couples, kidnapping people together, holding people captive together. Killing together. Could've been his mom. Why not? Could've been his lover. Why not? Why did Susan assume this man is working alone?

She runs, actually runs, through the halls. Her shoulders are bruised, elbows splintered, a palm is burned, too. She reaches the end of one hall and turns to face another. Another. Christ, it feels like she's going in circles, feels like she should be back at the room. Is she? Is the man in the mirror mask's mother or lover, or is *he* standing ahead in the dark, standing inches from her, that leathered wrinkled skin upon his own?

Susan doesn't care. Let the old woman come. Let the animal come. She'll tear into them all. She'll sink her nails into their throats and if they bite? She'll bite back. If they try to kill her? She'll—

"*Susan? You okay?*"

Susan stops.

She doesn't have to think about the voice at all to know whose voice it is. Dad.

"*You still at the carnival?*"

"Dad!"

She yells it but she knows how stupid this is. She knows this is a voice mail. Dad called her. While she's been down here. Dad called.

She feels too many emotions at once. Can't make sense of them. Dad's voice. Home. The fact that the man has her phone. Is playing Dad's message.

"*I'm not worried about the car. Just worried about you.*"

Dad's voice. From where?

Susan looks, as if she can see anything in this maze.

"*Let us know what your plan is, honey.*"

His voice isn't coming from up. It's coming from ahead.

"Dad," she says.

As if the man is standing ten feet ahead in the dark. As if he's talking to her in person.

"*We don't want to be nagging parents! But let us know.*"

She can see him, Dad, as if his form is a shade darker than the darkness surrounding her.

She thinks of the gasoline smell. The syrup she tasted. The growl of the animal.

Is there someone standing ahead in the dark? Is an old woman holding her phone, right there, not ten feet away in the hall?

Is it a man wearing a mirror mask?

As Dad tells her he loves her, Susan lunges forward, arms out, yelling, not caring if the man is stronger than her, if the man is armed, if this means she's going to die.

She feels the emptiness below her feet before it registers that she's falling.

Is there a basement beneath the basement of Holly Park?

This question clangs in her head like a struck gong, but the reverberations are quelled, cut off, cauterized as she first splashes, then sinks, into a pool of something thicker than water.

She's under for a second. Two. Three. She sees in her mind's eye the red paint of the walls, the thick hurried strokes of someone without delicacy, without refinement, impasto, red oil. Then Susan breaks the surface with a gasp, tastes the metallic nature of the stuff, and believes she's floating in a pool, a hole, a grave of someone else's blood.

SHE TRIES to climb out. It's not easy. It feels like something she won't be able to pull off. She's covered in it. Coated. Head to toe. That includes her shoes. And when she puts her toe to the side of the hole, looking for leverage, there is none.

Can she stand? She tries, but when her feet reach the bottom, her mouth and nose go under. She's tall. Not tall enough for this. So she treads, or maybe the stuff holds her up, she isn't sure. She's not thinking about sticking around, floating in the middle. She's trying to get out.

Beyond the lip of the hole, something breathes.

Susan holds tight as she can to the edge and lowers herself into the muck. It's complete darkness in here. She can't see what's near, but can it see her?

She waits. What else can she do? Her heart is hammering, her fingers can't hold on for long. She lets go. She floats (this doesn't feel like the right word; she's taken; if it's blood, the blood takes her) away from the edge. She waits. It breathes.

Man? Animal? Old woman in a chair?

It's her nature to call out. To break the tension. To do anything other than sit still. The sitting still is driving her mad. How long can she stay like this? She has to get out. All she wants to do is get back up to the surface, to daylight, and here she's fallen even lower.

"You gotta let me out of here," she says. She regrets it immediately. Because, as she speaks, she hears a difference in the breathing, the distinct sound of animal, indeed.

Then, movement on the dirt, something coming.

The unmistakable sound of a living thing slipping into a body of liquid.

Susan cries out as she hears the liquid part. She pushes her arms forward; propelling herself back, back, back, to the other side, a side she hasn't touched yet. When she gets there, she feels that it's more serrated, can feel it against her shoulder.

Leverage then? This side?

Susan turns her back on what's coming. She can hear it breathe (*paddle? Is it paddling?*) as she plants her palms on the dirt lip and jabs her right shoe into the side of the hole. She thinks of the sledgehammer she used above, testing her strength at the carnival. The game told her she was a weakling.

Susan slips, loses her grips, sinks back into the muck, goes under.

While under, she feels something bigger than her arm touch her own. Wet fur. Bone.

Susan breaks the surface. Pitch dark. Gasps. Reaches. Swallows the metallic-tasting liquid. Coughs it up. Feels the thing submerged, against her hip.

Susan freezes. Above, laughter. From everywhere, laughter. Sounds like old men laughing. Laughter that bleeds into coughing. Coughing. From everywhere. Fur against her shin. Coughing that becomes crying. Old men crying. Bone against her waist. Crying that becomes singing. Old men singing. Fingers longer than her own against her back. Old men chanting. Fingers on her shoulder. Both shoulders.

Susan pulls away. Tries to pull away. Hears the breathing in her ear. Both ears. She elbows what's behind her. Nothing is behind her. She feels it in front of her.

Old men humming. Old men chanting. Old men singing falsetto. Old men imitating women. Old men imitating little girls.

Susan swims to the serrated lip. She will not be denied this time. She can't.

She jabs her shoe into the wall. Higher. Grips the lip. Pulls.

Pulls herself out.

Halfway there, her belly flat to the dirt, she reaches ahead, digs her fingers into the dirt. Feels fur against her thighs.

Pulls.

Swings her leg up out of the blood. It's blood. Has to be blood.

Whose?

Uses the heel of the shoe that's out for leverage.

Pulls.

Rolls to the dirt. Gets up. Runs.

She hears the old men laughing again. Hears the slosh of something exiting the pit behind her. She thinks of tar pits, but can't fill in the details of what she thinks it is on her own. She needs someone to tell her what's down here with her, needs someone to name it.

Susan runs. Crashes hard into a wall. Feels some give with the wall. Like she could bust through it if she stayed here, in this spot, and tried enough times. She can't stay in this spot. She moves, runs, crashes into another wall. Another. She runs for what feels like too long, experiencing no obstacles.

Makes her think one is coming.

Another pit?

Another wall?

Another door?

The door out?

It feels like she's running in place. Like she's fooled herself into thinking she's moving forward, making progress. She imagines the man in the mirror mask watching her with night goggles. Laughing with the voices of a dozen old men who think it's so funny, so wonderfully delightful, the way the tall blonde girl is running in place down here in the dark.

The next thing she feels are curtains. She stops. These frighten her more than the wood walls. More than the doors she's already opened and closed.

Because curtains imply design.

Looking once over her shoulder, Susan parts the curtains, and steps into the darkness between them.

WITH THE fabric to her back, Susan doesn't move for a long time. There is silence behind her. No wet sloshing of something coming. Nothing breathing ahead. It's silly—incredible, really—that material as thin as curtains should represent a wall, a separation from the rest of this dark world, something to keep her safe. But it does feel that way. Like she's made it to a new level. The next phase. Like she's survived something. And for the first time today (if today is still today and not tomorrow; how long has she been down here?), she thinks, *This is a real experience.*

It's gross, in its way, respecting the moment in any way, shape, or form. But she can't help it. The discrepancy between the world she paid to walk through and the one she's run through is astonishing. It even smells scarier down here. The stuffiness, the paint, the momentary olfactory flood of gasoline. Christ, this is the most scared Susan has ever been. What could compare? Walking the halls of school without a friend? Sticking to the fifth corner? Checking her wholly ignored statuses online? Weighing whether or not to attend the Hoke County Carnival alone?

She thinks of Aunt Pam. What would Pam tell her now?

Keep your chin up, Susan! Some psychos can be defeated!

She shivers at the word *defeated* because that would require her to do the defeating. That entails a final meeting, a coming together, face-to-face, a standoff.

She steps into the darkness ahead, leaving the security of the curtains behind. There are no creaks from above; there hasn't been a distant scream in a long time. Is the world asleep? Is it nighttime now?

Susan thinks it must be. Her hands out, trembling, she worries for her parents. She's never not responded to a voice message like the one that was played for her earlier. She's never not checked in. Shit, she's rarely ever been in a situation that might hold her later than expected. No late night parties. Not really. There was one time at a girl named Marla's house. Susan forgot to text. But even then—

She feels hair against her right wrist. She can't help but cry out and recoil. She wishes she hadn't cried out. But is there really any question whether or not the man in the mirror mask knows where she is at all times?

She hears scurrying feet. She doesn't know which way to go. The creaking of a bed. What's further ahead? Sounds like she's standing between the curtain she passed through and the noises ahead.

She goes right, bangs her waist against wood. A counter? A shelf? The top of a dresser? She feels drawers.

Squeaking behind her. Susan knows this sound. Everybody does. The sound of someone shifting on a bed.

Susan turns and faces the darkness. The few clues she has as to what is in this room, this space, tell her there's something with hair upon a bed in a bedroom.

Is Susan in a bedroom?

"Mommy?"

The voice doesn't sound young. It's supposed to be a girl but it sounds like a man pretending to be a girl. Like when the old men stopped laughing and started singing like women.

Susan doesn't speak. Can't move.

"Mommy? Is that you by the dresser?"

Susan, coated in the muck (blood) of the hole, syrup or gasoline still in her hair, her palm burnt and her body badly banged up, can't bring herself to move.

"Mommy, it's dark in here. Turn on a light for me?"

Susan looks left to where she believes the curtain must be. Looks to the right. Is there a way out of this room without heading back the way she came, back toward the hole in the ground and the thing that followed her out of the hole in the ground?

"I'm gonna stare at you, Mommy, until you turn the light on for me."

A man, yes, imitating a little girl.

It's him, Susan believes. Because who else can it be? He's here in this small space. Reachable. Touchable. Defeatable.

He's sitting on a bed or lying on a bed and he's mocking her, trying to scare her, scaring her.

She doesn't respond.

"I'm staring at you."

She has a decision to make. Yes, it's pitch black. Everywhere is down here. That's not going to change. She doesn't know if he's armed. That's not going to change. She has to get out of here and she probably needs to stop him before she does that.

That's only going to change if she makes it change.

Susan steps toward the bed.

"No, Mommy. The light."

She stops. Because the way he said this, it's a game. She's supposed to turn on the light. Where's the light? On the dresser? Must be. Might be.

She's not going to play his game. She steps toward the bed. What she thinks is a bed.

"I'm staring at you, Mommy."

This doesn't sound recorded. Doesn't sound like it's coming through speakers, a microphone, or a cell phone. This sounds like a voice in the room with her. His voice. Pretending. So close. The man in the mirror mask who's trapped her. The man who will probably kill her if she doesn't do something. Now.

Susan does something now.

She rushes to the bed, hands out, feels metal against her legs, rubber, topples to the dirt, feels hair, the same hair that touched her, feels bones.

A light comes on.

Susan is in the dirt, beneath her is a skeleton. Is it real? She doesn't have time to determine this. A wig lies a foot away.

"Mommy, look."

Susan is afraid to look. Oh so afraid to turn and look. But she does, because she has to. Because she has to get out of here.

As she turns her head, she sees it wasn't a bed. It was a wheelchair. A skeleton in a wheelchair. Next are the curtains she passed through. Pink. Nearly transparent. Is there something crouched beyond them? Something that crawled out of the hole? Next is the edge of the dresser, she was right about this, a dresser, upon it a lamp, and next to the dresser, to the left of it, her hand still extended to under the lampshade, stands a little girl in a blue and white nightgown.

Susan, on the ground, her head craned back to see, can't talk. Not yet. Doesn't understand. That voice? Did it belong it to her?

And is there really a little girl down here, too?

"I'm staring at you."

Susan pushes up, pushes off the bones, feels like there are a thousand bugs on her; it's fear, hot fear, rising up her legs, back, arms and neck. But she's up, standing, facing the girl.

"Who are you?" she asks.

The girl's face doesn't change as she responds.

"You're looking the wrong way, Mommy."

It's not real. No. Jesus Christ. It's a doll. A mannequin. An effect.

Susan looks left. Looks right. Turns to see a man standing in the corner of the space.

But Susan only sees her own face, reflected in the mirror mask he wears.

She lunges at him. Doesn't give herself time to think. She can see her own hysterical expression, anger and horror in an eye each, coming at herself, an oval above a jean jacket, arms, torso, legs, a man, shorter than herself, but a man who might be holding something, *is* reaching for something, is fading, vanishing from left to right, as a red wall slides between them, as Susan crashes into it, pounds her fists on it, demands he let her go, screams she's going to kill him, kicks the wall, rams her shoulder into the wall, and, finally, relents.

The light goes out.

Susan tries to slide the wall in the dark. Isn't thinking of the bones by the chair, the lifelike little girl by the dresser, whose face looked so real Susan felt sympathy, empathy, like, for a moment, she wasn't alone.

But she is.

And she can't move the wall.

And the man in the mirror mask is gone.

And she feels like she could explode with anger, like every molecule of her body could light up. She wants to combust. She wants to erupt into flames, light her way to the man in the mirror mask, engulf him in her heat, torch him as she is torched, the two of them turned to dust in the dungeon, in the dirt, in the dark.

Instead, she turns, she walks, she searches the space for an opening and finds one. She enters, expecting worse ahead. But thinking, too, that she was close to him. And if she was close to him once, she'll be close to him again. And next time she has to reach him. Next time she has to be smarter than to just lunge. Next time she's gotta get her hands on the piece of shit psycho, bring his body to hers, and erupt into flames of anger, flames of revenge, flames of escape.

JOSH MALERMAN 🕷

SUSAN IS tired. She's hungry. She's worried about Mom and Dad. She almost wants the crazy man to play another message. Go on, mock me, she thinks. Please. Let me know what they're saying. Are they on their way? Where? Here? Maybe there's a way to know where she is. Maybe they can enter this world the same way she did: A hole in the floor of the Hoke County Carnival House of Horrors. Take the few rungs. Follow the couple of green arrows. Then you're in, Mom and Dad. Just like me.

Susan likes this idea. Not only because it would increase her chances of escape, not only because knowing where Mom and Dad are would bring her so much peace right now. But because she wouldn't be alone. Christ, she'd take anybody else down here. A couple. Assholes from school. Everybody in every line she saw before insanely believing that a hole in the ground was the next step to take. Send her anybody. Let's hear a scream, one good solid yelp, proof that she isn't the only person this madman is focused on, that there's a chance of him taking his eye off her, that there's a chance of going ignored.

Susan smiles. Look at her now, wanting to be ignored. So many bad dreams that find her on a stage, forced to perform some vague entertainment, some unknown (to herself) skill. All the sad mornings thinking nobody cared, nobody cared. Well, she's not ignored now. Oh boy. Probably being watched as she takes another turn, another hall. How deep is she? Does this lair reach the center of the earth? Is she in a cave?

"Cave!" she calls out. Checking for an echo. How high is the ceiling here? How high is the dirt? Who made this place? What was this place originally made for? What happened down here, in the past, before it became a hole in the ground in Holly Park and nothing more? What was in Holly Park before it became Holly Park? Is she walking the underground tunnels of an insane asylum? Is she in a sewer? Where the *fuck* is she?

Another turn. Another hall. Her hands are sick of touching the painted walls. Her feet are sick of the dirt. Her ears sick of the silence, her nose sick of the cellar smell, her eyes sick of the dark.

Time to go.

Got to go.

Got to get out.

But she's reached a dead end. An actual space surrounded by three walls. She checks the bottoms, checks if she's supposed to crawl. No open spaces

•••• | 442

there. She checks again. She doesn't want to turn back, doesn't want to back-track at all. Her mind still clings to the linear idea of a linear house of horrors in which you enter, you pass through a series of loud sounds and horrible sights, and you exit on the other side. Backtracking would suggest a maze. Or a walk back through all she's already done. She doesn't want to have to do this. She doesn't want to have to do anything at all.

She turns. No choice. And ten steps into backtracking she's surprised by a fourth wall.

Susan feels all around her. Feels the bottoms, the tops. Checks again. Again. Again.

But there is no new hall. No door. No window to slip through. She's stuck between four walls. Squared in. Trapped.

She raises her hand as high as she can, jumps, and touches dirt. Dirt beneath her feet. Four wood walls.

If this place felt like a grave before, she's now found the casket.

NOTHING SCRATCHES against the walls. Nothing creaks overhead. Nothing breathes. Nothing walks, nothing crawls, sloshes, rushes, slithers. Nothing comes.

Susan waits. She's struck the walls numerous times but she can't break through the wood. Too thick. There's some give, but not enough to give her hope. So she listens. She closes her eyes and *hears*. But nothing comes.

She imagines the man in the mirror mask setting up what will be her next encounter. She can see the horrible displays reflected in his ovular face. Bones in a basket. The face of a young man, too realistic, wedged into a wall. Bugs. Crawling bugs. Because whatever's next won't be less than what was last. If there's one pattern she's cracked, it's that one. The man is building. Building up. And maybe this is a good thing, as frightening as it is. Because if someone is building, there must be an end goal, too.

What's his goal? To kill her? Would he have done that by now? Maybe he hates women, all women. Maybe he hates his mother. Mothers have been a theme down here. The old woman. The little phony girl calling Susan Mommy. The text from Susan's own mom read at a blistering volume through speakers in the dark. Maybe the man in the mirror mask has a problem with his mom. Can Susan use this somehow? Can that help her get out?

She spreads her arms out, touches two of the walls, turns, and slides her fingertips across the other two.

What other clues does she have? How does the man do things? What is he drawn to? What's his pattern? Susan can only think of the mirror. And the jean jacket, too. Yeah. That was new, minutes ago. The jacket. Were there any labels on it? Slogans, bands, anything stitched into it like: KILL ALL LONELY WOMEN?

The jacket was sleeveless. Susan remembers that. And it means something to her. Not in a big way, but in some way. Like it narrows the scope. How many people wear sleeveless jean jackets in Samhattan these days? How many ever wore those?

She leans against a wall. Listens. Nothing coming. She can't be sure if the dead silence worries her more or less. The maniac has done a lot down here without making a sound. He might be doing a lot right now.

She listens. She hears…nothing.

Fine. Nothing. She'll do nothing, too. She'll wait. She'll rest. She'll—

"Sleep," she says.

The word scares her. Sounds more dangerous than *food*. Because she absolutely needs food and she's going to need sleep. And is she really thinking this way? Has it come to this? Wasn't she just standing in line at the carnival, waiting with everyone else to take a pass through a semi-scary haunted house in Holly Park? Come on. Has it really come to words like *food* and *sleep*? It's not fair. She doesn't want to say this, as she fingers the four walls, feels the uneven streaks of thick paint, imagines them as red as the red she imagines coating her body from the pool of blood she fell into not so long ago.

Survival.

No, she refuses to believe this is what it's come to. But what other word applies? When you've been locked in a place like this, when you think enough time has passed for night to become day, when someone mocks you with darkness, with the sound of your parents' voices, what other word have you arrived at but *survival?*

"No," she says.

She thinks: if he's not doing anything, shouldn't she be doing… something?

She strikes the walls again. All four in turn. Some give, but not enough. She knows that one of these walls wasn't here when she walked into this corner. She can't remember which. But if the wall wasn't here minutes ago, there's gotta be a way to make it go away again.

She looks for those ways.

Finds none.

Listens.

Nothing coming.

Should she sleep? Will it help her? Will her body heal and her mind rest? Will she have a better chance at outfoxing the man in the mirror mask if she sleeps for a minute or two or three?

Darkness. Closed in. Enough space to sleep. Lie down. Like in a casket. A box in the dirt.

Susan slowly crouches, then gets to her knees. She lies down on her side and curls up in a protective way, her knees in front of her belly, her hands in front of her face.

Survival. Because she has to start thinking this way. Day has become night in more ways than one. She closes her eyes and thinks of the words *carnival purgatory*. Like she's stuck between an innocuous funhouse and actual Hell, the sort of Hell Aunt Pam believes in.

Maybe Pam's right, maybe there is such a place, but Susan won't call this place Hell. Aunt Pam's Hell is eternal, forever in grief, with no way out. But here? There must be a way out.

Exhausted, bruised, rattled to a degree she didn't think possible, Susan begins to drift, thinking of phony horror tableaus, old lady masks and lifelike little girls. What is this place if not the scariest house of horrors someone like Susan could imagine?

Carnival purgatory.

Fine. Call it what you will. Either way, Susan needs sleep. She slowly unfolds from her protective position, her arms splayed out in the dirt, her legs stretching until her shoes touch one of the walls.

She sleeps. She actually sleeps because she's been down here long enough to need sleep. Because her body and mind have processed so much fear. Because if she's going to face this man, if she's going to survive, she's going to have to do things like eat. And sleep.

When she wakes, she is facing this man. The man in the mirror mask. A distant bell rings. Susan thinks of a dinner bell. Is that what woke her? There's a light above them, blue light, coloring the red walls purple. Blood purple. They sit at opposite ends of what Susan slowly realizes is a dining room table.

And the table is set for two.

MUSIC PLAYS. Classical, but not the nice kind. It's weaving, layered, disorienting. The man's dark hair shows at the sides of the mirror mask. When he moves his head to the right or left, she sees a belt holds it to his face. The kind of belt a man would wear to hold up his pants. His arms look thin, wiry, sticking out from the holes in his sleeveless jean jacket. He's holding a goblet in one hand. Susan can't see his other. It's at his side.

Does he hold a gun there?

She doesn't care. She moves. Tries to get up.

She can't. Looking down, she sees she's tied to the chair. The man must have carried her from the casket, placed her here. Did he drug her? Must have. She would've woken up. Anybody would've.

The table is long. The tablecloth looks blue in this light. Maybe it's white. He has a plate in front of him. So does she. On her plate is her phone.

Susan tries to lift her arms. Can't. She's tied to the chair.

She looks to the walls, sees no door. Looks to the man in the mirror mask.

Susan is looking at herself. She looks small in the glass. Her blonde hair looks dark and she knows it's because of the pool she fell into. The dirt. Maybe even the darkness. Maybe she has some darkness in her hair. Her arms are tight to her body. Her lips looks chapped but it's hard to tell for sure this far away. Has he painted something on her face? A smile? She knows she isn't smiling. But the glass shows someone who is.

"What are you doing?" she asks. She doesn't know what else to ask. She has to start somewhere. The music swells, as if he could control the timing of her question against the timing of the music, too.

He doesn't answer. Of course he doesn't. Susan looks to her phone. Sees she has twenty-two voice messages. This worries her as much as the man, as much as the sight of herself. Mom and Dad. Frantically calling. They're no doubt searching all of Samhattan. They might've found Dad's car by now, parked in the carnival lot. That would lead them to search the carnival grounds. Someone would recognize a tall blonde in an orange shirt and white shorts. The man who guessed her weight. The man who winked at her before she entered the House of Horrors.

Yes, one of them would say. *She was here for sure. She went in there. Right there, through the teeth.*

From there, Mom and Dad and the Samhattan police would search the House of Horrors. They would find the hole. Bust it open. Climb down and begin the trek to find her. They'd have flashlights. Weapons.

They're going to find her. Susan knows they are.

Maybe the face in the glass is smiling after all.

The man nods, seems to nod, does something so the glass tilts. Susan looks to the tabletop. Sees there is a goblet for her to drink, too. A long straw to accommodate the fact that she can't move her arms.

"What are you doing?" she asks. "Are you trying to scare me?" Her voice sounds firm. Much firmer than she thought it would. "Because you pulled it off. You scared me. Are you going to kill me?" Asking the question feels like a really bad idea. Like she's giving him the idea to do it. As if he hadn't considered it all before.

The music dips, then rises. Up and down. Disorienting.

The man doesn't move. The mask only shows Susan, seemingly pleading with herself.

"That's enough," she says. She sounds like Mom. Maybe that's good. Moms have been a theme down here. "Show me the way out and I'll pretend this never happened. I don't even know what you look like."

The man sets the goblet on the table, raises his hands to the mirror.

"No," Susan says. "Please don't show me your face."

He grips the mirror like he might. Slides his hands to the belt.

Susan holds her breath without deciding to. If she sees him, she'll be able to turn him in.

"Don't show me," she says. She closes her eyes. She keeps them closed. When she opens them, she cries out. Because she sees her own face, horribly close now, as the mirror is inches from her nose, as the man wearing it has one hand on the back of her chair and is leaning at the waist.

"Go away!" she yells.

But he doesn't. Not at first. He only remains that way, having delivered Susan her own face, it seems, for what feels like many seconds.

Susan sees that, yes, he has drawn on her face. A smile indeed. But more. Eyebrows and a line down the center of her nose.

She closes her eyes. Doesn't want to see herself. Can't stand the fear in her own eyes. The dark hair that should be blonde. The red walls, the blue light, the ghastliness, the goblets, the glass.

When she opens her eyes, he's seated again at the far end of the table.

Dust hovers to the side of the table where he just walked. Her eye tracks it, movement in the room, and sees, through it, the boomerang wedged into the dirt less than an inch from the wall.

She stares at the carnival prize because she can't look away. She doesn't want him to know that it means something, *feels* like it means something profound, but because of that very profundity she's stuck to it.

Why is the boomerang near the wall? It was dark when she jammed it into the ground but she believes (without proof, of course, not even a true mental picture) that she did not put it where it is. Yet, why would he have removed it from the dirt and placed it again, here? Wouldn't it be more like him to place the thing on the table? Like her phone on the plate? It seems overlooked is the thing. Like the man in the mirror mask doesn't know it's there. In fact, as the dirt settles, as the last fragments fall back to the ground, the boomerang itself becomes less visible, a trick of the blue light and the shadows of the wall.

As the music swells, Susan looks to the bottom of the wall. There is the smallest bit of exposed track there. Knows what track looks like because everybody's used a closet door and had to adjust it on the track. She thinks of Mom and Dad's closet sliding open. Thinking of the wall sliding open, too.

She looks to the man, to her own face in the glass. Can she see realization there? Hope? Can *he* tell she's piecing something together?

She tries to hide the feeling. The ideas. The pieces. Using the mirror like a camera turned on herself, like she's preparing for a silly selfie she'll never post, Susan is able to hide her hope.

But it's there.

The man in the mask raises his goblet. The music crescendos. A toast, he seems to be saying.

But to what?

Susan looks to the boomerang. Can't help it. Believes it's in the same spot she originally put it.

Sliding walls.

Track.

For fuck's sake, she thinks. *For FUCK's sake.*

She hasn't traveled miles at all. She isn't beneath the Samhattan Cemetery or Holly High, or home. She's still under the Hoke Country Carnival. And this madman fooled into her thinking she wasn't.

She tries to stand up. The ropes pinch her forearms, wrists, thighs. She sits back down. Can she bust out of this chair? She thinks she might be able to.

She's been trying to knock walls down, punching walls, kicking walls, trying to break through. Has she thought once of sliding one to the side?

She looks to the exposed track. There must be locks. Something that keeps them in place, buried beneath the dirt.

Ahead, her face reflects strength. She doesn't want to show this.

The man stands up. He brings his hand to the mask. Lifts it.

"Stop!" Susan yells.

But he only lifts it enough to expose his chin and mouth. A distant photo comes to mind, an image of the movie theater in Old Town. But nothing more. The man drinks from the goblet, the muscles in his thin arms moving beneath his exposed skin.

Dark liquid pours down his chin, his neck, his shirt and jacket.

Done, he sets the goblet on the table. Lowers the mirror again. Points to his side, where his appendix might be, then points to hers.

Susan sees her confusion in the mask.

He repeats the pointing. Himself. Then her.

He's telling her to look. She doesn't want to look. But she can't stop herself.

She looks down, to her own side, moves her arm enough to see a dark splotch there on her shirt, a different discoloration than all that made by the pool she fell into.

She looks back at him. He's holding the goblet. The dark liquid on his chin.

She looks down again. She thinks, *blood*.

If she moves a little she can feel padding there, under her shirt.

He cut you, she thinks. *And he's drinking your blood.*

Susan struggles against the chair. She stands, sits, forces her arms out, presses her shoulders against the chair back. She's got to get out this place. Now. He's cut her and he's going to cut her again.

The man steps around the table. He's coming toward her. In the hand she hasn't seen yet, the one earlier at his side, is a knife large enough to slice her. Dark enough to suggest it already has.

"*No!*" she screams. Struggling. Shoving. Kicking at the table.

Then she falls, to her side, her face in the dirt. Before turning to her knees, she sees the boomerang again; the track at the bottom of what must be a sliding wall.

How close is she to the rungs she took down here? How close has she been this entire time to the very beginning?

His boots kick up dirt as he walks toward her. Susan gets to her knees, forces herself away from the chair, feels the ropes digging into her, all over her.

She sees it when she breaks free. Sees the moment in his mask.

The knife is coming toward her, the tip like a diseased needle, the blue bulb reflected in its splattered surface. Her blood? Is that her blood?

She's up, facing him. He swipes once. Susan backs up. He swipes again. Susan steps around the table, watching herself do so in his mask. He follows.

They move this way, cat and mouse, the man in the mirror mask and Susan, Susan now at his end of the table, he only a foot or two away along the side.

He swipes again. Slow. Is he mocking her? Could he get to her if he wanted to? If he really, really wanted to?

Susan backs up to the wall, turns, flattens her palms to them, tries to slide it left. Slide it right.

The mask tilts. The unmistakable and universal gesture of curiosity.

He knows she knows.

The wall doesn't move. And he's closer now, too close.

Susan stumbles across the room. She looks to the table. What can she use? The goblet? A glass of her own blood?

She falls to her knees where the track is exposed and swipes dirt away. Swipes more. Feels his hand in her hair.

Locks. Yes. Locks.

She unlocks one. Swipes more dirt.

His hand grips her hair. The knife against her throat.

She unlocks a second lock. Feels the steel begin to slide, slides the wall open.

Then Susan is up and running. She doesn't know what happened. Why he let go of her hair. Was he so surprised? Are there more important things to take care of, now that she knows? Now that she's seen behind the carnival beneath the carnival's curtain?

She hits another wall, just barely illuminated by the blue light coming from behind. She turns, but doesn't want to pause yet, to stop and slide. More darkness, familiar darkness, endless darkness ahead. She enters it, moving fast, and comes to another wall.

This one is made of dirt.

Susan turns to see if he's coming. With that knife.

A dirt wall implies the end of the line. One line. One of four. How big is it down here? Big enough for her to be in one place and him, silent to her, in another?

She follows the wall. Her back to it, she slides along the dirt, her eyes ahead in the darkness, expecting the man's hand to appear, suddenly, in her hair again.

How close was she to death back there? How close now?

She continues, has to. She has hope now. She has desperation now, too. A cut in her side. A man with a knife.

She feels bars. Her fingers actually slide through what must be bars, metal bars, feels the lapping of a tongue against her palm.

Susan shrieks and backs up, slams into a wood wall.

A growl from behind the bars. An animal in a cage.

Susan tries to see it, tries to really see where she stands right now. A hallway for the man alone? Behind the walls? Where he keeps his wares, his weapons, his beast?

"Hello," Susan says to the cage.

Silence from within. Will it growl? Is there more than one? One caged, one not?

She continues, feels along the dirt wall, looks back into the darkness, hears the music still, louder now. A speaker above? Her fingers dig into the dirt as she goes, her back to it, going, moving, with hope, with horror. She reaches a corner, slides along a second dirt wall. How many until she's back at the beginning? There was a beginning. Before she was covered in blood and dirt, before she was cut, before she lost half her—

Susan stops. It strikes her that she hasn't lost her mind. This is incredible to her. Who could know how well they'd maintain in a place like this?

She continues, moves, moves, slides along the wall, knocks something over, cries out, continues, has to step around boxes, continues, sees light ahead, just enough, escaping between what looks like two wood walls, a slight opening. She continues, eyes on the light, going, her fingers in the dirt, back to the dirt, shoes in the dirt.

At the opening now, light against the wall she slides against. Red light. Dull. She moves slower now, peers in, moves a little more, peers further in, sees the back of the man in the mirror mask, only he's not wearing the mask, the mask in on a table in front of him. She sees his long dark hair, the back of his jean jacket, his bare arms working on something, sharpening something on the table. The room is loaded with props. Weapons. Buckets. Bags. Arms and legs. Faces. Her Sylvester the Cat.

Susan stops at the opening.

The man tilts an ear in her direction.

She lunges. Arms out. Her mouth open in a scream but she does not scream.

He turns toward her. Almost there. Almost on him. Almost sees his face. She sees her phone on the table.

The lights go out.

She hears the cinematic swoosh of steel through air. A knife drawn. An ax falling.

She feels a prick on either hand.

It happens so fast that she doesn't comprehend what's happened until her knees strike the dirt, until she's on her knees, holding her arms up in the dark.

"No," she says. Because this can't be. The sound, the sensation. And now, the lack thereof.

"I can't feel my hands," she says. "*I can't feel my hands!*"

But she can. Accidentally. As she shuffles to get up again, as her knee touches what must be fingers on the ground. No, not fingers, an entire hand. No, not a hand.

Two.

Susan's hands. She can't feel her hands.

The swoosh of steel.

The quick prickling.

And hands, her hands, no other hands to be, *her* hands, beside her in the dirt.

Susan closes her eyes and screams and the sound of her own voice acts as a rope, tugging her into a darkness more complete than any a man in a mirror mask could manufacture.

THIS IS a real experience.

The smells, the sights, the sounds. The touch.

It's dirt, really, all of it. A big grave. Susan (knocked out? Blacked out? In the process of losing her mind?) harps on the two words for a second, doesn't want to let them go: *BIG GRAVE*. Sounds like an attraction itself. But there's so much, too much, perhaps. To smell. To see. To hear. To feel.

Smells like dirt. Yes yes. *Smelled* like gasoline. Yes. Doesn't anymore? No, it doesn't anymore. Why? Doesn't matter. Smells like tears right now. Smells like fear. A hot smell. Something burning. Susan's reason? What's burning? Is it reason?

Despite the dark, there *are* sights. An empty carnival. Yellow flags flapping in a breeze. Empty stalls. No lines. No couples, either. A lot of darkness. So much of it that it feels physical. Like it touches you. Like hands.

Mirrors, too. And isn't it just like a carnival to have a hall of mirrors? And isn't it just like the House of Horrors to put you in a blue room with a single bulb as a woman older than the Bible smokes cigarettes and stares?

No creaking above. Long gone, that sound. That evidence of being buried beneath life. No distant screams. Only her own now. Sobs? Cries? Susan doesn't have the capacity to name things right now. Susan is hardly here right now.

Was Dad just here? Hardly? He talked. He did! He said something. Told her he loved her. Told her he wasn't worried about the car, just her.

Christ.

This is a real experience.

Remember the hands you felt against your leg? Remember those, Susan?

Susan doesn't know she's smiling as she physically turns her head away from the idea of loose hands in the dirt. Her face moves on its own, the ends of her lips lifting up up up because they have to go somewhere and a perfect circle for a scream feels wrong. So wrong.

"*Susan. Hey. It's Mom.*"

Susan doesn't have to open her eyes to see Mom saying these words. She's standing somewhere in this hall. Wearing night goggles? Might be. Might be being polite, not pointing out the hands.

"*Dad says he tried to reach out.*"

Tried to reach out! Incredible. No hands. Incredible.

"*Just let us know what you're planning.*"

Planning. Not planning right now. Grieving. Couldn't hold a pencil to a planner, Mom.

"*And if you're having fun, don't worry about us. Stay where you are!*"

Stay where you are! Don't worry, Mom! I probably will stay where I am.

The smells, the sights, the sounds, the touch.

Some silence. Long enough for the man to switch to a different voice message.

"*Susan. We're getting worried here. Where are you?*"

I think I'm right under the carnival, Dad! Can you believe it?

Then, Mom again: "*Susan, we're calling the police. We don't want you to think this means we don't trust you. But if you are receiving these messages, you must call us back.*"

Susan tries to stand up, can't use the balance of her hands. No hands. She hears a sloshing sound. Blood pouring from the stumps? How much blood is in the dirt? How much on her shirt? Is she losing consciousness? Getting dizzy? Losing blood?

No, she thinks. As incredible as it sounds, she doesn't feel any different than she did while sliding along the dirt wall. Where's the dirt wall now?

Ahead, a small square of light. Then it's gone. The screen of her phone? Yes, she believes it was.

Susan is standing. Facing where that square just vanished. But what's the point of going to it? She couldn't use the phone now. Couldn't climb the rungs. Couldn't fight the man in the mirror mask.

So she turns from it. Walks, does not run. She's in another hall. Wood walls. She could get to her knees, but how to undo the locks on the tracks? So she just walks, turns, walks, hall after hall, the same darkness filling all the halls like black cream, almost resisting her, forcing her to walk with a lean, forward, as if walking into a black wind.

Is she light-headed? No. Shouldn't she be? Yes. Is this shock?

Susan doesn't know, can't see anything other than herself walking alone, handless, to Old Town, walking the halls of Holly High with stumps, sticking to the shadows, the fifth corners.

This place is a fifth corner. Every space has four corners, even if it has eight. And every place has that fifth, that spot someone can stand where nobody will see them, nobody will ever notice they're there. The House of Horrors at the Hoke County Carnival has four corners. This place down here, this is its fifth.

And it's darker than hell. And it smells like dirt. And it sounds like Mom and Dad calling, worried sick, taking action, but not soon enough.

Susan cries. No hands. So she cries. One wall, another wall. How to slide them open? No way to do that. Not now. So she walks. She cries. But she does not believe she's lost her mind. That's something that must come gradually. Like removing a screw from a bridge. It won't fall now but...

A light comes on. Susan doesn't want to look up, doesn't want to see what the man in the mirror mask wants her to see. So she keeps her eyes closed and elbows out, and walks. Toward the light. Toward the next tableau. Blind, by her own choice. In her own darkness. Not his. Brushing against a poorly painted, splintered wall because she chooses to. Not because she has to.

She chooses not to see what's next.

But the man makes her.

Hands upon her face. Thumbs over her eyes, forcing her lids open.

Look! He's saying. Just look at yourself! Look at the fear in your eyes! You're so scared I have to make you look! You choose to close your eyes down here because you can't stand to see another thing! Anything! You don't even know what it is!

His arms against her shoulders, his fingers locking her eyes open, the mask so close to her face that all she can see is her eyes.

So wide.

Yet, still her own.

Still her own eyes. And her own face. Not just a bag of sorrows traveling through the dark. Not just a helpless person who was once able. Not just the next attraction, the next scare in this very real house of horrors.

Susan pushes back but he isn't letting go. She can smell him, smells like soap, smells like dirt, smells like someone who has worked very hard to ruin the life of another.

He squeezes harder on her face and tilts his own, just enough to show her where the scant light is coming from, the source of this light.

In the glass, Susan sees rungs.

Unevenly jammed into a dirt wall. A tunnel of sorts, leading up. Purple and white lights shine down upon the rungs and Susan recognizes that light, those colors, from the House of Horrors above.

She's back where she started, where she saw this same man crouched upon those same rungs, when she believed she was still a part of the world above, alone or not, still a part of the carnival.

He releases her. Something is jammed into her pocket. Her phone? Feels like her phone. He's guided her, almost pushing her, to the rungs.

Is this it then? Susan looks to the light, can see the opening now, a piece of it, a crescent hole.

She turns from it, elbows out, shaking her head no. She will not be forced to go up there, to perform, to be ignored by the thousands of people in attendance who wait for her to do something she does not know how to do.

The man is pushing her now, toward the rungs. Go on, he's saying without speaking, that's it, get out of here. This is over.

But is it?

Susan can't reach for his neck. Can't strike him. Can't even remove what must be her phone from her pocket.

She's at the rungs now, looking up, sees the entire open circle, the same one she entered way back when she was blonde, uncut, had hands.

He's got her against the rungs, is helping her climb them. Shoving her up the makeshift ladder to the light. She's going, not sure how, going up one, another. Is he lifting her? Is she carrying any of herself?

She's half out, belly flat to the wood floor of the House of Horrors. She's sliding across the floor, her legs following, until all of her is out, all of her back where she started.

Behind her, the lid to the hole closes. She hears the lock.

She rolls to her side, looks to the lid, listens to the space she is in. Hears no one. Looks to her pocket. Sees the square of light her phone makes.

She reaches for it. Almost stops. Then, incredibly, as if someone has injected her with a serum meant to ape joy, she feels a flood of relief she can hardly understand.

She has hands.

She cannot feel them, but they are there.

Susan sits up. Lifts her shirt with her numb right hand, tears the white padding and tape from her side. Sees she has not been cut.

She stands, removes her phone from her pocket, and uses the flashlight to guide her through a series of halls occupied by childish displays, silly rubber spiders and mannequins in masks, until she reaches what must be the back door, the exit, of the Hoke Country Carnival House of Horrors at last.

Susan steps out to find it's still evening. Not dark yet. She takes uneven metal stairs to the dirt (above ground, sandy here with patches of Holly Park grass). She has hands. And though she can't feel them, she uses her fingers to call Mom and Dad. But as she presses the last of the digits, the phone goes dark, the battery dead, and Susan stares at the screen as if she might hit it. As if the device in her hand is to blame for everything she's endured today and not the man who stands halfway across the otherwise vacant carnival lot. Stands with his arms folded across his chest, leaning against the ring toss stand, the cockiest smile she's ever seen across his face.

She sees this smile because he wears no mask. His features are wholly exposed in the falling sun.

She recognizes him.

It's Dandelion Andrews from Holly High.

Susan feels a tingling in her hands. Coming to life. Feeling again.

"What'd you think?" Dandy asks her, as she walks toward him, crossing the sandy lot. "I worked my ass off on that. What was your favorite part?" Susan is close now. Close enough to see the red paint on his fingers, close enough to see he has a dog with him. A small one. But one whose growl is very loud in the dark.

Feeling returns in her own fingers. Susan closes them.

Dandy says, "Tell me, what'd you—"

And Susan, close enough now, punches him in the face, breaking his nose, and causing him to drop to the dirt next to the wood wall of the carnival stand.

"YOU PAID to be scared," Dandy says, his words distorted by the broken nose, the puffy lips. "But you didn't really want to be scared."

He's tied to the All-Knowing Scale. His boots upon the steel square, his torso, legs, and arms secured with lines of colored carnival flags.

The scale reads one hundred and thirty-eight. Susan has him by close to sixty pounds. And she felt like it, too, as her fist connected with his face.

More than once.

"There's nothing worse than a phony," Dandy says. "And nothing worse than a phony scare."

"I'm not your audience," Susan says. The small dog is at her feet, lapping at an ax. "I don't care if the House of Horrors is scary or not."

Dandy spits. Blood. Real blood. The first real blood all day? Susan can't be sure. But she likes to think so.

"You say you don't care. But don't you get it? If you pretend to be scared, you pretend to be happy. If you pretend to be happy, you pretend to be okay with all the bullshit of this life and everything's that thrown at you." Susan makes another first, steps toward him. He turns his face away and winces. Opens one eye, slowly, to see if she's going to hit him again. She's not.

"You laugh in my horror movie, I'll scream in your comedy," Dandy says.

Susan rolls her eyes.

"Who cares?" she asks.

"I do," he says. The passion in his voice is undeniable. Susan knows he's crazy. But how dangerous? Is she hurt? Truly hurt? "I care because a person shouldn't pretend one goddamn thing," he says. "You shouldn't lie and you shouldn't pretend. Momma always said—"

"Ah," Susan says. "Momma. I guessed there were mommy issues involved."

Dandy struggles against the flag ropes. "She knew her shit," he says. "Knew what was real and what wasn't."

"I'm gonna leave you here, Dandelion Andrews," Susan says. The sun has gotten lower. Soon, night. Tomorrow, the carnival again. "So the cops know where to find you."

"Go on," he says. "You think I care about that?" He's smiling, but not really. Susan can feel the anger in him. Like he could melt the ropes that bind him. "I showed you a real time today. It's a time that's gonna stay with you the rest of your life. You'll forever gauge what's real and what's not by this day. Fear, jealousy, what to be mad about. Love. Yeah, when you think you're falling in love one day, you'll think of me, and you'll ask yourself, is this true? Is this love?"

Susan picks up the ax.

Dandy eyes it.

"You ever see those ax tossers, Dandy Andrews? The carnival acts that trust one another enough to throw axes at each other?"

Dandy eyes the ax.

"Trust me," she says. "And if I miss, you'll forever think of me when you need to check if something's real or not."

She grips the handle. Lifts it higher.

"Come on," he says. "I didn't actually hurt you."

Susan nods. "Maybe my real is a little more real than yours."

She cocks her arm back. Dandy cries out. She throws the ax.

It hits Dandy square in the forehead before falling to the metal at his feet. The scale's needle rises less than a quarter pound. In the last vestige of the sun, he sees it's plastic.

He looks to Susan.

And Susan laughs. She can't stop laughing. The look of horror in his eyes. The legitimate fear as the weapon flipped, end over end, toward him.

"Oh my," she says. "Did you wet yourself, Dandy Andrews?"

But Dandy can't use his arms to cover his pants.

"You suck," he says. "Now let me go."

Susan shakes her head no. She bends and picks up the dog.

"Hey," Dandy says. "Hey!"

But Susan is already walking away from him. The dog licks the syrup and food coloring from her chin. She pets it, thinking how incredible it is, how a thing so small could harbor such a ferocious sound.

Then she looks to the sky and releases a howl all her own. As she passes the ticket booth, she thinks about what Dandy said.

Is he right? He might be. She might think of him when next she gets mad. When next she feels all alone.

She crosses the gravel lot to her father's car. There she removes the key from the holder on the back of her phone. She sets the dog on the passenger seat, gets in behind the wheel. She starts the car.

She turns on the lights.

From where she sits, she can see him. Dandy, tied to the All-Knowing Scale. His head hangs limp. His hair covers his face, reaches his chest.

She asks herself if she's really going to call the police. There's some twisted psychotic wisdom to what he told, to what he did.

She puts the car in reverse but does not back out yet.

She watches him. Wonders if he knows she can see him. Wonders what she's going to do next.

But she'll decide that when she gets home. After she's seen Mom and Dad. After she's told them she's fine, that she made it through something today, the House of Horrors at the Hoke County Carnival, and has the mess in her hair, on her body, on her mind, to prove it.

She drives out of the lot, turns left.

Driving, she turns to the dog, Dandy's dog, and says, "Your dad is a piece of shit. But I'm going to tell you something and I want you to tell him it for me. And since you can't talk, you'll never tell him. And that's the way it should be. But I gotta say it to someone who knows him, so that I feel like I said it. Will you do that for me?"

The dog looks up at her, small tongue sticking out its mouth. The same tongue that touched her palm in a nightmare that wasn't real. Only it was the realest time of her life.

"Tell him thank you," she says. "Then bite his fucking balls."

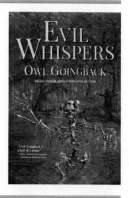

Made in United States
North Haven, CT
11 February 2024

48618100R00281